Also by MarcyKate Connolly

*Monstrous*

# RAVENOUS

MarcyKate Connolly

**HARPER**

*An Imprint of* HarperCollins*Publishers*

Library of Congress Control Number: 2015940703
ISBN 978-0-06-227274-4(trade bdg.)

Typography by Torborg Davern
16 17 18 19 20   CG/RRDH   10 9 8 7 6 5 4 3 2 1
❖
First Edition

*For Jason, Tootsie, and Milo—my family, my heart, my favorites*

# CHAPTER 1

THOUGH I SIT BY THE WARM, WELCOMING HEARTH IN THE HOME OF THE king's page boy, Ren, one small sentence is all it takes to drag me back to that awful place. To my nightmare.

"We are sending aid to Belladoma," King Oliver said moments ago, propelling us all into confusion.

Belladoma.

*I stand in the tower again, the nauseating smell of sea brine stinging my nose and a guard's hands pinning my shoulder to the rough windowsill. Below us, black water swirls against the cliff's edge and one long tentacled arm gropes up the rocks.*

*All those other girls King Ensel holds captive as meals for the sea monster, the Sonzeeki, are too soft, too coddled.*

*I have to help them. I have to try, no matter how futile it seems.*

*But every month, we're taken up to the tower like clockwork, and terrible, helpless rage curls around me like a strangling cloak.*

"We are sending aid to Belladoma."

"You must be joking," I say. The mere thought of that place makes my stomach lurch. I grip the edge of my chair, nails digging into the wooden frame.

Laura, Ren's mother, bristles in the chair next to me. I've known her almost as long as I've been friends with her son; she hates Belladoma too. "Greta's right. Why should we help them? They murdered our children. They aided the wizard."

How can I forget those empty-eyed courtiers in Belladoma, or the poor who hid, safe in their houses, while King Ensel sent yet another of my friends off the cliff to sate the ravenous beast in the bay? They did nothing to help us. Why would they? Without us, the Sonzeeki would destroy their city with floods unless they sent their own children to it. The sea monster that haunts every Belladoman child's dreams has spread like a disease to disturb the slumber of Bryre's children too.

I don't need to look at Ren to know what he is feeling. He tried to save us, only to fall victim to Belladoma's evil king too. Out of the corner of my eyes, I see his hands clench and unclench, much like my own. But he doesn't say a word to the king he adores and serves. In spite of everything.

And there is Delia, who should be as disgusted by this idea as any of us. We were both among Bryre's stolen girls. But she simply stands beside her father, the king, staring at her feet. Her golden hair drapes in such a way that I can't see her expression.

King Oliver sighs. "I do not expect any of you to be happy about this. But it is not the people's fault their king was a horrible man. He was a usurper, and he was mad; he was never going to be a good ruler. The people of Belladoma have long suffered, and we can help. Now that Ensel is dead and no one feeds the Sonzeeki, it floods their city every month, poisoning the soil with salt so nothing can grow."

He stands, and for a moment he resembles the king I recall from when I was a child. Tall, strong, decisive but kind.

If only the transformation wasn't on behalf of Belladoma. Bryre—our own city—needs its king's full attention now more than ever.

"They starve," King Oliver says. "The few children they have left who weren't victims of King Ensel's sacrifices are dying. I will not stand by and watch."

I cannot bite my tongue like Ren and Delia. "*They* joined forces with the wizard and his evil magic. *Their* king woke the angry sea monster with a taste for young girls. The wizard stole Bryre's girls, my friends. Haven't *we* suffered enough?"

"She's right," Laura says, putting a hand on my shoulder. "We should show them the same measure of kindness they showed us."

The disappointment in the king's face sears my heart.

"It grieves me to hear that," King Oliver says. I can't

meet his eyes. The emotions twisting inside will explode from my chest if I do. I wrap my arms around my middle, and Ren's mother rubs my back. At least someone here understands.

The king sighs again, then bows and leaves the cottage silently. Delia follows like his shadow, but her betrayal lingers, needling my skin like tiny knives.

"Greta, Mama," Ren says to me and Laura, "I don't like it any more than you do, but if the king says we must, we have no choice."

"If the king said we must give over our girls to help them, would you go along so easily? Our focus should be on our own city, on Bryre. We need our king here, not running off to some other place."

Ren frowns, and it pinches my heart. "Belladoma is repulsive to me, too, but we can't let people die needlessly."

"But how can we help another city when we can't even help ourselves?" I stand, pulling my cloak around my shoulders.

Laura pats my arm. "Just wait—perhaps the king will see reason tomorrow. Belladoma might refuse our help. They've always been a proud people."

The fire flickers, throwing shadows all over the small room. "I can't bear to watch it happen." A buzzing in my ears, like frenzied waves crashing, grows louder with every second.

"Greta." Ren tries to follow, but I flee. This is worse than the nightmares that still plague me after all these months.

But the worst part is that our own king would offer help to the city that attempted to destroy us before he heals Bryre's own deep wounds.

Our city may have come back to life, but its occupants have a long way to go.

I wander through the city streets, meandering toward the palace, trying to escape the sound of waves crashing that won't let me rest. I know what draws me in, but it's foolish. This won't help a whit. And yet . . .

The guards know me well now. Ever since I fought against King Ensel and the wizard with Kymera the monster girl, they have treated me with more tolerance than they ever would have before as a commoner. They let me into the gardens without batting an eye.

While I have visited the palace many times since the battle with the wizard, there is one place I have avoided.

A strange flower lies at the edge of the garden not far from the palace steps. A beautiful red rose that's always in bloom, never closing up for the night to sleep. It never wilts, and it probably doesn't need watering, though the gardeners water it anyway. After the battle, it rooted in a broken pillar, and King Oliver built the Altar of the Rose around it in an enclosure of fine silver-veined white marble, with an opening to let in the moon and sun and rain.

Strange occurrences are often followed by rumors, and Bryre's rose is no exception. A steadily growing faction in the city claims the rose has the power to grant wishes, to fulfill unspoken needs, and to right wrongs. They visit the flower regularly to leave offerings and pay respects, their red cloaks marking them as followers of the rose.

But I don't believe in rumors. I believe in myself, and what I can do with my own two hands. Yet the righting of wrongs, the tempting idea it might be possible, now draws me in at last.

I enter the alcove, the moon high above, its light piercing through the opening and illuminating the rose in all its perfect beauty. Just seeing it quiets the ocean in my brain.

There's enough room inside for a handful of people to circle the rose on a marble walkway. The walls have shelves from floor to ceiling, and many of the city folk, not only the cult, leave tokens and offerings here. There are a few statuettes of dragons, and many carved in the monstrous likeness of a girl with claws, a serpentine tail, and black wings. Other oddities line the shelves too—dried flowers and roses mostly, but also bits of bone, thorns, and pottery of dubious shape and origin. And there on the bottom row lies a book of fairy tales.

I kneel on the marble path, a foot away from the flower. The petals are like soft velvet; its leaves are green and strong, and its thorns are fierce.

"I don't know if you can hear me," I say. An odd desperation has settled in my chest: if the rose does look after Bryre, it would not approve of the king's plan, I'm sure. "I don't know where else to turn. Our king wants to help Belladoma, to give them supplies and food. They can't feed the Sonzeeki any longer, and it has been terrorizing and flooding the city." I ball my fists in my skirts as the image of that awful black shell rising from the depths dances in front of my eyes. "I pity them, but I can't stomach the thought of helping them. They sat idly by and did nothing while King Ensel held us captive, while he threw my friends off the cliff. They don't deserve our help." Unwanted tears burn the backs of my eyes.

The night breeze brushes over the petals of the rose.

"Would you aid the people who tried to destroy your city? If you have any power to stop the king, I beg you to do it. He hid from the wizard for so long, and now Bryre needs him here. We need him *more*."

The rose doesn't answer, but a cloud passes over the moon, removing all the light from the altar chamber. I leap to my feet.

My hands quiver. It's only a rose. Nothing more.

A single beam of moonlight pierces the cloud, striking the book of fairy tales on the alcove shelf.

A memory stirs within me. The book reminds me of something an old friend once held dear. I kneel by the wall and put my hands on the book. The clouds shift again, and moonlight fully illuminates the room. The change is so sudden, it startles me and I drop the book. A pressed rose slips from between the pages, and as I pick it back up I realize the book is filled with the pressed flowers.

Someone treasured this book once. I'll take the fairy tales—my brother, Hans, will love them—but I don't feel right taking these.

I carefully remove each pressed rose, making a strange sort of bouquet. When it's complete, I tie them together with a piece of string I find and rest the flowers back where the book once stood.

It must be the wind whispering through the palace garden, but I think I hear a sigh as I put the book in my satchel and leave the Altar of the Rose.

# CHAPTER 2

**I SPEND HALF THE NIGHT WANDERING THE DARK CITY STREETS AND** reliving my nightmares.

Once I had a family, a loving mother and father, and a younger brother. Mama and Papa were long gone before I was sent to Belladoma. Hans was all I had left.

Then the wizard's disease curse infected me and I was tossed into quarantine with the rest of Bryre's sick girls. That's when Kymera, the monster girl created by the wizard, stole me and unwittingly sent me on my journey to Belladoma. If only she'd known what really waited for us in that city.

*Belladoma.*

The memories creep in around the edges of my vision and I shudder. Like water, they flow through every barrier

9

I put in their way. My parents raised me to believe in the kindness of strangers. But the people of Belladoma merely watched while their wicked king sent us over the cliff, slowly killing every ounce of that belief.

Finally, I reach our cottage on the outskirts of Bryre. It isn't a large house, but it's too big for just my brother and me, and it's fallen into more disrepair than I can fix easily. The roof needs thatching, and the front window frame is cracked from a recent storm. But the house is painted a pretty blue and the walkway is neat and free from the weeds that would threaten it. I tiptoe into the cottage as the dawn crests the trees with hues of pink and gold. I checked that Hans was asleep before I left to see Ren and the king. The last thing I want to do now is wake him.

Hans suffered enough while I was captive. Reduced to begging, even stealing on occasion, his only other source of food was the small garden I had planted behind our house. When I finally returned, he was so thin, I feared he'd never recover. I wasted no time before volunteering to help out the local baker and butcher, if only to justify the scraps I took home. I promised never to leave him again—unlike our parents.

Until the day they left, we were happy together.

Happiness is not something I'll ever trust easily again.

I hang my cloak on the rack by the door and rub my sleepy eyes. The anger I felt at Ren's house has dulled to embers, leaving me exhausted and hollow. I should sleep for a few hours before another day of trying to coax the old Hans out of his new shell. Perhaps today I'll have better luck.

About a year ago, our parents vanished. No note, not a whisper of where they might have gone. Did they abandon us? Or did something terrible befall them? Are they out there somewhere, alive and waiting for us to join them, or are they already in their graves? If not for my brother, I would have chased after them, hunted down some small trace. But Hans needed me here.

I miss the Hans who was full of life and wonder, constantly curious. It's been my personal mission to bring that boy back. He grew sullen and more frightened after they left. His laughing eyes dulled to a somber gray. Lately, he's become more stubborn than ever—and taller, too. Sometimes, when he gives me a rare smile, hope trills over me, but his smiles are few and far between and always fleeting.

I shuffle across the worn boards of our kitchen floor toward the back of the little house where our bedroom lies. We still share a room as we did when we were young, even though our parents' room lies empty. Neither of us has opened the door since that day. It would be like reopening a raw wound.

But after my night of wandering, I've made up my mind. Hans and I will leave Bryre. There's no reason to stay. Mama and Papa are not coming back. And I cannot stand by and watch while my friends help the people who held me captive and forced me to watch other girls die.

We're better off in the woods.

When I wake, we'll take our belongings and the little money we have to buy a few hens and a goat. Build a little

11

cottage deep in the woods. No one will trouble us there. We won't have to pretend our parents are still around. It's been over three months since the battle with the wizard; the days tick by and it makes me restless.

Careful not to wake my brother, I pry our door open. Dawn trickles in through the windows, casting light on a sight that stops me in my tracks.

Hans's bed is empty.

Panic rises in a thick, suffocating stream up my chest. The doorknob rattles under my hands.

"Hans?" I whisper, hoping and praying for an answer. None comes. "Hans!" I yell, and fling myself into our room. His bed is tousled and messy. Could something have woken him? Why would he have wandered off in the middle of the night?

I can't help thinking of our parents' disappearance. Hans wouldn't leave me too. We need each other. I toss off the bedclothes to ensure he isn't asleep somewhere deep under the covers. No luck.

Under the bed—the same. I rush to the closet and throw the door wide. Again nothing. His clothes are all there, but no Hans hiding inside.

He can't be gone. He *can't.*

Fear crawls under my skin, worming its way over my body. I run through the house, wishing to find something that will let me escape this nightmare. But our cottage is small. There are not many places to hide. I check every single spot we used to play hide-and-seek as small children. The pantry in the kitchen is empty of all but some potatoes and carrots. The cupboards have a few handfuls of rice and dried beans that I would have cooked for our supper. The nook under the front stair. The hollow in the oak tree out front.

Nothing, nothing, nothing.

At last, only one place is left to check: our parents' room.

I stand outside the door, focusing on breathing. This is too eerily like that terrible day a year ago, when Hans and I returned home from school to the same: nothing.

Maybe Hans got the ridiculous notion into his head that he needs his own room. Maybe I'll find him sleeping soundly on their bed, cranky because I woke him.

Or worse, he won't be there at all.

I close my eyes, heart trembling, and reach for the door-knob. It turns slowly, and the hinges creak and groan as the door swings inward. I don't want to look for fear of what I might see. When did I become so afraid?

Everyone I grow close to vanishes. I refuse to lose Hans. He's all I have left.

I force my eyes open.

Hans is not here. Everything is just as my parents left it. Clothes neatly stacked in the closet. Bed perfectly made. The only addition is a thin sheen of dust coating everything. No, Hans has definitely not been in here. Not since they vanished.

I flee the room, slamming the door behind me and sinking down to the floor. Water rushes in my ears, threatening to pull me under again.

Gone. Just like Mama and Papa. Visions of my family waltz before my eyes. Mama cooking in the kitchen, Hans playing with blocks on the floor or sneaking into their room and jumping on the bed. Papa scolding Hans for rumpling the bed stuffing.

And me, wide-eyed and hopeful that life would bring adventure and a happily ever after. Papa taught me how to use a hammer and a sword, and Mama taught me how to grow my own food and shoot an arrow. Everything I'd need to be resourceful. I took to all of it, but Hans was never quite as good. Mama and Papa always told me that when they were gone, I'd have to look out for him.

Above all, I am a sister, and a fierce one at that.

I will find my brother.

I push myself up off the floor and return to the room I share with Hans. There must be some hint, some clue as to what happened. Hans wouldn't just leave. I sit on the edge of his bed, smoothing over the blankets. No note lies hidden between the sheets or on his pillow. Not even on the floor.

Wait.

A yellow-and-brown feather lies on the floor, half hidden by the bed. It looks like it came from a chicken, except it is much larger than any chicken feather I've ever seen.

Puzzled, I walk over to the window. Caught on the outside of the sill is another feather, as though the window closed on a bird's tail. Several more dot the small yard beyond. A block of ice hardens in my gut. It can't be a coincidence that the feathers have appeared just as Hans has vanished.

They make a trail right up to the wall separating Bryre from the forest. Unlike Ren's cozy home, our cottage is on the outskirts. That was useful. It kept us from being noticed

14

when our parents disappeared.

But now I'm certain. Something bad is in the forest. It has my brother, and I won't rest until I have him back.

King Oliver holds court each morning, allowing Bryre's citizens to air grievances, settle disputes, or plead for assistance when necessary. Today, I am first in line, trying not to fidget with the lace on my best dress.

My brother is missing. King Oliver must help me find him. With the help of the king's guard, we could comb the forest and get Hans back by nightfall.

There is only one small problem.

I've never told the king or Ren that I have a brother. Or that our parents are missing. We were terrified of being thrown into the orphanage and separated when that happened, so we scraped and stole our way together instead. If I tell them I have a brother, they'll insist on involving my parents. If they find that my parents are gone, it won't be long before they realize that I'm a thief. People lose fingers for that. And get locked in the dungeon as punishment.

At the very least, the king would have put us in the orphanage, and that was enough to give me nightmares. My brother and I had only each other—the thought of possibly being separated, even by well-meaning adults, was unbearable. But now . . . now I will have to come clean. Nothing less will convince them.

"Greta?" Ren's voice jerks me to attention. "What are you doing here?"

I attempt a smile. It would be good to have him on my

side. "I have urgent business for the king."

"You aren't going to try to convince him not to help Belladoma, are you?"

"No, this has nothing to do with that." I was upset with Ren last night, but my anger has thawed amid the burning fear I feel for Hans. I have no time to worry about Belladoma now.

"I'm glad to hear it." Ren glances down at his shoes, and I realize the tips of his ears are turning red. "I spent half the morning trying to talk King Oliver out of it, but he'll have none of it. He won't change his mind. I'm sorry."

He looks at me hopefully. Perhaps Ren is on my side after all.

But before I can respond, the doors to the throne room swing open and we are ushered in front of the king.

"Greta," he says, surprised. "Please stand." I rise to my feet, and Ren takes his place behind the king. Nervousness suddenly swims through my belly. Ren's father, Andrew, the king's steward, is also nearby, as is Delia, on a low bench not far from her father. She looks like she wants to speak, but she wouldn't dare interrupt her father's court without being asked. I wasn't expecting an audience of this size.

"What brings you here this morning?" King Oliver asks.

I swallow the knot in my throat. "I'm here to beg your help in finding a lost boy. My brother. I am sorry I never told you about him before, but we are orphans. We were scared we'd be sent to the orphanage and separated. But now he's disappeared under odd circumstances. Please send

16

men to search the woods for him. We must find him and bring him home." The backs of my eyes begin to sting.

The king sits up straighter on his throne, and Delia's eyes shine with curiosity.

"I am indeed surprised by this, Greta, especially to hear that your parents are gone. I am very sorry for your loss. But are you sure your brother hasn't just run away? What were these odd circumstances?"

I pull out the huge feather I hid in my skirts. "This, sire. A trail of them leads away from our home and into the forest. Something took him, I'm certain of it."

The king takes the feather and turns it over in his hands.

"Please, send as many men as possible. Who knows what might have him? We might need a lot if the size of that feather is any indication."

The silence that greets me is almost as deafening as the water rushing through the spaces in my brain. I hold my breath.

The king has to help. These are my friends. I've told them the truth.

"This is indeed an unusual feather." But then something like understanding transforms King Oliver's face. "Greta, I think I know what this is really about."

"This is about my missing brother." My heart hangs in my throat.

"You were upset last night that we are sending our army to aid Belladoma."

"Of course I—"

"You don't really have a brother, do you?" His expression

17

is sad, but he has made a decision.

My mouth drops open, fumbling over every possible response.

"Greta." The tone of that one word seals my fate. "You do not want us to help Belladoma. I understand why. Horrible things happened to you there. But we will help them nonetheless. We cannot be delayed by ploys to send our soldiers on wild-goose chases in the woods." He gestures to the feather. "Even if there were a lost boy, the choice would be between helping one person and an entire city. I must send our men where they can do the most good, to the place that needs our help more. I wish I could heal the invisible wounds Belladoma inflicted, but I can't let a whole city perish. I am sorry, my dear, but that is my final answer."

Rage, hot and bright, fueled by grief, sets my heart on fire. All their faces wear expressions of pity. My friends. These people who I should be able to rely on. Who I was beginning to regard as family.

None of them believe me.

They think I'm so desperate to prevent aid from reaching Belladoma that I'd invent a story for them to chase.

If I open my mouth to speak, I will explode right here in the throne room and blow the entire castle to smithereens. I do the only thing I can.

I curtsy to the king, then spin on my heels and march out of the palace, head held high.

I am many things, but I am not a liar.

The only one I can always depend on to know me is Hans.

*Dear Ren and my king, Oliver,*

*You will not find me in Bryre anymore. Since you do not believe me about my missing brother, I have decided to go after him myself. I wish you well, and I shall miss you. Please do not search for me; I do not wish to be found.*

*Greta*


I leave my hastily scribbled note on the kitchen table. Ren has never been to my home, but I know how good he can be at ferreting out information when necessary. When I don't appear at his fireside tomorrow or the next night or the next, he will go looking and he will eventually find my note here. I'll be long gone by then. Hopefully, I'll have Hans back too.

My meager belongings fit snugly into a pack under my traveling cloak, even with the book of fairy tales I got at the Altar of the Rose. I can't bring myself to leave it behind. I tuck my knife into my belt but don't bother with my bow. I haven't had the money for arrows in weeks. Other than that, there isn't much to leave behind. Just memories. But what are memories worth? All they've done is tie me to a place that no longer feels like home.

I close the door and lock it, tucking the key into the shrub nearby. I will find my brother and we'll start anew somewhere far from here. It's what we must do.

# CHAPTER 3

**DAWN REACHES BETWEEN THE TREES TO ROUSE ME IN THE WOODS. I** traveled all day yesterday and made camp in the deep forest. Nothing can hold the nightmares back, but now that I'm out of Bryre, I can almost breathe again. Though it would help if I could find Hans.

The strange feathers have led me on a merry, circuitous path, as if whatever took him had no idea where it intended to go. If it is a giant bird, I will pluck it naked and cook it on a spit.

Plotting my revenge, I pack my bedroll and nibble on a carrot for breakfast, then move farther on into the woods. The trees here are thick trunked and old. Branches above me twine together in intricate patterns that allow only a small amount of sunlight through. Shadows hang over my head like they're waiting to pounce.

The feathers are closer together now, and I wonder if it's due to the *thing*—whatever it is—scraping between the trees. I grip the hilt of my knife tighter. I must keep my eyes and ears open for signs of this beast. I hope it hasn't reached its destination yet. And that it's waiting to finish Hans off until it gets there.

Hans isn't a fighter. He's nearly my height now, but even though Papa trained him just like me, he can't wield a sword to save his life.

If he's dead, that thing will wish it had never been born.

I move with as much speed and stealth as I can manage in the deep woods. By midafternoon, I'm exhausted, and I still haven't found the beast. Frustrated, I throw my pack to the ground and curl up in the moss at the foot of a massive oak tree. What a sister I've turned out to be.

As I chew on a piece of bread from my pack, uneasiness coils in my gut. Something feels off. Something about the forest—

It's too quiet.

I sit bolt upright, the bread all but forgotten. The animal noises I became accustomed to throughout the morning have vanished.

Something nearby scared them off. My breath hitches in my chest. I remain as still as possible while I slowly turn my head.

Nothing. Just the unsettling silence and me.

I creep to my feet. Perhaps the big oak hides whatever has frightened the animals in the woods.

I clutch my pack to my chest. No sudden moves. I only hope there isn't a beast behind me with a gaping maw.

I peek around the trunk—still no sign of the bird-beast. But a horrible stench floats on the breeze that makes me gag. I swallow my nausea and step around the tree. That stink is the first new clue I've found. Only something huge and carnivorous smells that bad. I hold my cloak to my nose and press on through the woods. The path has become more and more overgrown, and now is marked only by erratic patches of crushed undergrowth and broken branches from the few recent travelers. It makes for slower going, but I do my best to keep up a steady pace.

The source of that smell may be what I seek.

It isn't long before the stench becomes overwhelming. The afternoon sun will wane soon, but I must find this thing before then. It would be impossible to sleep in this rancid air.

Finally I see more light peeking through the green forest. A clearing lies up ahead. I move faster through the trees, and the branches scrape and tear at my clothes, pushing me back like they don't want me to succeed.

Moments later I stand in the glade, frozen and gaping.

It isn't a beast I've been hunting—it's a house. With chicken legs and a feather-thatched roof.

I back up against the nearest tree, studying the thing as it scratches the ground with huge clawed feet. The sides are closely packed branches from a strange sort of thin wood I can't identify. Every time the thing turns in a circle—like a dog trying to find a place to sleep—another feather floats free of the thatching. A tiny chimney stack puffs smoke from somewhere within the feathers. And strangely, dancing around the house's huge feet are creatures I recognize: a rogue pack of those horrid goat-footed chickens the wizard kept as his watch dogs. They dodge and weave around the legs and circle the beast almost like they're playing. My hand immediately runs over the small round scars that still dot my arm from when they attacked me as I tried to escape the wizard's yard so many months ago.

This is the strangest thing I've ever seen in my life. Considering I was once friends with a monster-girl, that's saying a lot.

But the question remains: Where is Hans? Realization dawns. He must be inside that ridiculous moving house.

How on earth will I get inside? Even as I think it, a plan begins to form in my mind.

The house moves in a pattern, a figure eight that brings it close to the edges of the woods, then back to the center, the goat-chickens trailing after. When it makes its next circuit, I run for the trees on that side of the glade and scramble up the one closest to the edge. The first time it comes around, it's still too far for me to make the jump. But the second time, I'm better prepared and I throw myself onto the odd roof.

I hit it hard and begin to slide. My fingers scrabble for a hold and I manage to halt my descent. I pull myself into a

23

sitting position and consider my options. The house steadily moves in its figure eight, almost as though it's waiting for something. I peer cautiously over each edge. On one side is a door into the house and a rim about a foot wide. If I miss, it's at least a twenty-foot drop to the ground.

I prepare to lower myself over the edge. This is for Hans, and that means any risk is worth it.

I let go and drop to the rim. And promptly slip right off.

My pack catches on a piece of the odd wood connecting the house to the legs, and it forces the air from my lungs painfully. But it's better than hitting the ground that looms under me. If I fall near those scraping feet, I'm lost. I grab hold of the ledge, enough that I can pull myself up. I rest there for a moment as I will my hands and legs to stop shaking long enough for me to stand.

I wobble to my feet and manage to pry the front door open. A loose piece of the wood snaps in half, and only then do I realize what it really is.

Bone.

I fling it away with a shudder, wipe my hands on my skirt, and step through the door.

A wall of cages lines the far side of the room, which is much bigger than it appears from the outside. A stove is on the right, and another door, perhaps to a bedroom, is on the left.

Hans—dirty, bedraggled, and wide-eyed—sits cross-legged in one of the cages. Hope blooms in my chest.

"Hans!" I rush toward him. He gets to his feet, but he has to hunch over when he stands. He is too tall for the cage.

24

"Greta," he whispers, fear marring his face. "Get away from here. She'll return any second."

"Who?" I ask, scrambling through the contents of the nearby table for anything that might pick the lock to his cage.

"The witch."

Uneasiness tingles up my neck, but I ignore it. "There are no such things as witches. Not anymore." The realm has long been drained of any magic by wizards. Witches were said to be creatures who sprang from deep in the mountains themselves, beings made from magic, like hybrids or dragons. The stories often said they were cruel, though they also said that about dragons, and the one that fought with Bryre against the wizard was kind.

Could Hans really be held captive by a witch? I shiver. It would explain the bizarre chicken hut. And after all I've seen of wizards, dragons, and sea monsters, I can't say anything is impossible.

"She has the keys. She always keeps them with her," Hans says. I put my hands between the bars and grab his shoulders.

"I will find a way to get you free, I promise." Finally I spy something thin and sharp near the hearth, and I scoop it up.

"It won't work," he says. "They're too brittle. Don't you think I've tried?"

"Maybe you didn't have enough leverage from that side," I say, then attempt to use it to pick the lock. It breaks in half, a piece of it jamming the lock.

25

He shakes his head, and I stare at the object in my hand. The second I realize what it is, I hurl it to the floor.

More bone.

"Were these other cages empty when you got here?" My voice quivers, but I try not to let it show.

"No."

My heart flips in my chest. "What happened to them?"

Hans's mouth twists. "There was a little girl." He fiddles with a button on his sleeve. "The witch cooked her in the oven when she was fat enough. She ate her."

I squeeze his hand. "That won't happen to you. I'll find a way . . ."

"No." His voice is filled with determination. "No, Greta, you have to leave. She'll eat you, too."

Fear pricks every inch of my skin. Fear for Hans, myself, and worse, that this is something I can't fix. "She won't eat me. I'm skin and bones."

"She'll boil your bones for soup," Hans says gravely.

"What have we here?" calls a melodic voice from the doorway.

My blood freezes in my veins. Hans shudders in his cage. I slowly face the voice. To my shock, the speaker is not the wart-covered, shriveled mess I expect.

Instead, she's lovely.

She's as young as any maiden, or is that magic at work? Her raven hair shows no hint of gray, and nary a wrinkle mars her pristine face. She steps fully into the hut.

"I said, what have we here?" She puts her hands on her hips.

"I—"

"Run, Greta!" Hans yells.

The woman laughs and locks the door behind her. She smiles, and it chills me to the core. I back farther away.

"So you know my tasty little pet, do you?" She glances back and forth between us. "Your brother, perhaps?"

She steps closer, and a static charge runs through the air. My arms stick to my sides. Panic swims in my throat. "What're you doing to me?" I whisper hoarsely.

She grins again. "Oh, nothing much. Just what I do to all intruders, especially curious, succulent children." She pinches my arm. My stomach heaves. "You are a bit skinny, though I daresay I can fatten you up."

"Please, I just want to get my brother back. Let us go and we won't tell anyone about you."

She cackles, the sound both merry and terrifying. This isn't someone I can fight with my sword. My only hope is to outwit her somehow.

I'm not off to a good start.

"You won't tell anyone about me from my cages, either. I'm not terribly concerned about that."

"Wait! There must be something I can offer you. A trade? Anything you want. There has to be something you want." Yes, I have been reduced to begging, but I'm not ashamed. I will do anything for Hans.

She laughs again but then pauses. "You're a brave one, aren't you? Perhaps there is something you could do."

"Yes!" I cry. "I'll do it. Name it."

She eyes me appraisingly but this time not for my body

27

weight. "You agree even though you have no idea what it is?"

"I'll find a way. I have many skills." I may be boasting, but if it will buy us time, it will have to do. "Let me do this thing for you, and in return allow Hans and me to go free."

"All right. I will make a deal with you. Bring me what I want and I will set you both free."

I breathe out audibly.

"But," she continues, "if you fail to do it before the height of the next full moon, I will hunt you down and have you both for dinner." She claps her hands together. "Sound fair to you?"

I swallow hard. The full moon? That's just over three weeks away. I can't imagine what the task will be. "Yes. What must I do?"

The witch comes closer, until she's right next to me. I can smell the horrid, choking stench from the forest on her breath. Like rotting flesh. "You will fetch me something I greatly desire: the cornucopia. It's a rare thing. A never-ending source of food. It always serves the owner exactly what he or she desires. It will be an acceptable substitute for the loss of my supper." She tilts her head toward Hans, and my stomach drops into my feet.

"A cornucopia? But isn't that just a legend?" I've heard it mentioned vaguely in fairy tales and stories of times long past, but never thought it was real.

The witch waggles her finger at me. "There is much more to legends than people nowadays can see. Do you know the story?"

28

"Only a very little."

"It is in the form of a horn-shaped basket. One merely has to touch it and think about what food one desires, and the meal will appear in the cornucopia. They say it once fed the ancient gods when they were but mewling children." She paces the small space as she talks, and I never take my eyes off her for a second. "But someone clever stole it from them, and it was passed around from one selfish human to another for centuries. For a time, one country worshipped it, believing it granted them a good harvest every year. But then the king and queen of that country lost it. They hid it, most likely, wanting the horn's abundance for themselves. Humans were never meant to hold that sort of power."

Her eyes pierce me, making my skin want to crawl and hide away.

"Where is this cornucopia now?" If I had much money to my name, I would bet anything the wizard hoarded that right along with all the other magic he stole.

"That is the trouble. No one knows. Ensel, that fool king from Belladoma, stole it years ago, but he was mad and greedy for any power he could get his hands on. At first he lorded it over his courtiers while the rest of the city went hungry. Anyone who wanted to eat had to be loyal to him. Their reward was a full stomach and daughters safe from the sea beast—until another courtier took their place. But as his madness grew, he began to fear that if he flaunted what it could do, or let anyone but himself and his most trusted guards near the cornucopia, it would be stolen. So he hid his treasure and moved it around constantly. Only his adviser,

Albin, ever knew Ensel's hiding places, and he is long dead."

She walks in a circle and clicks her long nails together. "King Ensel and that wizard friend of his suspected I wanted the cornucopia. But the wizard cast a spell so that I can't see the thing until someone willingly bestows it on me. Crafty, unpleasant man. He even put up wards around these lands to keep me out. Now that they're both dead, the wards are down and I've returned to the woods, but no one remains who knows Ensel's last hiding spot." She turns back toward me. "And that is what you will have to figure out."

Nausea creeps up my insides. "It's impossible."

She barks a laugh. "Not so sure of yourself now, my pretty one?"

I stand up straighter. "No, I am. If it's out there, I'll find it. But what if the wizard took it? He was notorious for hoarding magic. What if—"

"That is not my problem, is it?" She smiles. "Now, don't think for a second you can hide from me. I never forget a scent. And I always catch my prey. Do be quick."

She snaps her fingers and I find myself standing outside the chicken hut, watching it retreat into the woods at a breakneck pace, with a trail of goat-chickens pecking and squawking after it. "Wait!" I cry. "How will I find you again when I have it?"

But it's no use. The hut, the witch—and Hans—are gone.

The reality of my plight sinks in like a stone in a pond. I can't seem to escape Belladoma. It keeps dragging me back, like the Sonzeeki's tentacles.

I must return to find the one thing that can free my brother. If the witch even keeps her side of the bargain, and that's doubtful at best. But I have to at least try.

I slump to the ground with my head between my knees, heaving gulps of panic. Memories crash over me. It feels like water fills my lungs but I'm choking on nothing. *Those other girls . . . Ensel makes us watch. The salty air assaults my senses. The wind whips wildly around the girl at the tower window, screaming No, no, no, no. Then she's falling, terror-bound. A slimy black tentacle shoots up from the depths, latches onto her body, and yanks her beneath the waves.*

*Be good and you won't be next.*

Ensel's lies ring in my ears as I recover my senses. I could do nothing to help my friends, those girls. The crushing helplessness is worse than any cut from a sword.

I must go back. For Hans. I could not save them, but I may be able to save him. I'll have to face my fears and pray no one sees fit to feed me to the beast.

# CHAPTER 4

**THE STARS GUIDE ME ON MY JOURNEY TOWARD BELLADOMA. I HAVE NOT** a second to spare, and I walk all night instead of sleeping.

Shadows follow me through the woods as the trees grow denser. Clinging vines drape from the branches, occasionally slapping my face with reminders to stay awake. I'm exhausted, but terrified that if I stop, the witch and her chicken hut will scoop me up. I don't trust her to keep her word. If she knows my scent, she won't have any trouble following me.

The night slinks away as dawn creeps over the sky. The rays of sun don't warm me, not like they used to do. I can't help thinking of the monster girl, Kymera. If I could fly like her, I'd reach Belladoma in no time. Perhaps I could even find the cornucopia just from hunting above the trees.

But I am not like her. And I will get by as I always have: with my own wits.

I sigh and pull my cloak closer. Dew dampens it, but the sun will dry it out as the day goes on. I can't shake the feeling that something watches me from the trees. The chicken hut may not have eyes, but I am sure the witch has a means of watching.

I just hope she hasn't changed her mind already.

Before long, my unease deepens. Bird calls are few and far between. The usual sounds of squirrels in the underbrush have all but vanished. Only my footfalls echo through this section of the forest.

Something is wrong here.

This time no accompanying stench marks it as the chicken hut and the witch. I duck low between the trees but keep as fast a pace as possible. I need to hide. Something is near, and it scared away the wildlife. If I'd slept last night, I might have noticed it sooner.

Before I know what has happened, the terrain takes an unexpectedly steep dive. I stumble head over feet, bushes ripping at my cloak and face. Rocks and roots punch into my sides and arms. Everything blurs into a mass of green and brown and blue sky.

Then I stop.

First I focus on breathing. My lungs ache, and I can feel bruises forming all over my body. The cuts and scrapes on my face and hands sting like nettles. Then I open my eyes.

I'm not alone.

I must be seeing things. They're supposed to be extinct.

But the man brandishing a spear at my chest definitely has the lower body of a horse. Several of the people behind him have goat legs, marking them as fauns.

Hybrids.

I thought the wizard killed all that remained to steal their magic.

Except, apparently, these hybrids.

"Who are you? What are you doing here?" demands the centaur holding the spear at my chest.

"N-nothing," I stutter. "I'm headed for Belladoma." Just saying that awful city's name turns my stomach. It does the same for the centaur, judging by the sneer on his face.

"Belladoma. Are you one of the wizard's people?" He nudges me with the butt of the spear.

"Ow! No. I hate the wizard."

He snorts. "Why should we believe that?"

"Because I helped Bryre get rid of him. He's long dead now; I saw it myself." If we both hate the wizard, we at least have some common ground.

A murmur rumbles through the gathering crowd of hybrids. Women with snake tails, and men with wings—I can't name them all, but I recognize them from the hedge sculptures in Bryre's palace gardens. All these creatures I was sure were fictional stand before me. Menacingly.

"You're lying. Wizards can't be killed," the centaur says.

"Yes, they can." Why is this wound still raw after all these months?

More gasps. He prods me again with the spear. "Get up. We can't risk you running off and telling people about us.

Secrecy is the only reason we're alive."

"You're going to kill me?"

"For now, you're our prisoner. Get up, and come with us."

Tiny ribbons of panic slice up my chest. "I have to get to Belladoma. My brother is depending on me."

"Get up," he growls.

Slowly, I rise to my feet, arms outstretched. "Please. You don't understand. If I don't get to Belladoma, my brother will die."

The centaur paws the ground with a hoof and scoffs. "You're lying. Probably about everything. We can't take any chances with you."

"I'm not, I swear it!" I cry. Several more centaurs materialize from the forest, far too close for comfort with their long spears. They aren't going to let me go.

Instead, I'm herded toward a path I hadn't seen before.

"Please—"

"If you value your life, do not speak again."

I clamp my jaw shut as a faun approaches with a hood of dark material. I stifle my objection. Of course they'll blindfold me. They don't want me to know where we go, nor how to escape.

But they don't know me.

I'll put every ounce of life I have into breaking free.


I feel like I've stumbled around in the darkness for hours, though I suspect not much time has actually passed. We have reached what must be a village. Activity buzzes around me, and the faun finally pulls the hood off my head.

"Don't get any ideas," he says.

My jaw drops. The entire village is full of hybrids. The legends are wrong. When the wizard hunted them, these must have banded together and hidden themselves in order to survive. How deep into the forest did I wander?

Houses of all shapes and sizes line the cobblestone streets. Flashes of fins and faces dot the river surrounding the town. Platforms suspended in trees rise over our heads, and the winged hybrids perch there. Above it all, a huge canopy of green leaves and branches squeezes out every inch of sky, providing perfect cover from any prying eyes. Everything below is filtered in green light and shadows. In the center of the village sits the largest tree I've ever seen—undoubtedly the source of the foliage.

My eyes drink it all in, marking the locations of paths and huts and, most important, any potential exits.

They lead me through the village, and the eyes of the hybrids we pass burn into my skin. Do I appear as strange to them as they do to me? Have they even seen a human before?

And more concerning—what, exactly, do hybrids eat?

I crane my neck as we pass the humongous tree trunk, watching the red-flecked leaves of a vine drape down and sway in the breeze. By the time we round the trunk, I understand where they're taking me: a knotted hole in one of the tree's visible roots. It's half as big as our house in Bryre, and an iron grate hangs open in front of it. Several holes like it dot this side of the trunk, but all are empty.

"Get in." The lead centaur points to the hole.

My muscles tense as every nerve in my body screams at me to bolt. I can't go in there. If I do, there's no guarantee I'll ever get out. That would guarantee the witch will eat Hans.

The faun holding on to me shoves me forward; I pretend to stumble and then dodge to the side and sprint around the tree.

First they gape. Then they swarm.

Hoofbeats pound after me, too fast, and harpies swoop down, trying to carry me away. I don't even reach the other side of the massive tree before what seems like the entire village surrounds me.

Judging by their weapons and expressions, they are not pleased to have to ask me twice to get in the tree-root prison.

The lead centaur yanks me and pins my arms behind my back, forcing me to march awkwardly back to the cell. Once there, he opens the door and shoves me forward, not releasing my arms until I'm inside the cage.

I rub my sore wrists as the gate swings closed behind me.

# CHAPTER 5

**THE NEXT MORNING, THE FIRST THING I SEE WHEN I OPEN MY EYES IS A** horse's rear end. The centaur boy guarding my gate gives me quite a start before I remember what happened yesterday. Before I remember where I am.

Trapped.

I cannot remain imprisoned like this, not ever again. Especially when I don't know what they plan to do to me.

I'll just have to plot my way out.

My bed is a straw pallet on a wooden shelf carved from the root of the great tree. The rest of the room is spare. A chamber pot lies in the far corner, blessedly away from the door. The floor is hard stone, which means I won't be able to dig a way out.

Still, I must try something.

"Hello?" I call out. Perhaps playing the hapless maiden will make them pity me enough to let me go on my way.

The centaur boy glances at me. I scramble to my feet and edge closer to the barred door. "Hello, please, can I have something to eat? I'm starving."

He nods sharply, then trots off.

That wasn't quite what I expected, but at least I'll get breakfast. That's something.

A few minutes later, he returns carrying a small bowl and a canteen of water. My stomach rumbles. He sets the bowl on a sliding tray attached to the door and pushes it through, then holds the canteen out to me through the bars. I accept both as demurely as possible.

"Thank you," I say. "I'm Greta. What's your name?"

The boy's silver eyes flash with surprise, but then he retakes his place guarding my cell.

"Can you tell me where I am? What this place is?" I crane my neck to see more of my surroundings outside. "It's beautiful here." This is not an exaggeration. Everything is green, and colored flowers, and other plants glow in the hazy light.

The centaur stamps his feet but doesn't answer. Stubborn. I clench my fists in frustration but continue to talk.

"You must have family," I say. This earns a flick of his chestnut tail. I'll take that as a yes. "Do you have any younger siblings, a brother or sister?"

He goes still. Way off base or too close for comfort, hard to tell.

"I have a brother. Hans." I lower my voice to a pleading

pitch. "He's in trouble. I was on my way to help him when I happened upon your village." I swallow the sob welling up in my throat as the image of Hans stuck in a cage wobbles in front of my eyes. "He's twelve years old. He'll die if I can't get to him in time. Our parents are gone. There's no one left to help him but me."

"I'm not supposed to talk to you," the centaur finally says. He stamps his hooves again, then, without looking at me, moves farther away from my door.

Frustrated, I return to my pallet to eat my breakfast and think. The porridge isn't bad and the water is as cool as I could ask for.

What can I do to change the guard's mind? My thoughts are interrupted by hoofbeats. Moments later the guard opens my door to let the older centaur with jet-black hair into my cell, along with a female centaur. The woman scowls fiercely at me, though the man's expression is more tempered than when he found me. I fight the urge to cower in the corner until they leave, and stand up straighter instead.

"The council of elders has made their decision," the centaur man says. "But we have some questions first."

I don't move an inch. "What are you going to do with me?"

I hear a shuffling noise, and an ancient hybrid inches forward around the corner of my prison cell. He must be one of the elders. He has the lower body of an enormous snake, and the upper body of a man. He's also the most wrinkled creature I've ever set eyes on in my life. I wonder if his human skin molts like his snake skin must.

He slithers closer between the centaur guards to examine me, and I do my best not to cringe.

The snake-man's tongue flickers in my face as though he means to taste me. "How did you find usss?" he asks.

I dare to breathe again. "I didn't. At least, I didn't intend to find you. I was on my way to Belladoma to help my brother."

He hisses at the mention of Belladoma. "Yesss, our guards told usss you claimed you were headed there. The rotting city." It's an apt description.

"I have no choice. My brother needs help and Belladoma holds the key."

The snake-man tilts his head at me, coiling his tail beneath him in a way that makes me think of a human sitting on a chair. "What could Belladoma have to offer you? It was once lovely but went to ruin under the pretender-king Ensssel. Now only chaosss and mercenaries rule there."

I clench my fists. I don't want to reveal I seek the cornucopia, especially if they've already made their decision. An unending food supply would surely be appealing to these people, too. They might try to take it from me, keep it for themselves. Their locking me up hasn't exactly inspired me to trust them.

"He's being held by a witch. The price for setting him free was to deliver a message to someone in Belladoma." Half-truths will have to suffice today. "I must have taken a wrong turn in the woods; then I fell down the hill and here I am. I don't wish you harm, I just want my brother back. I need to leave. Please tell me you've decided to let me go."

Hysteria paralyzes my vocal cords. If they don't release me, I don't know what I'll do.

But I do know exactly what the witch will do.

"A pretty tale," says the snake-man. "It smells of liesss. Like the one you told our guardsss about the wizard being dead. Do you mean to trick usss?"

"No!" I cry. "I've never been on the side of the wizard. He did me a great wrong, one that a hybrid like yourselves fixed."

Utter silence greets me. The two older centaurs exchange a scowl.

The snake-man's eyes glitter. I shudder. I can't help it.

"You will remain with usss until we determine whether you tell the truth."

"Are you going to kill me?" I ask. They could kill me—easily—and not think twice about it. Why else would my guard not be allowed to speak to me?

Never get attached to those you intend to dispose of. Sounds like something King Ensel would've said. My hands shake, but I keep them firmly pressed to my sides.

The snake-man smiles, and it is a terrible thing to behold, all teeth and forked tongue and wrinkles. "No, we are a peaceful community. Perhaps you will become one of us in time and participate in all we have to offer—"

I don't miss the frowns that remark elicits in the centaurs behind him, but I hold my tongue.

"—but for now, you are our prisoner until we deem you trustworthy of joining usss outside your cage, little bird."

He nods at the centaur man and woman as he shuffles out of my cell.

"No! Please!" I cry as the female centaur roughly grabs me around my waist. "Please! I don't have much time to save Hans."

She drags me to the back of my cell, but I shrug off her grasp and slip in the dirt. "This is a death sentence for my brother! His death will be on your hands!"

Something hard and blunt strikes the back of my head; then everything fades.

When I wake, my lunch sits on a tray by the cell door. It's probably been there for hours. The council's decision and my screams of protest return in a rush. Tears spring to my eyes.

I must convince them to change their minds.

"Stop that," my guard says.

I wipe my eyes and sit up. "What?"

He gapes at me and steps back from the bars. I leap toward them.

"Your elders took away my freedom and doomed the only family I have left, and you have the nerve to ask me to stop crying?"

He paws the dirt, taken aback by my outburst. "I—"

"Don't you dare say you're sorry," I warn. "If you were truly sorry, I wouldn't be trapped in here."

I throw myself back on my pallet, but I'm out of tears. My pack catches my eye. Someone must have put it in my cell while I was out cold.

I lean over and tug it toward me. I riffle through the items and quickly realize someone already went through it. My knife is gone. If I had that, I might be able to pick the lock, or even fight my way out. I don't want to hurt any of these people, but if I can scare them off long enough to escape . . .

I sigh. There isn't much left that's useful. Except perhaps my flint. I've used it to start cooking fires, but I might be able to wear it down into something more practical for my current circumstances. I can't do much while the centaur boy is right outside my cell. I'll have to wait until it gets darker and muffle the sound somehow.

Missing my brother makes me want to do two things: first, escape; barring that, read the book of fairy tales I took. Over the past few months, Hans and I read a similar book of stories together at night. He loved to bury himself in histories, maps, fairy tales, and anything else he could get his hands on in our meager library. I think he read only in order to lose himself and forget the tragedy of our real lives. If I concentrate very hard, perhaps he'll hear me through the space that separates us.

Or perhaps I'm just losing my mind. Either way, I reach for the book and begin to read aloud.

The first story is about a mermaid who doesn't value the gift of her fins and wishes them away for legs. She is punished accordingly. How strange she'd want to be a mere human, when she was such a rare creature!

In the next story, a miller's daughter spins straw into gold with the help of an imp. When the king finds out, he insists she spin the gold for him or forfeit her life. The imp makes a bargain with her and helps her once again, but then she refuses to pay the promised price, so that one doesn't end well either.

As I read, the centaur inches closer. Could he be listening? Hope whispers over me. If I can gain his sympathy through reading, perhaps I can escape in time to save Hans.

When another faun arrives with my dinner, my guard hands me the stew through the bars himself. I take it gingerly but waste no time tucking in. I'm starving.

"Where did you get those tales?" the guard asks. I glance up in surprise. The last thing I expect from him is conversation.

"I found the book before I left Bryre. I thought my brother would like them."

He's quiet for a few minutes, then, when I put my tray back on the shelf across the bars, speaks again. "My name is Dalen," he says. "Will you read another?"

My mouth drops open, but I manage to form a reply. "Is there a particular one you'd like to hear? I can search through the book if you have one in mind." Perhaps if I'm kind to him, he'll be inspired to return the favor. One does catch more flies with honey, after all.

Dalen's face turns red. "I—I don't know. I've never heard these tales before."

"Don't you read?" The books I've read always said that centaurs were very smart.

"Of course, but we only have histories and archives here. Those tales are something else, aren't they?"

"Yes, they're fairy tales. Made-up stories. I think some are rooted in facts, but whoever wrote them took many liberties." Spinning straw into gold—Ha!—that wouldn't happen without the help of a powerful wizard.

He tilts his head with a curious look on his face, almost as though he's forgotten I'm a prisoner and he's not supposed to talk to me.

"Fascinating," he says. "But you will read another?"

I continue to read until darkness sets in and another guard takes his place. As Dalen leaves, he glances back at me and smiles tentatively.

I believe I've just found my way out.

# CHAPTER 6

FOR TWO MORE DAYS, WE KEEP THE SAME RITUAL, DALEN AND I. EACH morning, he's outside my door when I wake. The filtered sunlight warms the straw in my pallet and makes the day seem full of possibilities, even though by noon any hopes I have are dashed.

But now something lingers in his expression, something softer and earnest. He's almost . . . happy to see me.

If I wasn't stuck behind these bars, and Hans wasn't in great danger, I might feel the same way. Dalen is quiet, but from watching his behavior, I can see he is kind. Curious hybrid children come by to stare at me like I'm an exotic bird in a cage. Dalen speaks to them softly, but the guard who takes his place after dinner chases them away and scowls at me. My stories have no effect whatsoever on him, but they do have the added benefit of concealing the noise while I slowly sharpen my flint on the stone floor.

This morning I lie still with my eyes closed. High above, birds sing greetings to the sun and each other. The hum of bees and the rush of the river form a soft blanket of sound. For one moment I wrap myself in it, leaving all my troubles behind.

It's fleeting.

My breakfast tray clanks on the shelf and the bars creak as Dalen lifts them up and pushes it through. I crack my eyes open, but my face is still hidden in shadows, and he can't see it. He cranes his neck with an odd, hopeful expression on his face.

"Good morning," I say.

He skitters back. "I didn't think you were awake yet."

I swing my legs down and sit up, stretching. He glances back toward something farther down the path.

"What's wrong?" I ask.

He shakes his head. "Nothing. Just checking."

"For what?"

He doesn't answer. Instead, he resumes his silent posture, but his eyes remain on the path leading to the humongous tree and my prison. Dalen is positioned in a manner that seems oddly protective. It makes me uneasy.

I take out my book and open it, running my fingers over the edges of the pages and the illustrations. But when I start to read, Dalen hushes me with alarm. "Not today."

"What's wrong?" I ask, fear gnawing at me. "Why are you acting so strange?"

"Keep your voice down." His tail swats at invisible flies.

"Something *is* wrong. I knew it." I put my book down and lean up against the bars. "Please, tell me."

He turns his head back, the concern in his eyes startling me. "The night guard, Roman, he thinks I'm"—he pauses—"getting attached. He's suspicious of you."

"And you're not?" Hope rises in my chest.

He shakes his head. "I don't think you pose any danger."

"You believe me, then? That the wizard is dead?"

"I don't believe you have any reason to lie, nor that the wizard would have any reason to follow you if you're mistaken."

"What do you think Roman will do?"

"I don't know. Have the council relieve me of my guard duties, perhaps?"

Dalen has been the one saving grace about this captivity. The one tiny speck of light. "I hope they don't do that."

"Me too," he says. He squeezes my hand between the bars, and I squeeze back, holding on to this first shred of kindness.

I spend the morning whispering fairy tales to Dalen, and it seems to soften his fears somewhat. He tilts his head toward the bars to hear me better. I pull the straw pallet off my bed and move it closer so he doesn't have to try so hard to hear.

I start a new tale, one that is frighteningly familiar to me, though I do my best not to let on. "Deep in the old forest there lived a witch who spent her days traveling in a hut that moved on chicken feet." I can't help shivering. Perhaps there is more truth in fairy tales than I realized.

"Are you cold?" Dalen asks.

"No, thank you, I'm fine."

He frowns but remains quiet. I continue.

"The witch was ravenous and had a taste for girls and boys. They were more tender than adults."

I know it's only a story. But this is my witch. It's all too real, and she'll come for me if I can't escape. A maniacal urge to laugh rises up my chest, and I fumble with the pages.

So many of these stories end badly. The mermaid who turns into seafoam. The little girl who dies in the freezing cold because no one will buy her flints. The princess who eats the apple and never wakes up.

I don't think I can stomach knowing how this one ends. I refuse to let it be my ending.

I have to return to Belladoma to ensure that. The awful ocean roars in my ears, a dizzying drop off a cliff before my eyes.

The book slips from my hands, wrenching me back to the present, and I scramble to retrieve it.

Dalen notices my distress. "Are you unwell?"

A way out. I can't read any more today. "Yes, I'm sorry. Perhaps I can read more tomorrow."

Dalen opens the door of my cell and helps me move my bedding back to the far wall. My eyes flick to the open door, but I don't run this time. I know there are more guards not far from here, and they have four long legs to move them instead of my short two.

"Can I get you anything? Do you feel faint?" The

concern on his face is touching, but nothing can ease my pain.

"Only one thing will make me feel better and you can't do it."

He places a warm hand on my shoulder, his silver eyes flashing. "Tell me what it is."

"Let me go." He snaps his hand away.

"You're right. I can't do that." He trots out of my cell and locks the door behind him. "What was it about that story that upset you so?"

Centaurs. They really are too smart for their own good.

"That story hit close to home. Every story starts with a grain of truth. This one has a whole rock." My skin feels strangely itchy, like it doesn't quite fit anymore.

He startles. "Your witch has a chicken hut too?"

I lean back against the wall of my cell, wrapping my arms around my middle. "Oh yes. That story is very real."

"Are you certain?" Dalen's silver eyes are wide, but he hasn't called me a liar. Yet.

I laugh bitterly. "Very."

I recount the story, from the feather in my brother's room to my encounter with the witch and her chicken hut. My hands shake and I clasp them together while I talk. If I am to escape, I must be stronger than that, and only feign weakness when it might give me an advantage.

Dalen listens to my tale as raptly as he did to the stories in the book.

"What happened next?" he asks.

"The witch was going to eat us both, but I struck a deal

with her. I would find something she wants desperately in exchange for my brother's life. I only have until the full moon, and I've wasted so much time here." I shoot to my feet. Sitting feels wrong. How can I sit idly by while Hans waits in his cage, being fattened up by that witch?

I collect myself, then turn back to Dalen. I know what I'll do. I've been sharpening that flint, bit by bit every night. Soon, I'll have it sharpened to a point and I will use it to unlock my cell while the guard changes.

"What must you find for the witch?" Dalen asks. Kind Dalen, who I must betray and mislead without a second thought if it means escaping to help my brother. I swallow the lump of guilt.

"A cornucopia. Supposedly King Ensel had one. It's how he kept the courtiers in line. Anyone who wanted to eat had to be a courtier. Or he'd feed their daughters to the Sonzeeki in return. It's why it was so competitive—who wouldn't want to eat and keep their family alive?"

The crashing waves filled with writhing black tentacles roll back in with the memory of Belladoma and its evil ruler.

"What would she want with the cornucopia?" Dalen frowns.

"It gives the person drawing food from it exactly the sort that is their favorite and in unlimited supply. If I don't deliver it by the deadline, not only will she eat Hans, but she'll come for me, too."

Dalen straightens his back. "She won't reach you here. We are too well hidden and protected."

"No, you're not. Her sense of smell is abnormally keen. I can't hide from her, no matter how far away I run. Keeping me here puts all of you in danger too." Granted, these are only the witch's claims, but if they scared me, I'm betting they'll scare these hybrids more.

A hint of fear flickers in his eyes. "You're wrong. The only creatures we need to fear are wizards."

I shake my head again and return to my cot, fists clenched and digging into my sides. "Don't say I didn't warn you."

Dalen tries to speak to me again, but I curl up and pretend I'm sleeping. Instead, I cry.

I don't move until dinner arrives and Dalen again enters my cell to "wake" me from my fake slumber.

"Greta, you must eat something."

I sit up to take the tray from him. How would we get along if we had met under better circumstances than these? He is very different from me, of course, but in some ways we are more alike than I expected. If they weren't my captors, I might not mind these hybrids so much.

"Thanks," I mutter.

"I'm sorry. About earlier," he says softly, still standing in front of me. He paws the ground. I wonder if he does that when he's nervous.

I shrug and pick at my food.

"Do you really think the witch will try to find you here?"

My eyes, alive and angry, meet his—all my frustration at

being held captive directed toward him. "Without a doubt."

He's visibly shaken. "I—"

"Dalen!" snaps a voice behind him. "What do you think you're doing?"

Dalen leaves my cell instantly. "Just giving Greta her dinner, Roman."

"You've named her?" The older centaur scoffs. "Go home—your shift is over."

Dalen starts to leave, but pauses. "I didn't name her. She already had one."

"You'd do better not to learn it. She's nothing to us. Go home."

He begins to say something, but at the unwavering scowl on Roman's face, he thinks better of it. He takes off down the path without a backward glance.

"What do you think you're doing?" Roman growls.

"Sitting." I've returned to picking at my meal.

"Sitting?" He clenches his spear more tightly than before.

"Yes."

"If you're trying to win over our young colt there, don't bother. The good of our village and survival of our species comes first in all things. Nothing will change that. Don't even try."

His words make my argumentative spirit flare. "If you're certain, why bother warning me away? Besides, he did nothing more than hand me my dinner tray." I smile sweetly at him. "I think you might be overreacting."

Roman's hooves stamp the ground, his scowl likely

permanently etched on his face. "Mind your place, human."

I bristle. "I would. But my place isn't in this village or this cell. And I think we all know that."

He rears and scowls angrily, but no longer tries to engage me in conversation. Once I finish my dinner, I toss the tray onto the shelf and lie down on my bed, pulling the blanket over me. With my back to Roman, and his back to me, I pull out the piece of flint hidden beneath my pillow and slowly begin to sharpen the point.

# CHAPTER 7

I HAVE BEEN HERE, LOCKED IN THIS CELL, FOR FIVE DAYS. EVEN THOUGH my makeshift lock pick gets ever sharper, my hopes for saving Hans fade with each sunset.

And for saving myself. I haven't forgotten the witch's promise to find me should I fail to execute my task. I shiver in the dim light of dawn. It's never truly sunny in this village, only light and dark, wet or dry.

But the hybrids aren't cruel; not even Roman. These people are simply scared. They faced a true threat through no fault of their own. I must convince them the threat is gone. From what I've gleaned from Dalen, they've done nothing to really look into my claims about the wizard's death.

This morning, as Dalen hands me the usual bowl of porridge and nuts, I gather my courage and hope it is enough.

"Will you help me?"

His silver eyes widen; then his brow furrows. "What do you mean?"

"I've told you about my brother's predicament, and how he needs me to save him." I set the porridge down and grasp the bars that separate us. "He's all I have left of my family. I'm the only one who can save him. Please, help me."

Dalen's eyes water, and he takes a cautious step back. "I don't know."

"I must get out of here. I won't tell a soul about any of you!"

"I'm sorry," he says again, but more with his eyes than his words.

I take a deep breath and start again. "I know you're scared. I understand why; the wizard was a horrid, frightening man. But he's gone. I swear on my life it's the truth."

Something inside Dalen shifts. He steps closer and places his hands around the bars.

"I believe you, Greta." He sighs. "I don't know if I can make them believe you too. But I will try."

My hope burns like a candle flame. Hot and painful, yet what I desperately need. "Thank you."

Dalen opens his mouth to speak, but before he can utter a word, screams and wails break out in the village.

Something is terribly wrong.

He looks from me to the path and back to me. "Go," I say. "I'll still be here when you come back."

It's a lie, of course, but it gets him to leave. I don't feel as victorious as I expected. I'm almost sorry to see him go.

And I'm dying to know what's going on out there.

But this may be my only chance.

As soon as Dalen trots out of sight, I take my flint pick and get to work on the lock. It's slow going, listening for just the right click of the tumblers.

To my chagrin, the sound of hoofbeats returns all too quickly. I hide my flint pick in my pocket, then crane my neck to see out the bars as Dalen comes around the corner and back into the permanent shade of the enormous tree.

"What is it?" I ask.

His face is drawn and pale, and he's out of breath. He has a large pack on his back now, and when he pulls something out of it, I have trouble breathing too.

A large yellow-and-brown feather.

I scramble back until I can feel the cool tree beneath my fingers. The witch is here. Already. Horror claws up my throat. What if she changed her mind? What if the deal is off?

Dalen grabs me by the shoulders—when did he come into my cell?—and calls my name. "Greta? Greta, it's the witch, isn't it?"

I can only nod, struggling to breathe.

"A hybrid child has been missing since yesterday. Roman told me her bones were just found outside our village." He holds up the feather. "This was lying next to them."

I sink to the pallet, head in my hands. More death I couldn't stop. "It's a message meant for me," I whisper.

"Come," Dalen says. "I'm taking you to the council. Right now."

He pulls me up and hauls me toward the path, grabbing my pack in the process as though he's ready to toss me out into the woods this second. Roman greets us with his perma-scowl. "Where do you think you're taking the prisoner?"

"To the council. They need to hear what she has to say. It cannot wait."

To my shock, Dalen pushes past the older centaur, who seems equally surprised. He doesn't stop us, and I don't look back. Why bother? I know he's still scowling.

Dalen leads me into the green-hued light, lovely and floating with specks of pollen from the flowers hanging down on vines. The place is beautiful, but the air is tinged with the smell of rotting fruit left out in the sun. Faint, but enough to make me shiver.

The villagers are out in full force, but as I pass among them, there are no looks of wonder and curiosity. Only grief lives in their eyes. And suspicion. I'm new; I must have brought this on them.

The worst part is knowing they're right.

"What do you think this will accomplish?" I whisper to Dalen.

"If she's following you, then letting you go is the right decision—it's best for the village."

"What if they just want to kill me and thwart her that way?"

His mouth flops open. "They wouldn't—I—no, they wouldn't do that."

When we near a platform in front of a round hut in

59

the center of the village, the crush of hybrids divides and I stand before the council of elders. A representative from each species of hybrid stands on the platform. All have graying hair, fur, feathers, or scales, and all examine me with an unfriendly gaze.

The snake-man slithers forward, while the others growl in my direction. Fear worms its way under my skin, but Dalen's hands on my shoulders reassure me a little.

"Our young guard has informed you of our sssad news, I sssee," the snake-man says, slithering closer. He smells of earth and rot, and frankly he scares me more than the rest of them together.

"Yes. He showed me the feather."

Murmurs ring from the crowd.

"It means something to you?" the ancient mermaid council member asks.

"It's from a witch who lives in a chicken-footed hut and eats children." Someone behind me laughs, but the rest remain serious. I have no more to lose. I may as well come clean and tell them everything. "I told you before my brother is in grave danger and I must save him. This witch has him. I made a deal with her. I don't know what she'll do if I don't fulfill my end of the bargain, but I can't imagine it will be good."

"Ssstupid girl," hisses the snake-man. "Witches never keep their promissses. They're almost as bad as wizards."

"I had no choice!" I say. "I'd do anything to save my brother."

Dalen squeezes my shoulder, but it doesn't help.

"We spared your life, and you brought a witch down on our heads," grumbles the centaur elder. The snake-man returns to the group, and they retreat into a temple-like building in the square.

"What are they doing?" I ask Dalen.

"Deciding your fate," he says. Ice crawls up my spine despite the mass of hybrids surrounding me. Their faces are drawn and sad, with anger painted across them in stark lines.

Awful certainty takes hold. They aren't going to let me go. Dalen may not believe they'll kill me, but the hate pulsing through the crowd convinces me otherwise. It's a raw heat—I can almost feel it.

And smell it.

A terrible squawking kicks up, and a small herd of goat-chickens tears through the crowd, pecking and circling furiously. A familiar, unpleasant stench laced with woodsmoke wafts behind them, much stronger now than before. The gathered hybrids hiss and stamp at the unexpected strange creatures.

"She's here." I squeeze Dalen's arm tightly as he eyes the goat-chickens with astonishment.

Smoke curls out of the trees, slinking through the crowd of hybrids. They're puzzled at first, then scream and scatter as the chicken hut scrambles into the yard. It scratches at the earth, which happens to be occupied by a faun, who is launched into the air, then crumples to the ground in a limp heap.

Merfolk dive and vanish into the river. Centaurs immediately take up their bows and attempt to shoot the hut, but their arrows have no effect. They merely stick out of the side like pins in a feathered pincushion. It doesn't slow a whit. The elders burst out of their chamber.

Down the path strolls a lovely young woman with long dark hair. She walks right up to the center of the village with a menacing confidence that takes the hybrid council by surprise.

"Who—" The snake-man barely gets out the first word before his mouth is stuck shut. The witch merely glances at him. The other council members shrink back while he claws at his face.

"I have left you alone in my forest," she says sweetly, "and until now, you have never bothered me, and I have never developed a taste for your gamey flesh. But I will make a point of it if this girl does not go on her way immediately. She is performing a task for me, one I very much wish her to complete. You have already delayed her too long. If you wish to survive, you had better ensure she succeeds."

The mermaid elder is the first to find her voice. "We— we'll let the human girl go. Right away. We don't want any trouble from you."

At this, the witch smiles. "It is too late for apologies." She snaps her fingers, and a surge of magic singes the air.

In a flash, flames begin to devour the great tree in the middle of the village. A second later the witch has vanished into her hut, and it races away.

Any doubts I had about whether the witch could make good on her threats are gone too.

All I can see is red and orange and thick black smoke. I

can hardly even move. Screams fill the air like a swarm of flies.

This is my chance to escape.

I sprint away from the great tree. Awful creaks and cracks punctuate the wails, and I know all too well what that means: the canopy is about to come crashing down and rain fire on our heads.

I run headlong through the village. I have no idea where I'm going; I just need to get out.

Screams ring out all over, but a sharp one nearby stops me in my tracks.

"Dalen!" cries a young, frightened voice. The smoke is cleared by a gust of wind, and I see Dalen helping a centaur girl over a fallen tree, hampered by the large pack still on his back.

When he notices me, they race toward me, and then a pair of arms lifts me up and carries me, so I move faster than I did before—much faster than I could do on my own.

"You need to do as the witch says," Dalen's voice says in my ear, "or she'll kill us all."

We reach the outer edges of the village, but there is no relief. It is ringed by fire, magic no doubt, and it doesn't spread beyond the village. It's there to hem the hybrids in.

But the witch wants me to go after the cornucopia—she said so herself—which means there must be a way past it. One she knows I can figure out.

"Put me down," I say, and Dalen obeys. He paws the ground nervously. Horses do not like fire, and apparently centaurs are none too fond of it either. Standing behind him are the wide-eyed centaur filly and a centaur woman. They both bear a strong resemblance to Dalen. He must have gone after them as soon as the flames started.

I cast around on all sides, trying to find something that will help. The curve of the river lies a few paces to the east, but without a bucket it won't be much use. And really, if the fire is magical, it might not help.

If we can't extinguish it, and we can't get around it, how can we get through it?

My eyes light on Dalen's shoulder—my pack is still slung over it from when he dragged me from my cell. "Give me my pack. Hurry," I say.

He shoves it into my hands, his silver eyes never leaving the swelling flames. I yank out my blanket and cloak, then run to the river. I hold them underwater until they've soaked up as much as possible, then return to Dalen and his family.

"We're getting out of here, but we have to work together to do it." I throw my soaking cloak over my shoulders and hand the drenched blanket to Dalen. "Use this to cover up as much of your body as possible. Then we're going to run through the wall of fire. It looks like it's magic; we should be safe once we cross that line."

With shaking hands, Dalen hands the blanket to the filly. "Take it, Damara. Then throw it back through, and Mother will go next." He glances at me. "I'll go last."

"Suit yourself." I shrug. Damara puts the blanket over her shoulders and head, then paces in front of the flames.

More trees catch fire every second. I tug the blanket down, covering her eyes and face. "Run, and don't peek or you'll never do it."

She bolts forward and barrels through the flaming branches that stretch across the path. Dalen gives me a grateful look, then catches the blanket as it flies back through the fire. I douse it again to be safe. Then he places it over his mother's head, and she leaps through as well.

One more dousing and then it's the two of us. "We can go together." Terror swims in his silver eyes. Impulsively, I grab his hand and drag him with me. When I get to the flames I jump, curling myself into a ball within the cloak as much as possible, then tumble onto the mossy, unscorched forest floor beyond.

Dalen helps me to my feet, and only then do I realize we're surrounded by the furious faces of what remains of the council of elders.

# CHAPTER 8

**THE COUNCIL MEMBERS DID NOT FARE AS WELL AS WE DID. BURNS AND** ash cover their skin. They are not at all pleased to see me.

"You will leave usss," the snake-man says. "Immediately. You must swear upon your life you will not reveal the existence of our village to anyone." He glances at the flames still burning behind us. "It will take us time to rebuild what has been dessstroyed today. We have lost many because of you and your connection to the witch, and now she has charged usss with ensuring your successs. What is this task you agreed to do?"

I swallow hard. I had hoped to avoid telling them about the cornucopia. But now is not the time for deceit. "Fetch a cornucopia. King Ensel was the last known owner. That's why I'm headed to Belladoma."

"Then you must be ssswift so she will not bother us again. More than your brother depends on it now."

"I've been telling you for days I needed to leave. Don't blame me for this. I warned you." I fold my arms and glower at the council. Cowed and in dwindled numbers, they don't seem as scary as they did before.

The snake-man pulls himself up in front of me and Dalen.

"We have never had cause to trust a human before. For all we know, you and the witch are in this together, and your real plan is to destroy our speciesss. We will have a hard enough time staying hidden while we rebuild our village as it is. We must be certain you do not betray usss a second time. Dalen will accompany you to ensure you keep your promissse and get the witch what she wantsss. And he won't come back until the task is complete."

"You're sending me away from the village? But I can help here." From the expression on his face, Dalen did not expect this turn of events. He looks like he's been slapped.

"No, pick someone else," Dalen's mother says. Damara slips her hand into Dalen's and squeezes, but his face has returned to its usual stoic expression.

"Thanks to this human, there's nothing left to send you away from. Sssomeone must go with her or the whole village will be in peril again. Besides, you already have a pack of suppliesss. You are the most logical choice."

"But I only brought them because I thought the council would see reason and send her on her way. I thought the swifter she left, the better and safer for us." So that's why he had a larger pack when he came back for me. Now he'll need to use it himself.

The snake-man glances at the centaur elder and faun behind him. "I hear you've bonded with this human and that you are quickly becoming one of our best scouts. We need to ssssend someone who knows how to stay hidden and keep us a secret as long as possible. Your family owes the village a debt. If you want to keep what remains of that family sssafe, you will do this." Dalen shivers, but I don't let on that I've seen it. I can't help wondering what the snake-man means.

"I understand," Dalen says. His mother's face is now a few shades paler. "Good-bye, Mama." He embraces his mother and then his sister. I have nothing to gather up, save my wet blanket, cloak, and pack, and no one to say good-bye to. Within five minutes, Dalen and I set off.

His demeanor is more subdued than I expected. He hardly says a word as we leave his family behind and cross into the woods proper. We walk for an hour like this, yet the smell of woodsmoke clings to us, no matter how far we get from the village.

I finally decide to break the silence. "I'm sorry they're forcing you to come with me. I never meant to take you away from your family. I know how hard that can be."

"It isn't your fault." He trots onward. We've kept this pace so far, but any longer and I'll be exhausted well before nightfall.

"Dalen, slow down. I'm just as impatient to get this over with as you are."

Surprise flashes over his face, then he slows. "I'm sorry, I didn't realize." He sighs. "I miss my family already. My mother and sister are all I have left. My father . . ."

I bite my tongue even though I'm dying to ask.

"He was branded a traitor. He helped a group of travelers and it started rumors. People began to hunt for hybrids; it took years to quash the rumors and all of our magic to divert the hunters from the village. Father was banished. With the wizard on the loose, that was a death sentence."

I know enough of the wizard to have no doubt Dalen's father is no longer alive.

"I'm sorry. It sounds like your father was kind." I pluck a small branch from a nearby tree and pull the leaves off one by one. "I lost my father too."

Dalen looks at me with curiosity. "How?"

"My brother and I came home from school one afternoon to find both him and my mother gone. No note, no good-bye—they even left all their belongings." I break the branch in half and toss it into the undergrowth. "It was the strangest thing—like they had vanished into thin air. Something happened to them, but we don't know what. Even if I could have left Hans behind to go after them, I didn't have the faintest idea where to start looking."

"That's terrible, Greta. No wonder you're desperate to get your brother back."

Heat burns behind my eyes, but I refuse to let it show. His whole village is destroyed and he's not wailing.

"Guarding me was a test, wasn't it?" I ask, changing the

topic. "The council wanted to know if you'd do the same and help a human."

He laughs wryly. "They are still testing me. I will do my best to keep the village's survival in mind for all decisions. The elders made it clear your success is the key to keeping the witch away from us."

"I'm still your prisoner, then?"

"For now, while their spies might see us, yes. Once we're out of range, I have no desire to keep you from your family."

"And I have no desire to keep you from yours."

He gives me a fleeting smile. "I can't go back until the witch is satisfied."

"Then a rescue mission it is."

We trudge onward until we must stop to make camp for the night. To my relief we've seen no further sign of the witch. Between the hybrid child's death and the village fire, we've gotten the message clearly: keep moving or else.

How many lives will be on my head before this is all over?

As we unpack our bedding and start the cooking fire, I brush those thoughts aside, unwilling to dwell on them. There are some supplies in my pack, and Dalen catches a rabbit for our supper. Before long, we're full and trying to sleep by the dancing firelight.

"Greta?" Dalen says.

"Hmm?" I murmur.

"I—I don't think I can sleep."

With all that's changed for him today, I can't say I'm

surprised. I sit up and pull my book from my pack. "I think I can help with that."

I begin to read Dalen a story. He closes his eyes, leaning his head on the tree he rests against. By the time I finish the tale, he's snoring, and I curl back under my now-dry blanket. It reminds me of the times I used to read to Hans at night after our parents disappeared.

I am half asleep when I swear I see a pair of eyes staring at me from the shadows between the trees. I bolt upright. The strange eyes tilt over a hooked beak in the shadows, then blink and disappear. A moment later I see the retreating end of a striped tail.

I am dreaming. It only feels real.

I lie back down and pull my blanket up to my chin. When an owl hoots nearby, I pull it over my ears instead.

# CHAPTER 9

WHEN I WAKE, I'M STARTLED AND PANICKED TO FIND DALEN MISSING. HE settled down in the nook of a nearby tree last night, and now the hollow is empty.

The leaves across the grove rustle, driving me to my feet in seconds, the knife that Dalen returned to me clutched in my hand. The memory of those eyes in my dream haunts me. But my panic is short-lived. Dalen trots into the glade with his bow and quiver slung over his shoulders and a wild goose in hand.

"Oh, you're up. Breakfast and lunch," he says, holding up the goose in one hand and a couple of eggs in the other. A lopsided grin rests on his face, and a few rays of sun break through the clouds overhead, dappling his skin. I smile back.

"You scared me." I eye the eggs, and my stomach rumbles. "But for breakfast, I'll forgive just about anything."

I start the fire and he takes a small pan out of his pack—he is carrying considerably more than I, which I can't deny has come in handy. I might not mind having Dalen around.

"Do you have a plan for when we get to Belladoma?" Dalen asks.

"Sort of," I say, hesitant to admit that no, I don't. I haven't gotten that far yet.

He looks at me expectantly.

"From the last time I was there, I know tunnels run throughout Belladoma and the castle, and an entrance to them is outside the city. I've seen it once before. I remember the general area where it's located. We can sneak in through that and find our way to the castle. Ensel would have kept the cornucopia close at hand. It's the best place to start." I can almost smell the salty tang of Belladoma, and it makes my stomach turn.

Dalen stirs the scrambled eggs thoughtfully. "Are these tunnels large enough for me to navigate?"

Drat. I hadn't thought of that. "I don't know. We'll find out, I expect."

He sighs. "Yes, well, I won't be able to wander the city. I shall have to stay hidden."

I frown. Dalen tagging along is creating more problems than I thought it would. "Perhaps you can stay in the woods while I sneak in and back out?"

He smiles wryly. "I promised not to let you out of my sight, remember?"

"You're going to have to break that promise at some point."

He's silent and pensive for a few minutes, and the smell of food makes my stomach growl, drowning out the thoughts of Belladoma. This centaur boy has survived a lot too—even the burning down of his village and possible death of his friends.

He divides the eggs between two small bowls and hands one to me, glancing at the gathering clouds in the distance. "We may run into that storm ahead later in the day. There are a few villages scattered about this region. Perhaps we should keep an eye out for an inn if the storm gets bad. You could barter for room and board, while I hide in the stables with the horses."

"Shelter for the night would be nice, but all I have left in the world are my clothes and a few items in my pack." I pat the satchel beside me. "We have nothing to barter with."

"No," he says. "*You* don't have anything to barter with. I, however, do."

I finish my eggs and give him an indignant look. "Like what?"

"We've collected many bits and bobs and assorted things that fall onto the paths near our village. It led to rumors of robbers and ghosts in the woods. Anything to make people not inclined to wander too close to where we live. Humans are quite careless, but we hold on to everything. I can cover any bartering we need to do."

Suddenly, I feel awkward, as though this is something I should have considered before chasing Hans.

"All right. Thank you."

He finishes his meal, then packs his things. I follow suit and we head into the woods once more. We walk in silence for almost a mile before it becomes unsettling.

"Dalen," I say slowly. "Do you hear that?"

He stops and tilts his head, listening to the trees around us. Only the wind rustles through the branches overhead. He frowns. "No, I hear nothing."

"That's the problem." I pull my knife out of my belt and glance behind us. My body is tense, ready to run if danger presents itself. Dalen nods, and motions that we should cautiously keep moving forward.

Back is not an option. The witch has made certain of that. The knowledge that she hovers somewhere at the edges of my life, waiting, watching, ensures it.

She may not keep her side of the bargain—she is a witch, after all—but at present playing her game is the only option I have.

We walk painfully slowly to make minimal sound for several minutes. Then an owl hoots nearby, startling us both. Those same eyes I saw in my dream peer from the face of an owl around a tree on the other side of the path. It blinks, and I blink back. What is an owl doing on the ground instead of in a tree? And why is it out during the day? I could've sworn they're nocturnal creatures.

But then, nothing is as it should be in this forest.

Before I can say a word about it to Dalen, the creature has vanished.

"What is it, Greta? Did you see something?" Dalen's face is lined with worry.

"No, not exactly." I fold my arms across my chest. Did I imagine that strange animal? "I thought I saw something, but whatever it was, it's gone now."

Sure enough, the birds are chirping again. We continue on.

But now I can't help but think of the wizard and his misdeeds. I thought I was dreaming last night, but what if that odd creature, half raccoon, half owl, was real? I only saw the top half of it—the rest of its body hid behind the tree. Could it be one of the wizard's creations, like the goat-chickens? Or is someone else inventing new hybrids now? If the latter, it is not someone we want to encounter. I'm not equipped to deal with people playing with dangerous magic.

This thought bothers me exceedingly. I need a distraction, but I can't take my mind off hybrids.

"Hybrids are made of magic, yes?"

Dalen nods as he trots along. He is much faster than me, and I can tell he consciously walks slower so I don't have to run.

"What can you do with that magic?"

"What do you mean?" he asks, puzzled.

I cough. "I mean, can you do spells or are you just made from magic?"

"Oh, I see," he says. "There's a difference between

being made of magic and being able to manipulate it. We are magical. To harness that power, we need to sacrifice a piece of ourselves." He shakes his head. "It isn't something we do often, and only when absolutely necessary. For example, our mermaids used many of their scales to set up the wards around the village to discourage travelers from wandering in, but it was a slow and painstaking process. They had to rest and recuperate so they would not use too much of themselves and their life force."

So that's how they knew so quickly that I'd fallen into their domain. The wards warned them when I got too close. "The magic in you is part of what gives you life—so if you use too much of it, you'd die?"

"Correct," he says gravely.

"Are you always like that?" I ask, gesturing to Dalen's horse end. "Or can you change to all horse or all human?"

He laughs. "That is the oddest question I have ever heard."

"You don't have to answer," I say.

He smiles, silver eyes glowing. "No. We remain as you see us, half one creature, half another. Or for some hybrids, different splits. But the result is the same. We remain as the magic crafted us."

He pulls a strip of bark off a birch and chews thoughtfully on it.

"However, we do have our legends, and they tell of the first hybrid. The Phoenix Queen, mother of us all. She cast the spell that allowed our varied species to be created. The Phoenix Queen wasn't just formed from magic, she *was* magic, and she could wield it as well. Almost like dragons, but she had far more power at her disposal. She could shift forms between human and any animal she pleased. To rule her hybrid people, she most often took the form of a winged woman."

"She sounds fascinating," I say. His description reminds me oddly of Kymera. "What happened to her?"

"No one knows. Every fifty years, her mortal form would burst into flames, and she would be reborn from the ashes. Each time a little different, and a little more powerful. But the last time she did not come back. Legend says her ashes scattered to the winds, dripping magic across the lands." Dalen paws the ground. "What of your hybrid friend? The one who killed the wizard?"

Sadness washes over me. "Her name was Kymera. The wizard made her. She had huge black wings, cat's claws, and a tail. And eyes that could change from perfect blue to cat's yellow." I pause. "She was rather kind, and sweet, for a monster. But she was not a natural creation by any means."

Nor were the goat-chickens, or that strange thing I may or may not have seen in my dreams.

"How fascinating," Dalen says. "Was she able to do magic, too?"

I shudder at the thought. Kymera was always well-intentioned, but magic in her hands would have been dangerous while the wizard had her brainwashed. She was dangerous enough as she was. "No, thankfully. The wizard was bad enough. He convinced her she was saving our city's girls, when really he had her steal them from a quarantine hospital and send them off to Belladoma. Ensel used this to his advantage and held them captive to be the Sonzeeki's monthly meals."

"The wizard was a truly wretched being. I'm glad to hear he is dead."

"Did you ever have a run-in with him?"

Dalen's face clouds over. "Not personally. But my father never returned, and never tried to contact us again. I can only assume . . ." He trails off, tail flailing.

"I'm sorry." I put a hand on his arm. "I lost many friends to the wizard too."

I'm beginning to fear I miss too many people. I must move forward or the past will swallow me whole.

# CHAPTER 10

BY NIGHTFALL WE ARE NEARLY BACK TO MY ORIGINAL ROUTE. THE SKIES broke open midafternoon, and though the rain has stopped now, our cloaks are still drenched. More people travel in this area, and buildings occasionally sprout up in the woods. Sleeping in the open will be tricky tonight.

"We should look for an inn," Dalen says. "Then you can pretend I'm a horse that you're keeping in the stables while you take a room inside."

"It's a good idea, but we may have to be very sneaky to make it work."

The innkeeper may not be keen on renting a room to a girl with only baubles to her name. I'm not wild about trespassing, but we'll do what we must.

The buildings become closer together and I'm grateful

it's late at night. Far too many people would be on the streets if it were not nearly midnight. I shudder. We'll have to sleep quickly and rise early if we want to leave without any trouble.

A tavern with a gaily painted sign appears on our right. A stable sits behind it. Dalen's tail flicks when he hears the horses whinny softly in the darkness.

I lead Dalen into the tavern yard, sticking as close as possible to the side of the building. A few shops lie across the street, all dark paneling and white trim like the inn and tavern. Raucous voices ring out from inside, and the sour smell of ale and sweat wafts through the windows. I give Dalen my pack and advise him to duck low in the bushes while I go inside. He keeps his head and torso down as much as he can, but nothing can be done about his horse half. If anyone glances out the window as he passes, they'll just see a horse's rear end.

The door to the tavern creaks when I open it and step into the smoky, half-lit room. All I want to do is find the innkeeper, barter for a room, and, barring that, hide in the stables with Dalen.

"Hey, Jakob, more ale!" cries a tall man with a deep voice and long arms. "Our mercenary friends here must celebrate." The words catch my ears. Mercenaries. Men who sell their allegiance and skill with a sword. Those are the sort of men Ensel employed in his army.

A thin older man with long graying hair looks up from his books. He shakes his head at the first man and nods at the young barmaid. The man must be Jakob, and if he's in charge, he must be the innkeeper. An older woman with hair the same shade as Jakob's walks out of the kitchen and into the hall carrying a basket of rolls.

"Do you have the coin for it, Aaron, or are you just blustering again?" the barmaid says. The men all laugh, and I imagine it is at Aaron's expense. I push my way through the crowd, headed for Jakob's side of the bar. At least twenty men crowd around the tables, many of them wearing cloaks with a scrolling red insignia on the shoulder, marking them as mercenaries. These are not men to be trifled with. I must be quick.

"What? Of course I do! Besides, these men are doing us a favor. You should be giving it away on the house."

"Really? A favor? What good have they done?" the barmaid scoffs.

Steel jangles and wooden benches screech as they're shoved back. Tall men with long swords tower over me and the rest of the patrons. I try not to cringe, edging closer to the innkeeper's station. That barmaid should not have asked such a question, not if they're like the mercenaries I remember. Those men were gruff and ruthless, unkind to all but the one who paid them—Ensel.

The man continues, oblivious to the dead silence around him. "Why, they're keeping us safe, cleaning up after that wizard—" His words suddenly choke off. A knife whistles through the air, knocking several plates off the bar and landing just shy of the barmaid's fingers on the tap.

"S-sorry, sirs," the barmaid stutters, "I didn't mean no offense."

"You should know," a new, deep voice says, giving me shivers, "that I am Vincali, captain of the mercenary league, and ruler of Belladoma." The man who speaks has dark, stringy hair that hangs down to his shoulders, and eyes like black bottomless pits.

Several gasps echo before the room falls to silence. My heart sinks into my feet. Nothing good can come of the mercenaries taking over that city. I reach the innkeeper at last. "Excuse me, sir," I say, but he only gives me a cursory look, then goes back to his books.

"Isn't that lovely," the first man giggles. He's clearly drunk. "Ensel died before he could pay them properly, so they took their payment by taking the city."

"Well, that's something worth celebrating, then," the barmaid says, voice quivering. I glance over and ball my hands into fists. The mercenary man who spoke, Vincali, has retrieved his knife and now holds it against her throat while she refills his glass.

Bullies. The whole lot of them. I hate bullies.

But I swallow my dislike and try again to talk to the innkeeper. "Excuse me, sir, but I would like to barter for a room for the night." I hold up several of the shiny objects Dalen brought with him, dotted with one or two coins. Even I know it's not nearly enough for a shared room, let alone a private one. But if some of these are real silver, he just might go for it.

The innkeeper raises his eyebrows and examines my offer. "This is no place for children."

I resist rolling my eyes. "My parents will join me shortly,"

I lie. "They just sent me on an errand to get a room."

Laughter breaks out behind me. "Jakob, are you renting rooms to babies now?"

Fuming, I glance behind to see Vincali sneering. His attention is the last thing I need.

Jakob pushes my hands away. "No. I was just telling her to run off and rejoin her parents."

Vincali steps closer, his sword jangling at his side with each step. "Yes, they must be looking for you. I doubt they'd appreciate you spending their money." He glances down at my hands. I snap them closed and drop them to my sides. "Or bartering their silverware."

My face flushes and it only makes me madder. "Excuse me." I push past him, moving toward the door. Every nerve is taut with fear. I can't afford to draw any more attention than I already have. Especially not from the people who currently run Belladoma.

Snickers crop up in the crowd. I keep my head high as I open the door and step out.

With a quick look to ensure I have not been followed, I duck around the porch and join Dalen in the bushes. I shoulder my pack and signal him to move toward the woods beyond the stables.

When we reach the corner of the inn, I glance around, then shrink back. A mercenary now stands by the front door, smoking a pipe, and puffing curling smoke into the air. Dalen wrinkles his nose.

"What on earth is that horrid—"

84

"Be quiet," I whisper. He gives me an indignant look but obeys. "The men in there are dangerous. We must be cautious."

Dalen goes absolutely still. "I know how to remain hidden," he whispers. "I have practiced it all my life."

I breathe out, relieved.

"Do you know who those men are?" he asks.

I shudder. "Yes. We don't want to cross them, I can assure you of that. We can't stay here tonight. Besides, the innkeeper refused to barter for a room."

When the man's back is turned, we creep softly over the grass toward the stables and the woods beyond.

"Do you hear that?" Dalen whispers.

Footsteps. Laughter. The clank of swords.

All headed in this direction. The front door of the tavern bursts open and we break into a run. I hope the distance and the shadows are enough to conceal us. We must reach safety as quickly as possible.

At first they speak in muffled voices, too far away for us to hear what they say. They do not look our way, and the tightness in my chest begins to unwind.

"Get on my back," Dalen says, bending his horse half down.

"What?" I say, bewildered. My pulse stutters with every shout and laugh from the direction of the mercenaries.

"You can't outrun them, but I can. It's the only way we'll escape without getting caught."

I jump up and awkwardly sit on his back, tying one end

of the ropes securing his pack around my waist.

"Go," I whisper.

"Put your arms around me," he says. "It will keep you from slipping."

I do, and then he ambles forward, only to step on a branch hidden by the tall grass. Suddenly, six pairs of unsavory eyes burn into our backs and a shout goes up.

"Run," I whisper. He throws himself into the forest at full speed. I cling to him, forehead pressed against his back, terrified I'll fall off any second. I hate running, but we're far outnumbered and have no weapons that can match their swords.

I've been told I'm brave, but I'm not stupid.

We plunge into the forest, branches whipping by our heads. Dalen ducks and weaves as much as possible, but a couple catch me on the back and shoulders. It smarts; it will bruise by morning.

But I'll take that any day of the week over what those men back at the tavern might do.

The sounds of pursuit follow quicker than I'd hoped. Pounding hoofbeats and men's shouts echo through the trees. A few curses and the word *hybrid* reach my ears. A hard knot of terror forms in my gut.

Moonlight streams through the trees, both a blessing and a curse. It lights our path, but it will also make it easier for our pursuers to spot us.

"We have to find someplace to hide," I say.

"I agree. But I am afraid I do not know this part of the woods."

"Keep an eye out for something."

Fortunately, the mercenaries' horses are not closing in yet. Dalen is fast, even with me on his back. What will they do with Dalen if they catch us? Sell him as a slave? No, the wizard taught us all one thing—hybrids are more valuable dead than alive. They'll kill him, and sell his parts for a fortune at one of the traveling markets.

Sickly heat crawls over my skin. Dalen is smart and kind, and he was the first to believe my story. It's up to me to keep him safe.

The sound of rushing water soon drowns out the hoofbeats pounding behind us. The river is up ahead. We might be able to lose them there. But the thought of all that water makes me dizzy.

The terrain becomes more hilly and rocky, and I fear Dalen grows tired.

"Should we try crossing the river?" he says. "It isn't far off."

"Soon, yes. But not right away. We need to throw them off our trail as much as possible first." I swallow hard, determined to keep my eyes focused on the dimly lit woods.

The river comes into view, rippling water sparkling in the moonlight. Dalen gallops along the bank, but the water is too wide and deep to cross yet.

"We need a shallower spot; otherwise the current will drag us to who knows where."

He turns south and picks up speed, following the river's edge. The trees are thinner, but the river shows no sign of narrowing. Horse hooves and snapping branches echo in the dark stillness of the woods. An owl hoots its disapproval. Our pursuers are not as far behind as I'd like them to be anymore.

Dalen runs down a hill. Then something dark and solid looms over the riverbank ahead. The river runs right through one of the larger hills, creating a cave. Perhaps this one has offshoot tunnels as well. Places we could lose the mercenaries. If Dalen can even fit inside. The bank between the cave wall and the river might be too narrow.

"Head for that cave. We might be able to follow it through and lose them on the other side, or find a tunnel to hide in."

He gives me a skeptical look over his shoulder, then shrugs. He doesn't have any better ideas.

Even with the moonlight overhead, the cave is hard to see. Something large and hungry could be waiting just inside, or rocks could be ready to trip us and toss us into the rushing water.

Or there could be a way out.

Dalen breathes heavily. I'm a burden to him now. At the least, we need a place to hide and rest. He skids to a stop at the entrance to the cave and peers inside.

"This is narrow, but I think I can do it. If it gets narrower, I will be in trouble."

"You'll be fine," I say encouragingly, though I don't feel half so certain. "I'll go first." I dismount and wobble into the cave. I take Dalen's hand and tug him after me. My legs are sore after riding, but I force myself to continue. I reach out for balance, but the sides of the cave are slick with damp stone and moss that gives off a faint light. I press on, feet solidly on the edge, keeping one eye glued to the rushing river beside me, hoping for an inner tunnel on the left. Anything to make them lose their trail. Anything to get away from all this water. Behind me Dalen groans.

"Shhh," I whisper.

"Sorry," he says. "This place makes me uncomfortable."

I squeeze his hand because I doubt he can see my smile in the darkness, but I have to release it to keep my balance.

Moments later, I hear the sound of something heavy sliding.

*Splash!*

I whirl. Dalen flails in the water with all six appendages. I grab at his hands, but the current yanks him out of reach. He can't get ahold of the riverbank and the cave doesn't have any sort of branch or vine for me to use to reach him.

Panic streams up my arms, but I shove it down. I don't have time to panic.

Instead, I run. I follow his waving arms and bobbing head and hindquarters in the faint cave light. I must figure something out. Or follow the river until he finds something to grab onto.

I will not lose him like I lost my friends.

The only good thing is that since Dalen had a hard time passing through this cave, so will the men chasing us. In fact, this may be the perfect way to lose them entirely.

Provided, of course, Dalen doesn't die in the process.

I run with all my might, ignoring my sore muscles and the vise of fear that seems to be squeezing my chest, but the river is faster than me. It tosses him around a bend, and out of my line of sight. The faint sounds of slow hoof steps echo from the cave entrance.

It won't be easy for them to follow, I remind myself. Maybe they'll give up. Sure, it might be nice to have a hybrid to sell off, but he's not worth risking their necks over.

I take the turn as fast as I dare, and relief floods over me at the sight of moonlight at the end of the cave tunnel. A way out.

Dalen flies right through it. He might be hurt. I can't imagine trying to maneuver a horse body underwater, not with the violent current tugging me along. And yet he doesn't cry out. Does he know it would give us away?

I don't know that even I could manage that.

What if he's unconscious? His lungs could be filling with more water every second I delay.

I pick up the pace and burst out into the moonlit night. No horses and riders threaten, no wild animals near.

No Dalen, either. Nothing at all.

My heart pounds in my chest, and I ball my hands into fists at my sides as I catch my breath. The memory of tentacles slapping wet rocks reverberates in my mind and drives me to my knees. A girl's scream echoes for ages. The stickiness of salt coats my skin, making it itch. Then I scratch too deeply, the sharpness stinging me back to the present.

I can't leave poor Dalen treading water. Or worse, underwater.

I take off, scanning the river for any sign of a horse or boy. Or any large obstructions that the water has to run over. My legs burn and all I want to do is lie down and sleep. But I can't rest until I have my centaur back. He wouldn't leave me behind if it were me in that river.

On my way, I find a sturdy-looking stick that isn't too unwieldy. I grab it, then keep on running. It's useless if I can't find him, but I'm operating under the assumption I will.

Up ahead, a tree branch appears to be stuck in the river.

And then a head, hair dripping with water, bursts over the waves, and gasps.

"Dalen!" I cry, then clamp my free hand over my mouth. What a stupid thing to do. Even Dalen knew better.

Fortunately, no sounds of pursuit follow. At least, not yet.

I reach the branch Dalen clings to and tug on it with all my might. It's more like a tree half submerged in the water than a branch, and it doesn't budge so much as creak. It makes me nervous. A wild look takes hold in Dalen's eyes. "Please, Greta. Get me out of this water," he sputters.

"Of course I will," I say, faking all the bravado I can muster, as though pulling centaurs out of rivers is something I do each day before breakfast.

I use the branch I picked up on my way over to reach out as far as I dare and still keep my own feet planted on the riverbank. I'm keenly aware of any slight shifts or give in the silt below my feet. One false move, and we'll both be in the water.

He grabs onto the end, and it's all I can do not to tumble headlong after. He's much heavier than I expected, and he's weighed down by all the water he has soaked up and swallowed.

"Come on, kick your legs to help move your body to the bank."

Another wave washes over his face, slurring whatever response he makes.

He shakes his head, terror and relief mixing in his expression, and I wonder if one of his legs is broken.

Slowly but surely, I drag Dalen toward the bank against the current, while he pulls himself closer hand over hand on the submerged tree. Finally, he reaches the edge, and with one last tug he pushes off with his legs and he is up and over the bank. He scrambles to get as far from the edge as possible. I'm relieved nothing appears to be broken, especially his legs.

I pat his back while he coughs up river water.

"Remind me to never go swimming again," he says.

I laugh with relief. "If I'd had any idea you were planning to dive in, I would've discouraged you."

He rests on the grass for a moment, staring up between the trees. "Where are we?"

For the first time, I look around us—really look around us—and realize the trees are different here. Not many pine and birch and oak, but more spindly trees, shorter and newer. And more vines and greenery.

Truth is, I have no idea where we are.

We are completely lost.

# CHAPTER 11

**WE WERE TOO EXHAUSTED TO DO ANYTHING BUT MAKE CAMP LAST**
night. I helped Dalen dry off and start a small fire. We risked
giving away our position, but if we hadn't warmed him up,
he might have become ill, and that was just as risky. At first
he shivered violently, but while the fire's heat warmed his
muscles, I read him fairy tales until he fell into a fitful sleep.

The pack was latched onto Dalen tightly enough that
he managed to keep most of the contents. It weighed him
down and didn't help his rescue, but I'm grateful to have it.

Even if it is still damp.

Our food, however, did not fare so well. Most of the
bread and cheese is ruined, and the bits of jerky we had left
are disgusting. We'll have to catch our meals now. Water we
have in abundance.

Our breakfast this morning consists of a bit of bread and some of the fruit I had stored in my own pack. We split it between us, and my stomach still growls. At least it isn't raining today.

"Keep an eye out for birds and rabbits," I say as we set out from the camp. "We might have to have an early lunch."

Dalen's stomach grumbles in response. He raises an eyebrow, and I laugh.

"Glad to see you agree."

"Who were those men who chased us last night? How do you know them?" Dalen asks.

"They're part of a band of mercenaries Ensel hired. He paid them to fight for him, guard his castle, things like that. The only loyalty he trusted was to gold." I lower my voice. "The man in the tavern said Ensel never paid them for the final battle; he died first. They claim they've taken over the city of Belladoma."

Dalen cocks his head. "This is bad, I take it?"

I sigh. "Very. These are terrible men."

"It sounds like this may impact our ability to hunt for the cornucopia."

I groan. "Impact? It will bring it to a screeching halt." If those brutes have the run of the city, finding the cornucopia will be next to impossible. I can't just walk up the steps of the castle and hope they let me inside to search for something they'd probably love to have for themselves.

"Then we shall have to stay ahead of them. Does this place seem more familiar in the light of day?" he asks, but I shake my head.

"No, if anything it looks less familiar. I have no idea where we are." The trees are of a different variety than those in Bryre or what I saw on the road to and from Belladoma. I'm accustomed to the old-growth pines and oaks with an occasional birch, but these come in two varieties: thick and short, or tall and spindly. The larger trees have branches that reach out to connect to the others nearby, creating an almost continuous cover of foliage. Everything is filtered in a hazy green light. Long vines hang down from the branches, and they make me nervous. Ever since those nasty briars crept through my city, I've been wary of them. These are different—and don't have thorns—but the way they whisper over our shoulders is unsettling.

Dalen frowns, then shrugs. "We should try to find that village again. That ought to get us back on track. Those men aren't likely to stick around and wait for us, are they?"

I ponder for a moment. "I don't think so. Not all of them anyway. But we'll need to be careful. They saw you. That's why they chased us."

"Why? What would they want—" His face darkens. "My parts . . ." he says slowly. "My parts are valuable because they're rare and have magic in them. I am worth more to them dead than alive."

A sick feeling pours over me, but I nod. "Not all humans are kind, I'm afraid."

He doesn't say anything more. He turns so I can't see his face and finishes packing up the blankets we laid out to dry the night before. Soon we head back in what we hope is the direction we came, this time cautiously taking the long way around the mountain with the cave. We're in deep forest here, and no sign of a road presents itself. We may have to walk for a while before we reach civilization again.

But before we get far, an owl hoots—near the ground—and it stops me in my tracks.

"What is it, Greta?" Dalen asks, frowning.

I turn in a slow circle, looking to find the source of the sound. "I'm not sure. But I . . . I keep seeing and hearing an owl near us. It's almost like we're being followed."

"By an owl?"

"Not quite." I shiver, remembering the striped tail. I'm honestly not sure what it was I saw, but everything odd has me on edge lately. "Owls aren't usually out during the day."

I take a few steps, then pause. Something shuffles in the underbrush between trees. I head for a small clearing a few feet away. Sure enough, the rustling follows now that I'm listening for it.

When we reach the center of the clearing, I turn toward the rustling. Beady eyes stare back from behind a low bush. This time Dalen sees it too, and tenses next to me.

"Don't owls keep to the trees?" he says.

"Not this one, apparently." I draw my knife from my belt, just in case it's rabid.

The creature tilts its head at us, then to my surprise steps cautiously out from under the bush. At first, my brain doesn't fully register what I see before me. Then cold horror slithers over my skin.

It must be one of the wizard's creations. Maybe it was one

of the rejects he used to practice his disgusting magic before he created Kymera. But what in the realm could it be doing here?

From the neck up, the creature has an owl's head, and no doubt its keen senses, too. But the rest of the body is gray and furry, and it has the small paws of a mammal. Its tail is striped like a raccoon's, but it's shorter than it should be. Almost like someone or something cut it off. Maybe it was caught in a trap and it got away with all but the end of it.

The raccowl takes a tentative step forward and tilts its head—all the way around.

"That cannot be natural," Dalen says. "And that says a lot coming from a hybrid."

I snort. "It isn't. It has to be one of the wizard's failed projects. That's the only thing that makes sense."

"What should we do with it?"

"Do with it? Nothing. Raccoons are scavengers. It probably thinks our leftovers would be an easy meal." Not that we have leftovers with our food getting ruined last night, but I can't blame it for trying.

Dalen examines the creature thoughtfully, and it seems to regard him with the same consideration. "It does look hungry. We could feed it."

My fingers run over the small scars from the peck marks the wizard's goat-chickens left on my arms. I'll never underestimate one of the wizard's creations, but I almost feel sorry for this one. Kymera found her original family, Pippa the sperrier has Delia, and even those awful goat-chickens have the chicken hut.

This creature doesn't have anyone. Kind of like Hans and me.

I shrug. "If you insist." The little beast shambles over to Dalen's front legs and weaves between them, flicking its stubby tail. "It doesn't seem to be rabid, at least."

Dalen tosses the raccowl a bit of dried meat, which it holds in its paws and pecks, devouring the treat in a matter of seconds.

Slowly but surely we press on until the trees become more familiar. The raccowl follows us closely, almost like it thinks it's joined our group. I wonder what lands are beyond the river, but this is not the time for that sort of exploration. Maybe someday, but not without Hans.

The old familiar ache returns. Are my parents out there? What really happened to them? Could someone have taken them like the witch took Hans? The way Mama would smile and tuck my unruly dark hair behind my ears while we cooked supper together haunts me still. As does how Papa would look so proud when he gave us sparring lessons and I scored a hit. They wouldn't have just left us.

I find myself sneaking glances at Dalen all morning. At first I'm not sure why. Perhaps I feel a bond with him because he lost part of his family too, and the rest is in danger until we deliver the cornucopia to the witch. I can't quite explain the relief that billows every time I see his face. I'm glad he didn't drown in the river, and I worry about what might happen to him if the mercenaries were to get hold of him.

Everyone who's dear to me has left or been taken.

I don't like the idea of entering Belladoma without him.

It's a strange, dizzying thing to feel I need someone's help. I've always been able to depend on myself alone. But he feels for my plight, risks much, and is willing to help for nothing in return save my continued silence about the existence of his hybrid species.

That isn't something one finds often.

If Dalen notices my distraction when we stop to cook a rabbit for lunch, he doesn't remark on it, and for that I'm grateful. He does remark again on how scrawny the raccowl looks as its unsettling eyes watch us from the tree line. It may want food, but it's wary of fire.

"Since he's followed us all this way, I think we should name him. I've decided to call him Stump," Dalen says, chewing on a piece of rabbit meat.

I laugh. "Stump. Because of his tail?" Then I shake my head. "Don't get attached. He's a wild thing. He won't stick around." I neglect to mention he's been following us for two days. I can't imagine what he wants, aside from food.

When we finally draw close to the village, Stump circles in front of me to cut off my path. I frown and sidestep him, and he nips the tail of my cloak.

"What was that for?" I say. Stump merely tilts his head in response.

Dalen grabs my arm. "Look, Greta."

The buildings of the village peek through the trees, and pungent woodsmoke steadily approaches, billowing through the forest like fog.

Strangest of all, brilliant flames dance over the rooftop of the inn and tavern.

We blink in disbelief. We're well hidden in the shadows of the woods, but we can see the villagers running to and fro, none of their water buckets able to douse the fire. It burns the water up too.

"Magic." I mutter it like a curse. It is the only explanation. But who would have—

Oh no.

Dalen and I exchange a look, and I can tell we're thinking the same thing.

"The mercenaries. *They* must have done this. A man at the tavern said they were cleaning up after the wizard," I say. Dalen grips his pack a little tighter, unable to pull his eyes away from the flames.

But how would they have gotten their rotten little hands on magic? Do they know where the wizard once lived? Or did they happen upon it by chance?

If the mercenaries are able to use magic, my task in Belladoma will be much more dangerous than I ever imagined. The city of my nightmares, bubbling over with horrors.

I shudder. I can't decide which is worse—wizard pretenders or that awful witch in the wandering chicken house. I'll have to take my chances with the pretenders and hope it all works out for the best.

Dalen paws the ground nervously. "We should leave here immediately."

I agree, and we take off at a brisk pace, putting as much distance between us and the village as possible.

# CHAPTER 12

**THE SUN IS HIGH, BUT THE HEAT DOESN'T BEAR DOWN ON US TOO HARSHLY** as it filters through the branches and leaves of the forest. After the bizarreness of the village, it almost makes our journey feel light and airy, or perhaps that is just the cool breeze wandering between the tree trunks. All afternoon, disconcerting thoughts of the mercenaries and magic trail behind me. Once we finally reach the main road to Belladoma, I know just what to look for: a landmark of two trees twining around each other like dancers under the moon.

It's the same place Ren waited when Kymera freed us and we fled Belladoma. It doesn't take us long to locate the trees and the entrance to the tunnels beneath the city. The trees are as twisted as the residents they grow near. It's a fitting tribute.

The trick, however, will be Dalen. And how to get him inside.

He eyes the tree warily. "In there?" He points to the darkened hollow at the base. You can't see inside, as you can with the ones in his village. Stump won't even come near the spot. Instead, the creature perches on a rock at the edge of the clearing, tilting his head this way and that, and occasionally all the way around. It's unsettling.

"Yes," I say. "Ren and Kymera, my friends who were here with me before, set this as the meeting point once we escaped the city. We came here through the woods by the cliff instead of the tunnels, but they told me about how they used the tunnels to gain entrance to Belladoma and find us." I frown at the entrance. "I wonder how wide and shallow it is after the opening." I sigh. "Wait here—I'll go in and check, then come back for you."

Before he can object, I plunge into the shadows at the base of the trees and let the darkness envelop me. It's shocking at first, and the damp tunnel smells like freshly turned soil. Like death. My eyes adjust to the faint light seeping in from the outside. The passage should be wide enough and tall enough for Dalen to stand once he gets down here. Farther ahead, the tunnel widens more.

Good. I won't have to go back *there* alone after all.

The closer we've gotten to the city, the tighter anxiety has wound around my chest. Every day it's been a little harder to breathe. If Dalen chickens out, braving my nightmare alone might be the one thing to finally break me.

When I return to the daylight of the forest, Dalen paces

the clearing. Sweat beads on his brow.

"What's wrong?"

When he sees me, most of the tension releases from his face and he stops pacing. Dalen clears his throat. "You're back. It could have been a trap."

"You were worried, weren't you?" I grin at him. "I'm fine. No traps in sight, I promise."

"Good, I'm glad of it. Though I'm sure it is much too narrow for me to fit, yes?"

"You'll have to duck down to get through the entrance, but once you pass that, you'll be fine. The tunnel is at least four men wide."

Dalen swallows nervously. "Are you certain? I . . . I can't bear the thought of squeezing all the way down there and getting stuck." He swallows again, and finally I understand.

"You can't bear confined spaces." At the word *confined*, he turns green, confirming my suspicions.

"I have never been in them much. The closest thing was guarding the occasional miscreant in the root cellars. But those were more open."

"Right," I say. "Tunnels and horses don't usually mix. But it's that or prancing into Belladoma in all your hybrid glory."

He walks toward the trees, Stump scampering behind. "Please, just give me a moment to collect myself, and then we can be off. Or down. Whatever you call it."

I swallow my laugh, because he might find it cruel.

Five minutes later, I follow him into the woods, nervousness nipping at my heels. What if he decided to leave me on my own, and risk his council's wrath? But no, he wouldn't. I find him in a grove, ducking and weaving between low branches and whispering to himself. Stump settles in to watch and twists his head to set his beady eyes on me when I approach. Is this Dalen's idea of preparing?

"Dalen," I say. He halts in his tracks. "It's nearly dark. Are you coming with me? I understand if you can't." I fold my arms across my chest, trying not to show how much I need him to say yes.

"Of course I will," he says. Is that a hint of hurt I see in his eyes?

I smile and head back to the twin trees. Dalen's hoof-beats follow, and I take two apples from my pack, offering one to him.

"We should eat here before we go inside." I wrinkle my nose, remembering the smell. He takes it gratefully, and we chew in silence for a moment. Stump does not return to the twin trees with Dalen, but a hoot calls from the forest while we eat. He must not like dark, confined spaces any more than Dalen.

"What scares you about the tunnel?" I ask.

He swallows a bite of apple. "I'm not flexible like some creatures are. The risk of getting stuck is higher. Also, this is near the ocean, and we know the Sonzeeki floods the city. It stands to reason that these tunnels flood too. Really, it's those two things combined."

My blood runs cold. I had forgotten about the flooding. Rushing water is suddenly all I can hear. "We shall have to be quick."

Dalen stares down the shadows gathering in the base of the tree. Somehow, it seems darker than it did a few minutes ago. My hands are so cold they've gone numb. My heart sits in my throat, throbbing so hard I can barely speak. This is like going directly into the belly of the beast for both of us.

I only hope we don't get eaten alive.

"I'll go first," I offer. Dalen nods. "But you do have to follow."

He gives me a withering look. I duck my head and step into the base of the tree.

My eyes adjust more quickly this time, but Dalen has difficulty finding his footing in the dark, and he almost tramples me twice before he finally tumbles down to the passage floor. I help him get his bearings and he blinks, looking around wildly.

"I can't see, Greta. I can't see." Panic chokes his voice into a whisper. I grab his trembling hands.

"Yes, you can," I reassure him. "Just close your eyes for a minute and take a deep breath. Then another. Stay calm, and your eyes will adjust." He doesn't know it, but I say this as much for myself as for him. Focusing on keeping Dalen calm almost manages to tamp down my own rising panic.

He does as I say, and soon his chest rises and falls, the deep breaths making the shadows twitch around him.

"Now, slowly open your eyes and focus on the sound of my voice. I'm right in front of you. You should see me first." I do my best to smile, even though I can't help keeping one ear cocked to listen for rushing water. The real kind.

Or the awful sound of tentacles clamping onto limestone.

A peculiar sound that will never leave my dreams in peace. Dizziness sweeps over me, but I keep to my feet for Dalen. I know the Sonzeeki only floods these tunnels at the full moon, but that does nothing to lessen the primal fear that threatens to strangle me the closer we get to Belladoma.

I hate that the city holds such sway over me still.

"Yes . . . ," he says. "I do see you." The relief in his voice is palpable, and mirrored in myself. His silver eyes are wide and focused on mine. I gaze back for longer than I should, letting his cool silvery hope steel my nerves, like a lifeline connecting us.

But we need to keep moving.

I lead him down the dark passage, the sound of hoofbeats and dripping water marking our path. Every drop of water needles my nerves, making me want to break into a run and find the end of the tunnel, but he doesn't need to know I'm afraid too. It would only make matters worse.

Little by little we make progress. The passage twists beneath the earth, but it doesn't steer us wrong or make us choose a blind path. Time blurs in the darkness, measured only in halted breaths and flaring pulses. Every step we take away from the entrance makes Dalen more nervous. He hasn't let go of my hand, and I don't force the issue. I understand; there's something comforting in the certainty you're not alone in the dark.

But then the air changes. Something shifts on the wind. Wait. Wind?

A breeze meanders down the tunnel, caressing my face

and teasing my hair. I want to laugh out loud but I fear frightening Dalen.

"We're close," I say instead.

"How do you know?" he whispers.

"Can you feel it?" I ask. "The breeze? That means an exit is nearby."

He sighs. "Thank the gods. I don't know how much longer I can stand being down here."

We follow the breeze and soon reach the end of the tunnel. A door is carved into the brick wall, and at the very bottom is a grate that lets in a faint trickle of light. Perfect for ensuring no one is near when we exit. I suspect the door appears to be a wall from the outside. But how will we find our way back in if we need an escape route?

"Look," Dalen says, pointing to something scratched into the brick above the door. It's over my head but right in line with his eyes. "That must be how we unlock the door to get in and out."

2 knocks—nicked bottom brick. Then 3 knocks—
top slab with half-moon.

"It's almost too simple," I say, but Dalen shrugs. I locate the brick with the nick and the slab with the half-moon easily enough.

"Sometimes simple is the last thing people guess. Can we leave this tunnel now? Please?" His hooves stamp with nervous energy.

I kneel down to the grate and peer out. As far as I can tell, the alley beyond is deserted—and filled with the stench of rotting fish. Perhaps this tunnel doesn't connect with the ones that flood the city and only leads out into the forest. Still, I'm not looking forward to breathing in that reek. I place my sleeve over my nose, knock on the brick and slab as instructed, and cautiously pull the door open.

We're greeted only by the dusk, and a few rats fighting over naked fish bones down the way. Muck and slime coat the wall, but I check for the markings on the outside, too. They exist, and I repeat the instructions over and over until they're imprinted on my memory.

Night has fallen, and with it the citizens of this tattered city have vanished, scurrying back to their houses to protect what meager possessions haven't been destroyed in the floods. The mercenaries are no doubt in taverns or the castle. I intend to avoid them at all costs.

We don't need a repeat of the chase we had arriving here.

What we do need is a barn. One where Dalen can hide in the daylight, and that we can rest in at night.

We creep through the alley network, avoiding noises and any hint of people, until we find what we seek on the outskirts of the city. An old decrepit inn with a cracked, faded sign hanging off the front—abandoned as far as we can tell—with a moldering barn adjoining it.

No one has been here in months, I'm sure. All the less likely anyone will show up.

Dalen beams when he sees the barn, and smiles even

wider when I return and declare it empty. In minutes, he settles into a stall in the far corner and falls asleep. I curl up opposite him, hoping sleep will find me, too, even in this city of nightmares.

# CHAPTER 13

AT FIRST LIGHT, I SLIP OUT OF THE BARN. A SALTY TANG HOVERS ON THE
air like a ghost. They say that nothing will grow in the soil
now that the Sonzeeki floods Belladoma regularly.

I pull my cloak tighter around me. My heart hasn't
stopped hammering since we entered the city. The nightmares haunt me even when I'm awake. An ever-present
tension keeps every muscle in my body taut and ready. The
air is oppressive, and I want to flee, but I must be practical.
I need the cornucopia, and this is the last place we know it
was. I must investigate.

The sooner we're done in Belladoma, the better for
my sanity. And the better for my family and Dalen's. The
sunken faces peering out from the windows I pass look like
they'd eat anything—even horse meat—making me very

glad it was necessary to leave Dalen behind in the barn.

A trumpet sounds from near the gates of the city, causing me to trip on a broken flagstone. I know that trumpet. All too well. King Oliver is here to aid Belladoma. He started that foolish mission sooner than I expected. I thought he'd take longer with the preparations. My hands clench into tight fists beneath my cloak. I am not ready to face him. Not after he accused me of being a liar.

I must reach the palace before him. I need to search Ensel's old rooms for any hint of where the cornucopia is hidden. An icy hand squeezes my chest, like the cursed city itself wishes to choke me. I won't be able to breathe freely again until I'm far away from here.

Wary of the main road, I duck down a side street and weave my way toward the palace. As we stole through the streets last night, I noted a couple more spots where the nick and the half-moon appeared. If the code remains true, the tunnels beneath Belladoma's crumbling citadel have an entrance not far from here.

I speed my pace. Bits of green and brown plant life hang from the gray walls in places, stuck on windowsills and what once were flowerpots. Seaweed. Everything reeks of decay. I can hardly stand to breathe. Fish bones cling to the gutters, unable to return to the sea.

Beyond me, the city springs to life. The arrival of help from Bryre stirs the residents out of doors. The thought of anyone I love helping these people, who would've killed me to save their own hides, nauseates me.

I'll find what I need, then leave. No reason for me to

linger here. Hans and I, we can start fresh somewhere else. Maybe Dalen and his family can come too, now that they need a new home.

The footsteps are upon me before they register in my brain. I flatten against the damp alley wall just before a boy jogs through an intersection of alleys a few feet ahead. I'd recognize that sun-streaked brown hair anywhere.

Ren.

I swallow my surprise and count to one hundred. Only then do I peel myself off the wall and continue toward the secret tunnel entrance. That was too close. Seeing my friends will do nothing good for me; they don't need to know I'm here. They should have helped me. But if they didn't believe me before, why would they believe an even grander story about a witch and a chicken hut? They might lock me up for fear I've lost my mind.

I tread carefully, all too conscious of the possibility I might run into someone I know. Who in Belladoma will greet the Bryrians? The mercenaries squatting in the palace or perhaps no one at all? Maybe they'll go back to Bryre if they see how little their efforts are appreciated.

A chill slinks down my neck. I doubt Vincali, the mercenaries' leader, will appreciate Bryre meddling in his affairs. I hope King Oliver knows what he's doing.

I walk away from the direction Ren was headed, hoping to lessen my chances of running into anyone from Bryre. When I pause to check my bearings, more voices ring out from the road. There's nowhere I can run from here; all I can do is hide. The alley is too long in the direction I am now moving, and only garbage, loose bricks, and an alcove or two give me a hiding spot. From their rough voices, I'm guessing the men coming are mercenaries. From the little I've seen of the native Belladomans, they're mostly pale, wan, and hungry-looking, and keep to their homes or stores. The arrival of the Bryrians drew them out, but not for long. After so much time under Ensel's heavy thumb, I can hardly blame them.

These men, however, stomp toward my alley with heavy boots and steps to match. My heart leaps into my throat as I frantically cast around for something better to hide behind. The best I can do is squeeze into an alcove and crouch as close to the ground as possible. And hope they don't glance to the side.

The alcove is still coated with salt from the last time the Sonzeeki flooded the city, and the smell of rotting fish and seaweed is stronger here. I pull my knife from my belt, then tuck my arm under my knees as the men march down the alley. The blade digs into the backs of my legs, but I feel better having something solid to defend myself with if necessary.

I squeeze my eyes closed, willing myself invisible as the boots tromp past. Just as I breathe out in relief, one set of feet returns. My lungs stutter and contract, and then I'm yanked from the alcove by my collar.

"What do we have here?" The horrible deep voice I recognize from the inn curls around me.

I swing my arm wide and catch my attacker on the cheek with the blade. Vincali yowls and drops me, pressing his hand to his face. Black, furious eyes burn down at me from a cruel face.

I run.

Vincali shouts and other mercenaries join him in the chase. Behind me comes a flash of light and a strange noise, accompanied by the smell of smoke. What madness is this? I dart down the next alley, hoping I can reach the tunnels before they catch me. They may be bigger, but I'm faster and sneakier. I careen headlong through the alleys, ducking across the streets to save time. I attract a few stares, but I don't have time to worry about that.

I cannot get caught or delayed by these men. The thought of being thrown back into the Belladoman dungeons, leaving Hans to die, is enough to spur my tired legs onward.

I round a corner and run straight into a large man wheeling a cart of fresh bread, knocking a few loaves into the street.

"Sorry!" But I keep on moving. He shouts, then goes silent by the time I'm around the bend of the next alley.

The mercenaries must have reached him.

But no sounds of pursuit follow. In fact, I hear boots clomping and growing more distant every second. Confusion reigns in my head. Did that man lie about where I went, even after I ruined his wares? It doesn't make sense. Unless he assumes I'm a Belladoman girl who was somehow hidden from Ensel. I could see any Belladoman going to great lengths to keep their own people safe.

I suppose I am doing the same for Hans. It would be easier if these people were all simply as bad as the visions in my head.

If my memory from last night is correct, the entrance to the tunnels should be up ahead. Two turns, then there it is in the wall. The entry code to any tunnel is the same as the one for the passage we used to enter the city.

I dash ahead, leaping over piles of seaweed moldering in the damp, muggy air, even though my pursuers are not close behind. I don't want to risk running into any more of them. I round the last turn with every ounce of speed in me and skid to a stop. Voices murmur from the guardhouse around the corner. Hurriedly, I locate the markings of the passage and tap them the allotted times.

To my great relief, the door swings inward, and I duck into the passage, quickly closing the door behind me.

The second it clicks shut, I lean back against the wall and sigh.

Outside, heavy boots tromp by my hiding spot and several men's voices bicker. When they fade, I can't help a small smile. They didn't see me come in here. Still, that was too close for comfort. Worse, now there are Belladomans who know my face, and know the mercenaries were chasing me.

I have no doubt they'd give me up in a heartbeat to save their own skins.

# CHAPTER 14

**NOW THAT I'M SAFELY IN THE TUNNELS, I CAN BREATHE EASIER. AT LEAST** until it hits me that I'm that much closer to the castle. The darkness is almost soothing—I could pretend I'm anywhere else—but the smell is terrible. These tunnels must connect, the ocean rising through them to flood the streets.

My footsteps are as light as possible on the muck-filled stones. I don't want to risk slipping and sliding down an unseen passage. No one knows I'm here except Dalen, and he'd have little hope of following me should I need help.

But I won't. I escaped from Ensel and his trader. I stood with Kymera and Bryre against the wizard and Ensel's army. I just faced one of the mercenaries running rampant through this forsaken city. If nothing else, I'm a survivor.

The least I can do is find one silly little horn-shaped basket.

My resolve pushes me onward, though little light reveals my path. Instead I listen—for the sound of water, or feet overhead. One means death, the other means I'm headed in the right direction. Before long, the tunnel splits. I wait and listen for ten whole minutes before choosing. I'm glad I did. The faint sound of waves splashing against rock echoes from the path that my gut initially urged me to take. I hurry down the left split instead, and soon face a door. Those mercenaries must not have discovered the tunnels yet. I intend to be long gone from Belladoma by the time they do.

Putting my ear to the door, I listen for any hint of life beyond. My pulse thrums under my fingertips, pressed to the wood. From the rumors we heard on the journey to the city, it sounds like only the mercenaries wander the castle now. The royal family is long dead, of course. Ensel usurped the real king—his own stepfather, no less—and killed every other possible heir.

When no sounds come through the door, I risk peeking inside. It's a small storage room in the palace cellar, empty of all but a handful of rotten potatoes and carrots. I crinkle my nose at the smell. I doubt Ensel hid the cornucopia here. I need to find his chamber and hunt for a clue there. It's the most likely place. I shudder at the thought.

I try to take a step, but my feet refuse to move forward. To tread upon the flagstones I remember all too well. The sounds rush back—screaming girls and fleshy tentacles hitting rock, ringing in my ears and making me wish I could run as far from this place as possible. I sway and sink to my knees, unable to move and unable to scream. Frozen by my past.

I close my eyes and gasp in breaths, but it only makes me dizzy.

Faces of the other girls swim before my eyes, their screams all too real. The girls and the beast, the witch and Hans collide, merging into an epic nightmare in my mind.

But Hans isn't dead. Not yet.

Courage lifts me to my feet. I hold my sense of bravery close like a shield. I will do this. I must.

One footstep at a time, I find the kitchens and dodge my way through the halls past wayward mercenaries. Only a few remain in the palace today. The delegation from Bryre must keep them occupied for now. I'm almost glad it chose today to show up.

I stop briefly in the servants' quarters on my way up from the kitchens. A handful still work in the castle, though I can't imagine the mercenaries pay them. More likely they've threatened and bullied them into slavery. I duck into the laundry room, still steaming from the wash earlier this morning, where I steal a serving girl's uniform and a large cloak. I throw them on and hide my own clothes in my satchel.

When I reach the part of the castle I recognize, the tremors in my hands begin. I close them into fists and press them to my hips, breathing deeply.

These mercenaries may be intimidating, but the one thing I really fear is the beast waiting in the depths outside the cliffs. It is much too close for comfort. I won't be around when that monster rises, expecting to be fed.

Swallowing my fears, I head for the courtiers' quarters. I recall much of the layout from when we escaped Belladoma. Ensel's own chamber is farther down the hall from them. I half expect the room to be stripped bare, but it's the best idea I have.

Ensel must've kept the cornucopia close at hand. His private quarters would've been the most reasonable place. Trouble is, I can't say he was the most reasonable of men. In fact, from what I saw and heard, Ensel was flat-out insane.

Several voices emanate from the courtiers' quarters, and I tiptoe by as quietly and quickly as possible, holding my breath. When I was first brought to Belladoma as a captive, I attempted to escape every day for an entire week. They threw me into the dungeon after that and then put a steel bar over the door to the girls' room too, but each time I got out, I went a little farther and became a little better at sneaking by undetected.

This time, my disguise should help, though not many servants wander this area of the palace. Hopefully the mercenaries don't know all their faces.

When I locate Ensel's door, I put my ear to it and listen. No one seems to be inside, and I yank at the knob. It doesn't budge.

It's locked.

I pull two pins from my hair and kneel close to the door. It takes more tries than I'd like to pick the lock, but after a while I'm rewarded with a click and a turning doorknob.

The past few months of stealing food for Hans and me have paid off. I volunteered to help out the baker and butcher every chance I had. The food, however obtained, was more like payment.

I check the hall once more for prying eyes and then slip into the room, shutting the door softly behind me.

To my surprise, Ensel's chamber is much the way I remember it—far too fine for a king who wasted all his money and let his kingdom starve. But it's more worn down than I recall, and the telltale signs of mercenary occupation taint the former finery. Empty wine bottles and flasks litter the floor, and a thin coat of dirt seems to have settled over everything except the bed. That is a rumpled, but well-used, mess.

A heavy weight descends on my chest, threatening to smother me. Someone still lives in these quarters. I'd be willing to bet it's Vincali. I can't be caught in here when he comes back.

The good news is that if anyone is dealing with Ren and King Oliver right now, it's bound to be him. They wouldn't settle for speaking with anyone other than the man in charge. He'd have to oblige them.

That means I have an hour, maybe two, to find what I need. If what I need is here at all.

Now, where would I hide something as valuable as a cornucopia if I were greedy and suspicious like Ensel?

My gaze wanders around the sitting room. Fine tapestries line the walls, woven with silver and gold thread depicting both pastoral scenes and seascapes with a beastly thing inching its way across the image. It makes me want to retch. Several shelves holding decorative items and the occasional book also line the walls. And there's the fireplace we came through when we made our escape.

My eyes light up.

If Ensel has secret passages, could he have a secret hiding place, too? A vault? Perhaps even a secret room? The mercenaries haven't found the tunnels yet, because they weren't part of the trusted guard Ensel kept in the know. They might not have a clue what to look for.

But I do.

I doubt it's in the floor because that's where we found the tunnel entrance. But the walls . . . any of them could open into another room. Those tapestries are perfect for hiding cracks and grooves. I consider the layout of the space. Where would be the most likely place for a hidden room? The sitting room stretches all the way to the windows. One side, with the fireplace, leads to the tunnels; the other side of the adjoining wall is the bedroom, which runs perpendicular to it.

Which means there's a pocket of space between the bedroom wall and the passages that could be perfect. I immediately begin to run my hands over the walls between the fireplace and the bedroom door, hunting for any seam or crack that could be the opening to a hidden chamber. I peel back every tapestry, scanning from floor to ceiling, but nothing presents itself on this side.

Frustrated, I run into the bedroom and examine the wall from that angle. I remember there was a piece that moved with the fireplace. Could a similar mechanism be at work here? This wall is bare of tapestries, but several hooks, the kind you'd hang a robe on, are built into it just below a shelf. I tug on one and it turns all the way down. Emboldened, I yank on the other three and they all move too.

But the wall doesn't.

Perhaps they must be pulled in a certain order. There are twenty-four possible combinations, and on the seventh I hear a click, like a lock in the wall releasing. I pull on two of the hooks and the wall creaks open. It hasn't been used in months.

The main door to the suite opens and I freeze. Two men's voices grumble in the sitting room, and panic spurs me to close the secret door behind me, creaks and all.

I'm alone, trapped in the dark. In Belladoma.

As the minutes tick by slowly, the silence becomes a roar of crashing waves, the darkness a solid mass of writhing black tentacles. Every second my heart beats louder and louder, until I'm sure it will explode out of my chest and give my location away.

I close my eyes—not that I can see a thing—and try to make out what they're saying.

At first I can't hear much but the blood drumming in my ears. Gradually, my pulse slows and I settle on the hard floor to focus. The men are arguing, I think. Their voices started hushed because of the wall between us, but there's an edge to them. They're not seeing eye to eye on . . . something.

Ice forms over my heart. One man has a higher-pitched voice, and the other has a gruff tone that is all too familiar. Vincali.

Part of me is dying to know what they are talking about, and the other part is dying to get out of the close, dark room. Yet here is where I might find answers.

If only I could see those answers.

I scowl at the nothing around me.

The men's footsteps approach the bedroom, but I still can't make out complete words through the thick stone walls.

The deeper voice—Vincali—laughs; then his footfalls cross the room and the bed creaks. I picture him perched on the edge.

One boot drops to the floor, startling me and making me gasp. Something next to me clatters. I clamp a hand over my mouth, terrified they might have heard me squeak, or bump into the pile of . . . whatever it is next to me.

They're far too quiet for far too long, and my pulse spikes in response. *Thump thump, thump thump.*

My muscles tense, tight and ready to spring. I have no real chance against these men. If they find me, surprise is the only thing I have on my side.

I may have to use it. I have no idea whether the hooks returned to their normal position when I closed the door, but I'm praying they did. If not . . .

The other man begins to speak again and relief fills me. But the clinking of a decanter and a wineglass sets my nerves even more on edge. How long will they dally out there?

I can't do anything from inside this room.

Anxiety bubbles in my gut. I hate being stuck here in the dark, helpless, and at the mercy of these two men.

What if they don't leave at all? What time is it, anyway?

Eventually the second man leaves Vincali to his business, and he hums to himself in his deep baritone voice.

When he dozes, I'm left wide-eyed and anxious, waiting in the dark.

# CHAPTER 15

MY REPRIEVE COMES IN THE FORM OF THE NOISY ENTRANCE BY ANOTHER mercenary, who calls Vincali away. He doesn't sound happy about being woken up, but I'm relieved. I wait a few more minutes to be safe.

When I'm certain I'm alone, I crack the secret door open. The room is still a mess, but now the candles are lit and two wineglasses sit on a table on one side, with an empty decanter between them.

Wonderful. Not only is Vincali vicious, but he's also drunk.

Now, finally, I can examine the room I've hidden in for the last couple of hours. I throw the door wide, propping it open with a boot. I knew it was full of oddities, but not until this moment, peering inside with the candlelight, do I realize what I've stumbled upon.

Ensel's secret treasury.

Granted, as far as treasuries go, this one is rather poor. For people like myself—and the mercenaries—it would set us up for a lifetime or two, but it's not enough to sustain an entire city.

The room is small, maybe ten feet by ten feet, and another ten feet high. The shelves on the walls are stacked floor to ceiling with gold bars. Piles of gold, silver, and bronze coins are heaped in the corners, along with jewels, necklaces, and brooches of all shapes and styles.

It brings to mind the dragon hoards I've read about in the fairy-tale book.

This display disgusts me. Ensel ruined lives to keep this safe? It's horrifying.

Even worse, I don't see the cornucopia. I systematically make my way through the piles, poring over every piece of silver, leaving no bar of gold unturned.

Nothing.

Riches to set me up for life, but nothing to grant me the one thing I need. The one thing that I can barter for my brother's life, and my own. But then, as I pull apart a tangled mess of jewelry, I do find something.

Something from my past.

I pull a necklace free and stare at it, hardly believing my eyes. It quivers in my shaking palm, making the silver sparkle. It's a thin silver chain, pure and fine, with a pendant set with a ruby-red rose. The tiny gems glitter and swirl in the patterns of the petals, and emeralds trace the lines of the leaves and thorns.

Awestruck, I run my trembling fingers over the jewels.

It can't be. It's impossible. How could this be here? This necklace that looks exactly like one I know well?

There's one way to test if it's truly the one I remember.

I press down simultaneously on the top and bottom of the pendant. A soft click echoes in my ringing ears, and the locket swings open. Sweat trickles down my spine despite the chill in these rooms. Uneasiness slips over my skin along with it. This can't be.

Inside the locket are nestled two little paintings. One is the likeness of a boy, the other of an older girl.

They are Hans and me. The portraits were done five years ago. Mama was a painter; she was astonishingly good at portraits, especially miniatures. She had a cart at the market and everything.

This locket was the finest thing we owned, given to my mother as a gift on her marriage to my father.

And now my mother's locket is in Ensel's secret treasure chamber.

Shock brings me to my knees. I don't understand. How could my mother have been here? Why would she ever go to Belladoma? King Ensel was certainly cruel, but what possible use could he have had for her?

And if she was here, what about my father? I scrabble on my hands and knees, tearing through the remaining finery. I ignore the burning in my eyes and the faintness in my head. I have to know what happened. Is she still here? Or did Ensel toss her over the cliff?

My heart sinks into my boots.

That would make the most sense. A horrible, terrible sense. All the jewelry must be from Ensel's victims. What other use would he have for women's jewels?

I swallow down the sickness, and keep scrabbling, but no sign of Papa presents itself. He carried a pocket watch that he wound every night. But it wasn't made of gold or precious jewels. It must not have qualified in Ensel's twisted little mind.

I put the chain over my head and hide the pendant under my shirt. No one needs to see it, but I like the idea of wearing it close to my heart. Now that I know my mother was here in Belladoma, it changes everything. Something terrible must have happened to my parents.

Or *someone*, like Ensel.

I strike my palm against the floor beneath me. That awful man ruined so many things.

Something in the floor clicks, then springs loose. One of the floorboards conceals a hidden compartment. I pull it back to peek inside.

The crowns. Of the former king and queen. People say they were kind. Then Ensel betrayed them, stealing the throne and awakening the horrible beast beneath the waves.

The crowns are gold and platinum filigree and covered in jewels that glitter like pure starlight. Diamonds. They rest on top of many pieces of parchment along with a box filled with several crystal vials of murky liquid. A rush trills over me. What if this is where he hid the secret to his cornucopia's location? I pocket all the papers and vials, desperate to leave this awful place and examine them in better light and with a night's rest behind me.

The distress of finding my mother's necklace has not worn off, and my hands shake as I close the door on the hidden room in a daze and put everything—boot and all—back exactly as it was. But while I do, I notice a pile of papers on the desk near the bed. The one on top, I assume, is half finished, because it bears no signature or seal yet. Curious, I hover over it and read quickly.

*Your Majesty,*

*As you expected, we had no trouble taking over the mercenary army. Over the past two months we've rounded up the scattered troops, and the price you've instructed me to offer them will be enough for them to live and breathe for our cause, no questions asked.*

*But I write now to inform you that we found where the wizard once lived. The rumors are true; he is dead. We stripped everything that was left in the remains of his cottage and laboratory and will send it onward within the next week. We did not find what you hoped would be hidden there, but we still scour the city and countryside. If it exists, we shall find it.*

*I also must advise you that there has been a complication. The king of Bryre and his army have arrived, and I fear he is here for more than just to offer his aid in feeding Belladoma. I have stationed troops in the woods near their camp and spies to watch their every move. If they do anything to threaten our endeavor, we will put a stop to it immediately. The surprises we found at the wizard's place may come in handy sooner than we expected.*

The letter ends abruptly, but not before it raises the hair on the back of my neck. All the power the wizard left behind is now under the control of the mercenaries? I was right. They were responsible for the burning inn.

And who is the mystery royal Vincali addresses? More important, what could he want with horrible, tainted magic?

I'll have to warn Ren and the king that they're being watched. Could they really be up to more than they have let on? I don't want them to know I'm here, but I can't leave them in danger like that. Not if I can help them evade it.

I must flee. I remember where the trapdoor in Ensel's floor was before. I pull back the rug and open the trapdoor, careful to place the rug back over so it will fall flat when the tunnel door closes.

These tunnels are coming in handy now that I'm the only one who knows about them.

By the time I reach the barn, night has fallen thick around the city. Finally, I've begun to collect myself, though I'm sure Dalen still notices I'm shaken up.

"Did you find something?" he asks while I set my pack down in the area between the stalls and remove my cloak.

"I did, though I don't know whether any of it will be useful." I pull the papers from my pack and spread them out on a table in the corner. "I found a secret room. It was Ensel's treasury—jewels, and gold, even the old king and queen's crowns. But no cornucopia." The heavy weight of my omission—my mother's pendant—hangs around my neck, and my eyes stray back to my pack, where the vials remain hidden. I'm not sure what he'd think of me taking the latter, and I'm not ready to engage in a conversation about my parents yet. I need to think more about both first—then I'll tell him. "We should look through the papers and see if there's any mention of it, but otherwise, it's a dead end."

I fold my arms across my chest and lean my head back against a stall door. Dalen eyes me curiously. "What is it? I can tell something else bothers you. What happened? You were gone a long time."

I sigh. "The chamber was in Ensel's rooms, and while I was there Vincali showed up. He took the king's quarters, of course. After he finally left, I discovered a letter. He has the Bryrians surrounded. He thinks they're up to more than just feeding the city. Even worse, it seems he and his men were sent here to round up what was left of Ensel's mercenaries and hire them to take over Belladoma."

Dalen frowns. "Why would anyone want to do that? This isn't exactly the sort of city people fight over, not with a sea monster outside."

"It would be a desirable location if not for the monster. But the letter revealed that they're looking for something. They found where the wizard once lived and took anything magic they found there. But whatever they were sent here to find eluded them."

"Any hints to what it is?"

I shake my head. "None. But I can't stop wondering.

What if they've heard rumors of the cornucopia, too? Who would have sent them? And what else could be of interest to anyone beyond our shores?" I throw up my hands. "Kymera, maybe? The wizard did create her, after all, and she was magnificent."

"So really, it could be anything, and it's likely something magical."

I nod.

"Perhaps there's a clue in the papers?"

"That's what I'm hoping. And that it isn't the cornucopia."

We begin to look the papers over, but mostly, they're deeds to property in the city, pleas from citizens to forgive their debts and not punish their daughters, and a handful of communications between the wizard and Ensel. One of these I surreptitiously pocket. It mentions the vials and sounds like it was sent to Ensel along with them.

When our candle burns low, and we can't help yawning, we each curl up in our own stalls to sleep. I wait until I hear Dalen's soft snoring, then creep from the stall to the barn window. By moonlight, I read the letter and learn what the vials are and what they can do.

It isn't until I am safely back in my stall and pulling the blanket up to my ears that I realize the moon is almost full.

# CHAPTER 16

I STEAL AWAY EARLY THIS MORNING WITH AN EYE TO CATCHING REN AS soon as he enters the city. But first, I sneak toward the section of Belladoma where they sell food. I don't enjoy stealing, but our meager supplies dwindle every day.

We must keep up our strength to save Hans.

So as dawn breaks, with my cloak pulled close, I slip into an alley behind the first store I see—a bakery—and pick the lock of the back door. It is loose anyway, as though it needs repair, and the door creaks open, making me wince. If anyone is inside, they do not stir. I step cautiously into the entryway, letting my eyes adjust to the burgeoning light coming in through the windows.

I stand in a narrow hall, and I tiptoe across it, past a small pantry that contains only a few staples for baking and a half-filled bag of potatoes. But the smell of bread and pastries swallows me up. My stomach rumbles. When I reach the edge of what must be the kitchen, a faint noise stops me in my tracks. Slowly, I crane my neck around the corner.

The baker is awake, with his back to me, kneading bread on a long counter next to an oven and a stove. Several pans nearby await the dough. Hunger besieges me, but then I spy something along the far side of the kitchen wall that is completely unexpected. Three straw pallets, one empty and the other two occupied by a woman and a boy a few years older than me.

The baker hums, oblivious, while he kneads, every note striking a chord in my heart that is all too familiar.

His family lives in the bakery. Their pantry is almost empty. They have no real beds with feather mattresses. They have no house, just the shop, all that remains of their livelihood. And yet, the baker still sings.

Sadness slides over my skin, leaving me clammy and cold. I can't steal from this family. Even if they are Belladoman. It wouldn't be right.

As quietly as possible I creep back down the hall and out the door. Only when I'm again standing before the dawning sun do I stop, filled with a hunger for all the things I've lost.

Remaining out from under the watchful eyes of the roving mercenary bands, I sneak through the slick alleys of Belladoma while keeping my target in sight.

Ren.

After I told Dalen about what the mercenaries have

planned for the Bryrians, we agreed warning them is a must, as is determining what else the Bryrians might be after in Belladoma. Since I left Bryre so suddenly, I'm not sure how much they'd let me into their confidence now.

I've followed Ren all over the city and already know something doesn't add up. They arrived yesterday but, as far as I can tell, didn't bring anywhere near enough supplies to sustain Belladoma for more than a couple of weeks. There are too many mouths to feed in this rotten city.

King Oliver and Ren must have a different plan. I intend to find out what it is.

All night I debated whether I should follow Ren. It's been weeks since we've spoken; I'm not ready to say hello, nor explain why I left. They didn't trust me. Why should I trust them? Maybe I could wear them down and convince them to help me with Hans, but I fear the price would be my help with Belladoma.

But the truth of the matter is I miss my Bryrian friends terribly. I must satisfy my curiosity. Most important, I must be sure that they'll stay out of my way, or at the least that I stay out of theirs. The best way to do that is to uncover all I can about their plans.

I waited near the entrance to the north gate for half the morning before Ren appeared. The early-morning sun soon gave way to pouring rain. I trailed him through the town—he is not half so careful about the mercenaries as I am, but he's learning fast—and now I follow him back to where the Bryrian army made camp. I'm soaked through, but I don't care.

He takes the road, accompanied by a couple of soldiers, while I shadow them from the trees. The sound of the rain pounding the branches aids me. The camp is about a mile up the road, spread out in a muddy field. Tents and pennants from my home city twist in the rain, making my heart sour. I'm sneaking into my own people's encampment.

The guards escorting Ren take up posts and he heads for the main tent. Now that I have to dodge and weave between tents instead of trees, the going is trickier, but my luck holds and the rain continues, even throwing thunder and lightning down to spice up the otherwise dreary afternoon. Guards huddle beneath tent overhangs while other sodden soldiers hurry between them. I pull my hooded cloak tighter around me and do my best to blend in, carefully noting which tents are living quarters and which ones hold supplies.

Ren ducks through the flap opening of the largest tent. It must be King Oliver's. The fire pit inside throws shadows on the sides of the tent. Soldiers guard the opening, but I work my way around until I find a tear in a seam where I can peek through. Ren and the king huddle over a table in the center of the room near the fire. I can't see what they examine but I hear them fine. My curiosity increases by the second.

"Do you think it's real?" Ren asks.

"Oh yes. That prisoner was prepared to use it to barter for his life."

"You mean you let him go?" The king nods, and Ren

scowls. "But he was one of Ensel's guards. What if he's lying?"

"What if he is? What if this is only a legend?" King Oliver paces. "We have no way of knowing, and holding that man would not change the facts."

"It is real, I'm sure of it. The guards knew of it. I heard them myself when they held me in the dungeons." Ren sighs. "Still, I wish we had him here to question if we needed to."

My ears perk. What in the realm are they talking about?

"We made a deal; we had to honor it."

They return to examining the parchment on the table. I'm dying to know what it is. A book? A map? A spell?

"This is useless," Ren says. "We can't make heads or tails of this. We'll never find the cornucopia."

No. *No.* They can't be seeking the same thing I am. I shake, but it's not from the cold.

It makes a horrible sort of sense. This is their master plan to aid Belladoma. It's how they hope to feed all those people.

They'd feed all of Belladoma forever in spite of the monster in the deep—at the expense of my brother. Though I suppose I'm planning to do the reverse—let all of them starve to save one boy.

"There must be some kind of key," King Oliver muses. "I am not clear what these symbols mean, but Ensel knew and must have had some way of explaining them."

"I bet that guard knew where the key is," Ren grumbles.

"He didn't. We tried to get that information from him too."

No question remains. They have what I need to find the cornucopia. I hate stealing, and especially from them. But what else can I do?

Unbidden, the image of the baker, humming and rolling dough while his hungry family slept nearby, comes to the front of my mind. I choke on the memory but shove it down.

I know Ren and the king. I know their kindness, and that they want to do the most good possible.

But that means they'd never let me give the cornucopia to a greedy witch.

Certainty accompanied by sickly guilt fills every inch of my limbs as surely as the rain pouring over me. If only they'd believed me back in Bryre, maybe we could have found a way to work together. Maybe we still might. But I need that parchment if I want any hope of finding the cornucopia first. Having that in hand is the only way they'd really listen to me.

And I need to act now.

The clouds gather in an ominous thunderclap, and a horse whinnies from the makeshift stables not far from where I hide. An idea springs into my brain. I slip away from the tents, weaving behind one, then the other, making my way to the stables. I'm more careful than ever not to get caught.

Ren and King Oliver will never forgive me if they find out I'm willing to let an entire city starve. I may never forgive myself, but it doesn't change what I have to do.

The guards near the stables are already drinking ale liberally from their flasks, probably the only way they can keep warm on a day like this, when a fire won't stay lit outside.

Needless to say, I sneak by the guards effortlessly.

The tricky part is unlatching the gates holding the horses inside. The "stables" are a partially open pen with an area canopied off to provide shelter and dry hay for the horses. Most of them lie in the hay for warmth. I'm chilled to the core myself, but I can't spare the time to notice. Too much is at stake.

Finally, with raw hands, I pry the iron mechanism open. The horses' ears perk up, but they don't approach. Why would they? Who'd want to be out in this weather? A wayward laugh bubbles in my chest; I feel slightly unhinged.

If they won't come out willingly, I'll have to find another way. An awful yet perfect idea sends me off to find the nearest empty tent. Not far from the stables, a handful of guards leave one of the large barrack tents and head for the perimeter. Changing of the guard. Perfect. I slip inside, relieved to see the fire's coals still burning. I can't help noticing the food left out on the table—bread and cheese and a few apples—and I hurriedly shove that in my bag. Their leftovers will feed Dalen and me for a few days. Then I grab the pot hanging over the fire pit and fill it with hot coals.

Holding it as far from my body as I can so I won't get burned, but also won't draw suspicion, I scurry back to the stables. One or two horses have wandered out of the covered area to inspect the gate, but they show no signs of taking off. I grimace. I don't relish putting anyone or anything in danger.

More guards turn out for the shift change. More people to notice me, but there's also more commotion to distract from what I'm doing. I sneak around the fence toward the dry overhang. I hope the hay isn't too wet. And that the horses can run fast. The ones in the stable area glance my way but don't make a sound.

They will soon.

I glance behind to be sure I haven't been spotted. The guards mill around but pay me no attention. Once I do this, I must flee fast. There's no turning back. A heavy weight descends, like gravity dragging me down.

I toss the pot into the stable and it lands with a clang on the dry hay. Hot coals pour out of it and the hay lights up before I even have time to take a breath. The horses scream and stomp and tear out of the stable—heading directly for the gate.

I dash behind a tent as the horses stampede into the camp, crushing tents in their way and causing an uproar among the guards. As I run, my mother's necklace slips out from under my dress. If I believed in ghosts, I might think I was being scolded. Mama would be furious if she could see me now. Or would she? If she knew it was for Hans . . .

Moving quickly, I sneak back to Ren and King Oliver's tent in time to see them run outside to find out what all the commotion is about. Within seconds, the entrance to their tent is out of their line of sight, allowing me to slip inside. The parchment lies on the table half unrolled. I puzzle at the markings, but even more at the fact that some look familiar to me, then stuff the parchment in my pack. Hurriedly, I scribble a note on a stray piece of paper: *Mind the woods. You're being watched. Vincali is not to be trusted. He suspects you're here for more than to offer help.* That will have to be warning enough. I don't have time to explain more. I just hope they heed it.

I swallow my guilt and run back out into the rain.

# CHAPTER 17

MY HANDS STILL QUAKE WHEN I REACH THE HOVEL OF A BARN WHERE Dalen hides. My actions follow me close behind, waiting to pounce and swallow me up.

Ren and the king won't find the cornucopia without that map. It rests heavily in my pack. It's one thing for me to not help my friends aid the Belladomans or for them to refuse to believe me about a missing boy; it's another to actively pit myself against them. It does not sit well with me.

The room is warm and welcoming, a relief from my thoughts. Dalen peels out of the shadows to greet me, a smile dying on his lips.

"What's wrong?"

I frown. Am I so transparent? "Nothing. Everything is right, in fact. I have a map."

His eyes widen with amazement as I pull the piece of worn parchment from my pocket and hand it to him. My hands are shaking, though I don't feel afraid. I just feel sick. "Can you make sense of it? It isn't like other maps I've seen. I'm not sure what it says."

He moves to the makeshift table by the window and spreads the parchment wide. On the top right hand corner is an embossed mark—a horn shape with a basket weave. No doubt it is the cornucopia.

"Curious. It may take me a few days, but I have an idea or two." Dalen grins. "Well done, Greta. Where in the realm did you find this?"

My breath catches. He hears everything I don't say compressed into the single moment of guilty hesitation. His face falls. "What did you do?" he whispers. "Please, tell me you didn't have to . . . do anything terrible for this."

I open my mouth, certain I'm about to crush all the hope in his gaze. "I found it. That's all you need to know." I start toward the back stall, but Dalen catches my arm. For a horse-boy, he's alarmingly fast.

"Tell me."

I try to shake him off, but to no avail. He's also very strong. I forgot about that since we've been traveling together. He never threw his weight around in the hybrid village like many of the others did.

"It's not important," I say. "The only important thing is finding that stupid cornucopia and getting my brother away from that witch. It's what will keep your family and species safe too. Or have you forgotten the witch's threat?"

He turns his eyes upward, as though he's praying. "Please, tell me you didn't kill anyone."

"Kill someone? For a blasted map? Do you think that little of me?" First Ren and King Oliver think I'm a liar, and now Dalen suspects I'm a murderer? He releases my arm like he's been burned.

"No. But since you refuse to tell me, I have no choice but to draw my own conclusions."

I step closer to Dalen. "I'd never take a life unless there was a direct threat to my own or to someone I love." Anger shivers over me. Dalen reaches out to steady me, but I evade his touch.

"Then why won't you tell me?"

I stare at the floor. Dalen's hoofprints cover it. He's been pacing, waiting for me to return. He worries.

He should.

"I stole it," I whisper. Heat stings my cheeks. Yes, I stole it from those who would use it for good, so I can give the cornucopia to a selfish, evil witch. I am no hero.

"From who?"

"No one you know." I examine the map again, praying it's worth all this trouble.

"But *you* do." He places his hands on my shoulders. I can only nod in response. Tears slide over my cheeks, but I won't meet his gaze.

"Were you close to them?"

"It was King Oliver of Bryre and his messenger, Ren. I was friendly with them back in the city." I throw up my hands. "But I had to do it. Hans will die if we don't find this. And then—" My words choke off. I can't bring myself to say it, but we both know the witch will come for me next. And then what's left of Dalen's village. Her reign of terror will never end unless she gets that cornucopia.

Dalen backs away. "You've mentioned them before. Next to Hans they sounded like they were practically family to you. You turned on them? Couldn't they have helped us?"

I hesitate before answering. If King Oliver knew of something to stop the witch, would he help?

"No." My face hardens and I wipe away my tears. He wouldn't believe me, and he certainly wouldn't just give me anything powerful enough to thwart a witch. "They turned on me long ago. Why would they help me now? They didn't believe me when I came to them, begging their help to search for Hans. They didn't know I had a brother and thought I was making him up. They couldn't spare the manpower because it was needed to help Belladoma. The same city filled with people ready to throw me and the other Bryre girls off the cliff to appease the Sonzeeki. They were going to save the people who tried to kill me, and if they were successful, then Hans and I are dead anyway. I couldn't let that happen." Though I hold no love for the Belladomans, the understanding of what this could mean for them, what I've taken away, is a burden I wish I didn't have to bear.

Dalen's face is unreadable. "How did you get it away from them?"

I sigh. "I scared away their horses, set them loose in the

145

woods. It will take them days to round them all up. When Ren and the king left the tent, I took the map."

Dalen is quiet for a long moment. My heart hammers in my chest, punctuating the silence.

"Would you turn on me if you thought I stood in your way?" he says at last.

Dalen disappears into the shadows.

"No, wait! I'd never—"

"Don't," he says from the darkness. The door to his stall creaks open, then closes sharply.

I'm left with my guilty shame and a map out of which I can make no sense.

# CHAPTER 18

LAST NIGHT, I DREAMED OF FIRE AND HORSES SCREAMING. I CAN'T TELL IF the horses were supposed to be the ones I set loose or Dalen's disapproval running rampant, but his silence troubles me. Did I go too far? I didn't think anything was too far for Hans, but I'm second-guessing myself. Guilt still gnaws at me. That and a nearby owl kept me up half the night.

Dalen lost his home because of me. Discovering how untrue I am to old friends must have been disturbing to say the least.

When sunlight finally filters through the barn windows, I give up on sleep and opt for breakfast instead. I chew on a morsel of cheese on the verge of going bad—even with the food I took from the camp, we can't afford to waste a single scrap—and consider the map. The hollow image of the Belladomans crawling hopefully out of their homes at the Bryrians' arrival flashes in front of my eyes and turns my stomach again.

At first glance the map looks like any other map of Belladoma and the surrounding area. The forest on both sides is clearly marked, as are the paths and roads through the mountains, including a long, winding one leading off into the distance to other lands. The city itself is set out in particular detail, each road and shop carefully noted. Here and there are odd markings that ring with familiarity in the back of my brain, but what they are refuses to surface.

One is shaped like a triangle, point up, with an extra line on the inside. Another is the same, but with the point facing the bottom of the map. And still two others are like them, but without the extra lines.

Why do these odd things seem familiar? And why can't I remember what they mean?

Frustrated, I set the map down, careful not to damage the delicate thing. It's sturdier than it looks, but the crumbling, aged edges make me nervous. I leave it in Dalen's pack, poking out the top so Dalen will see it when he wakes.

I once heard centaurs love puzzles. I'm counting on that being true. With any luck, he'll have it figured out by the time I get back.

Absentmindedly, I clutch the locket around my neck. There's something I need to do. However much I hate the idea, I must return to the palace. This time to the dungeons.

Ever since I found my mother's locket, I haven't been able to shake the feeling that some hint of where my parents went might remain in the city. I can't fathom what brought them to this awful place, but I owe it to myself and Hans to find out.

Even though discovering this necklace in Ensel's room doesn't bode well, maybe the wish I refuse to let myself harbor will come true. It's a fragile and foolish thought, but what if—*what if*—my parents are still there, chained in the dungeons? I could free them. I might be able to reunite my entire family.

If I could find them, they could help me save Hans. They always knew how to make things better, to solve problems in ways I just couldn't see. Their loss has left a hole in my chest, invisible to the eye but painful nonetheless.

One way or the other, I must know. Returning to the castle is the only way to do that.

I gather up my cloak and satchel and, with a wistful glance back at Dalen's silent stall, leave the barn. Perhaps a little distance will make him more forgiving than he was last night.

A gray haze hangs over the streets of Belladoma, a lingering reminder of last night's rain. No sun, no rainbows shine through to this dreary place. The tide in my brain rises with every step I take into the city, panic threatening to drown me on dry land. I duck my head and hurry into the tunnels that will take me to the castle. After the rain yesterday, the tunnel is even wetter and more foul smelling, and I shiver as I close the hidden door behind me. I've made a point of not getting near the cliff. I don't know if I can handle glimpsing the Sonzeeki lurking in the waters below.

It's the black, beating heart of the city, one that threatens to burst from its own chest and drown everyone who lives in the vicinity.

The moon waxes near to full; the beast will rise soon. The thought of those slimy black tentacles wrapping around my waist barrels into me and I hold a hand out to the slick wall to steady myself.

I have every intention of being long gone before that happens. Cornucopia in hand.

Once the passage lets me out in the underbelly of the palace, I pause to get my bearings—and throw on the serving girl's uniform I snagged the last time and kept in my pack—and search out the dungeons. The entrance is in one of the towers. Ensel used to keep a guardhouse there, but who knows if the mercenaries bother. Do they have prisoners? Are Ensel's prisoners still in the dungeons, left to rot like the evil king's remains?

I shiver. I'll soon find out.

All the while, the awful, gnawing itch crawls over my skin, telling me I need to get out, escape before it's too late. I swallow down the fear. With Ensel I knew what to expect, but now every step takes me farther into the unknown.

I keep to the shadows and avoid all other people. I wait patiently in an alcove hidden behind a moldering tapestry near the dungeon's tower entrance, just to see who comes by and how often.

I prefer to take action, but even I know patience is a virtue if I want to succeed.

Only a handful of guards are posted in the dungeon tower, and most of them are playing cards. A couple of girls have gone back and forth to wait on them, bringing ale and food, while they get more and more drunk and gamble away their spoils.

I won't be able to get by them easily, and I'm not equipped to fight that many.

My hands tremble as I pull a vial of green liquid from my pocket. It glimmers when the meager light catches it. I don't relish the notion of using magic. According to the papers I took from Ensel's hidden room, each potion has a purpose. It was Ensel's stash of magic, part of the trade-off for helping the wizard with his plans against Bryre.

Green is for invisibility. Red to see in the dark. Blue to breathe underwater. Yellow to move without making a sound. White to send the drinker directly to sleep. I might be able to use the yellow one, too—and it's also in my pocket—but I have no idea whether these even work, let alone what sort of combustible interactions they might have if used together. I shudder.

Magic is tricky. There will be a price. Ensel's papers neglected to say what.

Which is why despite my curiosity, I cannot bring myself to drink it. Would it make my body invisible, but leave my clothes wandering around for all to see? How long does the effect last? An hour? Two? Forever? It is too dangerous and I have too little information. But I do have a plan. If I'm not ready to risk making myself invisible, I can test it on something else.

I unroll the cloak I also swiped from the laundry room and slowly sprinkle the green draught over it. The effect is immediate. Where the liquid touches, the dark cloth shimmers and fades, and the effect spreads over the entire cloak. I swallow my gasp, then run my hand beneath the cloak to test it out. When my hand touches the underside, it disappears too, revealing only the cold stone floor beneath.

I grin, then choke it back. I shouldn't take any enjoyment from something created by the wizard or hoarded by Ensel.

But still, it is kind of incredible.

I throw it over my head. The hood is enormous, made for a grown man, and it swallows up my face. I tiptoe down the hallway toward the tower. A thousand horrid thoughts stomp through my brain. What if this doesn't work? What if they see through the cloak? What if the potion wears off the second I step into the tower, or before I come back up?

I ball my hands into fists inside the cloak, clutching it tighter around my face. I just barely see out of it. I'll have to be careful not to bump into anyone or knock anything over as I approach. That would give me away in a heartbeat.

The voices of the men in the guard tower grow louder

and more belligerent as I approach. They appear to be fighting over the latest hand played.

"Check his sleeves! Hold him down!"

Several of the mercenaries stand over one man, looking as though they're seriously considering throwing him out the window. While I'm grateful for the distraction, I pity the fool who tried to cheat them. I hug the wall and take the stairs down two at a time. At the bottom, I grab a torch from the wall and light it.

I run through each corridor, peering into every cell and hoping for a familiar face. Most are empty. But a few hollow eyes peer back as I pass. Not one is familiar. My footsteps, quiet as they are, echo softly, and the prisoners can tell someone is in the hall from my torch, even if they can't see me. But the planes and angles of Mama and Papa's features don't appear in any of the cells. A handful of hopeless strangers is all that remains.

I enter what appears to be an older section of the dungeon. The walls are crumbling, yet shot through with unforgiving steel bars. One would think it would flood, but none of the myriad hidden passages snaking through the castle connects to the dungeons. The builders of this fortress must have been careful not to leave any potential escape routes for prisoners. Only the streets, forests, and fields beyond bear the brunt of the floods. Even so, it's dank and dark, and in some places water pools on the gray stone floor. They can't keep all the water out, I suppose.

The air down here is stifling from the poor ventilation, and I pull back the hood of my cloak. Sweat beads on my forehead, though whether it is from humidity or nerves, I can't tell.

Given how empty this section appears, I'm startled when I turn the corner and find an old man, sitting up in his cell and staring directly at me.

I can't tell who is more surprised, but we remain there in silence for several moments before I muster my voice. Yet the prisoner speaks first.

"Are you a ghost? You look just like her," he murmurs in a voice like sandpaper, and with those few words, he pierces my heart. With the cloak, all he can see is my face. It should terrify him, but instead he seems to recognize me.

I manage to squeak out, "Who?" My mind races, not yet daring to hope.

He gazes intently at my face, and my skin crawls. Some prisoners may deserve to be locked up; I ought to be careful.

"A woman who was a prisoner too once—I don't know how long ago. Time"—the man shrugs, strongly resembling a rag being wrung out—"means nothing here."

I shiver, then brush my hair back from my face.

"Who was the woman?"

The man's sunken, shadowed eyes gaze at me with curiosity. "The man in the cell with her called her Mia, but I knew her real name."

Mia. That was my mother's name, short for something longer.

"What was her real name? How did you know?"

He smiles sadly, and the decayed state of his mouth makes me grateful I haven't eaten much today. "Euphemia.

I knew her back when she lived in Belladoma."

Mind reeling, I stumble back to grip the far wall. That's my mother's full name, but it can't be her. She's from Bryre.

Isn't she?

The old man steps closer to the bars, wrapping gnarled, thin fingers around the rusted poles. "Are you her daughter? The resemblance is uncanny."

"My mother was from Bryre. She's never been to Belladoma." Except she has—the locket I found in Ensel's chambers is proof enough. But I can't believe she was here before. Somehow she and Papa must have run afoul of that horrid man.

"But that only confirms it. When her stepbrother Ensel became king, Euphemia fled Belladoma. She'd already married a commoner and was living in the woods outside the city, disgracing herself in her family's eyes. Ensel had the rest of the royal family thrown off the cliff so no one could challenge his right to rule. If she'd stayed behind, she would've followed the rest of them to the depths."

A chill works its way up my spine, like a jagged fingernail taking its time to scrape over skin.

The man sees my discomfort, and compassion lights his eyes. "Euphemia vanished after Ensel took power. But then she was brought back with her husband, Bartholomew. Ensel hadn't forgotten what his stepsister had done. I'm afraid they met their fate."

"Why should I believe you?" Could this be a trick? I can't believe I might be related to that hateful man in any way.

He sticks his head and neck between the bars. Rust

155

comes off on his sallow, sunken cheekbones. "Because I worked for Ensel once. And his stepfather. I was the court adviser."

"What happened? Why are you down here?"

He sighs. "The king didn't like my advice."

"But my mother wasn't part of the court, not if she married a commoner."

"No, but I knew her when she was a wee thing. And when she turned her back on her family for love." He spits the word out, but something in his eyes suggests he approves. "She was the smart one. Got out and stayed low until she knew they'd have to run. Bryre would've been the perfect place. Large enough of a city to stay hidden, but well off enough that she'd feel at home." He pulls back from the bars and settles onto the cold stone floor again. "And guarded well enough that Ensel and his lackeys would not pursue her." He frowns. "Of course, they did find her eventually. Pity. I always liked her. Even with her unfortunate taste in husbands, she would have made a far better queen than Ensel ever was a king."

My nails dig into my palms. I'm not fond of the way this stranger speaks about my father, like he's less than worthy.

He eyes me shrewdly for one who has been locked away for years in this awful dungeon. "You don't trust me, do you?" He shrugs. "Well go on, then, take a gander at the cell where they were held. You'll see for yourself."

"Where?"

He points to the one diagonally across from him. "The three of us were quite cozy down here until their end."

I shudder as I move to the unlocked cell across the corridor. A ratty discarded blanket lies in one corner, and loose stones litter the damp floor. Not much remains to prove anyone ever stayed in this cell. I nudge the blanket with the toe of my boot, then scrape it aside.

Shoved into the corner, and hidden by the seemingly tossed-aside blanket, is a folded-up letter.

"One of the guards took pity on her and snuck her some parchment. Mia always was good at making people like her. Except Ensel, of course."

I pull the letter out, hardly able to breathe. I recognize the handwriting immediately.

It's definitely my mother's.

My knees sway, but I straighten my spine and tuck the letter into my pocket. I can't read this in front of him. I need space and time, and to be somewhere I'm not worried I'll be caught.

I need to get out of this awful place.

But then I pause. "What was the advice Ensel didn't like?"

"I advised him not to consort with wizards. The final straw was when I advised him not to hunt below the cliffs for the cornucopia. He found something else entirely, too, then threw me in here for being right."

I frown. That explains why Ensel had a potion for breathing underwater.

"So he disturbed the Sonzeeki?" I muse.

"Oh yes. Now the beast returns each month to get back what Ensel stole. So many lives lost, when all Ensel had to do was toss the cornucopia into the waves. He had enough treasure as it was." He shakes his head. "But it will never be said Ensel was a reasonable man. More like a stubborn child who didn't like to share his toys."

"Where is it now?" Desperation taints my voice.

The man plucks at his loose clothing. "Do you think I'd be so skinny if I knew that?"

I sigh as disappointment fills my gut. He has a point.

I remove one of the pins keeping my hair back, but the man waves me away before I can try to pick the lock.

"Thank you, but don't bother. This is Ensel's dungeon; the locks are spelled. Only the warden's keys can open them."

"I'm sorry I don't have the keys to get you out." I wish I did. But stealing them from the very awake band of mercenaries upstairs would be a suicide mission.

"I didn't expect you would." His eyes glow in the darkness. "But it was nice to have someone to talk to for a while."

"If I can find a way, I'll come back," I say impulsively. I'm not even sure why. Perhaps I'm just grateful this man showed me a glimpse of my parents, even if the pain of it is sharper than knives.

He nods, not believing, and returns to a corner of his cell. With a heavy heart, hood up, and the letter in my pocket, I walk back through the dungeons.

# CHAPTER 19

WHEN I STEP OUT OF THE TUNNELS AND BACK INTO THE STREETS OF Belladoma, my whole world has shifted. My mother once walked these roads too. She grew up in the castle over the cliff, never dreaming of what horror slept below the waves. She was stepsister to Ensel. Which makes him my stepuncle.

I clasp the locket in my hand. Maybe this wasn't a wedding present at all like my mother always told us. Maybe it's an heirloom from the Belladoman royal line. At the very least, it might have been a pity gift from a rich relative.

My skin shivers and sweats, and this time I can't hold back the nausea. Thankfully, I'm alone in this alley, and I get back to my feet quickly after emptying my stomach and shoving my still invisible cloak into my pack. But I cannot shake the prickling uncertainty that pursues me. The staring faces from the windows. These were my mother's people. Did she know them? She never took on any airs in Bryre— did she go to the market here too? Do any of these people remember her? Could they tell me who she was before I was born?

I step into a street, keeping to the walls. The people around me, who hover in doorways, linger in windows, and stride down the streets, look different to me now. I can't help seeing things I didn't notice before. How the mothers keep their small children, mostly boys, close to their skirts. They hold on to their sons' tiny hands like they're the most precious things in the world. One little boy feeds a bit of his apple—a true prize in this place—to a stray dog. Husbands and wives embrace in greeting as they walk through doorways to their dilapidated homes, an emotion written on their faces that I never really believed they were capable of—love.

If this is the city that made my mother who she was, the mother I loved dearly, can it be as thoroughly evil as I've long considered it?

I wander the streets for hours, hunting for the ghosts of my parents, searching for them in every shadow and doorway, until dusky tendrils thread across the late-afternoon sky, like ink spilled on parchment. Like it's erasing everything I knew about my life and family. I thought my past was behind me. I thought I'd accepted the fact that Mama and Papa were gone and that I'd never know why.

Now that I've discovered they were here in Belladoma, I don't know how to handle it.

By the time I reach the crumbling barn I share with Dalen, I quiver from head to toe. Too many conflicting thoughts attack me from all sides. The letter from my parents burns a hole in my pocket. My fingers itch to unfold it and dive in headfirst.

And yet the thought of doing so ties my stomach into knots.

I close the creaking door behind me as quietly as possible. I don't want Dalen to see how affected I am by this.

But this is about family. This is about *me*.

I take a deep breath to pull myself together. I have faced down worse things.

I duck into the first stall of the barn and settle on the musty hay. I hear no sign of Dalen. Perhaps he's still angry.

With trembling fingers, I unfold the letter.

*To my dearest children* . . . Unbidden, a plump tear falls and blotches the note. I slap my hand over my eyes, wiping it away viciously.

I will not cry.

*You may wonder why we left you in such a hurry. It was by necessity, not choice. We didn't intend to leave at all, really. But I get ahead of myself. Let me explain. While your father is from the countryside that lies between Bryre and Belladoma, I never lived in Bryre until I married him. I grew up in Belladoma, which at the time was a shining jewel of a city by the sea. We traded with people inland and across the waves, the whole town a hub of international culture, of varied tongues and spices and wares. My own mother died when my brother and I were babies, and my father remarried a woman who already had a young son. Her first husband had gone mad and leaped off Belladoma's cliff, leaving her rich and lonely. But my father was a kind soul, and she was lovely, and good with my brother and me too. The city rejoiced, for its king had a whole family again. Yes, I grew up in the palace, so different then from what it has become under my stepbrother, Ensel's, thumb. It was beautiful and full of light once; now it rots from the inside out.*

*Sometimes, I wish I'd never left Belladoma, despite the risks of staying. But that means I wouldn't have married your father, and would never have had you two, my dearest joys, in my life. You see, your father was a commoner. I met him one day in the forest, then I stole away there every chance I had to see him again. My father had plans to marry me to a prince from the kingdom over the sea, but once I knew your father, I couldn't stand the thought of marrying anyone else. We eloped, and when I returned to the palace, my father banished me from the city. My older brother, Erick, tried to intercede on my behalf, but to no avail.*

*Even then Ensel, my stepbrother, showed signs of being a bad seed, his father's madness passed down to him. Our cousin had died recently in a hunting accident. There were rumors he and Ensel had quarreled before they set off, but I ignored them at the time. Little did I know how he plotted to butcher his way to the throne. If I had, perhaps I would have fought harder to stay in Belladoma. But my heart was with your father, and while the banishment pained me, it wasn't the punishment my father had hoped.*

*We had a small cottage in the woods, and we loved it there.*

162

It was outside Belladoma, so I could still see my city and occasionally my brother but not worry about the politics. And I never did. Not until we heard what Ensel had done.

He had spent his nights in taverns, drinking and dealing with every unsavory character in Belladoma. He made a deal with a band of mercenary soldiers from overseas, then proceeded to round up everyone with royal blood in the city. I began to worry when my brother didn't appear for his weekly visit, but it wasn't until days later, when your father came home from the market, that I discovered the truth.

My whole family was gone, and Ensel's mercenaries were hunting for us.

Greta and Hans, you were just a glimmer on the horizon then. We fled to the only safe place we could think of that we knew would take us in: Bryre. And when Ensel attacked, we were certain it was because he had gotten wind of where we were hidden. We were ready to stand and fight with our adoptive city, but as luck would have it, the wards the wizard set up kept him out.

For years, we believed we were safe in Bryre. We believed we could have children and live our lives in peace.

We were wrong.

The day we left Bryre, we had gone to a market an hour's walk away, and had every intention of returning home for supper. But while we were there, we were spotted by a man we recognized: Albin, the closest confidant of Ensel and captain of his guard, on some errand for his king. He recognized us too. We fled, then purchased weapons and doubled back to try to take him by surprise. We couldn't let him follow us back to

*Bryre, not to you and your brother. Ensel would kill you both if he knew there were any living heirs to the throne of Belladoma. But Albin was craftier than us, and he had more men than we realized. He surrounded us, caught us, and brought us back to Belladoma. I don't know what will become of us here, though I presume Ensel will either let us rot for the rest of our lives or he'll throw us off the cliff as he has so many of Belladoma's children. It breaks my heart to see what's become of my city. I don't know whether you'll ever see this letter, or if you'll ever forgive us for abandoning you, however accidentally. But I had to put this down on paper just in case—if nothing else than to express our love to you both.*

*Your loving parents,*
*Mia and Bart*

The sobs come, wracking my entire body, and I can't stop them. How long were they down there? They were caught many months before the wizard sent me to Belladoma, and Albin was that hateful man whom Kymera sent over the cliff.

Could my parents have been here, trapped, frightened, and filled with guilt for never being able to say good-bye, at the same time I was thrown into the dungeons for trying to escape our prison room? The thought is sickening. To be so close to them, and to have had no idea . . .

The sobs turn to chokes. I feel the breeze of the stall door opening, and the light touch of a soft, strong hand on my back. "Greta . . . ," Dalen whispers, settling on the hay beside me.

In a moment of weakness, I throw my arms around his neck and cry into his shoulder. I have no family left but Hans. Really and truly. The faint hope I'd cherished that perhaps my parents were still alive, and that one day they might return, has burned to ash.

Dalen's arms fold around me, and he hums softly in my ear. Grateful he has the sense not to utter false words of comfort, I cling to my friend and cry until the darkness creeps over my eyes and sleep takes hold.

# CHAPTER 20

**WHEN MORNING SLIPS *THROUGH* THE WINDOWS OF THE BARN, BATHING** me in warm, soft light, I startle. I still lean against Dalen's side, and his arm drapes over me. It would be easy to stay here, hidden away from the rest of the world, far from the troubles of my family, and the witch terrorizing my brother and me.

But hiding isn't something I can do, however tempting it may sound.

I crawl to our packs and pull out the remains of a hunk of cheese for breakfast. Before I can think better of it, I check to be sure the vials of magic potion are still where I left them, hidden deep in my pack. The way the invisibility potion swept up that cloak haunted my dreams. Magic is dangerous but surprisingly helpful. And I'd be lying if I said walking around in an invisible cloak wasn't fun.

I brush off the thoughts of magic and finish my breakfast. My entire body aches, and I notice a small wound, almost like a sore, on the back of my hand. I must have nicked myself on the way home last night, or maybe in the dungeons, and not even noticed.

Dalen stirs, and a lump swells in my throat. He's been better to me than I deserve, after he learned what I did to my other friends. He's depending on me to stop this witch.

Once I find the cornucopia, maybe King Oliver and Ren will be willing to help me find a way to defeat or even banish the witch. In his years of trying to keep the wizard at bay, King Oliver might have come across something that will stop her. And maybe I can make amends for stealing the map. But after they called me a liar, I'm not sure. At the very least, I need something I can use to make a deal, whether it's with the witch or my friends.

I wonder, did Dalen get far figuring out that map, or has he been too angry to bother? I tiptoe toward his stall to hunt for the parchment but halt—the feeling of eyes on my back is unmistakable. I whirl around to find Stump in the corner of the barn, staring. His ability to find us is unsettling. I was sure he was bored with us when he didn't follow us into the tunnels.

"Where did you come from?" I whisper, but his only answer is to twist his head in my direction.

I enter Dalen's stall and find the map wedged in the corner, half hidden by hay, so no one can see it if they give the place a cursory glance.

I carefully pull it out, noticing a dirty smudge across the top left quadrant of the map. I gasp—that same quadrant now has real lines and hints of a path. But it's incomplete. The bottom left section is also revealed with new details, and wrinkled as though it has been drenched with water and dried. An inverted triangle is etched in the bottom corner of this portion, and a similar triangle with a line through the base is near the first exposed section of the map.

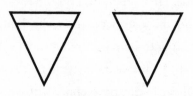

Upright triangles mark the remaining two corners. A triangle with a line and the quadrant smudged with dirt, an empty triangle and damp paper . . . elements. Now I remember—we learned about these symbols in school a couple of years ago. Each triangle corresponds to an element, and exposing it to that element reveals the real map. Excitement fills me.

We've got it. We've got the map to the cornucopia.

Dalen solved it.

I rush back to my stall, ignoring Stump and clutching the map to my chest. Dalen is awake and nibbling on bits of cheese. If we find the cornucopia today, we'll have all the food we could want.

I hold out the map. "You figured it out!" I throw my

arms around his neck, this time with joy. We can find the cornucopia and save my brother and Dalen's village. We're so close.

He laughs. "I can't resist a puzzle."

I release him and study the map again. "So these last two quadrants must also be elements? Air and fire?"

"Exactly."

"But how do you know which is which?"

He grimaces. "That's the tricky part. I think I know, but I thought I'd wait for you, and we could decide which to try first together."

I hold the map up to the light again and consider it. "I think," I say, "that these inverted symbols should be the opposite of each other, don't you?" I point to the triangles. "So if this one was water, then this one should be fire. And then if this one with a line was earth, the other should be air."

"That's what I was thinking too," Dalen says.

"Let's try air first. Can we just blow on it?"

"I tried blowing on it yesterday, and even held it out the window when the breeze went through the trees, but it didn't work. I think we need a stronger wind."

My face falls. "And that will increase our chances of losing it. If the wind rips it out of our hands, it's lost."

"That and the possibility of the fire quadrant going awry, is why I made a copy of what we've uncovered so far," he says, pulling out a piece of parchment. "I had some in my pack in case we needed it, and it finally dried out." He turns it toward me—he's made a perfect copy of the water and earth elemental sections, leaving the others blank. "If we do lose the original, at least we still have something to go on. Maybe we can deduce where it leads from there."

"Brilliant," I say, and mean it. All Dalen's anger from the other night seems to be gone now that he's invested in this map. I can't help but be relieved.

We decide to test the air section, and set out immediately for the forest and the route to the cliff's edge. It extends beyond the city, jutting into the ocean. The barn we've chosen lets out into the forest in the back, providing us access without fear of being seen. The cliff should have a strong enough wind to activate the element on the map. As best we can figure, the wizard put a spell on the map for Ensel after he hid the cornucopia, adding these elemental keys as directions for the initiated.

Now that we know the key, it's only a matter of keeping our grip on the map.

The morning is warm and sun filled, a relief after the dreariness of the past few days. This time Stump trails behind. I don't understand why he's so interested in us, but he did try to warn us once before. I'm starting to like having him around.

Every step closer to solving the mysteries of the map brings me closer to the edge of the cliff. Closer to the Sonzeeki, lurking in the waters below. I silently remind myself over and over that I am safe, Ensel is gone, and the mercenaries are nowhere near. No one will toss me over the cliff today. It helps a little, but I can no longer tell if the waves I hear crashing are the ones in my head or the real ones in the bay.

We follow the path to the cliff's edge through the thickly wooded forest, until brush and scrub begin to replace the trees. The dark loamy earth lightens with hints of sand. Soon the trees fade entirely, and the ocean spreads out before us as far as we can see. I clench my fists at my sides. I never did get used to all that water swallowing up the horizon. Dalen paws the ground nervously at the sight. Stump remains at the tree line and hoots.

"That's the ocean?" Dalen says, eyes full of a strange mix of wonder and terror. "It looks impossible!"

"Doesn't it?" I shiver. The ocean holds no majesty for me. It's cold and grasping and suffocating. But I'd better not tell Dalen that. Not if I'm correctly judging the fear flickering over his face. "It must end somewhere."

"Gods, if we drop the map, we'll never get it back." Dalen swallows hard.

I take his hand, as much for myself as him, and lead him closer to the edge. He balks about five feet away. Wind whips over us, pushing, pulling, and tugging my hair from its pins to toss it back in my face. Knowing what evil lurks below, I don't dare get much closer to the edge either.

"Give me the map," I say, and Dalen cautiously hands it to me. I unroll the parchment, keeping as tight a grip as possible, then hold it above my head to let the air currents buffet our treasure.

Something tingly runs over the map. Not the wind, but something that shivers all the way down my arms and almost causes me to release it. Dalen yanks my arms down and grabs hold of the other corners, as we examine the map together. The bottom right quadrant we suspected was air has become more intelligible, making sense of the other two quadrants already exposed with additional paths and notations.

Now all we have to do is run fire over the last one, and we'll have the entire map. Excitement trills over me like a living thing. Dalen's eyes mirror the same thrill.

"We should wait until we get back to the barn and use the fire pit to try the fire section," Dalen says. "We'll be out of this wind and better able to control it."

I tuck the map into my satchel, and we leave the cliff face behind, taking shelter in the cool forest. Despite our lighter mood, the shadow of Hans is inescapable. He would've loved the mystery of this map. He'd be fascinated by Dalen, too. And Stump. He's missing everything.

"How can we use fire on the map without burning it up?" I ask Dalen. This part of the mystery I don't quite understand. "The water got the map wet, and the earth got it dirty, and the wind nearly stole it away. What do you suppose fire will do?"

Dalen frowns as we meander into a grove with tall, thick-trunked pines. "I'd suggest we begin by holding it over a candle flame, but we don't have any left. We'll have to build a fire, run the map over it, but not close enough to light it on fire. Then move it closer bit by bit until the magic is unlocked."

"That sounds slightly better than tossing it in the fire pit."

He laughs. Then he pulls me to a stop in the middle of the grove. Stump hoots louder than before, and it distracts

172

me momentarily. But nothing strange appears.

"Greta, we'll get your brother back. I know how important he is to you. I understand how much you need him. I don't want there to be any bad blood between us. I'm sorry I was angry with you last night. I've been thinking a lot about what you did—how you stole the map from your friends. The more I think about it, the less I can say I'd do any differently. My little sister, my mother, and my friends are all in danger too."

My face is hot. "Dalen, I wouldn't do that to you. I—"

"Yes, you would. If I were working at odds with you, and Hans was at stake. But my point is, I would understand. I would forgive you for it. Help you, even, if you told me why."

An unsettled feeling wanders through the pit of my stomach. Once, I thought Ren and King Oliver might do the same. "I don't— Ow!"

Something sharp nips at my heel, and I see Stump duck away and off to the side of the grove again. He hoots menacingly this time. He didn't draw blood, but it hurt. "Something is wrong," I say, a feeling of dread washing over me. But there are no shadows out of place in the woods surrounding the grove, and as far as I can tell, nothing is amiss here. The sunlight warms us despite the chill I feel inside.

Dalen frowns. Stump has returned to his usual tilting and staring, which only perplexes me more. "I don't know. Maybe he just feels neglected?"

"He has an owl brain. I can't imagine he thinks much."

"Never mind Stump. You have to go to Ren and King

173

Oliver. Tell them. If they're truly your friends, they will understand. They may even help us save Hans and keep my village safe. Wouldn't it be better to have assistance? That way if the witch turns on you, we'll have more people to try to stop her."

Part of me sees the logic of what Dalen suggests. I was thinking the same thing only this morning. But I'm also terrified of my Bryrian friends' anger. Of losing them forever. Not to mention hurt that they refused to help me before. If they don't know what I did, they can't be mad. They can't know I betrayed them. Not until I have the cornucopia; it won't matter as much then.

I also don't want them to know that if what my parent's letter says is true, then Hans and I are the last living heirs of the Belladoman royal line. It seems so unreal.

"I already went to them for help once, when I first discovered Hans had vanished. They thought I was lying, hoping to keep their guards otherwise occupied instead of heading here to Belladoma. They won't believe me now. Not yet. They'll only see that I stole the map from them." Shame colors my cheeks. "But I've been thinking, and you're right. We can't trust the witch to keep her word. When I have the cornucopia, I'll go to Ren and King Oliver. Maybe they'll help when they see how serious I am and that I was telling the truth before. Maybe we can make a deal with them to help us with the witch, and then we'll give them the cornucopia instead."

The hope in Dalen's eyes grows, and I take a step forward. Something crunches under my feet. I jump reflexively and stare at the ground.

A choking sound leaps from my throat.

Where my foot just stepped moments before is a large, brown, and now crushed chicken feather. It was hidden in the deep leaves of the grove so I didn't see it until I was literally on top of it.

Every bit of air flees my lungs. This is what Stump was trying to warn us about.

The witch is near. She's either here for me—early, too early—or she's hunting again because she agreed not to eat Hans yet.

Dalen places a hand on my shoulder, then recoils at my expression. "Greta, what is wrong?"

"The witch," I gasp. "She's here. In Belladoma. In these woods." The world spins. Any second one of the shadows could transform into the witch, too ravenous to keep her promise. Too hungry to do anything but devour me, my brother, and Dalen. The raccowl hoots and the sound echoes painfully in my brain. It's too soon. She can't be back yet. I knew she couldn't be trusted, but I had hoped she'd at least give me time to find the cornucopia first.

The world sags and sways. Dalen's arms lift me up, then carefully set me down on the ground. I scramble away from the huge crushed feather. Dalen sees it and grows still.

"It's from the witch's house," he says quietly. Then he casts about, looking for others. "That's the only one—" He cuts off sharply. I have no doubt that's a very bad thing.

"What do you see?" I regain my feet, feeling like a fool for losing them in the first place.

Dalen's face is drawn and pale, matching my own. I

glance down at his feet and quickly turn my face away, balling my hands into fists.

Bones. Small and fine.

Dalen gallops to the nearest tree and retches. I narrow my eyes at every shadow, ready to make a run for it back to our barn. I can't help being relieved that the bones are too small to belong to Hans. But they belong to someone, and somewhere a family aches with their loss.

"We must get away from this place. She found me again. We have to finish unlocking this map and find the cornucopia." My eyes are drawn back to the small pile of bones at the edge of the grove. "Then she won't do that to another child ever again." My life is now based on slim hopes—that my Bryrian friends will know how to defeat this witch or, failing that, that she'll keep her end of the deal. But I have to try.

Dalen looks as unsteady as I feel, and I take his hand, willing mine to stop shaking. "Let's go," I say again. He doesn't object. We hurry, especially Stump, careful not to make too much noise and draw unwanted attention. I can't help glancing over my shoulder every few minutes and staring too hard at suspiciously shaped shadows.

Any one of them could be the witch.

But she doesn't materialize, and as we near the barn again, I begin to hope we found the feather and bones simply because she was passing through. We didn't notice the house's telltale stench. Maybe they've been there for months. Surely the house must range far and wide. Just because she happened to be in the vicinity doesn't necessarily mean she was here for me.

I almost believe it, too.

We hurry into the familiar safety of the run-down barn, but Stump just hoots, then slips into the shadows of a tree. Is he off to hunt or is that another warning? Puzzled, we latch the door behind us. My hands have finally stopped shaking, and Dalen breathes a little easier, too.

We're safe. For now.

I take a deep breath, and it takes a moment for me to register the smell of something—

"You had better hurry," says a dark, familiar voice. "I do not like waiting." Dalen skitters backward, and I slowly face the witch. My voice has vanished. Words escape me entirely. I'd nearly forgotten the witch leaves her house on occasion.

She smiles, and it's beautiful and horrifying at the same time. She's just as I remember—long black hair spills over her shoulders, and her eyes shift color with every step she takes toward us. And the smell. Sickly sweet, but with an edge of something rotten underneath.

"What? Nothing to say this time?"

"We're close to finding the cornucopia. We'll have it for you soon, I swear." I swallow hard against the rocks clogging my throat. Could she possibly know what we were just planning in the grove? "How is my brother?"

"Fatter," the witch says simply. Her eyes shift to Dalen and her head tilts inquisitively. "Are you aiding her search, hybrid? You'd better not be slowing her down, or your village will pay the price."

"He's helping me. We need a few more days to uncover where Ensel hid it. Then we—"

She cuts me off with a look sharp enough to slice a

sword in half. "You have four days. No more. Then Hans will be my supper. And I'll have you for lunch the next day. You had better hurry; today is already half gone."

I shudder involuntarily. "We'll have it."

She saunters toward the door of the barn. "Oh, as an added incentive to hurry, I will take a child from this odd, decrepit little city you've found every night you delay. I must be prepared in case you fail. I take it you found my warning in the woods, yes?"

"We did," Dalen says, recovering his composure.

"Then you should have no trouble believing I'll continue."

In the instant it takes me to blink, she crosses the space between us and clutches my face in her hands. Her long fingernails dig into the soft flesh on the underside of my chin and throat. I don't dare swallow.

"The sooner you bring me the cornucopia, the sooner the Belladomans can sleep easier in their beds." Her voice is lower than usual, filled with malice and menace, and the sound crawls over me like tiny spiders. Up close, I can smell the carrion scent on her breath. I hold my breath so I don't gag.

She shoves me away and returns to the door so fast I don't quite see it happen. "A word of advice, pet. When a witch gives you a deadline, you don't just keep it. You beat it. Otherwise, she might get bored."

I give one more terrified blink, and then she's gone, the barn door slamming shut in her wake.

Silence weighs heavily in the air, as though breaking it will summon her back, full of wrath.

178

I sink to my knees in the hay, and only then does Dalen speak. "She is far and away the most unsettling, terrifying creature I've ever beheld."

I laugh bitterly. "That's saying a lot, considering you lived with snake-people. I don't think I could abide all that hissing and skin shedding."

Dalen smiles, but only halfway. "Trust me, in comparison, all the hissing in the world is preferable. You get used to it. I don't think anyone could get used to her."

My face darkens. "Hans has had to deal with her every day since she stole him." Tears prick the backs of my eyes, but I blink them away. We will save him; there's no cause to cry.

"Let's finish decoding that map," Dalen says, and for the hundredth time this week, I thank my lucky stars for his presence.

While Dalen copies the newly revealed air quadrant, I venture outside the barn with trepidation and build a small fire. Stump has vanished. I miss him. He *was* warning us. He didn't want us to go back into the barn. We just barged right into her trap.

When the flames are hot enough, I return to the barn for Dalen. Fear clings to me like fog. Either this is going to work and reveal where the cornucopia hides, or it will send all my hopes up in smoke.

Dalen seems equally uneasy, but I suspect he tries to hide it for my sake. Have I become so transparent that he can see right through to my deepest fears? He follows me back outside.

He doesn't say a word, just looks at me, and I nod in return, letting him know he should do it and get it over with. He holds out the map with steady hands and waves it over the flames. And nothing happens. He lowers the parchment little by little, and I wince each time.

Leave it to the wizard and Ensel to invent a map impossible to decode.

I think back to the potions in my stall. Could any of them help solve this puzzle? But none of them are potions to light something on fire. Become invisible, breathe underwater, move silently, yes; resist fire, no. If only.

My mother's locket weighs against my collarbone and I wrap my sweaty fingers around it, grasping for some measure of renewed strength.

"I have to put it fully in the flame," Dalen says quietly after too many unsuccessful passes to count.

The blood flows away from my cheeks in a heady rush. "Do what you must." If the water and the air and the earth didn't destroy it, surely there must be something in the map to keep it safe from fire, too?

Dalen holds the precious map above the flames, and they flick over it as if eager to consume the parchment. It looks so fragile, I want to cry out and snatch it away from him, but I resist.

I close my eyes and picture Hans's sweet round face. The way he was before Mama and Papa were taken to Belladoma.

I hear the sizzle of parchment hitting flame, and the quick burst of a flare hits the backs of my eyelids.

Dalen whoops and my eyes flicker open, just in time to

see him reaching into the fire with his bare hands and yanking the map out by an untouched corner. He tosses it on the ground and immediately stamps out the flames before they can destroy the parchment.

I rush over to help. His hooves have saved it, and coated it with a thin layer of dirt. I gingerly lift it up, hardly daring to hope it worked.

The edges of the map are badly singed, and crinkle off at the touch of my fingers. But the bulk of it is intact. Thin lines have appeared where none were before, and now an *X* forms in the last quadrant.

I grin at Dalen, the tightness that has bound my chest ever since I saw that feather finally releasing. He grins back—and then seems confused when he looks at the map.

The *X* that formed moments ago is not alone. Several other *X*s appear on the page, designating other potential locations for the cornucopia, along with the words: *Five days before the path fades.*

My heart sinks into the earth. Ensel must've had many hiding places. He was so paranoid that he moved it around frequently. When it wasn't in use, he'd send it to a random location. One of eight, by the looks of it. And the notation makes it sound like the ink will fade. At least it should last long enough for us to meet the witch's deadline.

Between this and what he did to my family, I've never hated Ensel more. How will we check all eight within four days? I'm tempted to throw the map back into the fire, but Dalen pries it from my hands first.

"Careful," he says. "If you hold it too tightly, it might

crumble. That would be a shame after it survived the fire."

Better for him to carry it right now.

"Ensel had multiple hiding spots." I sigh. "We'll have to check them all."

Which, of course, means that I will have to check them alone for the most part.

"We can do that. Or we could split them up," he suggests. "It would go faster that way."

Peering at the map, I ask, "Which ones are in the city and which are outside it? If you can check the ones outside it, near the woods and places you can hide if necessary, that would help." I frown. "But if none are near places you could hide, I hate to ask you to do it. I dragged you all the way here, and I should be the one to ensure you remain safe."

He laughs. "I can handle a brief search. But I thank you for your concern. And you are correct, I will keep to the forested areas, and you can search the city and any other places not easily accessible to me." He holds up the map. "See, here is the line marking the forest, and this one the city gates. It's divided almost in half. We can do this twice as fast, then get your brother back."

"Thank you," I say, squeezing his hand and meaning it.

# CHAPTER 21

DESPITE ALL THAT HAS TRANSPIRED, IT IS ONLY EARLY AFTERNOON, AND we have no time to waste. We decide we'll each tackle one of the Xs. Dalen has copied the entire map so we can each have one. In my stall, I fill my pack with supplies, my hands lingering over the bottles containing Ensel's potions. I hate them because they belonged to him . . . yet they might come in handy. One did before. The urge to take them with me is sudden and strong.

Dalen doesn't know about the potions. He and his kind have even more reason than I to despise the wizard, and I don't know how he'd react if he knew I'd used one of them. Or that I might decide to use another. Surely, the ability to move silently would come in handy on this expedition. I toss the vial into my pack. If it will help me rescue Hans . . .

Who knows what aftereffects it might have? Thankfully, the cloak I used the invisibility potion on didn't seem the worse for wear, and the potion's effects faded in a few hours, but some of the other potions I'd need to ingest. The thought scares me more than I like to admit.

Dalen pushes the door of my stall open. I drop the vial of invisibility potion like a hot coal into my pack and whirl around, cheeks burning. I nudge the edge of my blanket over the small box, then cross my arms over my chest.

"I'll check the ravine mentioned on the map," Dalen says, holding his copy in his hands, his pack slung over his shoulder. He paws the ground.

"I was just about to leave, too," I say, feeling oddly nervous, yet hopeful.

I absentmindedly rub my finger over the sore on the back of my hand. It's gotten worse over the course of the day. I'll need to bandage it soon.

Dalen notices and catches my arm. "What happened to your hand?"

I shake my head. "Nothing, just scratched it on something. Don't even remember it happening."

He frowns briefly, then says, "We'll meet here at dusk."

I nod my agreement. Why do I suddenly feel awkward around Dalen? Didn't I just spend last night curled against him, weeping?

Maybe that's exactly why.

Vulnerable is not something I ever want to be again. I duck my head, grab my pack, and barrel out the door.

The afternoon sun flares in my eyes when I step out of the tunnel into an alley on a side of town I've yet to explore. The buildings are large and spacious, but just as run-down and wet as everything else in this city, though the smell is less cloying. Perhaps most of the unfortunate fish are caught up by the streets of the central part of the city and don't leave as much waste here. Only dark, ghastly water to rot the houses.

Did my mother ever tread here, too, when the streets were filled more with life than death?

The path beneath my feet is damp in patches. Nothing ever really seems to dry out in Belladoma. The map takes me on a circuitous route, weaving around houses, back through crisscrossing alleyways, until finally stopping at a huge stone mansion in the same place as the *X* on the map. It towers over the others, like one giant standing stone pile, with the forest at its back. The huge, close-knit trees look dark and foreboding, like an army ready to spring to life. The hedge monsters in Bryre's palace garden leap to the front of my mind. That sort of thing is much more possible than I'd like.

But the wizard is gone, and as far as I know, I carry with me some of the last traces of his magic in the form of Ensel's potions. Except, of course, whatever it was that the mercenaries got from his cottage. I shudder. After seeing what the mercenaries did to that inn, I'm sure it must be more sinister than anything I've found.

I examine the house. Should I use one of the potions before I break in? There are no signs that people live here, not like the others I've passed. No carts, no horses. The grounds are overgrown to the point where the front walk and steps are almost entirely overtaken. But that doesn't necessarily mean the house is empty.

At the foot of the walk, I take out the vial of yellow liquid. Yellow is for silent steps. I could try this potion, just in case. A flare of excitement ties my stomach in knots.

It's dangerous. I shouldn't risk myself needlessly. Though perhaps . . .

I take off my boots. Holding both potion and shoes away from my body, I pour a single drop on the sole of each. A golden shimmer runs over them, tingling up my arms. I drop them in surprise, as a heady rush sweeps over me.

That must mean the potion worked. Better to test it on my shoes than on myself. I lace them back up and take a tentative step. Nothing, no sound at all. I stomp, then try jumping. Again, nothing. I shouldn't grin, but I do anyway. Now I can really be sneaky. This is almost as good as invisibility.

With one last check of my surroundings to ensure no one follows, I start up the walk, carefully picking my way through overgrown shrubbery and patches of prickling thorns. No one has called this place home for a long time. By the time I reach the front door, I wonder if I have the wrong place.

But one of the elemental symbols adorns the door knocker—an inverted triangle with a line through the top for earth—and all my doubts vanish like fog dispelled by sunlight.

Determined not to hope too much, I open the door. The leaded glass windows spill light into the room. Dust motes swell into the air, swirling in sunlight. The entryway was polished granite once upon a time but now is coated with a dull sheen. A thick tapestry hangs on one wall; it's so faded I can't make out what it depicts. I follow the long hallway and peek into every room, the potion keeping my steps silent.

It looks like it was abandoned in a hurry. The dining-room table is still set, waiting for the occupants to return and sit down to supper. I don't linger; it's far too eerie for my taste.

The trouble with the map is that it gives only the general location of the hiding spot. There's no map of the inside of the mansion; only the notation that the cornucopia could be here. Somewhere.

Frustrated, I stop to gather my bearings in the library. I've searched each room on the ground floor for any indication of a hiding spot, which I suspect will be marked by the triangle element symbol. Yet nothing since the door knocker has presented itself. The library is long and narrow, oddly so. Still, there are plenty of books to spare, row upon row at the back of the library. A skylight above my head reminds me I'm supposed to meet Dalen at the barn by dusk. I wonder how he fares with his search.

This section of the library is situated in front of a fireplace, cold and full of old ash. Several chairs and a chaise sit in front of the fireplace with layers of dust so thick I initially mistake them for a blanket. I move toward the rows of books. On the back wall between two windows is another tapestry, though this one is easier to see. It's cleaner than the rest of the room, though plenty of dust still clings to it.

The threads on the panel depict an ocean and the sea life inhabiting it. I shiver as I recognize the giant outer shell and rippling tentacles of the Sonzeeki. I lift my gaze to the top of the panel. It shows a scene above the ocean: the cliff and castle. Two figures with crowns woven in gold threads stand on the top of the cliff eying the waters below as if they rule the seas peacefully.

Odd that the Sonzeeki seems calm. It rests in a cavern, arms curling around something that looks suspiciously like a cornucopia.

Understanding comes to me suddenly. The cornucopia wasn't just another piece of treasure the Sonzeeki hoarded like dragons did jewels. Ensel took away the Sonzeeki's food source, and now it rises to the surface, starving and desperate and angry. It makes a horrible sort of sense. My fists clench, nails digging into my palms, as I turn away from the tapestry.

This is *his* fault. The ruin of Belladoma, the deaths of my family and many other girls—all of it comes right back to Ensel and his insatiable greed. If he wasn't already dead, I'd hunt him down and kill him myself.

But I can't change what he did, and I can't even fix it. I can't return the cornucopia to the Sonzeeki—I have to give it to King Oliver in exchange for his help, or to the witch so she'll release Hans. There are no good choices. Every one I make will cause misery somewhere. All I can do is what is right for me and mine, and hope for the best.

What would my mother have done, faced with this choice? Her city or her son? If she was horrified by the state of Belladoma when Ensel was alive, she would be deeply saddened to see how ruined it is now.

When the shelves and walls reveal nothing new about Ensel's hiding place, I head back to the main entrance to the library. A cloud moves away from the sun and the light in the room intensifies. It shines down, hitting a section of the parquet floor in the very center of the library. I gape.

It's shaped just like the earth elemental symbol—the inverted triangle with a line at the top, this time contained within a circle. I stumble to the floor, hands pawing at the symbol, seeking any seam or rent that signifies an opening. My hands find nothing. I slap my palm as hard as I can against the center of the earth symbol.

Wood panels slide down and across, revealing a hidden compartment below. Laughter bubbles up in my throat and hope soars in my chest.

I've found it.

I put my hand into the space and feel around the corners, but it's empty. Nothing is inside it now, though it was clearly the spot designated on the map. Ensel must have used a different one the last time he hid it.

I hope Dalen has fared better than I have.

The panels slide back into place on their own, which I find both disconcerting and good to know. I might have to put more than an arm into any one hiding place before we find what we need.

As I leave the house, I make a closer examination of the portraits in the hall. Many of them seem familiar, and when I see a younger yet unmistakable rendition of Ensel's face, I understand.

This was his childhood home, which must have been left to relatives when his mother married the king. Then he took the throne by deceit. The deserted table . . . he rounded up his own family during dinner. He must have feared they might get ideas about ruling, too. The more I learn about Ensel, the more sickening his callous nature becomes.

These must be some of my steprelatives. Ensel was related to my mother by marriage. I may as well be wandering into my own past, one I have little interest in recovering.

I straighten my spine and march down the rest of the hall, ignoring the remaining portraits. I don't look up until I am out the door and back on the street.

One down, too many more to go.

# CHAPTER 22

NEITHER OF US FOUND ANYTHING SUBSTANTIAL YESTERDAY. DALEN WAS intrigued that the hiding place in the mansion held sentimental value for Ensel—and by the tapestry depicting the Sonzeeki.

"So they knew about the creature all along, possibly for centuries. Maybe there was once an entire pack of them beneath the cliffs, all sustained and pacified by the cornucopia."

I shrug and continue preparing for today's excursion, not wanting to revisit anything to do with that disgusting creature.

"I wonder how he got the cornucopia away from it," Dalen muses.

"Does it matter?" I say, with more irritation than I

intend. "He did, and now the Sonzeeki wants to destroy the city, and I'll let it so I can use the cornucopia to save my brother. Would you like to drive that point home a little more?" Guilt has become my constant companion, always needling into my sides. Worry, too. What if we ask King Oliver for help in exchange for the cornucopia, and Bryre's army can't stop the witch?

Besides, I know exactly how Ensel did it—with the help of his potions. But something still holds me back from telling Dalen about them. He might make me stop using them, and they still might prove useful in my hunt for the cornucopia. When this is all over, I'll come clean.

Dalen pales. "I'm sorry, Greta, I didn't think—"

I sigh. "No, I'm sorry. I shouldn't snap at you." My hands tighten around the strap of my satchel. Now that I know what Belladoma meant to my mother, it doesn't sit right with me to do nothing. Even if Bryre won't aid us, my conscience may force me to try to help—after I free Hans. "I make no claim to be a good person, and I know I can't save everyone. I'll leave that task to King Oliver and Bryre. But I can try to save Hans, and that's what I'll do."

Dalen nods thoughtfully as we leave the barn and part ways. The hiding place he visited yesterday was as empty as mine. The map led him on a merry dance through the forest, skirting the river, and down into a deep ravine. He had to dig beneath a huge boulder marked with an elemental symbol until he found the case where the cornucopia once rested. All that remained were a few bits of straw, nothing more.

Hopefully today will prove more fruitful. If not, I have no doubt the witch will make good on her threat to kidnap another child from Belladoma.

The map doesn't lead me into the tunnels this afternoon, but it does take me into town. I keep to the alleys and near crowds of people when I can. Ren and King Oliver could be here, or worse, Vincali and his minions.

I'd prefer not to encounter any of them.

My cloak weighs me down, but it also hides my satchel and the map I peek at periodically. If I need it, I have the invisibility potion with me, and could use it again. The silencing spell faded off my shoes by morning, but the temptation to use it again niggles at the back of my mind.

The path takes me through the main square, filled with local shopkeepers and those who can spend the meager savings they have left. I've seen no traders from the big traveling markets here at all. The people are probably too poor to afford their prices. Why sell below cost to a starving city, when plenty of other places will buy at full price? No, the market here looks like it's homegrown.

Everywhere I go, I'm met by hollow faces and rotting buildings barely holding together. I pass the bakery I snuck into a few days earlier, and a fragile-looking child stands outside it, peering in the dirty windows at the baguettes on the counter. His eyes are wide and wanting, and seeing him there makes my heart hurt. I switch to the other side of the street, heading for a parklike area on the map. But I can't help a quick glance back.

The baker is out on the street, stooping down to the

little boy. The boy shakes, probably terrified he'll get in trouble for staring too long. But the baker puts a small bun in his hands, and the boy's eyes widen further, now shiny with unshed tears. I swallow hard and walk away.

I know full well the baker can't afford to give away his wares. And yet . . .

I close my eyes as water begins to rush in my ears and take a deep, steadying breath. Then I continue on.

But the picture of the baker slipping the beggar boy a morsel of bread haunts me all the way to the park entrance. They lost friends and family too. The only females I've seen are babes in arms or adults. How long did Ensel torment these people that they ran out of an entire generation of daughters and had to resort to taking Bryre's instead?

The map instructs me to go directly into the center of the park. Pools of stagnating water from the last flood linger in random dips in the earth. The trees are wasted and sallow, and no greenery adorns them now. Stale brown leaves cling to the branches in patches and litter the ground below.

I wander through the park, trying not to follow the path the map sets out in a straight line. No need to draw attention. I almost wish I'd lagged behind and taken the time to coat my cloak in the invisibility potion before I set out. Then I could plow through without the need to worry about someone following. The X on the map is over a building, but I don't know what it's doing in the park.

I crest a hill and understand. At the top is a large public building—more stonework—in the shape of a gazebo, but larger and with columns on the outside surrounding an inner chamber. I bet the hiding place is somewhere inside.

As I draw near the gazebo, the fine lines cracking the foundation appear more stark, opening into shadowed crevices. Part of one wall has crumbled, littering the ground with pebbles. A handful of people linger outside, murmuring quietly and eyeing the coastline. The palace can be seen easily from here, and the deep blue ocean beyond.

For a moment, it almost seems peaceful in this city.

I step into the gazebo, hesitating outside the door to the inner chamber long enough to see the imprint of another element—air. Inside the chamber are several curved benches attached to the walls. Broken pieces of ceiling speckle them, and mildew slicks the walls with a sheen of shadows. It is chillier than I expected. The interior is one large room, with no windows, only two doors, one on either side. I inspect every inch of the place for another air symbol, but to no avail. The floor doesn't have any markings, just cracks and a large circle in the center. I collapse onto one of the benches and it creaks. I groan and pull out my map, studying it again to see where I went wrong. One of the sores on my forearm—there seem to be a few now—catches on the edge of my bag and I wince. The fact that they're spreading is unsettling, but it's the least of my problems.

What did I miss? The path leads directly here. Maybe I overlooked something outside. I leave the cold interior of the gazebo and return to the sunlight. Circling the perimeter, all I find are more cracks and mildew, and a few weeds pushing their way up through the cracks.

An awful thought grips me. What if the clue I need

was marked on a piece of the gazebo that rotted away? That air symbol could be anywhere amid the rubble. Or gone entirely.

I search through the pieces near me just in case. As far as I can tell, they all seem to be plain granite, with no special marks at all.

Maybe perspective would help. I march down the hill about halfway, then turn and face the gazebo.

And gasp.

The gazebo itself is the clue. It's shaped like the air elemental symbol—a triangle with an extra line at the bottom. A decorative strip of granite in this case, but present nonetheless. This is definitely the right place, and somehow the shape is the key.

The other triangle pointed down, and the hiding place was located in the floor. If that's a pattern, then the hiding place here should be . . . the roof.

I groan again. I can't just climb up the gazebo and see if something is hidden at the top in broad daylight. I'll have to wait until tonight . . . or use that invisibility potion again. Hans doesn't have the luxury of time—I'll take my chances with the potion.

I hurry back inside the gazebo and lay my cloak flat in the center of the floor, then sprinkle some of the green potion over it. I sit back on my heels and give it a moment to shimmer and fade. Then I sweep the cloak around my shoulders, pulling it up over my head along with a strange sense of satisfaction.

Back outside, I consider the columns, debating which is

the least likely to crumble under my weight. I was always good at climbing trees; that will come in handy now. I choose the column on the side with the fewest people nearby. Even though no one can see me, I check around me again just in case. Then I take hold of the column, pushing up with my feet and pulling with my arms.

Soon I reach the slanting roof. I slowly climb upward, holding my cloak close to my face so the wind doesn't blow it away. It's colder up here, and the wind is fierce and feisty. Maybe it doesn't want to give up what it holds. I crawl to reduce the pull of the wind and make it easier to keep the cloak close. Shingles and stones shift under my knees, my nerves jangling with every hint of movement. What if I fall off the roof, wounded, and no one can find me because I'm cloaked by magic?

I choke down the bitter terror and finally reach the apex of the roof. I throw myself on the spire at the top, and grab hold. My reward is the small imprint of a triangle with an extra line at the bottom carved into the side. I press it in, and the spire flips open, revealing a space inside.

Empty.

This can't be right. This search was much more difficult than the last. Didn't I earn the cornucopia?

But this isn't something I can earn, it isn't anything logical. I'm seeking the random last place Ensel chose to hide his precious stolen treasure. All I can do is guess blindly.

I pull myself together, then slide back down the roof and clamber down the column.

I head for the barn, anxiety hovering around me like

197

a cloud of bees, and comfort myself with the fact that we are halfway through. Perhaps Dalen has already found the cornucopia.

All the while, I'm trying to ignore the gnawing fear that Ensel never had a chance to return the cornucopia to a safe hiding place after all.

# CHAPTER 23

BY THE TIME I REACH THE BARN, IT'S POURING. I SHRUG OFF MY CLOAK
when I open the door, and shove it in my satchel so Dalen
won't see.

"Greta?" Dalen calls. I tuck the vials of potion I didn't
use into their box hidden in the moldering hay.

"I'm here," I call back, and meet him outside the stall.
"Did you find it?" His expression tells me all I need to
know. "Me neither."

"I found the hiding place, but it was empty like the one
yesterday. I had to hide from a group of city refugees. I lis-
tened to them for quite a while, actually. They didn't seem
as callous as I expected from your descriptions."

I brush past him back to my stall. "I didn't say they were

all that way. Just that they didn't do anything to help when Ensel held us captive. They let him sacrifice us to save their own skins." My doubt about the Belladomans resurfaces. Could they have stopped Ensel even if they'd tried? Perhaps the blame I've placed on them for months isn't as well earned as I thought.

"The family fleeing Belladoma was afraid their baby daughter would be taken by the mercenaries. They've heard rumors the mercenaries plan to use the townspeople's children again to pacify the Sonzeeki. They were fleeing for their lives."

"Of course they were. Those mercenaries are vicious. Better to leave Belladoma as far behind as possible."

"Have you encountered any of them?"

The image of the baker and the beggar boy flashes to my mind. "I try not to."

"Haven't you seen their kindness to each other? They pull together in the worst of situations."

I whirl around. "Don't talk to me about their kindness."

"I understand," Dalen says, "why you need them to be terrible people. But sometimes people don't fit the molds we make for them."

I pale, and my knees weaken. I brace myself against the wall with my arm. "You don't understand what happened to me," I say. The generosity of the baker haunts me, but all I can hear is the sound of tentacles slapping rock.

"You're right. I can't know what you went through. All I'm saying is that you don't understand what happened to them, either. If Hans were in danger, would you do anything less?"

I know what he says is true—I'm willing to do exactly what I hate them for doing—but if King Oliver won't help, I don't see any way around it. Maybe they didn't either.

Maybe we're a lot more alike than I want to admit.

But I don't know what else to do. It makes me feel more helpless than I ever have before. So I do what I have always done: channel those feelings into determination.

I face Dalen grimly, water still dripping into my eyes from my wet hair. "I'm going to ask Bryre for help once we have the cornucopia. But what if they still don't believe me? What if they say no? Do you think I should let Hans die? Give myself up? And your village?" My voice rises, approaching hysterical.

He places a warm hand on my shoulder, but I shrug it off. "No," he says, "I don't. You're in a terrible situation with your brother. Every choice you make hurts someone. Even feeding the Belladomans with the cornucopia would hurt the Sonzeeki if the cornucopia was its main food source, as you suspect. I wouldn't do any differently in your shoes. I just think you need perspective. They're not horrible people."

I clench my fist around the wood frame of the stall door until splinters dig into my palms and fingers. Dalen is exactly right. It's an impossible situation. I hope our plan works, but if it doesn't, I'm responsible for the result, no matter who gets hurt. The worst part is that I don't want

201

anyone to get hurt, not even the Belladomans.

I grab my satchel from the hay. Before Dalen can say a word, I duck under his arm and back out the door.

I quake outside the barn, feeling as though something inside me has come unhinged. I can't go back, but it's cold and pouring. I don't bother putting on my cloak because it's still magicked, and soaked anyway. Maybe one of the Belladomans will use their famous kindness to take me in for the night.

I head back toward town. A tunnel entrance lies not far from here; I can hide there for the night. Then when I'm better rested and less upset, I can seek out the next hiding place.

Dalen's words chase me, leaving me restless and uneasy. I can't stop thinking about what he said, or about the hollow faces I see when I wander the streets of Belladoma. I won't be able to sleep, but perhaps I can walk it off.

*Hoooo.*

I jump and give the nearby bushes a closer examination. A pair of beady eyes regards me. "You're back!" Stump only tilts his head in the shadows in response. The last time he was here, it may have been to warn us. What could he want now?

Stump drops to all fours and ambles toward me, sitting back on his haunches when he reaches my feet. A chill prickles over my arms as I realize he holds something in his beak. He twists his head in an impossible manner, and when I hold my hand out, he releases a piece of cloth into my palm.

It is a small chunk of fabric, with a hemmed edge that looks like it was bitten off a cloak. Specifically a royal blue cloak with gold filigree edging.

My heart slams into my ribs. Only one person wears a cloak like that. The king of Bryre.

If King Oliver is in trouble, Ren no doubt is too. And trouble can only mean Vincali is involved.

I have to do something. Fast.

I tear my cloak from the satchel. I still can't see it, but it feels like it's dried a bit. I wonder how long it will last. Hopefully long enough. I throw it around my shoulders and pull it over my head.

"Can you show me where they are?" I ask Stump, praying he's as smart as he seems.

He twists his head all the way around. *Hooooooo.*

"That better be a yes."

He scampers down an alley and I follow, feeling foolish that I'm relying on such an odd creature. But he has proved true before.

I scratch at the sores on my arm, then pull my sleeve over them, hoping the itch will stop. After we've gone several blocks, sticking to the shadows, we turn into another alley that leads to an abandoned threshing house where they used to separate grain after a harvest. I've seen it before in my travels around the city. With the local crops all but ruined by the salt water, it's fallen into disuse.

Except tonight, there is torchlight slipping out the windows, and the sound of angry men's voices shatters the darkness. On the road ahead lies a lump of fabric. The edges glimmer in the moonlight, and I would bet anything that it's the king's discarded cloak. He'd never leave it there so carelessly.

Which means he was definitely brought here by force. He and Ren must be inside. If anything happens to them, I'll have only one course left: to give the cornucopia to the witch.

My cloak curls around me like a shadow as I run toward the threshing house, keeping it close about my face. This time Stump does not follow.

Arguing voices echo through the building. Old, half-rotted wooden boards creak under my feet, and I consider using the silencing potion too. But magic still leaves a sour taste in my mouth, and I'm too nervous to try two kinds at once. The last thing I need is to spontaneously combust during a rescue attempt.

Shadows shiver as I tiptoe closer to the door of the granary. That's where the voices are coming from and must be where they hold Ren and King Oliver. Torchlight spills out onto the threshing floor. My feet tread on mildewing bits of old wheat. I pause outside the doorway and listen, holding my breath and reminding myself that my cloak conceals me. I will not be afraid.

Something smashes in the granary, making me jump. My hood slips down my neck, but I pull it back over my head. I peek around the doorway to see what I'm up against.

Ren and King Oliver are each tied to a pole supporting the rafters of the granary. What smashed was Vincali's fist into a grain barrel, long and hollow. The mercenary leader paces before my friends in his billowing black shirt, revealing hints of red light from his chest. I blink, confused, until he stops and the light settles into an amulet that hangs from his neck. It's plain as far as necklaces go, just a large red stone, probably the size of my fist, with no additional adornment. But inside the stone, it looks like fire flares and ebbs. Like a blazing coal is suspended around his neck, yet not burning his skin.

I'd bet there's magic in that. Did he steal it from Ensel or is that one of the spoils from the wizard's cottage?

"I don't believe you're here to help. We've seen your page boy skulking around parts of the city he has no business being near, and getting far too close to the castle. You're after something, aren't you?"

"That's ridiculous," King Oliver says. "We came to offer our aid, and this is how you repay us."

I told them this would happen, so many weeks ago. I warned them helping the Belladomans wouldn't lead to anything good. I've never regretted being right more in my life.

I imagine Ren and King Oliver are regretting it right about now too.

"If you tell me what you seek, I might be lenient, old man."

"The only thing we hoped to gain from our visit to Belladoma was a potential ally by helping your city in its time of need."

"Lying is very unkingly behavior, don't you agree, Rasco?" Vincali says to his captain, a stocky, dark-haired man, a few feet behind him.

"Oh yes, not kingly at all, I'd say," Rasco agrees.

Gripping my knife in my sweaty hand beneath my cloak, I step into the doorway. Vincali can't see me, but I'm terrified nonetheless. I take another step while he confers with his captain on the other side of the large, long room. Then another. Step by step, I make my way around the back of the granary, hugging the walls, until I can see the knots that tie Ren and the king to the posts.

It's painfully slow work, but twenty steps later, I'm positioned directly behind Ren. One quick slice and his bonds slip free. I repeat the motion with the king, but they both have the presence of mind not to exclaim or say a word. I watch them exchange a glance, and understand. They're waiting for the right opportunity to run. They just need Vincali's back to be turned.

Now that can be arranged.

On the far side of the granary is a huge stack of old barrels, just like the one Vincali punched. I work my way over to them, faster this time, and my luck holds. When I reach the end, I maneuver into place behind the barrels, as Vincali turns back to Ren and King Oliver.

"It would be a shame to make you wait to meet your fate, and seeing as our slimy friend is almost risen and hoping for a morsel, I'm loath to make him wait. Off you—"

Vincali doesn't finish his sentence because I launch my body into the barrels with all my might. They crash into the pair, smashing Rasco over the head, but missing Vincali by an inch. Rasco stumbles toward the wall for support, looking dazed, but Vincali has nothing but murder in his eyes.

"Who's there?" he says, his gaze rippling over me. He can't see me under the cloak, but I've given myself away. To my relief, King Oliver and Ren yank their hands from the poles and flee out the door in the confusion. I sigh in relief, then I slap my cloaked hands over my mouth, which turns out to be a bad idea too.

Vincali's eyes snap to the point of the sound, and he steps forward. I jump to the left, toward the door, but he focuses on where I was moments ago. Then to my surprise, he removes the amulet from his neck and holds it out in his palm like he's warding something off.

Light and piercing heat explode from the stone, and I leap to the side to get away. Flames lick the barrels. What is that thing? Magic, definitely. And not magic I ever want to be on the receiving end of.

Though perhaps I was before. A memory of our flight through the forest from the mercenaries at the inn comes to mind, and with it the smell of smoke and fire on our heels.

I run.

Shouts ring out behind me and another lancing flame crashes into the wall as I pass. The hem of my cloak is on fire. It gave me away. There's no time to stop and stamp it out, and I tear through the threshold and out into the street. The fire, white hot, sweeps up the cloak, consuming it far faster than I would've expected—

Oh no. The magic in the cloak. It may be reacting to

207

the magic in the flames. Without another thought I throw off the cloak and hang it from a passing beam in an alley as I race back to the tunnels to hide. Boots pound the road behind me. I hit the wall and press the right bricks, then slip into the passage, just as flames reach the edge of the alley. The door closes, and I slide down the wall, gasping and quivering.

Vincali is definitely going to be a problem.

# CHAPTER 24

THE SONZEEKI RISES FROM THE BLACK DEPTHS BEYOND THE CLIFF ALL three days of each full moon and floods the town if it doesn't get the meal it desires. My deadline is tomorrow, at the height of it. I stand outside the barn and glance up at the sky, a tiny knot of fear forming in my heart. While last night's rescue and the threat of the mercenaries is still fresh in my mind, nothing compares to the terror in the deep.

I must be quick. The bones of the child the witch left for us in the forest dance in front of my eyes. No one deserves to have their children eaten by the witch. The Belladomans didn't deserve what Ensel did to them either. But I can't change that, and now the witch has taken two more of their children—because I can't find the cornucopia fast enough. This may have begun as a mission to rescue my brother, but it's quickly ballooning to include so many others. It's an unexpected responsibility.

Earlier today the map sent me to a crumbling old church graveyard at the edge of the city. Once again, all I found was an empty hiding spot. Now, I steel my nerves as I enter the tunnels, tapping the marked brick and slab in the correct order. According to the map, this—the last of the hiding spots on my list—is deep in the secret tunnels, somewhere only Ensel and his closest henchmen knew about.

Dalen's task in the late-afternoon gloom is to find a cairn on the top of a mountain and look underneath. This morning he had to trudge through a swamp to check a tiny island. Ensel was annoyingly thorough in his methods of concealing the cornucopia.

A cool mist clings to the air in the city today, the pale afternoon sun fading by the minute. I must hurry. Just to be safe. These tunnels, while infinitely useful, still give me chills. Walking into them is like passing through a thick wall of foreboding. I shut the hidden door behind me, sealing myself in. A strike of a match lights the small torch I carry. A quick check of the map gives me direction, and then I'm on my way.

The mist follows me into the tunnel, and the walls are coated with a thick layer of black sludge that shines in the torchlight. It's cold, and my damp hair clings to my scalp and face as I pull my new cloak close. I'm grateful Dalen had the presence of mind to pack a couple of extra, especially after the oversized one I swiped from the palace burned up last night. I'd be freezing without it. The fog makes it more difficult than usual to see my way, but I've traveled these tunnels enough in the past week not to step in any holes. The smell is foul. Fish and rot and decay, all preserved by the brine of the ocean. I use my free hand to put a section of my cloak over my mouth and breathe through the fabric instead. It only helps a little to keep out the disgusting smell.

Please let the cornucopia be here so I can leave this place and never return.

I want nothing more than to go somewhere that doesn't reek of ocean backwash. Somewhere Hans and I can be safe. And Dalen and his family, too. He's done more for me than I can ever repay. I'd never have gotten this far without him.

When I reach a fork in the tunnel, the map takes me down a passage I haven't explored yet. It smells stronger of salt.

All I have to do is check the hiding spot, then run as far as I can from here. I'll be out in no time.

In my mind, a thick black tentacle worms its way up the face of a cliff, while a second crashes and clings to the rocks below. The awful green-black shell gleams in moonlight. I shudder and pull my cloak closer. Yes, the Sonzeeki is out there. But so am I. And I'm motivated by something far more precious than simple hunger.

Love is a powerful thing, but fear and love combined are enough to drive anyone to strange feats of will.

The fog follows me down this course, concealing my feet. While I brought Ensel's potions, I doubt I'll need them here. I'm not likely to encounter another living thing today. The corridor is long and winds downward, giving me an odd sense of slowly falling. It's unsettling, but according to the map, I'm about two-thirds of the way there.

The deeper I go into the tunnels, the colder it gets. This passage definitely doesn't lead to the palace like the others I've taken. It either leads toward the forest or the cliff face by the ocean. I'm turned around enough underground that I can't tell which. Fear edges its way into the back of my mind, but I refuse to let it come forward.

Fear will only slow me down.

The air grows heavier and the stench intensifies. Dead fish pile on the floor, and I slow to pick my way over their rotting bodies. I cough into my cloak. Grasping seaweed clings to the walls, half dried and crusted, yet still coated with sea slime. It's hard to tell deep underground, but I believe I approach the hiding spot. I refer to my map once again; the winding curve of tunnel line takes a sharp right before it's marked with an X. This is in the water quadrant of the map, all too fittingly, and the spot should be marked here in the tunnel by the elemental symbol for water: an inverted triangle.

The map holds true. A few minutes more of marching, and the tunnel veers to the right. The instant I pass the sharp curve, the walls and floor shake, as though something nearby, above or beneath, has hit them violently. I grab onto the slimy wall to steady myself.

It isn't easy, but I force my feet to keep moving. I'll be on my way out soon. I will not meet my end in the Sonzeeki's belly.

A few more feet and I stop to examine the walls, hoping

to find the mark of the water element. So much scum and detritus clots the walls that I have no choice but to get my hands dirty. I stoop down to clear away some of the dead marine life when the tunnel quakes again, sending me reeling back into the muck. I manage to keep hold of my torch. Panic fills me, but I get to my knees and paw through the debris by the bottom of the wall. I'm covered in it; I may as well embrace it. I uncover a section as long as I am tall before I see the mark: a tiny upside-down triangle carved into the floor. I claw at it, hoping to hit on some hidden opening, but to no avail. No seam or rent in the floor reveals itself.

Frustrated, I settle back on my heels and hold my head in my hand, taking deep breaths of the sour air. I shoot to my feet and examine the wall above the mark, following it all the way up to the low ceiling. At the corner where the wall and ceiling merge, hidden by a sticky piece of seaweed, is another symbol for water. It's a good thing the tunnels have low ceilings and that I'm tall for my age. A grown man would have to hunch over to make it all this way, but I can walk upright easily enough. I reach up to the ceiling, feeling for the fine seam above my head. Frantically, I pound my fist on the mark and it slides inward. A small section of the ceiling pushes up and back. The sound of stone grating over stone never sounded more welcome to my ears than it does right now.

Another shock rattles through the tunnel, shaking free more rocks and debris. I duck instinctively, throwing my arms over my head. One rock pelts my forearm hard enough to make it bleed. A nasty bruise will form there later to keep the troubling sores company.

But none of that matters if the cornucopia is here. I stand on my tiptoes, reaching up into the space to feel around. My hand fumbles onto something solid. It feels like a basket edge. With my heart in my throat, I grip it tightly and pull it down.

Relief, cool and perfect, floods every inch of my body. The cornucopia is in my hands at last.

It's smaller than I expected, but the horn-shaped basket is just as the witch described. It looks empty, but then I haven't wished for anything to eat, either. The thought of eating anything down here is revolting. I'll test it out once I'm free of the tunnels.

I press the stone button again and the panel overhead slides into place. That must be how the cornucopia stayed put despite the flooding. Hiding it in the ceiling kept it from being swept away.

I slip the cornucopia into my pack and hurry back up the passage, the floor quivering under my feet and making my stomach flip. How late has it gotten?

As if in answer, a low rumble echoes down the passage.

I break into a run, spurred on by the thought of real water at my back. This isn't the waves crashing in my head. Soon the tunnels shake again, as though something wishes to rip the city from its foundations.

Something does.

The rumble becomes a roar and I tear through the passage like the devil is on my heels. How long did it take me to get here? Hours or minutes? Has the sun disappeared already?

The sound of splashing echoes around me, startling me enough to glance down. My boots are ankle deep in black water. Images of the beast outside haunt my every step. I press on as fast as my limbs will carry me.

But the water is faster. It rises an inch for every few steps I take, swirling around my legs and weighing me down.

I must get to higher ground. Fast.

Then it's up to my knees, and the bottom of the cloak slows me like a lead weight attached to my neck. I yank it up and wrap it over my shoulders, but the time it takes me to do that only gives the water a chance to climb higher. Frantic fish swim next to me, nibbling at my ankles, and seaweed curls around my legs, threatening to trip me. My lungs ache, a combination of panic, exertion, and the foul stench of the tunnels.

I turn a corner I recognize as about halfway from where I entered. I quickly check my map as I slog along, but there are no other exits near where I am. The closest exit is the one I entered by, and I still haven't reached the place where the tunnel forks.

By the time the water reaches my waist, I know I'm not going to make it.

The frigid water seeps into my veins. The dread of drowning is no longer a fear I can brush aside. It's a harsh, cold reality. I can't move faster, not with the heaviness of my clothes and the shaking of the walls every few minutes throwing me off-balance.

I'm going to die. Hans will die. So will Dalen, the rest of the hybrid village, and every Belladoman child the witch can find.

Unless . . .

Still moving, I feel around in my soaked pack. My hands close around one of Ensel's potions and I pull it out. Red. Not the one I need. I reach in again, and the next is yellow. Still not what I need. I find a third, and pull it out—blue. Blue is supposed to allow the drinker to breathe underwater. What if it doesn't work? What if the side effects are more than I can bear? I have yet to drink any of his potions. I don't know what it could do. Does it matter? If I don't try, I die anyway. One mouthful shouldn't do too much harm, I hope. I pop the top of the vial and take a swig. And nearly spit it out. The stuff is as foul as I expect, but I manage to swallow it. A dizzy rush tingles over my arms and legs; then I secure the top on the potion and return it to my pack.

But I'm not about to stop here and place all my bets on magic. By now, swimming is faster than running, and I am forced to abandon my torch. I shudder to think what might be swimming next to me. Hopefully nothing bigger than mackerel or sea salmon, which is all I've seen so far.

Please, for the love of the realm, no eels. I can't bear eels. They look far too much like the Sonzeeki's tentacles.

The water rises, and as it does, pieces of the walls shift and tumble. The water lifts me higher, and I can see the fine cracks and rents that mar the entire length of the tunnel.

If someone doesn't stop the Sonzeeki's rampage soon, the entire city will crumble into the ocean.

My arms and legs pump through the water, desperately swimming toward the fork. My hands have gone numb, and my legs feel like they're made from soft butter. My head smacks the top of the tunnel, and it's all I can do to tread water. Gasping, crying, I can do no more than let the waves push me along. At least they move in the right direction.

My last thought before the water surges over my head is how strange it is that my parents were claimed by these same waters and now they're about to pull me under too. My only hope is pinned on the magic potions of the man who tossed them off the cliff.

I float in the dark and cold and wait for death to find me. It doesn't.

I hold my breath until I have no choice but to gasp a lungful of water. But somehow—*somehow*—I can breathe it. I can breathe underwater.

Spurred onward by the understanding that I'm not about to die after all, I swim forward underwater as quickly as I can. The water buoys me, and now that I don't fight to keep my head above it, I can go much faster. Frenzied laughter tumbles from my lips as the current pulls me past the fork and rushes toward the main passage where the hidden exit lies.

I'm going to live. I haven't failed Hans and Dalen after all.

I open my eyes in the murky water. While the potion didn't give me sight underwater and doesn't stop the sting of the brine, I can breathe, and that's half the battle. I work my way to the side of the tunnel where the door lies and grab hold of the cracks in the stone. Water rushes in my ears, and I force my feet back to the floor. I grope the rest of the way up the tunnel until I feel the familiar indentation of the carvings in the rock. I press them each as instructed and the door swings open. I tumble out into the alley in a rush of water and limbs.

For one flittering, delicious moment, I believe myself to be safe. Then I look up into the angry, surprised eyes of the last person I want to see.

Vincali.

# CHAPTER 25

**VINCALI YANKS ME OFF MY FEET BEFORE I'VE EVEN STOPPED SPUTTERING**
seawater. A chunk of my hair rips free from the scalp and
tears burn my eyes. I harden my expression, refusing to let
him see me cry. He drops me and two of his men immediately latch onto my arms, while two others manage to close
the door in the wall against the onslaught of water.

Vincali's sharp-angled face examines me from head to
grimy toe. He grins.

"Just the girl we've been looking for. You've been skulking around for some time. First the inn on the road, then
that alley." His fingers brush the cut on his cheek where
I nicked him a few days ago. "And I'd bet anything you
were involved in last night's little adventure in the threshing
house. I don't like it when nuisances get away. Now how did

219

you get in that wall?" he asks, narrowing his eyes. His voice has all the sweetness of a rabid kitten. "And more important, why?"

"I got lost," I say through clenched teeth.

"Lost? Behind an alley wall?" He lifts me off my feet again by the front of my cloak. I can smell his awful, garlicky breath, but I refuse to turn my head away as it pours over my face. Instead I stare him down. "I have no patience for liars."

He tosses me back, and my head strikes the brick wall, leaving me dazed and aching. One of his henchmen seizes my cloak, and I vaguely hear Vincali bark the words "Search her thoroughly."

Panic upends my insides. They can't find the cornucopia. Not after all I've been through to get it. I struggle, landing a good kick to the henchman's legs before being caught up by a second man. More men fill the alley by the second. My mouth is too dry even to swallow, and my head still spins from hitting the wall, but I thrash and fight, and I'll keep thrashing and fighting until I lose consciousness or get away.

I pull my cloak close to conceal my satchel, but the men yank it free again. I'd give anything to have a sword in my hand right now, and a flash of silver at the hip of the man next to me catches my eye. I keep flailing. Anything to keep them unbalanced, off guard, and not expecting me to dive for that sword at the first opening.

They search my cloak, hoping for a hidden pocket, but find none. I kept everything—the map, the potions, the cornucopia—in my satchel. Which is exactly what they set their sights on next.

As the first mercenary—the one with the sword—lunges for the bag, I reel backward, taking the second henchman with me. He grunts as his head connects with the brick wall. I stomp on his foot as hard as I can, and he releases his grip. Then I dive at the first man, rip his sword from the sheath, and hit the muddy road in a roll.

My shoulder throbs where I struck the ground, but I ignore it and leap to my feet, brandishing my newly found weapon. I edge toward the busy street, filled with Belladomans who look to be in a hurry. The two henchmen gape. But Vincali laughs.

"Stay back," I say. "I don't want a fight, I just want to leave here. That's all."

"You're a feisty little one," Vincali says. I like him even less when he's amused. "You're not going anywhere. You're surrounded. Do you even know how to use that thing? I'd hate to see you hurt yourself."

Rage boils beneath my skin. "I fought in the battle for Bryre. Yes, I do know how to use a sword."

Vincali doesn't seem impressed, though a few of his lackeys murmur. From somewhere at the other end of the alley, one shouts, "She's a fool and a liar to boot!" which is greeted by a chorus of laughter. My grip on the sword tightens. It's heavy, but I've learned how to use the weight of it, how to swing and swipe at a man's gut, or sever the tendons on the backs of his knees. My parents prepared me well.

All I need is opportunity.

But Vincali's gaze strays from me, his would-be opponent, and he grins down at something in the water by the wall of the alley. Water begins to lick our feet, and I realize why they're all out on the street—they were headed to higher ground when I stupidly burst out of the tunnel like a wild animal. That explains why so many Belladomans are out on the street too. The noise from their carts and chatter is a dull roar behind us.

Vincali picks up the thing that pleased him, and my heart stutters in my chest.

No. No, it can't be.

He holds the small cornucopia in his hands. It must've fallen from my satchel in the struggle. The one thing I need to free Hans is now in the hands of the mercenaries.

"This is why you were sneaking around the alley, isn't it?"

"No, it's nothing. Only a trinket. I don't care about it at all," I say, hoping he'll think it has little value and toss it back to the alley floor.

"Then you are indeed a true fool. This," he says, cradling it in his hands, "is a thing of beauty and tremendous value. Do you even know what it is?" He considers me a moment. "Yes, I can see in your eyes that you do. You must have your own designs on it. Unfortunately, this is what I've been hunting for since Ensel's demise."

"Give it back or I'll cut it out of your thieving hands."

Vincali laughs. "No, I don't think you will. My men will disarm you quickly enough, and toss you into the dungeon to rot out your youth. How does that sound?"

"Like cruel and unusual treatment of children," says a voice so familiar it makes me want to weep. King Oliver stands behind us where the alley meets the road, a full contingent of his army spreading out behind him on the street. Ren is at his side, and to my surprise, Dalen is, too. "Let her go, and give her back her property."

A dark cloud of anger flickers over Vincali's face, and then he's all amiability again. "What? This trinket?" He holds up the cornucopia. "The girl said she didn't care about it at all. Therefore, since I care about it a great deal, it's only fair that I should look after it."

"What exactly do you intend to do with it?" King Oliver says.

"It's no business of yours, old man," Vincali says. Ren takes a step forward, fury etched on his face, but the king puts an arm out to stop him. I allow myself a small smile. Ren is loyal to a fault.

"I beg to differ. If you are taking it to feed the Belladomans, then I can't object. But if you intend to take it and leave, I'm afraid I must stop you. It is a treasure of Belladoma, and one we are here to protect."

"I'll do with it as I see fit. You and your army have overstayed your welcome, I think."

"No," King Oliver says. "I believe it is you who have overstayed your welcome." Though the water rises and the ground shakes, our debate draws attention. Out in the street beyond the forces from Bryre, Belladomans have stopped fleeing and begin to congregate, glaring at the mercenaries like they smell blood in the water. "Moments ago, you threatened to imprison one of Bryre's citizens for no reason. You are planning to take the Belladomans' hope for food away from them and leave them starving. I cannot let you do that, and"—he gestures behind him to the Belladoman crowd swelling on pace with the tide—"I don't believe they will either."

The rage in Vincali's face turns his skin a horrid purple shade. "You want a fight? Then that's what you shall get."

At their leader's words, the mercenaries throw themselves on the Bryrian army, but they're prepared.

Men seethe around us, but Vincali still holds my cornucopia. To my horror he also now holds that strange red amulet in his hands, and he aims it at the fighting Bryrians—specifically at the king.

"Don't you dare," I yell, throwing myself at him and sending him careening to the far side of the alley. The amulet's fire goes wide, scorching the brick wall instead. As Vincali regains his feet and I try to wrest the cornucopia from him before he can catch hold of me, my sword slips under the chain holding his amulet and breaks it. The amulet slides to the other side of the alley and splashes in the rising mucky water. He kicks me off and I land in a puddle.

I leap to my feet and brandish my weapon at him. "Give the cornucopia back."

"Get out of my way, little girl, before I decide to make an example of you."

"I'll run you through with my sword first."

Vincali rolls his eyes and puts the cornucopia in the pack

at his hip. As he does, I realize he has sores on his wrists too.

"If you insist, I will teach you a lesson." He draws his own sword, and it hisses as it slithers free. My palms sweat against the sticky, leather-wrapped hilt of my weapon. The water is up to my ankles. When the mercenaries closed the door it slowed the tide, but water still rises from the grate at the bottom of the doorway. I shiver in the breeze, clothes sticking to me like glue.

Vincali lunges and tries to knock the sword from my hands. But he doesn't count on my swiftness, nor my stubborn ability to not let go. I duck and parry, then manage a swipe at the cuff of his sleeve. No matter that I was aiming elsewhere, I still slice it open enough to surprise him.

He comes at me faster, no longer holding back because I'm a mere child. I evade the blow again, this time severing the strings holding his bag to his belt as I roll by.

Vincali doesn't give me a moment to breathe. Our fight spills onto the street as he attacks again, not realizing he's lost his bag. The one holding the cornucopia. I need to get it. I parry blow for blow; every time his frown grows deeper, and his frustration becomes more palpable. The melee around us dies down, and I realize that fewer mercenaries remain on the street, and more Belladomans and Bryrians do instead.

I think we might be winning.

He swings again, and I barely leap out of the way in time. He laughs savagely. "This should teach you some respect, girl."

Suddenly, strong arms lift my feet off the ground and up into the air. I struggle and kick until I hear a familiar voice at my ear. "It's all right, Greta, you're safe," Dalen says, and I relax slightly.

I'm pulled into the middle of the crowd from Bryre, standing shoulder to shoulder in the ever-rising murky water. King Oliver is at the head of the crowd, several guards with swords drawn standing beside him. Vincali is alone. The other mercenaries are either cornered or have fled. Vincali eyes the alley where his amulet fell, but Bryre's guards fill the space in front of it.

"Picking on children?" King Oliver says. "When we first met, you claimed to be an honest man, trying to do his best by Belladoma now that it was without its king. I'm beginning to doubt you are as dedicated as you claim." The king plucks the bag that once was attached to Vincali's hip from the water as it floats by. He pulls the cornucopia out and holds it up. Vincali is visibly enraged.

"You know," Dalen whispers, "everyone is making an awful lot of fuss over such a small thing. I thought it would be bigger."

All the anxiety I've been holding inside suddenly breaks and I can't help laughing. "No such luck. But it does make it very portable."

Now it's Dalen's turn to laugh.

"That's rightfully mine," Vincali huffs. "I slaved away for that stupid king for years, waiting for him to trust me with where he hid it. I've got more claim to it than that girl or the people in this town."

A rumble runs through the gathered Belladomans, and I catch a few words here and there. *He can't take what's ours.*

*Don't let him hurt the girl.* My stomach twists. So many people claiming this one thing, the only thing that can save my brother. Now that King Oliver is involved, he'll be sure to do the right thing.

He won't just let me have it.

Which means I've lost my only bargaining chip. Will he still help me, even when he realizes I stole the map?

"It was never Ensel's to begin with," King Oliver says, "and you will not take it as plunder. Not when the cornucopia can do much more good outside of your hands."

"You'll give that to me, old man, or I'll—"

"No, you will leave this place. We know you have procured ships that are docked in the cove a few miles down the coast. I imagine you planned to take whatever magic you could from this country and flee, leaving the Belladomans to rot. Now, you and your men will go there—without the cornucopia and without stopping at the palace to collect any ill-begotten loot—and you will sail back to the country you came from. You will never return."

Vincali scoffs. "Why would I do that?"

"Because while your men are trained, and *were* better armed, we have more forces from Bryre in our camp, and combined with the Belladomans we have many more than you. The men you had lying in wait for us in the forest have been dispatched. And we stripped the weapons from those men who were here earlier, but they seem to have fled. You are alone, Vincali, and I think if you stay here, you will not survive the wrath of these people."

Vincali pales, but his jaw tightens. "I will go for now,"

he says. "But I make no promises about the future."

"We are allowing you to leave because enough people have died in this city. But if you ever attempt to return, we will be here to stop you," the king says.

Vincali glares at him, then straightens his back and marches down the alley, splashing through the water to reach the street not clogged with townspeople. King Oliver is too lenient. If it were me, I'd have locked Vincali in the dungeon and thrown the key over the cliff.

King Oliver lets out a deep breath as soon as Vincali vanishes from sight. "Now, all of you, please leave the city before it's too late. Our encampment is on higher ground, and we will gladly share our tents and food with you."

As the crowd thins, I finally manage to turn around. Dalen stands exposed in the middle of the Belladoman streets. He smiles crookedly and shrugs.

"How . . . ," I start, unsure what to say and still completely baffled as to how or why he is here.

"I heard the water rising. People were streaming past the barn, fleeing as soon as the quakes began. I knew you were in the tunnels, and you weren't back yet. I had to get help. I figured they"—he points over his shoulder to Ren and the king—"would be the least likely to want to chop me into parts and sell me at the market, and the most likely to be willing to help you. Besides, the plan was to go to them anyway. Did you really expect me to hide in safety while you drowned?"

I throw my arms around Dalen's neck.

"Thank you," I say, and bury my face in his shoulder. Half to keep myself from crying, and the other half to keep myself from yelling at him for being so careless with his own life.

# CHAPTER 26

NOW THAT REN AND KING OLIVER KNOW I'M IN THE CITY, I RETURN WITH them and Dalen to their camp, right after rescuing the discarded amulet from the muck. It might come in handy later.

The Bryrian tents are drier and warmer than our barn. And they have fresh clothes and real food. A respite from jerky, stale bread, and overripe fruit is more than welcome, and my belly rumbles when they sit me, now clad in a dry change of clothes, in front of a fire and put a bowl of chicken stew in my hands.

Dalen didn't tell them I stole the map. All they know is that I'm here, but not why. Ren's eyes overflow with questions, only reined in by the king's restraining hand on his shoulder.

"Let the girl eat first—then we will chat," he says, and I

smile gratefully over my stew. I always did like King Oliver, even if he is a little too kind sometimes.

Once my belly is full, I place my bowl on the table, pull the blanket they've lent me close, and wait for the barrage of questions to start.

"We were surprised to find you in Belladoma, Greta," King Oliver says. "I never dreamed you would venture near here."

I shrug. "Things change." It's difficult to look them directly in the eyes. I don't want to see their expressions, or the disappointment there, nor do I want to betray the pain in my own. Or the confusion. I am no longer so certain how I feel about the Belladomans I once professed to hate.

"Why did you leave Bryre?" Ren asks. The hurt in his voice is palpable.

"I was needed elsewhere."

"More to the point, how did you find the cornucopia? How did you even know about it?" King Oliver asks. "We have been searching for it for months. You can imagine our surprise when you appeared along with the cornucopia."

What's left to lose? They have the cornucopia. I need their help to save my brother, and I've lost the only thing I had to bargain with. Even if they didn't believe me before, I may as well tell them everything. The whole truth is the only thing that might convince them to help me now.

"You had a map, one a prisoner gave you. You couldn't decipher it, but I stole it and we"—I point to Dalen and myself—"solved it."

Ren gasps. "*You* took the map? Did you set our horses to the hills, too?"

I fidget. "Yes, I did. I need the cornucopia desperately. I've been searching for it for weeks now too."

"But what could you possibly need the cornucopia for?" Ren says. "If you'd stayed in Bryre, you'd have plenty of food. We'd never let you starve. I don't understand."

"Ren," King Oliver says, "wait. Something else is going on, isn't it, Greta? Does this have anything to do with the story of your lost brother?"

I nod miserably. "It wasn't a story, and I'm sorry I stole the map," I say, clenching and unclenching my fists. "I did it for Hans, you see. My brother. Everything was for Hans."

"You really have a brother?" Ren asks. "Why didn't you ever bring him with you to our meetings? He would've been as welcome as you." His voice grows softer. "Why didn't you tell us about him before he went missing?"

"I made a rule not to talk about my family. Our parents"—I swallow the lump in my throat—"disappeared a few months before the girls in Bryre began to get sick. It's just been Hans and me since then. I didn't tell anyone because I didn't want him to get taken away. We . . . we thought they'd come back. They never did. They ran afoul of Ensel and were thrown off the cliff." I wipe a tear from my cheek.

"My silence was to protect my brother. I was afraid you would make us both go to an orphanage for our own good, and I couldn't risk it. By the time I decided I could trust you, it was far too late to say anything. But then he was stolen from our home by a witch. She moves around the forest in a hut thatched with feathers that walks on chicken legs. She's going to eat Hans unless I bring her the cornucopia. That's why I came to you at the palace that day begging for help. That's why I left Bryre, and why I had to take that map. Hans's life was at stake."

Is *still* at stake, and more at risk with every second I waste here.

"That is a grave situation indeed," says the king. Firelight dances across his face, making his graying hair appear lighter than it really is. "And most unfortunate. We cannot hand over the cornucopia to a witch. Not when there's an entire city of people who need to eat."

This is what I feared he'd say.

"Then you understand why I chose not to tell you. But I know the witch cannot be trusted. I need your assistance, if there's any hope of defeating her and getting my brother back. I'd planned to give the cornucopia to you in exchange once I found it."

Dalen clears his throat. "It is not only Hans's life at stake, I'm afraid. My village took Greta captive, and as punishment for the delay, the witch burned our village to the ground. She's threatened to return for all the hybrid children if Greta does not complete her task."

"She'll come for me, too, and Dalen. She's even begun to take children from Belladoma. No one will be safe if you don't help me," I say.

"I am sorry I doubted you, Greta. Your request for help looked like a ploy to delay us. I should have trusted you more—then perhaps we could have avoided this whole situation." The king sighs. "But what's done is done, and now we can simply take our guards and force her to return Hans."

I shake my head. "That won't work. She's pure evil, and has just as many tricks as the wizard ever did. Manpower won't impress her, and it certainly won't stop her."

"Then we'll have to sneak in and rescue Hans and any other children when she leaves the house," Ren says.

I laugh without mirth. "How do you think I struck the deal with her in the first place? She caught me, and now she knows my face and can track Hans and me. No, she'll just find us again. The only way for him to be safe while she still lives is if she gives him up willingly."

"Which she won't do without the cornucopia," Dalen says. "She tracked Greta down when she was in my village, and then again here at the old barn where we've been staying. She's already started feeding on Belladoma's children and is holding at least two right now. I don't doubt for a second she will kill many more if we don't stop her."

The memory of the bones in the woods near the cliff makes me shiver.

"We can't give in to her demands," Ren says. "That's crazy."

"I'm not suggesting we do," I say. "You're both more familiar with magic than me. I had hoped you'd have some idea about how to get rid of her. She didn't bother this region before because of wards the wizard set up. Maybe something else can banish her again. Sire, for years you sought a means of ridding your city of the wizard. Surely you came across something that might help."

"Your Majesty," calls a voice from the entrance to the large tent. One of Bryre's soldiers stands in the doorway. "I'm sorry to interrupt, but the captain has arrived. You sent for him earlier?"

"I did indeed." King Oliver turns back to us. "Please excuse us for a moment. The captain will ensure Vincali removes himself from Belladoma. I need to speak with him first. Ren, come with me. We'll be right back."

Ren and King Oliver confer with their captain about sending more troops to force Vincali to leave as instructed. Dalen and I remain in the tent with a guard posted outside. No doubt they fear I will run off or steal something from the them again.

I hate waiting. I fiddle with my mother's necklace and pace in front of the fire pit.

"Greta, you'll wear a hole in the ground. Come sit. We'll think of something."

I sigh at Dalen. "What will we think of that we haven't already? If the king doesn't know of something that might stop the witch, then the only way to get Hans back is to exchange the cornucopia for him. We can't reason with her, or appeal to her kindness."

Dalen laughs, which only makes me frown more. "I had no intention of suggesting that. But I think I've found something that will interest you. Come here and I'll show you."

I realize he holds the book of fairy tales in his hands. It feels like a lifetime ago that I read to him in the hybrid village. I left the book with him in the barn. My curiosity piqued, I sit next to Dalen on a bench near the fire.

"Fine. What do you have to show me?"

He grins, but I can't imagine what could make him happy when everything has gone wrong. "This," he says, pointing to a page in the book. "Sound familiar?"

I stare at the page, more confused than ever at first, until I begin to read. *There once was a witch who lived in the woods,* it begins. I jerk upright, now paying full attention to the details of the story. I remember I started this one and could not bear to finish it when we were in the hybrid village. The witch in the story wasn't a kind one, and she had a taste for children. She also had a house on chicken legs. . . .

"Look here," Dalen says, then reads aloud. "'The witch hid her own heart in the house, and brought it to life with a spell of the darkest magic, forging a bond between herself and the house.'" He grins. "This is your witch. I'd almost forgotten about how you began reading the story and couldn't finish. I completed my task early this afternoon and thought I'd read a fairy tale while I waited for you to arrive. Then I realized there might be a clue here."

I pore over the words again, imprinting them on my memory. "Her heart is in the house. . . . What if we could find it? We could destroy it and free Hans!"

"She's a witch; her magic could kill you."

I take a deep breath, dizzy with certainty. "I am dead anyway if we don't destroy her."

Dalen glances again at the book. "The tricky thing will be determining where her heart is hidden. We'd need to get it right on the first try—otherwise all we'll do is anger her.

That won't be a good plan if we want to stay alive."

I shudder. "No, it would not."

"Keep reading and see if you find any more hints. I did not, but you look at things differently. Perhaps you will."

I raise an eyebrow but do as he suggests and read the rest of the story. It picks up after the first section I read so many weeks ago—those children managed to flee, but this time two spoiled children become entangled with the witch, happening upon her and the chicken hut in the forest by accident. They ran away from home because their poor, hardworking father couldn't afford to buy them sweets, so they set out in search of new parents. Instead, they found the witch.

And she found them delicious.

Fairy tales. They never do end well.

But the tale reveals no clues to where her heart is hidden. The children in the story never figured it out. I close my fingers over my mother's locket absently, then suddenly jolt upright.

"What is it?" Dalen asks.

I put my hand into my pocket and pull out the amulet I took from Vincali. It glows red in my palm, yet it's lighter than I expected. I look up at Dalen.

"This is how we'll destroy her."

Dalen's eyes sparkle and he pulls the amulet from my hand. "What is this?"

"Remember the flashes of light and smoke from when we fled the inn?"

He nods.

"Vincali was using this to try to burn us out. This is also what he used to set fire to the threshing house where he had Ren and King Oliver captive. Burned the cloak right off my back. He tried to use it in the alley earlier today, but I caught him off guard and took it."

Dalen turns it over in his hands, frowning. On the back is an engraving of a bird with spread wings and flames on the edges. "I've seen this before, though never on an amulet, only in ancient history books. It's the symbol of the hybrid queen, the Phoenix."

"How would Vincali have gotten his hands on that?" I take it back from him. "Or rather, the wizard. I believe Vincali found it in his old cottage."

"It is old, whatever it is. And it has fire magic?" He shakes his head. "The Phoenix Queen was associated with fire; whoever made it must have known that and marked it because it is so powerful."

"It's dangerous."

He folds the amulet into my hands and squeezes. "Whatever you do, Greta, keep this close, and don't let anyone take it from you."

"I won't. I promise."

When Ren and King Oliver return to the tent, the time for hesitation and apologies is over. I march up to them, sure now that I know what to do.

"I know how to destroy that witch, and I need your help to do it."

# CHAPTER 27

DAWN SETS THE FOREST ALIGHT WHEN I RETURN TO THE BARN AND PACK my meager belongings, then head out into the forest proper. It took us most of the night to finish planning. Dalen insists on coming with me. I can't decide whether I'm grateful for the company or wish he'd stay safely behind. I'm even conflicted about Stump, who swiftly becomes our shadow as we leave the barn.

Dalen's become an odd fixture in my life. Steady, constant, and someone I've grown to lean on. I don't like depending on people; too many of them leave without warning. And yet, I find myself wanting to talk to him when he's not around, and wishing for his silver eyes and funny smile.

The early-morning light filters through the trees, toying

with pollen motes. There are no feathers in sight yet, and it feels oddly peaceful. It's deceptive. I know the witch is out there, watching, waiting.

Ravenous.

The amulet weighs heavily in my pocket, and I wrap my fingers around it to reassure myself. Its odd warmth is comforting. Last night I practiced with it in the field, figuring out how Vincali used it to shoot flames. All it takes is a directed thought, and the fire lances from it to strike whatever target you seek.

It's a terrifying sort of power, one that makes me feel both uncomfortable and thrilled at the same time.

Dalen still doesn't know about the potions of Ensel's I've been using. What troubles me most is that I *want* to use them again. It's an itch at the back of my brain, hunting for an excuse to drink one more drop and feel the rush of power flowing through my blood, or seeping into my skin from my cloak or shoes.

I don't want to stop it. And that means I must.

A warm hand on my shoulder startles me from my thoughts. "Don't worry—we'll find the witch. She'll hardly avoid you now that you're so close to her deadline to deliver the cornucopia," Dalen says.

"I'm not worried," I lie. "I was just thinking."

He raises an eyebrow. "About something other than the witch?"

"Yes, oddly enough. I hate that I must rely on magic to beat her. That I'm not strong enough on my own."

"Perhaps not. But you are strong enough to stand up

to her no matter the cost to your own person. Being brave enough to use it counts for something in my book."

I stop. "But don't you hate these magic things? They came from the wizard. He hunted down your kind."

Surprise rearranges his face. "Hate magic? Not at all. I *am* magic, Greta. That would be like hating myself. I do, however, hate that wizard, and the people who would use magic for ill. No good ever comes of that."

"I never thought of it that way," I say, though now I realize I should have. How stupid I must sound to him.

We resume walking, but soon Dalen stops and paws the ground. "Look," he says.

Not ten feet in front of us is a large yellow-and-brown chicken feather, lying innocently on the forest floor. The stench of rotting meat wafts through the trees, leaving no doubt.

"She's here," I say, a shudder rolling over me. Beyond the first feather lies another, then a few feet after that yet another. We follow the trail, winding and erratic, over several hills, down a valley, and into a large, wide grove of pine trees. Ren, the king, and the Bryrian soldiers follow behind us by the bits of crumbled stale bread I leave on the ground so the witch won't suspect we didn't come alone. Hopefully they don't have much trouble keeping up. Especially once they find the feathers.

We've come to an understanding, Ren, King Oliver, and I, and I hope our friendship can be repaired over time. We just have to survive the witch first.

Judging by the sun, it is midmorning. Sunlight shimmers

through the trees, and the grove is covered by a thin coating of pine needles. The pungent smell fills the grove, growing stronger with every step we take, crushing the needles under our boots, and almost disguising the scent of carrion on the wind.

A strange sound echoes through the trees, making my spine stiffen in recognition. Scratching. Like a whole flock of chickens scraping at the earth in tandem. Dalen rears, and a few feet behind, Stump hoots. Moments later, the chicken hut skitters into the grove, scrabbling wildly at the ground every few steps and shedding feathers as it does. I will not be cowed.

Dalen slips his hand into mine and squeezes. I squeeze back.

Yes, depending on someone else is a strange thing. Even stranger is the knowledge that he'll stay as long as I want him to.

We're stronger together than alone. I understand better now that I can't take on the world on my own. Sometimes I might need help. From Dalen, or Ren and King Oliver.

I'll take it.

My breath speeds up while we wait for the witch to leave her hut, my heart pounding.

And then she's in front of us. No warning, no long, painful walk from the chicken hut. Just *here*.

Her black hair spills like ink down her back, and her face is still deceptively lovely. Her eyes are piercing and yet I still cannot put a name to their color. But the smell of death that clings to her gives her away.

Panic flares. This is too fast. The Bryrian army isn't here yet, I need more time, I need to stall—

Wait. A flicker of motion between the trees. Then another, and another. The tightness in my chest eases slightly, knowing we're not alone.

"I assume either you're here for dinner, or you've brought me the cornucopia."

"We have it," I say. "But first Hans. I'm not handing it over without him."

From the corner of my eye, I can see Ren climb up the back leg of the house and slip in through a window. He's armed with a contraption King Oliver's blacksmith made that can cut through steel. If Hans and the others she's stolen are in there, he'll get them out. The witch cannot be trusted to keep her word.

The only way to stop her is to kill her.

"Hans is fine where he is. I told you I would make the trade. I am an honest witch; I always keep my word."

Dalen and I exchange a look. She'd make the trade . . . then come back for us all later when she's bored. It would never be a permanent solution.

"We need to be certain. The only way for that is for you to bring Hans with you, like we brought the cornucopia," I say.

Her eyes brighten with interest as we mention her prize. It's in the folds of my cloak, tucked into a hidden pocket. My hand tightens around the amulet. As soon as Ren and Hans are clear of the house . . .

"You didn't think I would bring him, did you?" She

pouts. "I'm disappointed. I thought you were smarter than that. I could reduce you both to ash in an instant if I choose. But you amuse me, which is why I agreed to the trade, why I let you live." Her face darkens, giving a glimpse of the evil inside. "Don't make me regret that. I tire of this already."

A flash of blue and green—the colors of Hans's and Ren's shirts—along with three dots of pale brown leaps from the window of the chicken hut. They tumble to the ground, then the figure in green—Ren—helps the others to their feet. The tightness inside me explodes into relief.

Hans is free. *Hans is free.*

I reach into the hidden pocket of my cloak and produce the cornucopia, holding it out of her reach. The witch's eyes gleam with want. She licks her lips.

"Give it to me."

"Not yet." With my free hand I surreptitiously pull out the amulet and think one word with all my might toward the house: *Burn.*

The chicken hut erupts into flame, flaring high with an audible pop, reaching up to the tops of the trees in the grove. The witch screams, and, I think, the house screams with her. I toss the cornucopia to Dalen, and he takes off at a gallop—our plan is to get it back to King Oliver and safety while I stay here with the amulet and ensure she dies.

The witch yowls, and Dalen is yanked off his feet and launched into a tree. Stunned, I see what tossed him—three disembodied hands that have materialized in the air and hang there, seeming to wait on the witch for instruction. Her skin smokes, and her hair begins to lose its black luster, fading fast to gray. Fine lines appear on her skin; they carve inward, forming deep ravines and folds. Her breath reeks of something I don't want to think about, and her teeth, which I expect to be chipped and rotted from gnawing on bones, are made of gnashing iron instead. She advances toward me, and I hold out the amulet, the only line of defense I have. I inch my way closer to the chicken hut.

She should be dead by now, but she isn't. Something's wrong. I must find where she keeps her heart and crush it.

"You," she growls. "You ungrateful, stupid girl. I will tear you apart and then take my time devouring you."

The three hands twitch and the witch screams again. Something furry and strange dashes out of the woods and latches onto the back of the witch's cloak, catching her off balance. I was wondering where Stump went.

I run. Straight for the chicken hut.

Bryrian soldiers pour into the grove, charging the witch. Arrows strike her in the chest. She stops and growls, then rips them out like they are nothing.

She separated the only human part of herself—her sole vulnerability—and hid it away. The only way to kill her is to kill what's human about her. We talked about this long into the night, and in theory, the magic shouldn't hurt whoever destroys her heart. She's a creature of nature, wild and magical, not an unnatural abomination like wizards. Dalen believes the magic should go back into the ground, just like it does when a hybrid dies.

And if it doesn't, then at least Hans, Dalen, and everyone else will be safe from the witch.

It's a risk worth taking.

The witch's floating hands pluck soldiers from the ground and toss them aside like ants. One grabs at my cloak and lifts me up. I swing at it with my sword and land a glancing blow. The hand makes what sounds like a shriek and drops me. I hit the ground running, then slide underneath the burning house. Its chicken legs stomp and scratch, and the sound it makes is ear-curdling.

Home is where the heart is, they say. Something sparks in my mind. Home is also where the hearth is, and judging by the untouched square of hut above me, I'd stake my life that's where her heart lies, protected underneath the bricks of the hearth.

I leap up and grab one of the legs, holding on with all my might despite its best efforts to toss me aside. The hand returns and tries to pry me loose. I put the amulet around my neck and think toward the untouched spot, *Burn.*

Nothing happens. The fire can't get past whatever powerful barrier the witch has put there. I take my sword and, swatting at the hand again, jab the blade up into the belly of the house. I twist and turn it until one of the bricks comes loose. The house jerks and hops and the witch suddenly wheels around, a silent scream on her lips. I turn my thoughts back to the amulet, holding it in my outstretched hand, as the witch materializes before me, wailing. A trickle of blood stains her shirt; I chose the right spot. The amulet flares to life, fire pouring from it as the witch tears me off the leg of the house and squeezes her hands around my neck.

Darkness pricks the edges of my vision, but I keep my

thoughts on one thing alone: *Burn, burn, burn.* The fire is blinding, lancing into the belly of the beast house.

It explodes in a blast of fire, feathers, and blinding light. The witch screeches, the light and flames consuming her body as it turns pitch black with cracks of red fire—then nothing remains but falling ash.

In the air above where she stood is a swirling ball of light. It hovers, then races toward me. I throw up my hands defensively, terror echoing through every bone in my body.

Pain ricochets down my arm like I punched a brick wall.

But I live. No burning, no death, unless it was so fast I missed it. I open my eyes and cradle my outstretched arm.

In my palm is the amulet, my fingers still gripping it fiercely. But now it burns with a swirl of black shadows as well as the red flames.

# CHAPTER 28

HANS CLINGS TO MY HAND AS WE RETURN TO THE CAMP, AND I CONFESS, I cling back. I can hardly believe he's alive, much less that he's returned to me. The witch was true to her word in one respect; he is fatter now, but better that than the half-starving boy who was taken away from me. The three children the witch stole from Belladoma are on their way back to their families already.

Dalen grins widely each time I look his way, but he keeps his distance to let us have our space. He carries poor Stump, who has an injured leg after he delayed the witch for me. She did not appreciate his efforts as much as I did.

When we reach the camp, Dalen heads toward another tent, one just for him.

"Dalen, hold on, I need to talk to you." I turn to Hans.

"Our tent is just over there. Go inside and get warm, and I'll join you in a moment." Hans nods and backs toward the tent but doesn't take his eyes off me until he ducks inside.

Dalen looks at me in that quizzical way of his, and I almost lose my nerve. But I'm nothing if not nervy.

"I haven't been entirely honest with you. I found something when I searched Ensel's chambers, more than the papers and crowns and the things I told you about."

Dalen's eyebrows raise, and then he smiles. "I know what you're going to say."

"You do?"

"Of course. I found the potions where you stashed them in the barn. I was looking for something to help me hold the map still while I held it in the wind, and there they were."

"You don't understand. I didn't just find them—I *used* them. Several times."

"Of course you did. What else would you do with a potion but use it? And a good thing, too. I'm assuming that the breathing-underwater one is how you got out of the tunnels alive with the cornucopia?"

I feel relieved. "I didn't think you'd be happy with me using magic from such a tainted source as the wizard. I kept thinking about them, finding excuses to use them. I should toss them in the ocean, but I can't bring myself to do it."

"That is the nature of magic. It is a tricky thing and can worm its way into even the truest of hearts. That is, after all, how wizards were created." His face brightens. "But you don't have to worry about that. There's no need to destroy them. I'll take them, and keep them safe, until such time arises as you truly need them. Just be careful. You don't know what the magic could do to you. Don't depend on it too much. It might betray you. Especially if the potions were made from black magic."

I'm rooted to the spot. I have been depending on the potions. In fact, every time I use a potion, it gets easier. I can't deny I'm a little more eager and willing each time.

Dalen places a comforting hand on my arm. I shrink back. A crestfallen expression crosses his face. "I only worry, Greta. You are not a wizard nor a creature made of magic. Humans were not meant to handle such things. It could have terrible and unexpected consequences. Why do you think King Ensel thought stealing from a sea monster was a good idea? Or that feeding it girls from a rival city was a perfectly reasonable thing to do? He was already crazy, and the desire for more power, more magic, drove him completely mad."

Every word he says is another knife in my gut.

The strange joy that leaps in my chest each time I touch one of the potions. The sores that have broken out on my arms, and get worse with every potion I use. The same ones Vincali had. The magic is wheedling its way under my skin.

Thank goodness Dalen will take them away. I'll no longer be tempted. There's just one problem.

I draw a circle on the ground with the toe of my boot, a little sheepish and now a little scared. "I do have a need for one more first. Then they're all yours."

"All right," Dalen says. "One more. Then I'll take them away."

"But how will you keep them safe? What if I'm determined to steal them from you?" If black magic drove Ensel mad, why not me, too?

He laughs. "Don't you remember? I know more than a few hiding places around here."

I laugh with him, yet uneasiness fills me as I pull the blue potion from the box in my satchel and slip it into my pocket. Soon, this and the others will be hidden away, too well for me to find.

But this one will allow me to do what needs to be done to protect this city. My mother's city. Maybe even my city.

I hand the box to Dalen, his kind face and silver eyes gazing back at me happily. "You'll keep them safe as long as I need you to?"

He smiles. "As long as I live, I promise. I won't let you use them again unless there is a very great need."

I smile back, grateful he understood the question between my spoken words. The one I couldn't quite bring myself to ask.

He'll stay. He won't let me give in to the weakness Ensel and the mercenaries fell victim to. He'll be here to stop me.

Now that Hans and I are safely ensconced in a tent for the evening, we can finally talk. The scent of smoke and burning meat clings to us both, but it will fade over time.

I may never eat chicken again. And I doubt Hans will either.

We curl up on the pillows near the fire and he stares at the flames. Belatedly I wonder if the fire is a good idea at all considering what he witnessed today, but then he speaks and chases all those fears away.

"I knew you'd come back for me, Greta," he says, a smile on his chapped lips. I was worried he might have forgotten how to smile. "And I'm glad you killed the witch. She taunted me, you know. That you'd never come back alive. That I was almost fat enough. She was planning to take the cornucopia from you if you found it, then eat me anyway and save you for dessert." He lifts his wide gray eyes to meet mine, dark lashes framing them. "But I knew she was wrong. Even when she started taking more children. Other people don't always return, but you do. You did when you got sick and the wizard sold you to Ensel, and I knew you would this time, too." He stares at the fire again. "It's better this way. Now she can't hurt anyone else."

He's so serious, my brother. He's grown up by leaps and bounds in the past year, but he's always quiet and serious. Sometimes startlingly so.

His fingers, plumper than I remember them being, pry my fist open. I gasp at the stone in my hand; I'd nearly forgotten I still clutched it close. It felt like an extension of my arm. But now Hans pulls the amulet out of my palm, holding it and its swirling red and black insides up to the light.

"What do you think its purpose is?" Hans asks.

I shake my head. "All I know for certain is that I'm lucky it took the brunt of the magic. It seems to be a container of magic, but it can be used as a weapon, too."

His brow creases as he studies it. "It looks like ink rolling in red water."

I take it back. Best not to let him fixate on magical things. Or perhaps that's the overprotective part of me. Though he isn't wrong. That's exactly what it looks like now, though before it was just red.

"Hans, I need to tell you something."

He raises an eyebrow warily.

"It's about Mama and Papa." I pull the folded letter from my pocket. I've carried it with me ever since I found it, unable to let go of it, unable to let go of *them*. "I discovered what happened to them. Mama was King Ensel's stepsister. She fled Belladoma with Papa years ago, before we were born. Ensel tricked them and captured them. And then he—he—" Suddenly my throat is too dry to form sounds, and I helplessly hand Hans the letter instead.

He fixes me with a solemn gaze. "He killed them, didn't he?"

I can only nod.

He reads the letter, silently squeezing my hand. His eyes shine with tears, which stick to his lashes before they fall to the pillows beneath us. When he finishes reading, he doesn't say a word. He simply folds it back up and presses it into my hand, then curls his arms around my middle. We hold each other tightly, the only family we have left, in front of the fire until we fall asleep.

Someday, I'll have to let him go. But for now, I'm grateful he needs me too.

# CHAPTER 29

**IT HAS BEEN TWO DAYS SINCE WE DEFEATED THE WITCH, AND SINCE**
Vincali and his mercenaries vacated the palace. Now I have
a promise to keep. If it isn't already too late.

We make an odd procession through the city, newly
flooded and adorned with fresh clinging seaweed and dying,
stranded fish. Many of the Belladomans returned with us
to the city to survey the damage to their homes. Last night
was the last day of the full moon, and the Sonzeeki will rest
until the cycle begins again.

"This is even worse than I imagined," Hans says
beside me.

I nod. "It is an awful price they pay for Ensel's greed."

"I wish we could do something to help."

I suppress a small smile. It took weeks for my hatred of

these people to transform into something like understanding and sympathy. But for Hans, one look was all he needed. He's always had a kinder heart than me.

But he's right. We do need to do something. I even have a plan. I just need to convince King Oliver it's a good one.

As we walk up the cracked palace steps, I realize this is the first time I've come here through the front door. The flagstones shift and crack under our weight, slippery from last night's floodwaters. A contingent of the Bryrian army waits outside in case there's any trouble while we push open the creaking rusted gates. The palace hasn't changed in the past few days. Cold and dusty, and smelling of old salty seawater. No servants remain behind; they probably fled the moment Vincali left. I run to the abandoned guardhouse and tear down the stairs, Ren and Hans hard at my heels.

"Greta, wait! You don't know what's down there," Ren says.

"I know exactly what's down here: a man Ensel locked up."

"But there could be a trap. What if Vincali—"

I take the stone stairs two at a time into the depths of the dungeons until I can no longer hear Ren. Hans knows better than to try to stop me. The newer areas are mostly empty, with a few scattered faces. Bryrian guards will be along shortly to let them out too. When I reach the last section of the prison, I round the final corner and enter the familiar hallway that held my parents and the king's former adviser. The sounds of the boys' footsteps echo behind me, but they haven't caught up yet.

My eyes drift to the cell where my parents were held, where I found the last letter from Mama and Papa, then the cell across from it. The heap of rags lies motionless in the corner. Did Vincali and his men even know he was down here? Did they bother to feed him? Or were they content to let him die?

I don't even know the man's name to call it out and rouse him if he's asleep.

Hans reaches me first and swallows hard. "This is where Mama and Papa were all that time?"

"In that cell over there," I say, pointing. He places a hand on the bars and peers inside, but there isn't much to see.

Ren finally catches up, holding something in his hands. The keys. "Opening his cell might be tricky without these," Ren says.

"Thanks. I suppose I was in too much of a hurry." He hands them over. I clench my fists around the circular key ring so my hands won't shake.

"Hello?" I call, but the shape makes no answer. I fumble for the right key, and after several tries, the lock clicks and the door swings open.

I drop to my knees by the pile of rags and gently shake his shoulder. To my intense relief, he moves.

"Are you hungry?" I ask, pulling out a piece of bread from my satchel.

The groggy man sits up with some help from us, his milky eyes registering recognition. "So you are a girl of your word." He takes the bread and tears into it greedily, while eying Hans and Ren with interest. I hope he doesn't get sick from eating too fast.

"I told you I'd come back if I could. The mercenaries are gone. Thank you for telling me about my parents. If not for you, I'd never have known what happened to them. Nor would my brother, Hans." My eyes burn as I gesture to my sibling, and I turn my face away from the others. No one needs to see me cry. "Giving you back your freedom is the least I can do."

The man's eyes glitter. Perhaps the bread is reviving him. "Do you have any water?"

"Oh, yes, of course." I hand him my flask, and he downs half of it in one gulp.

"Ah, now that is what has been in shortest supply down here. Fresh water."

Ren frowns, then shudders. He must remember the time he spent in these dungeons.

"I must ask," I say, when the man is done with his small meal, "what is your name? You never said when I was here before."

"Manson," he says. "Manson Cartwright, disgraced former adviser to the king."

"Well, Manson Cartwright, can you walk?"

"Let's find out," he says, grinning lopsidedly. We help him to his feet and slowly head back to the stairs. We half carry him up the stairwell, and I'm glad Ren and Hans came with me. It would take far longer without them.

Slowly but steadily the four of us make our way down the dirty hall toward the main doors of the palace. Manson seems delighted each time he manages to put one foot in front of the other.

"How long were you down there?" Hans asks.

Manson shrugs. "Who knows? Months? Years? Time does not pass in the same manner when one's surroundings do not change. I tried to keep track at first, but grew bored and lost count."

We push the heavy double doors open, and daylight pours over Manson's face. He sighs, breathing in the fresh air deeply.

King Oliver, Dalen, and the Bryrian soldiers wait on the steps of the palace. To my surprise, a large crowd of Belladomans has gathered too. They must wish to know what we plan to do with their city now that Vincali is gone.

Many of them gape at Dalen, but he insisted on coming with us. After all, plenty of Belladomans saw him when we overpowered the mercenaries the other day. His secret is out; there's no more reason to hide.

But that doesn't mean we need to spill the details of the hybrid village just yet. Caution is still necessary. He paws the ground nervously when he sees the skin-and-bones man hanging between Ren and me.

But then Manson stands up straighter, cautiously putting his full weight on his own two feet. Murmurs roll through the gathered crowd as the people recognize him. The king comes forward and shakes his hand.

"Greta tells me you were once an adviser to the kings of Belladoma," King Oliver says. "I am Bryre's king and I wish to help this city. Since you know it better than all of us, I would welcome your advice on how best to do that."

Manson's eyes trail over to me, something sparking in them. He looks back at King Oliver. "Manson Cartwright, and I'd be happy to, Your Majesty."

I step forward, leaving Hans to stand by Ren. "If I may, King Oliver, I have an idea or two that I'd like to share with you." I realize now that I was overstepping the last time I brought an idea to the king. This time I'm determined to do it right.

King Oliver raises an eyebrow. "You want to help this city?"

I swallow the needles in my throat. "I understand it seems unlikely, but much has changed in the last few weeks."

He regards me appraisingly and I swear the milling crowd holds its breath. "All right. Let's hear it."

I take a deep breath as Hans appears at my side. I smile gratefully at him. "You came to Belladoma to bring food and supplies. But that is a temporary fix. While generous, it only addresses the short-term effects of a much bigger problem." The crowd murmurs. They know all too well what that problem is.

"Even if the cornucopia can provide enough food to sustain the entire city, it will never be a permanent solution. The city is falling apart. There are tunnels that run beneath the castle and the streets and alleys. I've gotten to know them well while I've been here, and they are not in good shape and need to be repaired. It is not enough to feed the people of this city. Soon we'll need to house and clothe them too, if we don't stop the Sonzeeki."

Hans squeezes my hand and I can feel the weight of his eyes on me. I have not even shared this plan with him.

"That is a fair assessment, Greta," King Oliver says. "But how can we stop a beast like that? No arrow has ever pierced its shell. And trying to scale the cliff when it rises is a suicide mission."

"Give it what it wants."

Ren gasps. "But it wants the cornucopia! The people here need it to eat."

"The people need to be able to grow their own food and trade with others more. The Sonzeeki is the cornucopia's rightful owner."

"Ren has a point. That cornucopia is what we had planned to use to help Belladoma," King Oliver says.

"At first, I was conflicted about relinquishing it, too. We could use it to feed Belladoma's people. But like all magic, there would be a price." Hushed whispers ripple through the gathered crowd. "I can't stand the thought of the entire city being tainted by reliance on magic. It's already much too late for the Sonzeeki. If the cornucopia's used to feed the beast instead, Belladoma could again grow crops and truly rejuvenate itself. Even you have to admit that's a far better solution than more bloodshed or permanent dependence on magic."

King Oliver considers my words for a long moment. Then he frowns. "You make a good case, but how do you propose we return it to the beast? If we send it over the cliff, it might get swept away by the tide. If we wait until the next full moon when the beast rises, someone might get eaten in the process."

"The same way Ensel reached it the first time."

"And how exactly did he do that?"

Manson, realizing what I plan to suggest, begins to laugh. "King Oliver, this Greta is a smart one, I tell you. Very smart indeed."

I sneak a glance at Dalen, and he nods encouragingly. I don't like using magic, but it needs to be done. Though I resented Belladoma for a long time, I can't leave my mother's city—my family's city—to rot and ruin. It would make me no better than Ensel.

"Ensel had potions, one of which allowed him to breathe underwater. The wizard gave them to him. That is how he snuck into the Sonzeeki's lair and stole the cornucopia in the first place. I found these potions. I . . . I have tested them before."

Understanding flashes in King Oliver's eyes. "Do any of those potions happen to make one invisible?" No doubt their escape from the threshing house so many nights ago now makes more sense to him.

"Yes, sire. And since I have used them, I volunteer to return the cornucopia to the beast. I am an excellent swimmer for one, and I have the potions."

"Greta, I cannot ask you to do such a thing." King Oliver folds his arms across his chest.

"I must. I need to face the beast down. It will haunt my nightmares forever if I don't." I shudder involuntarily.

"Magic is too dangerous; you don't know what it might do."

"Actually," Manson says, stepping forward and grabbing

my arm, "we know exactly what these potions will do. Or at least I do."

My face flashes hot as he pushes my sleeve up to the elbow, revealing the many sores dotting my hands and arms. I hiss as the fabric brushes over them. They've gotten much worse since I drank the last potion. Hans sucks in his breath sharply and the king frowns.

"As I suspected," Manson continues. "The potions are made from dark magic. They work very well, as I recall from my days with Ensel, but they take a blood price. Fortunately, they require only a small amount of magic, and the price is small, too."

He releases my arm, and I let my sleeve fall back into place to hide the sores—and my trembling. I'd braced myself to admit to using magic, but I wasn't prepared to have the sores revealed like that. "Are they permanent?" I ask Manson.

He shakes his head. "No. The ones on Ensel cleared up within a week or two of using a potion. It takes what it needs for the spell, and then the user can heal. It isn't wise to use them too often or in the long term, but one more use will do you no lasting harm."

King Oliver's face bears an unreadable look. "You know how I feel about using magic, Greta. I have never seen it lead to anything good."

"I agree, sire," Manson says. "And that is why I fear what reliance on the cornucopia could do to this city. I saw how it twisted Ensel, making him greedier and more paranoid than ever. I understand perfectly the temptation to use it, but the price might destroy Belladoma in the long run."

The king sighs. "I have to agree that it is best to ensure the cornucopia is returned to the beast so it will leave Belladoma alone. But I don't like the idea of sending you down there. There must be another way."

My fingers clench around the vial in my pocket. I have to be the one to do this. If my mother were here, she would do the same without hesitation. I was going to leave these people with no way out, hungry in a crumbling city. I need to make amends. "No. This is the only way. I will not give the potion to someone else. I need to do this."

Manson clears his throat. "King Oliver, I believe I may be able to shed a little light on Greta's meaning. And I also have my own proposition."

"You do?" the king and I say together.

Manson winks at me and turns back to the king. "Might I suggest restoring the eldest surviving member of the royal family to the throne?"

I begin to choke, even as the crowd's murmurs turn to outright cries of surprise, tinged with delight.

King Oliver frowns. "I didn't think any of the royal family lived. Ensel murdered all who could lay claim to his throne."

Manson's eyes glitter, and Hans pats my back to help me with the choking. I manage to catch my breath, but before I can tell Manson, *No, no, no,* he gives up my secret.

"She stands in front of you. Greta's mother was Princess Euphemia. She married a commoner and fled to live in your city to keep her family safe from Ensel's wrath. I'm afraid he caught up to them eventually. Greta will be old enough to rule on her own in a few years. I imagine you, and I, could provide her with the necessary guidance until she comes of age."

A scream wells up in my chest. Rule? *Belladoma?* Of all places!

The king gazes at me with surprise. "I take it you knew nothing of this until recently, Greta?" I shake my head.

"I think you can see, Your Majesty, why it is no small thing for Belladoma's future queen to want to be the one to save her city. And why it is important that she carry it out. These people have been downtrodden, used, and neglected by their rulers for too long. They will not follow her for less," Manson says.

"If I may, sire, I can attest to her bravery, and fierce loyalty to those she intends to protect. You could not find a better queen," Dalen says. I stare at him in shock.

King Oliver regards me for a moment as though seeing me for the very first time. "I believe you are right, Manson," he says slowly. "Greta will make an excellent queen."

"But—but I know nothing about being queen. Or how to run a city." The weight of all that responsibility bears down on me.

Dalen, now at my side, takes my other hand. It's comforting. "You won't be alone," he says, smiling. I glance over at Hans, who is speechless, but his eyes are bright and shining.

"You most certainly won't be," King Oliver agrees. "We will guide you. I know your memories of this place have not been good, but you have the power to transform it. To make Belladoma a place worth living in again."

"I cannot say it will be easy, Greta," Manson says. "Only a fraction of the wealth this city once knew remains in the treasury, but it should keep you and your brother for some time. I suspect you do not share the lavish tastes of your stepuncle or the mercenaries. With Bryre's help, the city could be rebuilt and be flourishing again soon."

I gape, still stunned. Can I really do this? It's tempting, in its way, to renew this place. Our mother's home. Our heritage. The idea of having a treasury—however small—at our disposal is staggering. No more stealing for our next meals, no more scrounging what we could from our meager garden. We could sleep peacefully at night, without the terror of being separated and thrown into an orphanage turning our dreams to nightmares. We could move on with our lives at last.

But can the blood Ensel poured through the streets ever be washed clean? It's one thing to help Belladoma with the Sonzeeki, but another entirely to commit the rest of my life to the city. Could I bear to live in the same halls where I was held captive? I stare at the gathered crowd, struck by one cruel fact: there are plenty of boys among the men and women, but only a handful of girls older than a year or two. None at all older than five or six. Ensel fed the Sonzeeki almost every young girl in this city. Then he went after Bryre. It wasn't because the people here supported it; it was because Ensel took everything from them. They've suffered just as much—maybe even more—than we did. Shame fills me. This is what Dalen was trying to explain the other day. They are not bad people. They're victims too. They deserve a ruler who can understand what they've been through, not someone who will take advantage of them yet again.

My mother loved this city once, its alleys and roads and the castle in its prime. Could I try to love it too, for her sake? Can I see this castle as a place where she grew up instead of as my former prison?

The crowd of Belladomans murmurs no longer. The collected people have heard every single word that's passed between King Oliver, Manson, and me on these steps. Their faces are filled with something I've never seen on them before, not in this tortured city.

Hope. Smiles.

At first, there's a few scattered cries of *A survivor of her generation! Our girl returned! She'll rid us of the beast!* Then their voices join together to form one word over and over like a beating heart: *Greta, Greta, Greta!*

Hans beams, and begins to chant with the crowd. Dalen and Ren join in.

The decision seizes me with an unshakable certainty. "I'll do it," I say, not taking my eyes off the gathered crowd chanting my name. "I'll learn to be Belladoma's queen."

And I'll have my friends, and Hans and his kindness, to guide me.

# CHAPTER 30

THIS MORNING, SUNLIGHT GLINTS OFF THE DEBRIS–FILLED CITY, DROWNING everything in gold and pink. The ocean waves shine like glittering diamonds. If only the sun could burn away the smell of rotting fish and seaweed, too.

Yesterday I chose this path, and now I stand with Hans and Dalen on the cliffside by the secret tunnel door, certain of—and terrified by—what I must do. They insisted on coming with me, and I can't deny I'm grateful not to be alone. Stump hovers by the tunnel; he doesn't seem to like being so close to the cliff.

I place a hand on Dalen's arm. "I want you to know that after this I'll do whatever I can to protect you and the rest of the hybrids. You and your family deserve to live without fear. Maybe, when I'm queen, you can live here? I know

King Oliver and Bryre would also help to keep you safe from people like the mercenaries. And you could help the citizens renew their fields in half the time."

Dalen's eyes gleam. "No more hiding? I rather like the sound of that. The others may require more convincing."

"Well, they are in need of a new home, after all," Hans says. I filled him in on all my adventures, and he was most curious about the hybrids.

"Indeed they are." Dalen smiles at us both. "I think Belladoma may soon become a very pleasant place to live. You'll make a good queen, Greta."

I smile back. My city will surely be the strangest the realm has ever seen. I wouldn't have it any other way. I glance at Hans. He has taken all of this—what happened to our parents, who our mother was, and what that means for us—in stride. I almost envy him that.

They say Hans and I are the last of Belladoma's royal line, but I don't feel like it. I've known myself as a daughter, a sister, an orphan, and a fighter. Queen isn't a title that fits me.

Not yet.

"I must earn that title, Dalen."

"That's why we're here."

If I'd had my way, we'd never have dreamed of helping Belladoma at all. We'd have let the Belladomans die for the sins of their usurper king, Ensel. I was wrong. I don't deserve to be called queen, not while the Sonzeeki still plagues us. I have to stop the horror Ensel set in motion. I must set right what he set to ruin. Then I'll be fit to lead.

My shoes are weighted—I'll sink quickly. Ensel's underwater potion quivers in my shaking hands. This time real waves crash below me, every slap of water jolting my nerves. What if the potion doesn't work the second time? What if I drown and Hans is left with no one? I swallow my fear.

This is the cliff my friends were thrown from. And my parents. The ghosts of hundreds of girls have haunted me these past few months. The Sonzeeki must be stopped. How else can Belladoma survive? If we are to grow anything to eat here, the soil must have time to recover from the salt poison the beast has thrown on it every month.

If I am to be queen, I must save my people.

Hans nudges my arm, startling me. "Don't worry," he says, a smile on his face. "You always come back. I know you will this time too."

"And we'll be here to pull you back up when it is done." Dalen gestures to the long rope waiting beside him. When I resurface, they'll throw the rope down and help me back to safety.

"Thank you."

The potion bottle glints in the morning light. Manson says it should last at least two hours. I must find the lair quickly. My other hand grips a sword taken from Ensel's hidden room, which, according to Manson, was forged in dragon's breath long, long ago. Imbued with such magic, it may very well be the only thing that can pierce the beast's armor should our plan to return the cornucopia go wrong.

Ready as I'll ever be, I down the potion in a single gulp. Then I jump off the cliff.

Cold water slaps my skin and I sink quickly. Water on every side. Terror rears its head like a vile living thing. But then relief. I can breathe.

If the beast eats me, I hope Dalen will watch over Hans. With every second, I draw closer to the source of my nightmares. My pulse throbs in my ears.

The deeper I sink, the more the light begins to fade. My sword glimmers with magic and shows the way. I can almost see the bottom. Schools of fish dart here and there, shimmering in the last vestiges of sunlight. Strange plants root in the reefs and rocks. Broken pieces of wood—a shipwreck, perhaps?—shoot up from the ocean floor. Everything sways with the tide as if it dances.

My boots are heavy with water and weight, but when I hit the bottom, I trudge onward, plumes of sand kicking up in my wake. According to Manson, Ensel found the Sonzeeki's lair in a deeply shadowed cave carved into the base of the cliffside. Soon I locate my destination—it's humongous.

Just like the Sonzeeki.

I head for the cave, every nerve tingling painfully with trepidation. Now more than ever I understand how much I have to lose.

I force my feet to keep moving, though I may as well be trudging through molasses. My heart shudders against my rib cage. I cling to my sword, determined not to show fear.

Secretly, I pray the beast never wakes and I can return

the cornucopia while it slumbers.

The cave entrance looms ahead and I hold my sword aloft to light the way. Phosphorescent algae line the walls, giving off a faint glow as well. No fish venture near the cave, confirming the Sonzeeki lives here.

What prey would willingly walk into a predator's lair?

Only me.

I take a deep breath of seawater, then swim inside. The cave floor is studded with smooth round rocks, as though the sand has been worn away by something massive. The walls are easily fifty feet apart. Finally the passage opens into a cavern that must be directly below the city. It's so high I can't quite see the ceiling.

This is how the Sonzeeki floods the city. From here, if the creature stirred the cave waters violently enough, they'd flow up and onto the streets and fields. I'm close.

Several shadowed passages dot the walls of the cavern. The beast must sleep in one of them. The question is: which one?

I inch around the edge of the cavern, feeling like an ant scoping out a snake's lair. The fear I'm about to be crushed is ever present and inescapable. The first and second tunnels only lead farther on, but when I reach the third, I pause. This is another cave.

I investigate, sword firmly gripped in my hand. My stomach drops into my feet.

Bones. Many, many bones.

I stagger back but manage to stay on my feet. I must be strong.

A huge, shadowed rock lies beyond the scattered bones. Like the walls, the rock is covered in algae and barnacles. Something catches my eye. In the center of the boneyard lies a pile of other objects. These must be the things the beast couldn't digest. My stomach squirms, but I lunge for the pile anyway. I have to know.

Earrings, necklaces, and other adornments are the most common. A forgotten coin in a pocket here. A handkerchief there. I recognize the initials of some of the girls I met when I was Ensel's captive. Whole pieces of discarded clothing, mostly dresses, in varying stages of decay. A handful of belts and boots, too. Those must be from the courtiers Ensel threw off the cliff before he discovered the Sonzeeki would only be satisfied with young girls.

My hands stop short as they light on one particular object. I lift it from the pile. The pocket watch is silver-plated with a simple filigree design along the edges. I'd know it anywhere. Papa carried it with him always. It was as precious to him as Mama's locket was to her. He used to tell us how one day I would inherit Mama's locket and Hans his pocket watch.

Now we have them both back.

A sob rises in my chest. The glass is cracked, letting in the seawater, and the two hands are frozen at eight thirty-one. I can only assume that is the time they died.

"Papa," I say, doubling over and clutching it to my chest.

Grief twined with fury brews inside me. They died so senselessly. To protect us when no real protection could be had. It was for nothing.

I shoot to my feet and head to the back of the cave, bubbles from my sudden movement in the water floating up around me and tickling my ears. There can't be anything worse in here for me to see. Except, of course, the Sonzeeki itself.

The piles of bones continue until I reach an alcove at the far end. It's different from the rest of the cave and passages. No algae cover the walls, but the ambient light reveals the rock face is a shimmering jet-black stone.

In the center is something I definitely didn't expect to see.

An altar.

It's carved from the same black stone. An indentation is the only thing marring the top. I stare at it for a moment; then it hits me. I know exactly what was here. I know *exactly* what would fit.

The cornucopia. This is where it was when Ensel, that selfish idiot, stole it. The beast had easy access, and no need to plunder the coast and city for food. Everything it needed to survive was right here.

I look closer at the indentation. At the bottom is inscribed: *To sate the ravenous beast.*

The legends are true. The Sonzeeki is ancient. A creature from myth, long forgotten, but still sleeping beneath Belladoma. The kings and queens of old found a way to keep the beast at bay.

Then Ensel went and ruined it with his insatiable greed.

My hand curls tighter around the hilt of my sword. I wish Ensel had never been born.

I step out of the alcove, needing more space, but my fury trails close behind.

The only one of its kind, the beast must have been down here for centuries at least. Understanding ripples through me. It wasn't always alone—it couldn't have been. Maybe the rest died long before Ensel took the throne, or perhaps afterward from lack of food. Whatever the case, this beast is *lonely*.

In an odd way, it makes me think of Kymera. She was a lonely monster too. There wasn't a single living thing like her anywhere. And like this monster, everything she'd become was tied up in the past and death.

And yet somehow I managed to forgive her for what she'd done.

I sink to the ocean floor, still clasping my father's watch.

The huge rock on the far side of the cave begins to move.

Horror holds me in its grip. I'm not alone. The Sonzeeki has been watching all along.

The rock shifts and slowly spins, buoyed up by the undulating tentacled arms that sprout beneath it. The thing must tuck them inside its shell when it sleeps. One giant milky yellow eye turns to me. It blinks but makes no movement.

If I wanted to, I could kill it. Right now. I could rush the beast and plunge my sword through its eye, the only part not protected by the shell.

But I can't.

Its tentacles are no longer the robust, muscular arms I remember. They've begun to wither. It must exhaust itself every time hunger and fury drive it to flood Belladoma. It's an ancient thing.

And it is slowly starving to death. Whatever food this monster needs to eat, it must no longer live in the ocean. Or it depended so long on the cornucopia that it has all but forgotten how to hunt live fish. Either way, the beast is already dying.

A strange emotion fills me. Pity. Oh yes, I hated the Sonzeeki for eating the other girls and my parents. But it was used by the wizard and Ensel as much as the rest of us were. We were all tools in their twisted games.

No doubt the wizard could've killed the Sonzeeki any time he wanted. But why would he? It isn't a magical creature. No power could be gained from its death. And without the threat of the beast flooding his city, Ensel wouldn't have needed a steady supply of girls to feed it, nor would he have dreamed of leaving Belladoma to take over Bryre. Killing this beast would've ruined all of the wizard's plans because it would've solved Ensel's problems.

The Sonzeeki is only doing what it was made to do—eat and sleep. How awful to be at the top of a food chain that has all but died out.

The eye blinks, and the tentacles settle over the nearest piles of bone.

I can't kill a beast that is the last of its kind. But I can set right what Ensel ruined.

I must return the cornucopia to its rightful owner. I saw firsthand the lengths it drove Ensel to, and now I'm the lone witness to the sorry state of the beast who owned it for who knows how long.

Cautiously, I reach into my satchel and pull the small

horn-shaped basket out and hold it up like I'm warding the Sonzeeki off. I creep backward until I reenter the alcove, and rest the cornucopia in the indentation.

Its true resting place.

I edge my way around the cave, doing my best not to disturb the Sonzeeki. Its eye follows me, but to my surprise, it doesn't attack. Is it too weak, or is it grateful I've given its food source back? I don't know the answer, but I count my blessings when I reach the exit to the cave unharmed.

Now I must return home, and hope I've finally righted enough of Ensel's wrongs.

# EPILOGUE

*Two Weeks Later*

SUNSET LIGHTS THE TOWERS OF THE PALACE, WHILE ON THE NEW GRANITE
steps below a ceremony begins: the new queen of Belladoma
will be crowned at last.

The drowning city has begun to dry, and the fear of
unkind rulers and beasts in the deep abates. Over the last
few weeks, neighbors have helped one another clear out old
debris from the last flood, shore up cracked foundations,
and replace swollen wooden beams, revealing a new city.

They turn over the earth in the fields, confident in
the knowledge that their crops will not be ruined; this
time they will have the chance to flourish, and there will
be extra hands to till the soil. New inhabitants join them,
hybrid refugees from a hidden village, bringing their own
resources and talents to make Belladoma the beautiful

place it was in times past.

A steady supply of food from Bryre pours through the streets until the citizens can replace it with their own. The treasury, long hoarded by unscrupulous guardians, has been opened and distributed to the people of the city.

Beyond the castle, in the cavern deep below the cliffs, a creature of times forgotten finally sleeps, its long, slippery arms cradling a small horn-shaped basket, and its beady, blank eye mourning for the other creatures who shared the basket once upon a time.

Today, hope is written on the face of every man, woman, and child as they gather on the steps of the palace. A rightful ruler—a young and brave one—will soon be back on the throne.

An old man places a shining circlet of gold on the head of a dark-haired girl, then a thinner one of silver on the blond-haired boy next to her. Together, they inspire the hope and loyalty of the crowd. Nearby stand, a delegation from Bryre and a centaur boy. The onlookers, a mix of human and hybrid, cheer their names like a victory cry:

*Greta, Hans! Greta! Hans!*

The sun dips into the ocean behind the palace, smudging the horizon with red haze, but tomorrow, a new day will dawn in Belladoma.

# PRECIOUS

*A* Monstrous *Novella*

# CHAPTER 1

THE SPAN OF MY LIFE CAN BE MEASURED BETWEEN THESE WALLS. WALLS
that protect Bryre from the wizard. Walls that keep him out
and me, the crown princess Rosabel, very much in.

If my mother and father had their way, I'd have nothing
to amuse me save my garden and my sister. They would
have me remain here, where I am now, where I am every
day, coaxing roses from the ground, never dreaming of
leaving the palace.

Never having any dreams at all.

They did not count on Ren.

I twirl a bloodred rose in my hand and wander through
the garden maze. It begins behind the palace and leads to a
forest of topiary beasts and rosebushes marching all the way
to the main gate. It's patrolled by guards, but if I remain

between the hulking shadows of the sculpted hedges, they won't see me at all.

But Ren will find me. He always does.

Mama and Papa believe the palace is the one place I'm safe, but they're wrong. They can't watch me all the time. Someday, I will take their place as ruler of Bryre. How can they expect me to properly rule a people I'm not even allowed to see? Their fear of the wizard clouds their vision on this topic.

Fortunately, my own eyes are crystal clear.

I rest on a bench in the shade of a centaur-shaped topiary and wait for my escape.

Before long, the telltale rustle of Ren running through the maze reaches my ears. I can't help but smile. Soon he sits beside me, out of breath and bright-eyed from delivering messages for my father. His wild brown hair falls around his face.

"A perfect morning to walk to the market, isn't it?" He grins in a lopsided manner that never ceases to pluck my heartstrings.

We keep our eyes and ears open for servants passing by as we stroll through the maze. Papa and Mama know how much I love the gardens, so this never raises suspicion.

But if they heard we were opening a trapdoor in the old fountain nearly swallowed up by the hedges, they would definitely be alarmed.

It was drained of water long ago, and now the cherubs play only in dust. No one ventures this deep into the maze but us, and I suspect the gardeners have simply forgotten about it. The fountains in the squares and in the front of the palace gardens are much better maintained.

Cracks mar the edges of the small fountain, but Ren and I know the true secret that lies beneath it. All castles have escape routes. When we were small, Ren, my sister, and I found the hidden passages in the castle and followed them all to their ends. They were musty and filled with dirt, dust, and secrets. This one leads to an old church in Bryre in one direction, and inside to the pantry and kitchens in the other. It is also one of the few that we discovered after those childhood antics, and that Delia does not know exists. If we want to get to the market, the garden entrance to the tunnels is our best route.

Ren tugs at the arm of the highest cherub and it swings down easily. Stone groans as the floor of the fountain lowers and shifts into stairs.

"After you," he says with a bow.

I laugh. We only play at gallantry. Ren never stands on ceremony with me. It's a relief not to have to tiptoe around each other like we do with everyone else in the palace. We creep down the steps into the darkness. I pull a box of matches from my pocket and light the nearest torch, while Ren pushes on the counterlever and the fountain slides back into place. No one will guess where we've gone. No one ever does.

Ren's brown eyes shine devilishly in the half light. "Better hurry," he says, "the good stuff won't stick around all day." With that he runs down the passage. I follow blindly; I know this route by heart. Within minutes we reach the exit and surface in the crypt of the old church, filled with shadowed catacombs and the bones of the dead.

The one good thing about having been hidden away most of my life is that very few people in Bryre know my face. Besides, I have no interest in dressing richly when no one but my family and the palace staff see me. My gowns, while finely made, are simple. That is how I like it, and Mama doesn't mind quite as much if I happen to ruin one while gardening.

We slip out by a side door we discovered years ago. Occasionally we run into the old padre who cares for the church, but hardly anyone attends services here. That made it the perfect place for Ren and me to take music lessons when we were younger. But even that stopped a couple of years ago. Unlike the larger, more fashionable church in the main square, this one has character and history, all tied up in its huge, stained-glass windows and intricate tapestries. But we're not here for that today.

We sneak down the alley and are out in the market proper in minutes. Sunlight glints off the gaudy reds, blues, and yellows of the stall canopies. People are out, haggling and laughing. Spices scent the air with a sweet and salty mix in one direction, a peppery one in another. Someday we'll come here and all we'll do is sample every stall.

But not today. I've been harboring a purpose. I have been tending a small garden plot, hidden in one of the dead ends of the maze. I love tending to the roses, but Papa does not wish me to get dirty in the planting and caring. He only wants the results, for me to enjoy the flowers like a

284

proper princess. But I want the whole process. Mama and Papa would be unhappy if they suspected I prefer my small, haphazardly filled garden, so I spend plenty of time adoring the roses they've had planted specially for me. But each week we come here and I purchase a seedling or bag of seeds to try my hand at growing. Some fail miserably, like that poor orchid last week. It was dead in two days. But others flourish. The pretty flowering moss, for example, grew quite nicely.

It may seem a small thing, but it's mine. Something I do all on my own. Everything else I have is handed to me or done for me. There is no glory in that. There may be no glory in moss, either, but I am proud of it just the same.

It doesn't hurt that it gives me an opportunity to escape the cloying confines of the castle.

Ren guides me through the bustling crowds, weaving deftly between people and carts. When we stop at the flower vendor, she lifts her ancient head and smiles sweetly at me. "Back again, pretty one?" she says, as she does each week. Her gray shawl slips off her wild silver hair and falls to her shoulders. She frightened me at first, this old woman with crooked teeth and a mass of hair as thick and wiry as snakes. But something in her eyes makes me inclined to trust her. Something like kindness. Knowledge.

That's what I thirst for the most. The knowledge my tutors cannot share. The kind that comes of having lived in the world, the best and worst parts, and learning how to tell the difference between them.

"Yes, Old Mae," I say as I help adjust her shawl. She pats

my hand with papery-skinned fingers.

"I have something special for you today." She summons Ren, and he exchanges a hopeful look with me. We're both curious. "When I saw this, I knew it was meant for you. There, boy." She points to a small pouch on the rack attached to the bottom of her cart. "Grab that for me, will you?"

"Of course," Ren says. "Please sit, don't trouble yourself."

She sits, a little out of breath, but hums and smiles to herself. "You'll like this one. Though I warn you, pretty one, they weren't cheap."

Ren holds up the pouch, but before he can peer inside, she raps him on the knuckles. "Only she may touch them."

He frowns but laughs it off and hands the pouch to me. Inside are several tiny seeds. Each one is small and dainty, the size of a tiny pearl bead, and they shine like them, too.

"They're lovely," I say. "What are they?"

"The trader I got them from said they grow into Crown-of-Roses. Very rare, very beautiful. Don't they look like little stars?" She cackles and starts to cough. Ren fetches her canteen. "Thank you, boy. You're too kind."

I must know what these seeds will look like when they sprout. I put on my best haggling face as I pull my nose out of the seed bag. "How much?"

"Well, they cost me a pretty penny. I'll give them to you for fifty pieces of silver."

"Thirty, and not a penny more."

She narrows her eyes at me. "That's less than I paid for

them myself. Forty-five."

"Forty. That's my final offer."

She's still for a moment, then breaks into a laugh. "You get better at haggling every week, my dearie. It's a done deal."

I hand her the coins and tuck the seed bag into my skirts. I certainly hope the price is worth it. My parents give me a small amount of money each week so I can send servants to make purchases from the merchants when I wish. These seeds cost a whole week's allowance. We bid the old woman good-bye, but as we walk away, I still feel the weight of her ancient eyes on my back.

"Come on," Ren says. "Now that your errand's done, let's see what else is here. Last time, I swear I found a treasure map in one of the stalls. I want to see if it's still there."

I laugh. "A treasure map? What do you need that for?"

He shrugs. "To make my fortune, of course."

"Why do you need a fortune? You already work in the palace."

He's silent for a moment while we amble between the stalls. "What if I don't always want to work in the palace? What if I want to have my own?"

"What if you do? Is the map going to lead you to one?" I fiddle with my sleeves. Despite the best of tailors, they never do quite seem to fit. "Besides, having your own palace isn't all it's cracked up to be. All sorts of responsibilities and rules and restrictions. I'd be happy just to have a nice cottage in the woods with a garden and a stream and maybe some chickens. Something simpler."

Ren smiles. He always looks so warm when he does that, like the sun fills him up and spills from his face. "If I had enough money, I could have my own palace, and a cottage for you, too."

Cold creeps up my chest, battling the warmth in my heart. I hide it behind a smile. "I'm the princess. I can't leave Bryre."

This time Ren's silence lasts for several stalls.

We slip quietly back into the church and head for the garden maze. No one sees us come up through the old crumbling fountain. Ren helps me off the rim and at last seems to be returning to his normal self.

"I'll fetch your watering can." Ren runs off down the path. He has a knack for guessing exactly what I wish for. And delivering. If only Mama and Papa could see and understand my heart so clearly.

I pull the small bag of seeds from my skirts as I meander toward the garden hidden deep in the maze. Tiny, sparkling things like miniature stars in my hands. I can't wait to see what they become. That's what I love most about growing things—you never know what you'll get, even from the shabbiest-looking of starts. Some of the ugliest seeds I've seen have become the loveliest of flowers. Rose seeds, for example, are plain, but quite the opposite when they're grown.

You can't judge them by how they start, only by where they end up. When I'm queen, I hope to be a ruler who judges people in the same manner. For now, though, I'll content myself with flowers.

"Here you are, Rosabel," Ren says, handing me the brimming watering can. He eyes the seeds in my palm. "What do you think they'll look like?"

We turn the corner to the garden and I consider the seeds again. "Like something I've never seen before, I expect. Something new and unusual."

"For the price you paid, I should hope so."

Ren helps me turn a small plot of soil. Then we carefully space the seeds out and tuck them into the earth. Now all we can do is wait and water them every day.

"If these are anything like the ones we got a couple of weeks ago"—I eye the sunflowers in the corner, reaching greedily toward the sun—"they should sprout in a day or two."

"I bet it'll be sooner. You could coax anything out of the ground."

I laugh. "I hope that's true. I do look forward to meeting them."

We make the rounds to the other flowers, checking for weeds, making sure they all have enough water. It isn't long before the maids begin calling for me.

"Race you?" I ask.

We run back to the palace, laughing the entire way.

I beat him to the veranda, as always. Together, we creep back inside the palace, avoiding the maids on the prowl and careful not to cause any commotion or raise suspicion by walking too close together. I'm the princess, he's my servant, and we march steadily on, headed somewhere important. At least, that's what I want the rest of the servants to believe. When we're sure no one is in sight, we duck into my quarters, giggling like naughty children. The maids will find me soon, but for now, I can pretend I'm just a girl sharing a secret with her best friend.

"Where have you two been?"

Delia, my little sister, sits by the window, partially hidden by the lace curtains. My heart catches in my throat. That window looks out on the garden maze; could she have seen us? My quarters are the only ones high enough on this side of the palace to see that old fountain.

Ren stutters an excuse, but I wave him off. "Delia, why are you in my chambers?'

She looks petulantly at me. "You always answer questions with more questions." She folds her arms over her chest, and her tight blond curls shake as she stands up. She's nearly my height, despite the two years or so that separate us. I suppose she is not little anymore. "I was bored, and I thought you might like to . . . to play that piece with me on the piano while I practice singing." A frown mars her pretty face. "We haven't played together in a while. I miss it."

My heart sinks. I've been neglecting Delia. We used to include her in all our plans and games. But as Mama and Papa began allowing me fewer freedoms over the past several years, I stopping letting her in on my plans to circumvent them.

Mama and Papa can never know that I sneak out, and least of all that Ren aids me.

"Delia," I say, crossing the room to take her hands. She

dodges and plants herself on the gold-embroidered settee instead. I sit beside her. "I'm sorry. I've missed you, too. How about after dinner? We could play then. It would give Mama and Papa great joy to hear it."

She gives me a sidelong glance. "Where were you all afternoon? I saw you in the garden for a while—then you disappeared. You know what Mama and Papa say about the wizard. I was scared, and I . . ." She trails off and my skin prickles.

"You were watching me?"

"You must not say a thing," Ren says. "Please, Rosabel was in no danger, I promise."

She glares at him but says nothing in response.

I grab her hand, clasping it tightly. "There's no wizard. It's a foolish superstition. We're in no danger—we're just prisoners of our parents' fears. Bryre is warded. No one meaning the city harm can enter."

My parents know all this and yet their terror haunts them still, ever since the army of Belladomans returned several years ago. The wizard turned them away from Bryre once, and he set up the wards. But now they fear he has allied himself with the city that would destroy us.

These invisible dangers form the ever-tightening noose around my neck.

"Where did you go?" Delia's pretty face is red and puffy. I wonder if she has been crying. As if I could possibly feel any worse.

"To the market," I say softly.

She gasps. "How?"

I share a glance with Ren. He shrugs helplessly. Confiding in Delia now is the only way to regain her trust.

"Remember the passages we used to play hide-and-seek in? We found more. Some of them lead outside the palace, even outside of Bryre." I squeeze her hands encouragingly, but it does nothing to help.

"How could you do that? Mama and Papa have forbidden it." Her bottom lip quivers, and I fear she will cry again. She's much more sensitive than I. I'm the practical sister, raised knowing one day I'll rule. It's in my very bones.

But Delia is more prone to petty fears, and more easily absorbs the emotions of others.

"It's perfectly safe, and I never go alone. No one even knows about the tunnels except for us." I turn her chin to face me. "Now you must promise me that you will not tell a soul. Promise?"

Misery swims in her watery blue eyes.

"Delia, you didn't."

Ren stares at her with horror. If we're found out, I have no doubt he'll suffer more than I will, possibly even lose his post at the palace. I shove my fear down. The fault is mine. I knew the risks, and I'll bear them. I'll protect Ren in whatever way I can.

"I'm sorry," she murmurs. "Mama was looking for you, and I told her you were in the garden, but then you weren't anymore. I didn't know what to do. The servants were looking for you, but no one could find you."

I bury my face in my hands, while Ren begins to pace. "Oh, I wish you hadn't done that." For Delia's sake, I swallow the scream that wants out.

Delia begins to cry. "I'm sorry—I don't want you to be punished; I just wanted you to be safe. I was afraid the wizard might have gotten to you."

I put my arms around her and her tears spill onto my shoulder. "I know. But you have to trust me that we are in no danger from a wizard. From now on, promise me you will trust me. And that you'll tell no one about the tunnels."

She nods. "I promise."

Ren runs his hands through his hair. "I should go home. My father is going to kill me, if he isn't out looking for me already."

"Or worse, your mum," I say.

Ren sighs. "My apologies, princesses, but I must leave." He bows awkwardly, then runs from the room.

My hope of ever leaving this palace again flees with him.

With trepidation, Delia and I walk toward the dining hall. I changed as quickly as I could into a clean dress. Mama would be angry if I showed up in my filthy gardening one. She and Papa await us, and they'll be anything but pleased with me this evening. My sister clutches my hand but is strangely quiet. She used to be light and mischievous, but over the past few months, she has become increasingly withdrawn. Or is it because I've become obsessed with finding some measure of freedom? Whichever it is, I must remedy this change before it progresses any further.

We pass through the halls, tapestried and adorned with

paintings and scrolls. A proper and orderly palace for a proper and orderly king and queen. And me, the daughter who just can't stomach proper and orderly any longer.

The servants duck their heads as we pass; they know how furious our parents are. I sigh and pat Delia's hand as she mumbles yet another apology.

"I don't blame you. You were scared." I wipe the remaining tears from her cheeks. "You must pull yourself together for dinner. Mama and Papa wouldn't want to see you upset. Can you do that?"

She sniffles, then straightens her back.

I smile. "Good girl."

We enter the dining hall together. It's terribly quiet. Mama and Papa, usually full of laughter, sit stone-faced on either side of the long, lace-draped table. Tureens of hot soup steam at each end, dishes of buttered vegetables and a whole roasted duck wait in the center, and baskets of fresh bread lie scattered about the candles and glasses. It smells delightful, but my appetite is long gone. We kiss our parents on the cheek, then take our seats obediently.

Mama and Papa don't say a word until we are seated and spooning soup into our bowls. I knew the silence would not last.

"Rosabel," Mama says, "I needed you earlier this afternoon. We combed that entire garden maze and could not find you anywhere." Her lovely, placid face cracks with traces of anger. "Where were you? You gave us all quite a fright." She puts her soup spoon down a little too hard.

I take a deep breath. Haven't I prepared myself for this

moment ever since I first devised my plan for freedom? I'll be as honest as possible, because I believe what I'm doing is right.

"I'm sorry to have caused you or Papa any unease. I only went to the market."

The silence is marred by the hushed gasp of a servant. Everyone knows my restrictions: I must never leave the palace grounds.

Mama's face pales, but Papa speaks first, though he does not glance up from his plate. "Dear child, you are forbidden to do this. Why would you leave the palace when you know the risk is so high? How did you even get out?"

"We slipped out the side gate when the guard changed." I'm unwilling to give up all my secrets. I set my napkin down. "I don't believe there is any danger. In fact, I fear it is more dangerous if I do not get to know the people of Bryre. How can I rule a city of strangers?"

"I assure you, the threat is very real, and grave." The terror in Papa's eyes stuns me. It isn't like other times when he simply forbade me to leave; the fact that I was outside these walls truly scares him. Goose bumps pop out all over my arms, and a gnawing doubt seizes my chest, but I swallow it all down. There may have been a wizard nearby once, but I am certain the danger is long past.

"How can you know that?" I ask. "No one has seen this wizard in ten years. How can you be sure he'll come back? And really, how could he? The wards set around the city keep out anyone who would do Bryre harm. Surely that makes the market as safe as any other place inside the city."

Mama scoffs, but her shining blue eyes betray her fear.

"The wizard . . . the wizard is not a man who would forgive a debt."

Something sick creeps into my stomach, and I don't think it's the soup. "Debt? What are you talking about?"

Delia squeaks across the table from me, wide-eyed.

"Delia, please wait in the hallway," Papa says, patting her hand.

"No!" I cry. "She should hear this too. Won't it affect her as well?"

My parents exchange a weary glance. "You may stay if you wish," Mama says.

Delia bites her lip but remains in her seat.

"What is this debt you owe the wizard?" I ask again. Something hot and angry stirs amid the sickness in my gut.

Papa answers. "We were young rulers, and frightened. King Ensel of Belladoma was marching on Bryre. He'd ruined his own kingdom and was determined to take over ours. The wizard offered to help for a price." He dabs his brow with a napkin. "We were desperate. Belladoma had an army of thousands of mercenaries in their employ. Bryre's army was nothing compared to theirs. We accepted his help because we felt we had no other choice."

"We assumed his price would be in gold," Mama whispers. It echoes around the dining hall in a way that gives me chills.

"What was his price?" I ask. I'm not sure I want to know the answer.

Papa sighs heavily and places his head in his hands.

"You."

# CHAPTER 2

THE MORNING SUN TRICKLES BETWEEN MY CURTAINS, ROUSING ME FROM my nightmares filled with the wizard and his magic coming to collect. I shivered so hard during the night that my covers slipped off the bed.

Nothing can take away Papa's terrible words or the fear on Mama's face.

They blindly promised him anything to save the city from Belladoma's forces. He chose me.

The knock on my door makes me nearly leap out of bed.

"Rosabel?" my mother calls through the door. I am surprised she didn't come to my tower sooner; I fled the table after dinner and locked myself in my room, refusing to admit any servant or even my sister.

"Go away," I say.

A key turns in the lock, and I roll over to face the wall, scowling. How dare she invade my space after what they did?

I hear the soft click of the door closing. The bed dips as Mama sits on the edge.

"I know you are upset, but I hope you have a better understanding of why we insist you remain in the palace. The wizard is after you, specifically, and he is a diabolically patient man. Ten years is nothing to one such as him."

"If he was so horrible, why did you turn to him for help in the first place?" I grumble.

She sighs. "We were deceived. Wizards are masters of trickery. We thought he was a good man, a good wizard, but he bewitched people in outlying villages, even our trusted advisers, to recommend him to us. In our desperation, we thought we could trust him and made an exception to the ban on magic. We had no reason to suspect what he really was."

I sit up, clutching my blanket to my chest. "Why did he do it? What could possibly make him want me as his reward?" This is what troubles me most about this tale. It seems ridiculous he would demand a child who was as yet unborn.

Mama shakes her long golden curls, and twists one of her ruby rings around a finger. "That, I'm afraid, is my fault." Her voice trembles. "When I was a young girl, only a few years older than you are now, I was wooed by two princes: your father, and another prince who claimed to be from a faraway land. I had known and loved Oliver since I was a child, and at first I paid little attention to this other suitor. But then Oliver's father passed away and he was crowned king of Bryre. He could no longer remain in our court. With him gone, the other prince began to win me over. He offered me fine gifts, and somehow I was always in a daze around him. I could hardly remember what he said, only that I adored him and wished to see him again." She stops fidgeting and smoothes the silk of her skirts. "If Oliver had not returned to our court when he did and cleared away all those cobwebs the strange prince wove in my head, I might have married him instead. At the time I did not see him for what he was; I only knew that Oliver was back and that I loved him more than anything. I returned all the other prince's gifts and married your father.

"The truth is, that strange prince was not a prince at all. He was a wizard—the wizard—and he had bewitched people to pretend they were his servants and courtiers, and probably even altered his appearance. There was something familiar about the old man who showed up at our gates, and when he finally named his price, he gave us a flash of who he had been before. I don't know which was the illusion, the old man or the young, but he was clearly not what we thought. He did not tell us what he needed a child for, and I pleaded with him, saying that if he had ever loved me, he would ask for something—anything—else. He laughed in my face, and told me that I was a means to an end, and that end was the child. Whether I loved him or not, I'd give him one. We had already promised him anything he wanted in return for protecting Bryre. The deal was binding and sealed with magic."

Horror creeps over me in spite of the warm sun shining through my curtains.

"You can do nothing to break this deal? Why have you never told me this before?" Anger burns in my chest, but letting it out might stop the flow of answers I'm finally getting.

"We did not wish to scare you. I confess, I am embarrassed by the role I played. This is my fault. I brought the wizard down on our heads by choosing your father. And that means I will fight all the harder to keep you safe. We hired every historian within twenty leagues to hunt for something that could break a deal with a wizard. We had many false leads and hopes but found nothing tangible. The only thing we could do was keep you hidden away and constantly under our protection."

"But what in the realm did he want with a child?"

She sighs, and pales. "We did not know at first, but we consulted all our histories to figure it out. There is a spell, an ancient and horrible one, that can steal all the magic within a certain radius and bestow it on the caster. The catalyst of the spell is a terrible deed: the sacrifice of a child. The younger the child, the more powerful the spell and the wider the range of magic it would steal." She swallows hard.

I cannot breathe. This wizard wooed my mother, then tricked both my parents into promising me to him, all for greed of power. "Now you punish me instead."

She brushes her fingers across my cheek. "I know you hate this. I know it is hard for you to stay in the palace. But sometimes queens must make hard decisions. Someday, when you are queen, you will understand."

The anger flares. Understand? Unlikely. I turn back to the wall, wishing the sun could chase away the aching cold in my heart. I turn back only when I hear the swish of silk skirts and the click of the door closing.

I am done hiding. Oh, I will keep up appearances for Mama and Papa's sake and mope around the castle as much as possible. But now I have a new purpose—no more skulking about the market looking for new things to grow.

I need something to keep the wizard away from us permanently. Perhaps something to break a binding deal. Powerful magic is involved when one makes deals with wizards. But what could be strong enough to break that? They may have hunted for something, but I have to wonder—did they search hard enough? Did those historians know anything about wizards? The use of magic has been forbidden in Bryre and most of the lands beyond since long before I was born.

My parents must have been beyond desperate to accept help from a wizard, even a supposedly good one.

I swing my legs over the edge of the bed and sit up. I need help. And I know just who to ask.

I dress quickly, not bothering to call my maid, and race into the hall. Ren should be delivering messages around the city, but I might be able to catch him when he returns. Scampering through the halls and doing my best to hide from the servants, I make my way to the back garden, then settle in behind a hedge where I can see through to the back kitchen door. Ren always does like to see what he can con

301

from the cook; I'm certain when he comes back, it will be through there.

I don't have to wait long. Soon Ren slips out of the door, chewing a sticky bun.

"Psst! Ren," I hiss. He looks up from his breakfast and glances around. I step out from behind the hedge and wave him over.

"What are you doing out here, Rosabel?" he asks, licking icing from his fingertips. "I thought the king and queen would lock you up for good this time."

"Hardly." I put on a brave face, though I thought so too. I'm relieved I'm still allowed to roam the castle grounds. My parents are not so cruel as to lock me in my room and deny me my garden, my sole comfort, for a first offense. But if they catch me again, I have no doubt they will. "But I did find out why they believe I'm in danger from the wizard." A lone chill works its way up my spine, but I shake it off.

Ren's warm brown eyes go wide, his breakfast all but forgotten. "Why?"

"They made a deal with the wizard before I was born to help them protect Bryre from Belladoma's invading forces. They assumed his price would be in gold, but what he named was their firstborn."

"You?" Fear flickers across Ren's face. The last bit of his food slips from his hand and a small squirrel darts out from the hedge to snatch it up.

"I have to find a way to break the binding spell on their deal. Or something to keep the wizard away for good. The vendors in the market are well traveled and might know something the historians around here would not. Will you help me?"

Ren smiles bravely, but terror swims beneath his gaze. "Always."

My first course of action is to disobey my parents. They have posted extra guards at every entrance to the palace grounds, just to be sure I cannot sneak out. But they know nothing of the tunnels, and the second Mama and Papa leave the palace on business that afternoon, Ren and I slip out through the old fountain to go to the market. With so many traders of old and unusual things, if anyone in Bryre has an inkling what can rid us of the wizard or break the binding deal, we'll find them there.

Have Mama and Papa tried this already? Perhaps. But if the traders fear the wizard, would the traders have told my parents, knowing who my parents are? I can picture Mama regally questioning common folk about magic, and getting only nervous nods and tight lips in response. No one knows me, and only a few are aware of Ren's connection to the palace. If we ask about wizards and magic, it's more likely to be shrugged off as foolish, childish interest. That could work in our favor.

And I'm willing to bet the only thing that can break a deal like that is magic.

Though the morning promised sunshine, the afternoon brings clouds and drizzle, providing a gloomy cover for us as we sneak out. Delia is otherwise engaged with her tutor. She won't have a chance to spy on us this time.

Ren takes my hand as we exit the church. The warmth of it makes me shiver.

We try the map vendor first. He stands outside a large, tented stall with bright-red banners, blocking our entrance. He's covered head to toe in dusty robes, so we can see only his icy blue eyes.

"Do you travel far to make the maps?" Ren asks. "Have you ventured to any lands that still have magic?" A tricky question, since most magic these days has been absorbed by wizards or outright banned. Only pockets of magic remain, like the wards that keep Bryre safe.

But the man in front of the tent only gives us a silent stare in response.

Ren takes my arm and guides me to the healer's triangular, vented tent, and together we browse the healing draughts. The healer, a small, keen-eyed woman with a mass of curly red hair, approaches. "Looking for something particular?" she asks, keeping her eyes on our hands in case we steal something.

"Nothing specific, just curious." I smile, hoping to charm her. "We were wondering, have you ever healed anyone who was under a spell? Can it be done?"

"I never touch spells. I want nothing to do with wizards," says the healer.

"Of course." But she is already on to the next customer.

"Darn," Ren says, "I thought she'd be our best bet, too."

Next, we try a shadowy stall with deep burgundy curtains trimmed in gold filigree. Strange items are lined up out front and extend to the tent in back of the stall. They look odd enough that I'd believe they're magical.

I pick up one bauble, a deep-blue stone the size of my fist with a silver setting. It could have been a crown jewel.

"Like calls to like, doesn't it?" says the merchant with a sly smile that turns my stomach.

"What do you mean?" Ren asks.

"Why, only that pretty ladies like pretty things. And that," he points to the stone, "matches this young lady's eyes perfectly."

I return the stone to the pile it came from and wipe my hands on my dress.

"Are any of them special?" I ask.

"They are all special in their own way," he replies.

"We're thinking of a more specific sort of special," Ren says. "How old are the items here? Are any from the time before wizards? Do any hold magic?"

The antiquities trader steps back. "You're on the path to trouble if you keep asking questions like that," he tells us with a deep frown.

Ren scowls as we leave. "Why are they all so afraid? The wizard hasn't been seen in these parts in years. At least that's what my parents tell me."

I too had hoped for better results, but I am not surprised. "I cannot blame them. They leave the safety of Bryre all the time to make their livelihood. Even if the wizard hasn't ventured near here, it doesn't mean they might not encounter him elsewhere." If anything, I was depending on it.

"Fear shouldn't stop them from doing the right thing." He walks quickly in the direction of the flower stall. Perhaps the day won't be a total waste after all.

"They probably do their best not to know anything about the wizard for safety's sake. They can't tell us what they don't know."

Ren huffs. "Fine, when you put it like that . . ."

Drops of rain fall more steadily and dampen his hair. I pull up the hood of my cloak.

"Something troubles you, dearies?" The old woman's familiar voice floats behind us, and we whirl around. She hobbles in our direction, holding a bowl of soup from one of the food vendors. "Come to my stall; tell Old Mae what this is about."

"I doubt you can help," Ren says. The disappointment and weather must be affecting his mood.

"Thank you—we appreciate any help we can get." I give Ren a sharp look.

We help her settle onto her stool. She slurps soup from her bowl as we tell her we're looking for something that can nullify magic. Deals with wizard are sealed with a spell, which makes them binding. But if we can remove the magic from the document my parents signed, perhaps we could break it. At least, I hope so. That would require locating the document, for one, and magic is volatile at best. Any attempt to change it by a nonwizard could, I've heard, have dire consequences.

Perhaps this is where my parents quailed, choosing instead to lock up their daughter rather than run the risk of meddling with magic. The fear and regret in my mother's eyes this morning are unforgettable.

But for me it is the only choice if I want even the smallest chance of freedom.

Old Mae grins at me like she can see straight through to my soul. It is difficult not to squirm.

"I know just what you need, princess. Wizard's Bane."

My mouth drops open, my throat stripped of its voice. Ren sputters.

She cackles into her soup. "You both think you're very sneaky, but nothing gets by Old Mae." She nods in the direction of the other vendors. "Don't worry—those fools haven't got a clue, and I'm not interested in opening their eyes. Your secret is safe with me."

I manage to find my voice. "Thank you for keeping it secret." I swallow hard. "But how did you know?"

She grins again. "Not much happens in Bryre that gets by me. Just because I deal in flowers doesn't mean I've got my head in the weeds."

"What is this Wizard's Bane?" Ren interrupts. "Do you have it here?"

"Heavens, no. Far too dangerous a thing to carry around." She gulps down the last of her soup and wipes her chin with her apron. "It's difficult to find, but if I get it for you, it will cost you, my dearie."

"I'll pay anything," I say immediately. This time Ren gives me a sharp look. I know what he must be thinking. What if she's just a mad old woman who's an excellent guesser and is making this up for attention? It's possible, but it's a risk I'm willing to take.

My parents said the same thing to the wizard, all those

years ago. And now I offer the same unlimited price to undo the damage done.

She rocks back in her chair and folds her hands over lap. "I thought you might. Come and see me next week. I should have more information then."

"But what does it do, exactly?" Ren asks. "We must know how we're to use it."

She shrugs. "Never used it myself. All I know is that it's said to take away magic. I'll see what more I can find out."

"Thank you," I say as we get up to leave. "We'll be back next week."

"Be careful," she says, waving. "Even the walls have eyes, you know."

Something inside twists at her words. Ren takes my hand again and hurries us toward the crumbling church, my thoughts and fears haunting our every step.

# CHAPTER 3

**SINCE REN CAN TRAVEL FREELY OUTSIDE THE PALACE, THE BORING PART** of the research falls to me. The next day, while Ren is occupied running errands for my father, I venture into the library. Delia insists on coming with me, though I have not told her about the Wizard's Bane. I don't need her tattling to our parents if my plans go south.

Our heels click on the stone tiles as we walk down the hall. The whole host of our ancestors peers down at us from the portraits lining the walls. While Delia has done everything she can to make up for her misstep, she is still reticent around me. She feels terrible, which is the only reason I didn't object to her joining me now. I never meant to make her feel abandoned, and she's right: we haven't spent much time together lately. Hopefully this will be harmless, and boring, but enough to appease her. Mama would be very proud, I'm sure.

The library doors loom before us, carved from thick black oak with silver handles. I open them wide. The library is a rather pretty place, though a rather dusty one too. The trouble will be deciding where to start. Thousands of books line three stories of shelves. Sliding ladders on each level make it easier to get to the books, but finding the place where the ones about plants and biology are stored is the trick. Of course, that's if Wizard's Bane even is a plant at all. But it sounds like one, or perhaps some sort of weapon.

Either way, I must make a choice and start somewhere.

"Are you looking for a novel?" Delia asks. Her eyes are as big as serving plates as she takes in all the books. She rarely comes in here.

I laugh. "No, I am not in the mood for that today."

I head for the catalog table and flip through the catalog, searching for anything related to plants or spells. She trips at my heels. "Then what are you looking for?"

"Plants."

She frowns at me. "Mama doesn't like it when you get all dirty in the garden. She said you've ruined too many gowns that way."

I snort. Mama doesn't like it when I do anything she deems less than befitting a princess. "They were old gowns. It wasn't as though I was going to wear them anywhere else."

She giggles as she runs her hands over the dust on the table. "Why do you like plants so much, anyway?" She frowns. "They seem so . . . dull."

"I like watching something new come to life." I shrug. "It's the discovery. Who knows what lies inside a tiny seed until it sprouts? It's like discovering a secret."

This earns me a big grin. "I like secrets," she says.

I smile back. "I know you do."

"If you share more of them with me, I won't slip and tell Mama and Papa. If I'd known where you were, I'd never have done it." Her eyes water.

"I know, I'm sorry. Next time I'll tell you everything." The lie is bitter in my mouth, but I swallow the taste. I don't know where the hunt for the Wizard's Bane will lead, but I will do anything to keep my sister out of harm's way. Any hint that this will be dangerous, and I intend to shut her out entirely.

"Good." She folds her arms over her chest. "What kind of plant is this?"

I open the listings and scan the pages. "A very special one."

"Is it pretty?"

I frown as the turn of a page puffs dust in my face. "I don't know. I've never seen it."

"Then how do you know it's special?"

I give her a withering look. "Because it is, that's why."

"Let me help," she pleads. I cannot say no to that face. I will tell her some of it, but not all.

"Fine. The plant I'm looking for is called *bano magus* in the old language. It has some special properties."

"Like what?" Delia pulls another catalog toward herself.

"Absorption, for one. And it's a very old plant. You could say its history has roots."

She gives me the side eye, and I wonder how much she actually believes. "What do you use it for?"

"To . . ." I falter. "To absorb things."

"You mean like when the scullery maid spills milk on the floor, she could absorb it quickly with this *bano magus*?"

"Yes, just like that."

Delia smiles and pores over the listings. I am definitely the worst older sister in the entire world.

I shove down the guilt, then begin to search in earnest. I let her review the plants and surreptitiously search for ancient weapons and artifacts as well. The more territory we cover, the faster we'll find it. And Delia doesn't need to know I have an interest in anything other than plants.

I may not know what Wizard's Bane is; I just need to find it before she does.

It takes a good portion of the afternoon, but we manage to scour through more books than we can count. Yet we barely make a dent in the mountain before us. Frustrated, I pace the long rows of the library, wondering if Ren had better luck. I would much rather be out there than stuck in here.

Delia, however, is delighted to be a part of my search, and she's more diligent than I am. She comes up to me at least half a dozen times with possible plants that could be *bano magus*. None of them are, but her efforts are sweet.

I feel even worse that I deceive her.

It's nearly dinnertime when Delia begins to yawn.

"Why don't you take a nap before we have to get ready for supper?" I suggest. Delia gives me a shrewd glance.

"Are you trying to get rid of me?"

"Of course not! You're yawning all over that book."

She closes the tome with a heavy thud. "This one is the most boring of them all," she says, putting her elbow on the book and her chin in her hand. "Why can't you research interesting things?"

I make my way back to her side of the room. "I find them interesting. But you don't have to help if it bores you. I'll find it eventually."

She sticks her chin out. "You're stuck with me."

"And of that I am quite glad."

I tousle her loose yellow curls and take another circuit of the room. I can only stare at those books about swords and stones and staffs so long before my eyes cross.

What a disappointment. The only thing I can say with any reasonable amount of certainty is that I am quite sure Wizard's Bane is not a plant. It is . . . something else.

But what? Weapon? Rock? Animal? Or perhaps a person? I clench my hands in frustration and pace faster.

"I like this room," Delia says, hand still beneath her chin and head tilted to the ceiling. "Even if I could do without all the books."

"Why is that?" I call down to her from the highest tier of the library.

"I can watch the stars all day, even when they're not out. There's something romantic about reading under the stars." She sighs, and I can't help but laugh.

"Is that what the stories say?"

She nods, eyelids drooping, while I pause my pacing to gaze at the ceiling. It is painted in a lovely fresco of stars and constellations, but now that I stand on the highest section of the library, I notice something odd about it. At each of the four points of the room, a compass mark in gold filigree is affixed to the juncture where the wall meets the ceiling. But here on the north side of the library, it is slightly different. Behind the filigree is the faint outline of a rectangle. Just big enough for a person to crawl through.

I suck my breath in sharply and head in another direction. I can't have Delia noticing that, or I'll never hear the end of it. If something's behind there, it won't be a secret for long if she finds out.

I must wait for Ren. I will need help getting up there and someone to keep watch.

A secret space in the library. I am all a-tingle just thinking about it.

Before I reach Delia again, the doors open and a maid steps through. "If it please miladies, the king and queen have asked me to be sure you're ready for dinner."

"Thank you, Molly. We were just heading up to our rooms."

The maid curtsies and leaves, and Delia groans. "Finally! I'm famished."

"Of course you are. Come on." I shut the doors behind us, casting a fleeting glance at the northern compass mark on the ceiling. I make a silent promise to come back tonight.

Ren approaches us as we enter the hall, and Delia greets

him like a brother. "We've been researching all day."

"Find anything?" He speaks to her but looks anxiously at me. I grin behind her back, but only for a second.

"No," she says, scowling. "Just books."

"Imagine that, books in the library." Ren winks and she giggles.

"Go along, get ready for dinner," I say, and to my relief, she runs off toward the stairs.

"What did you find?" Ren asks in a low voice as soon as she's out of earshot. He smells like the warm bread his mother makes.

"I'm not sure. I found something strange on the ceiling. It resembles a door."

"Let's find out." He starts for the library, but I catch his hand and pull him back.

"Wait. Meet me here at midnight. No one will see us then," I say, far too conscious of his pulse under my fingertips. "Did you find anything?" I release his hand in case a servant happens by.

"Nothing new. No one wants to utter a word about magic. The baker closed his cart when he saw me coming near, and I wasn't even going to say a thing to him. Just wanted a strawberry tart." Ren pouts. "Where are you going?"

"Dinner, of course, but first to my garden. It needs watering and I have been cooped up all day."

"I'll help."

"If you like," I say, though I always enjoy having Ren around. And as we reach the safety of the gardens, I do not object when he takes my hand again.

# CHAPTER 4

WHEN THE NIGHT DRAWS ITS CURTAINS AROUND THE CITY, AND MY FAMily has gone to bed, I creep from my room. On light feet, I run to the library in my robe, determined to find out what lies in the ceiling above all those books. Who knows if it can help, but I must satisfy my curiosity.

Mama and Papa were subdued at dinner tonight but still refused to listen to reason. They shut me down when I tried to speak of the wizard. "Not in front of your sister," they said. "You'll scare her."

Haven't they noticed she's already scared? Delia is more observant than any of us give her credit for, which is why I glance behind me every few seconds tonight.

When I reach the huge doors of the library, I hear a soft noise, and Ren's form breaks free from the shadows. He wears a mischievous grin. "Come on," he says, reaching out his hand. I take it.

We creep through the aisles, between the stacks of moldering tomes, then upstairs and around corners. Every inch is packed with the knowledge our kingdom has collected over the centuries.

With all this mess of books out here, what could be behind that door?

When we reach the top level, the last step creaks, echoing off the rafters in the otherwise silent room. Ren and I hold our breath for almost a full minute before deciding no one heard us.

At the northernmost edge of the top level we are faced with another problem.

"How are we going to get up there?" Ren says.

I scan the walkway for a moment. "This," I say, heading for the ladder used to reach the highest shelves. "This should give us the boost we need."

We wheel it over together, positioning it beneath the northern compass point. "Ladies first," Ren says.

Getting to the compass point, a gold filigree star-shaped design, is easier than I thought. Figuring out how to get it to release the panel is more difficult. Pulling and pushing have no effect, and it won't even budge enough to turn. "We're missing something," I say.

"Missing what?"

"I don't know—that's the problem." I tap my fingers on the top of the ladder. "It needs to move for us to get behind there, but it's like it's locked."

"Let me try," Ren says. I come down and he hurries up the ladder in my place. But it's no good. He twists and cajoles with the same result: nothing.

He hops back onto the floor. "You're right—we're missing something."

"I've been thinking," I say slowly. "What could unlock a compass point?"

"Compasses are used for navigation. So perhaps something to do with the ocean?" Ren considers this idea, then his face lights up. "Perhaps the key is hidden in a nautical book of some kind, or a pirate history?"

I straighten up. "Yes! Or maybe even a map?"

Ren takes in the whole of the library—we can see almost every book from our vantage—and groans. "Do you think we'll find the key before dawn?"

I bite my lip. "I hope so."

We get to work, but none of the histories or archived captains' logs shed light on the trouble here in the library. We end up seated on the floor with piles of scrolls and tomes surrounding us. When I sneeze for the seventh time from all the dust, Ren leaps up from his chair. "It can't be a book. Let's try the maps and nautical instruments on the third tier. Or maybe one of the weapons exhibits."

"All right, but how could those things help?"

"I have an idea." Ren heads for the section that holds the maps. I follow, intrigued. "The ceiling is divided as a compass, right?"

"Yes," I say.

"Another navigational tool was a sextant. And that

318

we could find with the antiques . . . if we're lucky," Ren says as we reach the maps. Two whole walls are piled high with them. He handles the maps with great care as he looks through them.

"You've looked at these before, haven't you?" I say.

He glances up, surprised. "I may have snuck in here once or twice before."

Of course he has. Ren and I grew up together, and for a time we even shared a tutor. Papa holds Ren's father in the utmost respect and wanted to be sure his son had a good education. Ren always livened up on days the tutor taught us history, and the oceans and sailing were remotely involved.

"The sea intrigues you," I say.

The edges of Ren's ears turn pink. "It does. I've read everything I can find on the topic. I'd give almost anything to sail the seas one day."

"Perhaps you shall."

"Not today." Ren moves on to the glass cases along the next wall filled with oddities from the ocean and old weapons. I gave these a cursory examination yesterday in hopes one might be Wizard's Bane. It was as fruitless as I expected.

Rusted chain links, a telescope, compasses, a globe, and even an old anchor rest inside. And many, many strange triangular devices—sextants.

"How on earth will we figure out which one?" I grumble.

Ren opens the case and begins to examine them one by one. "Some have rusted through and can't move. I doubt those are the right ones." He studies the compass design in the corner again. "I'd be willing to bet the one we want will match that. Maybe it will be gold, or will have the same filigree design."

Together we pore over the compasses and sextants, seeking something that resembles the ceiling compass. Nothing stands out to me.

But Ren squeaks as he moves aside sextants on the bottom level. "Look, Rosabel!" A faint outline mars the bottom of the shelf, but I'd never have noticed with all the debris on top. Ren pries the paneling on the shelf up carefully, revealing a secret compartment that holds a crumpled map. He frowns as he pulls it out. "Who would do such a thing to a map . . . ?"

A gleaming gold sextant tumbles out of the parchment, but Ren catches it with his nimble hands. Adrenaline ripples through me.

"What do you think it will do?" I ask.

"I hope it's the key we need to unlock that door. If this map is any indication"—he spreads the crumpled paper flat on a table—"then I believe I'm right."

The map isn't of the ocean; it features the night sky. It looks just like the ceiling in the library, right down to the compass points in the four corners. A drawing of the gold sextant lies near the northern compass point.

"Now that is a remarkable likeness," I say, unable to suppress a smile.

We return to the northern corner of the room and this time Ren goes first, scrambling up the ladder, quick as the monkeys we once saw in a traveling caravan. I crane my neck to see while he fiddles with the settings on the sextant. I can't make sense of it, but it clearly means something to him. Then he turns to the compass point where it juts out from the corner. I couldn't get it to budge, but he finds a way to fit the sextant onto it in just the right manner so that it clicks, then gives, and suddenly the panel above swings open.

I start up the ladder and Ren gives me a boost into the opening. I crawl through into a room far larger than I expected. It looks like it spreads across the entire library. Above me is only sky—the ceiling is a glass dome and covered with sparkling dew and stars. This room, too, is full of books. If the ones in the library proper are old, then these are ancient. They fill the shelves with titles on their spines that I can barely understand. A thick layer of dust covers everything. How long has it been since a human set foot in here? Gooseflesh breaks out on my arms.

If any place in the city has the information I need on the Wizard's Bane, this is it.

"Amazing," Ren says behind me.

"What do you think is in here? And who built it?"

"And why?" Ren adds.

Moonbeams stream down and light up the tomes like stars reflected back at the sky from a pond. Did my parents build this room or was it already here? Do they know it exists? And if they do, why have they never told me about it? I'll rule this city one day; shouldn't I know every nook and cranny in my castle?

"I wonder what they thought they needed to hide," Ren muses.

I wander toward the first table and run my fingers through the dust. It puffs, making me sneeze, but by then the cover is half cleared.

*Magi Ministeria.* Wizard's Ministerings.

My heart leaps into my throat. "I know why they hid these books. They're dangerous."

Ren frowns. "What do you mean?"

"These are spell books."

Any question of whether my parents knew about this room vanishes. Mama would faint from fright and then burn the library if she had any inkling these existed, and in our own home.

An awed silence passes over us, just as the moon ducks behind a patch of cloud, abandoning us to the darkness. I shudder. It has been a very long time since magic was forbidden in the realm. We're surrounded by the bones of a magical past. We all know the stories of how wizards came to be, but magic itself is older and even more cunning. One tiny error in a spell and it could go horribly awry. Of course there's hardly any magic hanging about, not like there once was. They say before the dragon riders transformed into wizards, before they became greedy, magic flowed in the waters, whispered in the air currents, and made the soil fertile for exotic plants.

I would have particularly liked to see the last.

"Are they safe to touch?"

I frown. I hadn't considered that. "I think so. Spell books

are just books, after all." I sound more certain of this than I feel. "Besides, not much magic is left to be conjured anyway. You can't just create magic—you have to use what already exists and transform it into a spell."

"A spell and its cost."

A chill runs over my shoulders until the moon sneaks back out from behind the cloud. "Yes, there is always a price."

"I wonder what the price will be for the Wizard's Bane."

"Perhaps I will grow a tail. Would you still like me with a tail?" I try to shove away my fears and twirl around, pretending to have a tail.

Ren guffaws. "A princess with a tail? The commoners would revolt."

I punch him playfully on the arm. "Or perhaps you'll grow another head."

Ren sobers. "What if the price is something terrible? Worse than the wizard at our gates?"

I glance at the books, so well hidden here, probably lost even to my grandparents' memories, and take a deep breath.

"What choice do I have? Waiting under an invisible wizard's thumb is unthinkable." The memory of what Mama said about the wizard being terribly patient comes to mind in a cold rush. "He'll come for me sooner or later. We have to be rid of him once and for all."

Ren sighs, a weary acceptance of things beyond our control. "Let's see if we can find something that will help."

We decide the best possibilities are where we'd normally look last—in other words, the darkest corners of the hidden room. We divide them up and are soon coated in a layer of dust, and frustrated by lack of progress. Books about how to catch a dragon, or the origin of the various hybrid species (a spell gone awry, it turns out), how to make a potion from only mermaid scales, and other assorted useless things are all we can find. Soon the sun begins to peek through the clouds, brightening the dome over this room.

Then, as I am about to give up and call it a night, my hands clasp one small book in the farthest corner. It's bound in black leather with a cover etched with ink that only shows up in the shadows and fading moonlight, becoming invisible when it's struck by the first few rays of sun.

"Wait!" I say. "I think I have something."

*The Origin of Wizards.*

Ren reads over my shoulder just as the last vestiges of ink fade away, leaving only the black cover behind. My fingers tingle. "This one is special—I can feel it," I say. "If it has how they began, perhaps it will include how to end them."

Ren smiles, dust stuck to his chin. "Let's hope so."

I tuck the book into my pocket, and together we leave the hidden room behind.

# CHAPTER 5

MY DREAMS ARE BROKEN BY AN EARTHQUAKE. I REEL BACK INTO THE
pillows, taking in my surroundings.

They include one laughing sister jumping on my bed.

As my pulse slows to a normal pace, I scowl. "What are
you doing, Delia?"

She stops bouncing and her smile fades. "Why are you
so dirty?" she asks.

I glance in the mirror by my dresser and realize I was
exhausted enough that I forgot to wash my face last night. It
still bears the marks of the black dust from the hidden room
in the library. "I had an urge to garden last night and went
out after everyone else was asleep."

She frowns. "Midnight gardening? You are very strange,
Rose."

"What are you doing here?" I sit up, swinging my legs over the edge of my bed.

"It's time for breakfast." She rolls her eyes. "Mama and Papa sent me to get you. You're late, you know."

Heat floods my cheeks. How late did I sleep? How long did we spend in the hidden room? I cannot recall. "Let me get dressed. Tell them I will be there shortly."

Delia curtsies as I frantically search for an appropriate gown. "Don't forget your face." She sticks out her tongue, then disappears into the hallway.

I splash water and lavender soap on my cheeks and scrub until I cannot see any more dust in the mirror. I just hope I don't suffer too close an inspection by our parents. Mama has a knack for noticing even the slightest speck of dirt.

Without waiting for my maid, I throw a dress over my head, tying the sash as I race down the stairs to the dining hall. All I can think is how glad I am that the book is tucked under my mattress. Nowhere else would have been safe from Delia this morning. My thoughts remain with the book more than my family when I reach the breakfast table.

"Rosabel, nice of you to join us at last," Papa says, with a smile that doesn't quite reach his eyes. He is a kind man, but years of fearing the wizard have worn him down, and he is too weary to manage a true smile.

"We hear you had some late-night gardening," Mama says, and I give a sharp look at Delia. She stares at her plate, chasing a piece of bacon with her fork.

"I—yes, I did. I'm trying to get a special new seed to grow. I thought watering them at midnight might help."

The chair squeaks when I pull it out to sit down. "I'll have to see if there's any progress after breakfast."

"Watering plants at midnight?" Mama frowns. "Where would you get an idea like that?"

I smile to cover my uneasiness. "I don't recall. Must have read it in a book, I suppose."

"We spent all day in the library yesterday," Delia says.

"Really?" Papa raises an eyebrow, his suspicion that I'm disobeying them in some way no doubt rising with it.

"Yes, I wanted to know more about the seeds and the plant they'll grow into."

"Which plant?" Mama asks. I squirm in my chair, placing a biscuit next to the eggs on my plate.

"Crown-of-Roses. Ren brought me the seeds, but they're quite stubborn."

My parents exchange a glance, and Delia's mouth—open to speak—snaps closed. She looks as though she's swallowed a rotten egg. I'd almost forgotten I told her another name yesterday.

"Never heard of those," Mama mutters.

"Well," I say, scrambling for something believable, "they are rare."

Truth, or at least part of it.

"Did you find what you were looking for, sister?" Delia stabs a piece of egg.

"Not yet. I'm still looking." I turn to Papa. "When was the library built? Some of those books are very old, and I wondered where they came from."

Surprise lights Papa's eyes. I have not always shown

much interest in the library or history, but today it is my favorite subject.

He chews thoughtfully before answering. "The room housing the books was built by King Henler, well over two hundred years ago. Many royal families since then have used it and added their own knowledge to it."

"Is there . . . is there anything dangerous in there?" I clear my throat. "I mean, there are a huge amount of books, and many other things in nooks and crannies."

Papa frowns. "I'm not sure I catch your meaning, my dear."

Mama, on the other hand, does, and she bristles. "You mean books about magic." She throws her napkin down. "If that is what you seek, you shall be disappointed. Once the wizards began to make a nuisance of themselves, Bryre's king had the good sense to clear all those books out."

"Too much temptation, you see," Papa adds. "Besides, now there isn't any magic to be conjured. Even if they did exist, they'd be of little use. All the magic that once was has been sucked out of the land by the wizards, and now they take it from each other." He shakes his head. "It is a sad, messy business, magic."

Something icy radiates from the base of my spine. "Good thing then they got rid of all those books." I cover by beaming at Delia. "That means I have nothing to worry about if Delia helps me in my research again."

Mama doesn't appear convinced, but Papa seems quite happy with my words. "Good—I am glad to hear you are educating yourself. It will serve you well later on, when you rule this city."

328

"Though you would do well to read up on history, too," Mama says. "Gardening will not get you far when you are queen."

I swallow. I've been ducking my tutor lately. Mama must have caught on to that. Maxwell isn't the brightest, but he certainly does drone on about history.

"Of course, Mama. I want to ensure my education is as broad as possible." My education would be helped considerably by being allowed to leave the palace, but I bite my tongue. I fall back into idle chatter instead. Before long, breakfast is over and Delia and I are dismissed.

I want nothing more than to head back to my room and read the book hidden under my mattress. Delia, however, has other ideas.

She stops me outside the dining hall and folds her arms over her chest. "What are Crown-of-Roses?"

I do my best not to flinch at my lie. "They're the same as the *bano magus*, just a newer name, that's all."

Delia frowns, but the set of her shoulders relaxes. "Are you going to the library again today?" she asks hopefully.

I shake my head. "I must study. Maxwell gave me a lot to read last week, and I've been putting it off."

She pouts. "Then what am I going to do all day?"

I pinch her arm playfully. "Why don't you try doing your own lessons, hmm? Mama would be proud. Aren't you supposed to have lessons with Maxwell today, anyway?"

"I'd rather hunt for the *bano magus* or Crown-of-Roses or whatever they are."

"If you must, but I won't be accompanying you today."

329

"Fine." She stomps off down the corridor in a most unprincessly fashion, and I smother my laugh for fear she will hear.

I duck down the hall and into my room, locking the door behind me. The book is in my hands in seconds. The black cover shows no sign of a title in the sunlight, but the moonlit one is still imprinted on my memory. *The Origin of Wizards.*

Yes, I do believe this will contain the information I need.

I draw the curtains across the windows, blocking out the sun.

The pages shimmer when I open it. As long as I keep the pages out of direct sunlight, the ink shows up nearly as well as in the moonlight. I settle into a chair, tuck my legs underneath me, and begin to read.

The knock on my door rips me from the pages that have held my full attention for longer than I expected. With hurried hands, I shove the book back under the mattress, smooth my skirts, and open the door.

Ren's smile and freshly-baked-bread scent greet me.

I shoo him inside and shut the door, locking it from the inside. I am jumpier than usual. The last chapter I read was about how wizards can enthrall humans and force them to do their will. Usually the humans do not even know what they have done. The enchantment makes them forget.

"Have you found anything in the book?" he asks.

"Yes, much, in fact." We settle onto the window seat

together, our knees touching. His eyes glitter with curiosity. "The Wizard's Bane is not a plant. It is an ancient stone that absorbs magic. It is rumored that these stones were coughed up by the first volcano, then hoarded by fire dragons ever since."

The spark in his eyes fizzles out. "But there are no more dragons. The wizards got them all."

"That is the tricky part," I say, sighing. "That and finding a volcano."

"And getting into said volcano without being burned alive." Ren pushes off the window seat, frustration all over his face. I catch his hand on reflex and twine my fingers with his. Gooseflesh breaks out on my skin.

"Don't get discouraged yet. I was thinking it might be time to ask Old Mae. Perhaps she has heard something by now. Was she there when you went to market yesterday?"

Ren shakes his head.

"We must find her and ask her as soon as possible."

A mischievous smile creeps over Ren's face. "You want to sneak out again today, don't you?"

"More than anything, but we must be extra careful. Delia has been nipping at my heels."

"Then we should get moving before your sister realizes you're missing." He pulls me up, and we sneak through the halls into the back garden.

"Wait—I want to check on my Crown-of-Roses seeds." Together we enter the maze of hedges and wander to the hidden plot in the center. The sunflowers on the eastern side reach higher every day, and now they peek over the tops of the hedges. Sunlight paints the petals of my roses a pale gold and pink, and the morning glories stretch in their daily ritual, blooming blue and bright. Everything is bursting with life—except the small patch of dirt where I planted the Crown-of-Roses.

"Nothing." I frown at the brown spot marring the rest of my green garden.

"They must be duds," Ren says. "The old woman gave you bad seeds. That's the only answer. Everything else has at least sprouted."

"Perhaps they require more time below ground than most." I'm not convincing myself, but it seems to work for Ren.

"Let's ask. If they need special care, she should've said so when you bought them."

We leave the garden behind for the old fountain and the passage it hides. I keep a constant eye out for Delia and listen for shouts from servants who may be looking for me. Mama would be so disappointed if she knew I was breaking her rules yet again, but I must.

"Do you think the king and queen will check up on you?" Ren asks.

I bite my lip. "I fear they will. Mama was especially suspicious at breakfast. I had to tell Delia I did some midnight gardening to explain the black dust on my nose."

"Midnight gardening?" Ren laughs.

I try not to join him. "Mama didn't approve." I sigh. "I hadn't even read the book yet."

"Delia's determined to know everything you do. She looks up to you."

332

I twist my hands as we reach the old fountain. "I know, I know. And I love her dearly. But she can't keep a secret like we need her to. Maybe when she's a little older we can take her to the market with us."

Ren moves the cherub's arm and the passage opens. "Only if your parents don't lock you in your tower for good first."

I give him a weary glance. "That isn't funny."

His face is grave for a moment too long. "No, it isn't. But if they get desperate enough, I wouldn't put it past them. Desperate people do crazy things. That's how you got into this whole mess in the first place."

"Don't remind me."

I grow silent and sullen until we step out of the church and into the sunshine of the market. Perhaps I am part plant—I need sunlight to flourish. Hiding me in the dark will only make me wither and die. If only I could make my parents understand that.

"There she is." Ren points to the familiar shape of the flower-and-plant cart.

The old woman sits on her stool, humming and tapping her fingers along to a melody only she can hear. When she sees us, she waves.

"Good afternoon, my dearies," she says. "What brings you back today? Already looking for new seeds, hmmm?" She grins and one crooked tooth hangs out over her bottom lip.

"Not today. We wondered"—I steal a glance at Ren—"if you learned anything more about the Wizard's Bane. We may have found something, but I'm not sure it's possible to pursue."

She raises a gray eyebrow and rocks back and forth. "Oh my, no, I haven't heard much. Slipped my mind, really. It's like a sieve these days."

I fend off my disappointment with another question. "We found something in the castle. A book with a title that only shows up in moonlight."

I had hoped for a reaction, but she just blinks, waiting for me to continue. "I read it—well, most of it—and found a reference to Wizard's Bane. The book says the stones originated in volcanoes and can absorb a wizard's magic. It also says that fire dragons hoarded them, and they could only be found in their lairs, which are hidden deep in volcanoes."

"That does pose a problem, doesn't it?" she says. "Fire dragons have been extinct for a hundred years at least. They were one of the first breeds to go."

I sigh. "I was afraid you might say that. Do you think one of the Wizard's Bane stones might still be around, though? We'd hoped you might know where we could find a fire dragon's lair."

"One we won't die trying to reach," Ren adds.

The old woman's eyes brighten with mischief. "You're going to sneak out of Bryre, are you? Oooh, the king will be hopping mad!" She jumps around on one foot, puzzling Ren and me exceedingly. She claps her hands together. "I may know just the thing, though no guarantees the Wizard's Bane will be there." She leans closer and whispers. "To the south, at the far end of the mountain range, is another country. I've heard a dead volcano rests there. It spewed up the whole range to begin with long, long ago. If any Wizard's Bane remains in this region, you'll find it there."

"Is it far?" I ask, while Ren shakes his head.

She shrugs. "A journey of a day or two, maybe more. Who knows who you might meet on the way." She winks.

"What do you mean?" Ren says.

"Did you think the wizard wouldn't be looking for you?" Old Mae's eyes shine in a way I don't like at all.

"People say the wizard ran off to some faraway place," I say. Everyone except my parents, that is. They fear he hovers at the edges of our lives.

Mae grins toothily. "They're wrong. But I can give you something that will help you stay undetected. You'd like that, yes?"

Ren and I exchange a look. "What is it?" I ask.

"Come with me." She motions for me to follow her down the alley behind her cart. "I'll show you."

I hesitate, then follow her. It's just Old Mae. I know her.

When Ren follows too, she stops. "Only the girl. Remain where you are, boy." Her tone is surprisingly harsh.

"What? Not a chance, I—"

"It's all right, Ren," I tell him. "We'll be back in just a minute, right?"

She nods, silver hair swirling around her face and making her seem more wild than ever.

Ren starts to say something, but then he frowns and heads back to wait at the stall. Mae takes my arm, her paper-like fingers wrapping around my elbow. It gives me the chills, which is foolish. What harm could a mere old woman do?

Ren watches us like a hawk until we round a corner in the alley. The bricks are dark and coated with soot. Public houses and shops lie beyond the walls. The faint smell of something burning lingers here, but I don't see where it comes from.

"Where are we going?" I ask.

Old Mae clucks at me but doesn't offer an answer. I begin to wonder if Ren is right to worry, when she stops at a section of wall covered by enough soot that I can barely see the door she opens. She pulls a vial from her pocket and waves it in front of my face. "See this, dearie? It's made from a special plant. If you drink it, the wizard won't know you're out and about in the hills." She giggles. "But this isn't enough for both of you, nor for the time it will take to get there and back." She gestures to the darkness beyond the door. "There's more in there. Go on in and fill your pockets. That should do the trick."

As I stare down the darkness, an odd feeling of panic trickles over me. I squint and tilt my head, yet I can see nothing beyond the door. "What does the plant extract do exactly?" I ask.

"It dampens your signature, your unique life force. The wizard has you in his sights, that's for sure. He just can't reach you in Bryre."

The chill turns to a ball of ice. How does Old Mae know so much about the wizard? She never mentioned him in all the times we spoke before until recently. I can't help thinking of the passage I read this morning about unwitting humans under the thrall of the wizard. Something feels very wrong here. Could that something be Old Mae?

"Will there be any side effects?"

Old Mae cackles. "Beats me, dearie. Never taken the stuff. I only know it works."

"How?"

She grins so wide, I can see every speck of blackened gums between her teeth. "Do you think you're the only one who's ever crossed the wizard? Other people have had to hide on occasion, princess." She hisses on the word, and it chills me. "Go on, get the vials in there. You'll need them."

The sun moves behind a cloud, casting more darkness into the alley. "Have you ever met the wizard? Do you know what he looks like?"

"Get the vials, princess," she growls.

"I don't think I should go in there." The blackness seems to expand, like it wants to swallow me whole. Her aged hand tightens on my elbow.

"But you must," she says. "I am too old to bend over and lift them for you." I try to wrench my arm free, but she's startlingly strong. She places a hand on my back and pushes me toward the doorway. I thrash and twist, trying my best to get free of her iron grip. The odd behavior, the burst of strength—Old Mae must be in the wizard's thrall. Is it my fault this happened to her, or was she under his sway all along?

"Release me!" I shout.

"Tsk, tsk," she says. "None of that. In you go."

I dig my heels in to the alleyway dirt. "What's really in

there?" I am certain there are no helpful potions waiting for me. Only darkness and danger.

She laughs. "You'll find out in a moment." A crack resounds in the alley; then her face contorts from shock to anger to slack. She stumbles, releasing her grip.

Ren stands behind her, holding a flower pot, now cracked, and watches as she sinks to the ground unconscious.

"I knew she couldn't be trusted," he says. "It was too odd that she wanted you alone."

"Thank you," I say, shivering. I liked Old Mae. She seemed so harmless, but that's what happens when someone is enchanted. They seem normal until the wizard wants to use them. I rub the spot on my arm. I suspect it will bruise. This is a lesson I shall not forget.

"Let's go." Ren tugs at my hand.

We hurry back to the market, but I can't help looking over my shoulder now and then. The door she opened has completely vanished. It must have been magic.

I don't want to think ill of the old woman I thought was my friend, but I don't believe I'll ever return to the market. Not if she might be lurking here.

I still shake by the time we reach the tunnel, and Ren stops me once we're inside. "Rose," he says quietly. "Are you all right?"

I clench my fists at my sides. "I am not all right, and I'll never be all right until that wizard is out of our lives for good." I release a quivering breath. "Old Mae must be involved with him somehow, either willingly or under his thrall. I was a fool to trust her." Perhaps my parents have more reason to be afraid than I'd like to admit.

My garden—my precious garden—is now tainted by association with that woman. But it isn't the fault of the plants. I'll care for them even so.

"I trusted her too," Ren says. "I introduced you to her."

"We'll simply have to figure things out on our own." I stand up straighter. "I have faith those books can shed more light on things for us." I'll throw myself completely into the one I took when we get back.

Soon we exit into the garden. One of my rosebushes— the blush one—is in full bloom, and I pick a couple of flowers for Delia as a peace offering. However, when I get to her room, she isn't there.

Warning bells go off in my head. Where could she be? She should have been studying all morning with Maxwell.

I groan and stomp out of her room. I hope she didn't go looking for me again. After this morning, the last thing I need is a panicky little sister.

I march down the halls, racking my brain for where Delia might be. A peek out the windows reveals she is not in the maze in the back of the palace; a glance out the opposite side shows she is not out front, either. Perhaps she's in the music room.

My steps slow. I've been neglecting my younger sister. We used to play music together all the time. I would play harpsichord, and she would sing. Sometimes one of us would take a turn at the harp.

First my garden grew between us, now my festering

obsession with stopping the wizard. Yet I cannot stop trying. Mama and Papa gave up their efforts to stop him years
ago. I snort. Unless you count hiding me away.

I do not.

Their problem was that they were so blinded by fear
that they would not resort to magic. They feared that would
mean another wizard, another person who would deceive
them. I suppose I cannot blame them too much, but I am
determined to find an alternative to hiding.

They may have kept me alive this long, but it is hardly
a life at all.

I make my way to the music room. I'm not ready to
consider that Delia could be with Mama and Papa.

When I enter, she sits at the harpsichord, picking out
a mournful tune. She doesn't glance up, not even when I
stop in front of the instrument and place my hands on the
instrument.

"Delia." I say softly.

She pounds on the keys a little harder.

"Is something wrong?"

This time she slams the lid of the harpsichord, nearly
catching my fingers. She moves to the harp. The light
streaming through the windows makes her appear positively
angelic as she sits down.

My heart sinks in my chest. I hope she didn't do something very bad for me.

I stride over to her and pluck her hand away from the
strings, holding it firmly in mine.

"Delia, why are you acting like this? What has made you so angry?"

She cannot hide her scowl as she yanks her hand from my grasp. She returns to playing the harp.

"Maxwell taught me a section on plants today. I asked him if he had ever heard of a *bano magus.*"

I suck my breath in sharply. I never should've told her that lie. Stupid, stupid me.

"Maxwell says it is no plant he has ever heard of, and definitely doesn't mean Crown-of-Roses. In fact, he says the term means something else—something you didn't mention." Her eyes turn to mine, glaring. "He says it means Wizard's Bane."

I stare numbly out the window, watching the hedges rustle in the warm afternoon breeze. Sometimes it makes the creatures carved in the hedge seem to dance.

"Then you understand why I didn't tell you."

She shoots up, knocking over the bench. "No, I do not. Why don't you trust me?"

Anger ripples through me. "Why must you insist on knowing every single thing I do? Why can't you worry about your own life?"

I ball my fists in my skirts. I regret the words even though they are barely out of my mouth.

Tears well up in Delia's eyes. "Because you're my sister, and I'm scared I'm going to lose you." She runs from the room. I start to follow, but I know she doesn't want me to. How can I expect her to respect my need for privacy when I can't respect hers? Taking a seat on the harpsichord bench,

I rest my head on the lid.

It's an unpleasant business, but my choice is to either shut her out, or let her in entirely. She won't agree to half measures and half-truths.

Worse, she knows my secrecy has something to do with the wizard.

After almost getting kidnapped or drugged or who knows what by Old Mae, I need rest. Then I'll be able to make sense of this, and a sensible decision.

Unless, of course, Delia has already told Mama and Papa. I just pray she has not.

# CHAPTER 6

FOR THE SECOND DAY IN A ROW, A COMMOTION WRENCHES ME FROM slumber.

"Rosabel! Wake up!" Delia pelts my door with furious knocks. This time, I made a point of locking it. But I spent the evening with nightmares and little sleep from sneaking into the library, so I am more groggy than usual.

"Hold on," I mutter, pulling my robe over my nightgown and rubbing the sleep from my eyes. The flagstones are cold beneath my feet, odd for the summer, and they send a chill rippling over my body.

I open the door and find Delia and Ren in the hall. Fear grips my chest at the expressions on their faces. "What happened?"

Delia bursts into tears and launches herself into my arms.

What inspired her to forgive me already? I pat her back and give Ren a questioning look. He swallows hard.

"The guards," he whispers. "All the guards who were on watch at the city gates last night—at least twenty—they're all dead."

"All of them?" I cling to Delia a little tighter as she sobs again. Ren nods. "But how?"

He shakes his head. "I don't know. The court physician is examining them now, but there were no visible wounds. Poison, maybe?"

"Or magic," Delia says with a shiver.

I will not admit it to my sister, but I fear she is right. The wizard may not be as far away as I've always believed. If so, Ren and I must redouble our efforts to find the Wizard's Bane. If he can get to the guards inside the walls, who can say how far his reach extends? After all, while the wards may keep out those who wish to harm Bryre, they belong to the wizard. If anyone could find a way to nullify them, it's him.

I take my sister by the shoulders. "Delia, listen to me. Go to your room and stay there. Only come out for us or Mama and Papa, all right?"

Tears brim in her eyes. "Why? What will you be doing?"

"We're just going to see what we can find out about the guards. I need you to be safe." We must locate the Wizard's Bane, but I can't tell her I plan to leave the castle again. This time I don't know how long I'll be gone. I have every intention of breaking my promise to my parents and leaving the safety of Bryre far behind.

344

"Let me come with you," she pleads. I can't bear to look her in the face.

"We can't. They could be contagious. I won't put you in any danger."

"You can't keep leaving me in the dark!" she cries.

"Taking you would put you at risk. Don't you understand I need you to be safe?"

Delia's lower lip quivers, but finally she nods. She isn't happy with me, but I'm relieved she stopped fighting me on the matter.

We walk Delia as far as her room, then shut the door securely behind her. Knowing she is safe in there makes me feel much better.

"You're planning something, aren't you?" Ren says as we hurry down the halls.

"Am I that transparent?"

"What's the plan?"

I take his hand in mine. It shakes as much as my own. "I'm going to look for the Wizard's Bane at its source. You don't have to come with me. But I could use your help."

Ren's face pales. "You mean you're going into the mountains to find the volcano?"

"What other choice is there? The dead guards must be the wizard's work. We have to do something, and nothing in Bryre can help. We've done all we can from here. The only thing left to do is find the Wizard's Bane."

Last night, when all the palace was asleep, I snuck back into the library's secret room, but I found nothing more to aid us against the wizard. But I did find a map that confirmed Old Mae's assertion that a volcano lies a couple of days' journey away.

"Then I'm definitely coming with you. I know some of the trails. I can at least guide us as far as the river. And I'm a good tracker."

I squeeze his hand. "Thank you."

As we march down the hall, Ren asks, "When do you want to leave?"

"As soon as possible." My head spins with plans and preparations that need to be made, and in utter secrecy. "But first I want to see the guards."

"You want to see their bodies?" Ren chokes.

"I need to know what we're up against. I need to see his handiwork up close."

"It isn't pretty."

"I never expected it would be." I take the stairs two at a time. Ren matches my speed and we reach the lower level of the palace in no time. "Where are they? The infirmary?"

He nods and leads the way, but we're stopped by a procession of skittish guards escorting an upset farmer. Something more must have happened. Surely the dead soldiers aren't going anywhere. They head for the throne room, but Ren and I linger outside. We can hear Mama and Papa questioning the farmer.

"What trouble brings you here this early?" Papa asks. His voice sounds weary already, and this man is merely the first to seek the king's counsel this morning.

"Sire, someone has stolen my herd of goats."

"Who do you accuse?"

The man coughs. "I . . . I don't know. Last night, I locked them in their pen. This morning, they were gone. No trace at all. No footsteps or wagon-wheel tracks. Just . . . gone."

Gone? An entire herd of goats vanished?

I can only think of one person who could pull of a stunt like that—the wizard. But what could the wizard possibly want with a herd of goats?

"No trace at all?" Mama says from inside the throne room.

"None. Their milk was my livelihood. I need them back. Please help me find them. A search party, anything."

"We are . . . short on guards at the moment." Uneasiness taints Papa's voice. "But we can find a few to comb the forest. If the goats ran there, we shall find them."

"Thank you, sire."

The guards escort the man out, and we hold our breath until they pass. The sound of my parents talking reaches us.

"I fear what this means, Aria," Papa says. "An entire herd of goats missing. And now the guards."

"What could be next?" Mama says.

"That is precisely what concerns me."

"I think we both know who is behind this."

I freeze at my mother's words.

"I won't let him have her," Papa says. "I don't care if he destroys this whole kingdom, Rosabel must stay out of his reach."

A tight knot forms in the pit of my stomach. The entire kingdom is in danger because of me. Because my parents refused to give me up and pay the price they promised. I can't sit idly by while all of Bryre suffers for their mistake.

I'm the problem, and I'll do something to fix it. My resolve to find the Wizard's Bane solidifies.

Mama may not want me to take any action, but she raised me too well. I will be queen one day—I must protect my city.

Ren touches my hand, startling me out of my thoughts. "Do you still want to see the guards?" he asks.

"Yes."

We tiptoe away from the throne room. When we reach the infirmary, we wait until the doctor leaves, then sneak inside. Everyone, it seems, is more on edge than usual. Like something unpleasant lurks around the corner.

The room is very hot, probably because the fires burn steadily despite the summer heat. Odd, but I can't pretend to know the ways of medics.

Light spills in through the infirmary windows, casting an odd sheen on the guards' faces. Not a single wound mars any of them. It feels as though something squeezes around my chest as we approach the nearest one. Ren puts a hand on my shoulder.

"You don't need to do this."

"Yes, I do. If this is the wizard's work, then it's my fault."

Ren turns me around to face him, his hands gripping my elbows. "It is not your fault. You can't think that way. You are not responsible for your parents' decisions."

"I know," I say. "But I must do what I can to remedy them."

He releases my arms and I examine the nearest guard.

He is so still, and pale, and oddly serene. The sheen I thought was light is something else. Some kind of residue clings to his skin. Swallowing my fear, I reach out and touch his cheek—then quickly draw my hand back.

It isn't a sheen at all.

"What's wrong?" Ren asks.

"He's frozen. That shine on him—it's ice." Understanding shivers through me. This is why the medics have the fires going down here. They're trying to thaw the bodies.

"What a horrid way to go," Ren says. "It hasn't melted a bit. It really is the wizard's doing."

"I've seen enough," I say.

I hurry from the room, desperate to get away from the overwhelming heat and the frozen bodies. In the hallway, I lean against the wall and breathe. Ren's concern is clear, and his fears mirror mine.

All doubt of what I must do is gone.

Maybe, when I am back home and we are free of the wizard, Mama will even be proud. Once she recovers from her fury.

Smoothing my skirts, I start back up the stairs. "I'm going to prepare. Meet me in the garden at sundown."

Without another word, I run for my rooms.


My flight is swift, and I reach my room and close the door behind me. I gasp when I find my mother seated in the chair by my window.

"Rosabel, where have you been?" Her pretty face is marred by a frown.

"I—I was just in the library, studying with Ren."

"With Ren?" She looks at me strangely. "Take care with that boy's heart. And your own. You know you will one day marry a prince. Do not get too attached to the servants."

A sickly, guilty feeling wallows in my stomach. "Did you come here to lecture me about my choice of friends?"

She smiles sadly and steps forward to take my hands. "No, Rosabel, I did not. I came here to warn you. The wizard, he . . . he hurt many of our guards last night. He is closer than ever. I am not sure it is safe for you to wander the castle and grounds freely right now. Your father and I have decided that you must remain in your rooms until we've determined this threat has passed, and you're only to come out for dinner. You can study here."

"But—"

"Don't worry. We will have the gardener take care of your precious flowers. I know how you dote on them." She pulls me to her, the silk of her dress brushing against my cheek. "I hope it won't be for long. Now that we have told you everything, we are trusting you to understand and to obey. We must keep you safe."

Tears burn the backs of my eyes. "But what if there is another way? What if we could find magic to fight magic and—"

"Do not speak of such things." Horror crawls over my mother's face. "You do not know what you say. You do not know what magic can do." She shudders. Her voice is low and frightened now. "You have never been bewitched. You have been shielded from it your whole life. There is no good, no help to be found in that route."

Realization dawns on me with a prickling chill. "You were bewitched?"

She wraps her shawl around her shoulders a little tighter. "Once. I told you how I almost married the wizard when he was posing as a strange prince. That was no accident, and certainly not due to any true feelings on my part. Before I knew him for what he was, when he sought my hand, he cast a love spell on me. I could never quite remember the things he said when we were together, only that I needed to be near him and could think of nothing else when he was away. Thank heavens I had already fallen for your father before I met Barnabas, or I would have lost my soul to the wicked man. Magic is not something to trifle with."

I frown. "What do you mean?"

"Legends say the only thing that can break the bonds of a love spell is true love, and I can attest to that. When your father returned to my country as a newly crowned king, one look from him was all it took to bring me back to my senses. To break the spell." Her face darkens. "But for weeks, I was in the wizard's thrall. I could do nothing of my own to gain my freedom—I didn't even know I needed to. Once free of it, I could hardly understand why I had been so obsessed with him. It made no sense to me, not until years later." Mama's agitation rises, and she paces my room. "I could have been lost to him. I might have even given him the firstborn he needed to work his terrible spell." She stops directly in front of me, her face twisted with revulsion. I take a step back. "Do you want to know the worst part? I

351

would have handed over my child and let him sacrifice it gladly. I would not have known what I was doing. That is what playing with magic will get you. It is never, ever worth the price."

Shock roots me to the spot. I cannot muster the breath to utter a single word until Mama has swept out of the room. When she told me her tale of how the wizard wooed her before, I did not fully understand. But now I do. She was in his thrall, just like Old Mae. She experienced wicked magic firsthand. What could it have been like for her to be nothing more than a puppet for the wizard to play with?

Clarity dawns like wiping cobwebs off an old tapestry after a long winter. This is why Mama hates and fears magic so much. For my sake, yes, but also for her own.

I shudder. What price will be in store for me if I find the Wizard's Bane?

Dusk comes and goes far too fast. I hardly have the chance to put everything together before it is time to leave, even though I stay in my rooms, just to avoid suspicion. Outside my rooms, the palace is abuzz with whispering servants. Paranoia rules the day, and my parents are more protective than ever. True to their word, they again attempt to keep me in my room after dinner, even taking my key, but I learned long ago how to pick the lock from the inside.

Now I wait for Ren in my garden. The sad little plot where I planted the Crown-of-Roses seeds still lies barren. No matter how much I water and plead, they refuse to sprout. It vexes me. No plant has resisted at least sprouting before.

My pack contains clothes, a cloak, and two canteens of water—one for me and one for Ren. I swiped a plain gray serving girl's gown from the laundry room when the laundress had her back turned. It's a little big, but it will keep me from sticking out.

Before long Ren appears, carrying a bag—provisions from the smell of it. I smile. I can always count on Ren to think of the food.

"Are you sure you want to do this?" he asks.

I nod. Then together we head into the fountain passage and leave the palace grounds.

By midnight we've made camp deep in the woods. I've never been this far from home in my life. I wonder how long until my parents realize I'm gone.

The forest should hide us well. The trees are old and wide, with thick branches reaching high into the clouds. It was pretty as we fled, but now that the night thickens around us, I grow uneasy. Before I could see down the paths through the moss and foliage, but now the darkness is a wall obscuring everything beyond our fire.

What if the wizard is out there tonight, hunting for me? I shiver and shove the thought down. If he did find me, maybe he would leave my city alone. But what would that do to Mama? Her tale is still fresh in my mind.

The firelight teases Ren's hair. I hope he doesn't get into too much trouble for helping me. I swallow the lump of guilt lodged in my throat. It's for the good of Bryre. Surely that can be excused. If we succeed.

Ren hands me the bread he's toasted on the fire. It tastes delicious—but different from the usual palace fare.

I lie back and watch the moon shimmering through the trees from above, feeling a freedom that has eluded me my entire life in spite of the things that may hide in the darkness.

"I think I love the forest," I say. "I wish we were here for happier reasons."

Ren stares at the fire. "You know, you don't have to go back. We could run away. Get as far from Bryre and the wizard as possible."

I let myself consider that life for one precious, fleeting moment. Then I sink back into reality. "I can't. Bryre has suffered enough for me already."

Ren tosses a leaf into the fire. "It isn't fair that you have to pay for your parents' mistakes."

I shrug. Even if I agree, it doesn't change a thing. Mama's words haunt me. I'm a princess; Ren is a servant. Running away with him, even when this is over, is impossible.

"They're my family. Bryre is my kingdom, my home. I can't leave everything I love behind."

The sudden shock of hurt in Ren's eyes startles me, but I don't correct him. I didn't mean it like that, but perhaps it's for the best if he thinks so. Ren nods, then pulls up his bedroll and turns over so he no longer faces me. My heart sinks. I did hurt his feelings.

I curl up in my own bedroll and drift off into sleep.

⟡

In the middle of the night, I find myself suddenly awake, unsure of what pulled me from slumber. All I know is that my heart races, and shadows cling to every tree in sight.

I hold my breath, glancing over at Ren. He remains undisturbed.

That's when I hear it again.

*Hoo, hoo, hoooooo.*

A shiver dances up my spine.

Something rustles between the trees, but I can't make out what it is. Then the cry comes again from the other side of our grove. It sounds like an owl, but they're solitary creatures and no flapping of wings betrayed its movement. More rustling. Fear wraps its icy fingers around my chest.

*Hoo, hoo, hooooooo.*

This time it comes from the trees directly behind me, and I'm certain it is from the ground, not up in the trees like it ought to be. I huddle under my bedroll, hoping whatever it is will move along and find some other travelers to harass. Yet I can't help peeking when the moon comes out from behind a cloud.

Between the trees, not ten paces away, sits a creature. Its owl head tilts as it settles back on its haunches. A furry tail, striped like a raccoon's, curls around its body.

I blink several times. I must be dreaming. This is all a nightmare.

I rub my eyes, and this time when I open them, it has vanished.

# CHAPTER 7

WHEN DAWN WAKES US, WE HEAD OUT AFTER A QUICK BREAKFAST OF dried fruit and cheese. We have no time to waste; my parents will have sent a search party after us by now.

A vague memory of the night before haunts me. What I think I saw is impossible. It must have been a dream. No trace of either owl or raccoon remained when we left the camp.

It takes us most of the day to reach the mountain range. I'm worn out and my feet are peppered with blisters. I refuse to complain. This may not be what I'm accustomed to, but it was my decision to come here, and I don't want to be a burden. Besides, I made a point of packing several stalks of aloe from my garden, which should soothe those blisters in no time once we make camp.

According to the map I brought from the library, the volcano is to our south, right along the border to our neighboring kingdom, Mabori. Hopefully it's inactive, as the map and Old Mae suggest. If not, this may be a shorter trip than we anticipated. Returning home to Mama's wrath without a solution is unthinkable.

Ren has spoken only a few words to me since our conversation last night. I suffer his silence. As Mama said when she scolded me, someday we must accept that we're worlds apart. But he is my best friend. I cannot give him up yet.

The closer we get to the volcano, the warmer the air becomes. The plant life becomes more green and viney than the usual forest trees. The strange new colors and shapes fascinate me. Perhaps we will find what we seek after all. Legend says that the fire dragons hoarded the Wizard's Bane . . . until the wizards drove them to extinction. What would it be like to meet one of those majestic creatures in person? Would it gobble us up in a single bite, or would it be the wise creature I imagine? It was said they sprang from the volcano itself, obsidian scales with real flames smoldering beneath and lava flowing in their veins.

Surely they were a sight to behold.

Another thing the wizards ruined.

Soon the forest thins to rocky terrain, and Ren and I cautiously pick our way over it toward the volcanic mountain. It smokes lightly in the distance, and I expect we'll reach it by dusk. Then it is just a matter of finding the dragon's hoard and figuring out which is the Wizard's Bane.

Easy, yes?

"Do you think it's still dormant?" I ask.

Ren looks a little queasy. "The closer we get, the less certain I become. I didn't expect an inactive volcano to smoke like that."

I shiver despite the heat. "That's what I was afraid of."

"We'll have something to cook on without going to the trouble of building a fire," Ren says with a lopsided grin. I can't help but laugh.

"That is one way of looking at it."

The afternoon goes on and so do we. My mind drifts back to Bryre. My family must be tearing their hair out with worry after finding the note I left them. And no doubt combing the forest for any sign of me and Ren by now. Delia wouldn't be able to guess where we're headed from our adventure in the library, but she could tell our parents what we seek.

"How do you think we'll use the Wizard's Bane when we find it?" Ren asks.

"I have an inkling or two."

Ren raises an eyebrow.

I laugh. "I brought a couple more books with me from the secret library," I say.

"That's why your pack is so heavy." Ren snorts.

"I took *The Art of Casting*, *The Origin of Wizards*, and *Arcane Defenses*. They looked the most promising."

"We'll have to read them tonight."

"My thoughts exactly."

We grin at each other and I hope he has forgiven me, at least a little bit.

When we stop to camp at night, the heat is overwhelming and will likely rule out sleep entirely. But rest we must.

We lay our bedrolls out on the new, strange terrain. The landscape is mostly devoid of trees now, which makes me feel exposed. The ground is no longer soft earth, but has changed to what looks like a black stone river. Pieces of basalt shift underfoot in other sections, but this one was the most solid. And not far away lies the volcano. The top is a beacon in the night sky that fills me with both hope and dread.

"Not much I can do about foraging tonight," Ren says. He riffles through his pack. "We have a few pieces of bread, and one hunk of cheese left."

"No more of that jerky?" I ask.

"I finished that off last night," he says. "I didn't realize it would be so uninhabitable here." We glance around.

"We do have water, still, yes?" I ask.

Ren nods and relief fills me. "I filled the canteens at every river and stream we've passed."

"Good thinking."

Ren beams.

After we tire of reading the old books on magic, we attempt to sleep, but the heat keeps me tossing and turning for hours. I rest only in fits and starts, and the few dreams I have are plagued by glowing red eyes and huge black beasts.

My imagination gets the best of me, leaving me wide

awake and shivering in the darkness. Ren's form shifts next to me, and only then do I realize my shaking disturbs the rocky basalt beneath us.

"Rose?" he whispers. "Is that you?"

"Sorry," I squeak. "This place gives me nightmares." In the distance, the red beacon of the volcano glows steadily.

"Maybe there's magic here. Something about this whole region is otherworldly." He inches his bedroll closer and places his hand over mine.

I turn on my side to face him but don't relinquish his hand. His warm eyes drown out the memory of the nightmarish beasts rampaging through my head.

"I'm only a page boy. I can't promise that I can truly protect you from the wizard," he says. "But I can promise I'll do everything in my power to help keep you safe. I'll always be here."

A small smile creeps over my face. "I feel better already."

He smiles back, and warmth floods through me. Why did the wizard have to claim my life? Why can't I be a simple girl sharing a moment with her truest friend?

But my responsibilities as princess will not leave me be. They will bring me back to Bryre every time. Duty is the name of the burden I bear.

Ren tucks a wayward lock of hair back behind my ear, fingers straying over my cheek. "I'll keep watch until you fall asleep."

I close my eyes, hand still entwined with his, and hold on until sleep carries me away.

By the time the sun lazily runs its finger across the sky, brushing the darkness aside, I'm restless with the need to move. I slept for only a few hours, but somehow Ren managed to keep the bad dreams at bay. I pack up my bedroll and nibble on a piece of bread while I wait for Ren to wake too.

Despite the desolate landscape, it's oddly peaceful here. The growing light refracts off the lava field, shimmering in pinks and blues and greens. It seems a little less foreboding in the dawn.

I almost choke on my bread. I'll never see this again. When I return home from this journey, I'll be grounded until I become queen.

To distract myself, I pull out one of the books I brought with me. We need to figure out what to do with the Wizard's Bane once we find it.

Or rather, if we find it.

I tried one book last night that seemed promising, but I couldn't keep my eyes open. It was a spell book that mentioned Wizard's Bane and warding spells. Now I pore over the pages—binding spells using centaur bones, warding spells using mermaid scales, and many others.

By the time dawn is fully broken, my patience is rewarded. On the last page of the chapter on defensive magic, I find a mention of the Wizard's Bane:

*One may use the Wizard's Bane, ancient stones that absorb magic powers if invoked with the right spell, as a last resort against a wizard. They are very rare, and must be used only with the greatest of care.*

Below, it lists the spell along with a handful of odd ingredients.

Ren yawns and rolls over. "You're up early," he says.

"Couldn't sleep."

He sits up. "You're packed already?"

I nod. "Look at this." I shove the book under his nose. "Finally, something on how to use the Wizard's Bane."

Ren looks it over briefly, then hands it back. "Now we just have to find the actual stone." He stretches. "We better get moving. The sooner we find the Wizard's Bane, the sooner we can go home."

Home. I already miss my parents and Delia. Eventually they'll forgive me.

We sling our packs over our shoulders and head out onto the lava field toward the volcano. It's slow going and slippery, and the sun reflects off the surface, occasionally blinding us. But we inch closer. When we reach the base of the mountain, the sun is high and morning is almost over. Vents in the earth puff smoke and steam at regular intervals.

"I hope this place isn't about to erupt on our heads," Ren says, eyeing one of the vents suspiciously.

I shake my head. "I doubt it. An active volcano produces a thick cloud of smoke above before it erupts. There are warning signs."

His face scrunches up. "Then why is it so hot? And why is the ground smoking?"

"Lava flow. The magma lies below the surface even when the volcano isn't about to erupt. We still must be careful."

"And hope the Wizard's Bane isn't too deep inside that mountain."

"If we can even find a way inside."

We pause to eat a meager lunch, then carefully wrap up the leftovers. The cheese is soft due to the heat. It won't keep much longer.

What we need most is a way into the mountain and to find the ancient fire dragon's lair.

Tripping over basalt and other rocks, we have several false starts. Fissures in the mountainside that, at first glance, appear to be possible entrances. But when we follow them through, we hit only dead ends.

By midafternoon, we're frustrated and worn out, and stop to rest. The sun burns down. My skin, which is turning a deep pink, will soon blister. This place is so hot, nothing alive could flourish here.

Then we hear the noises.

Familiar ones, of boots marching down a path. Tree branches snapping. Rocks slipping under booted feet. Ren and I exchange a look, then scramble to peek over the rock concealing us from the forest in the south. Guards. From Bryre, judging by their colors and uniforms. My heart sinks. They tracked us so quickly! We haven't even gotten into the mountain yet. We're too close.

"We have to hurry," I say.

"Let's keep going around the mountain," Ren says. "We should be able to stay out of sight a little while longer." He sneaks another glance back. The guards have a hard time walking on the lava field. "That slippery stuff should keep them occupied for a while, I think."

We duck our heads and hustle around the mountain, keeping as much distance between us and them as possible. Grumbles and curses echo over the low plains of the lava field, spurring panic to simmer in my chest.

"We need to try every nook and crevice to get inside." I swallow the trembling in my voice.

"Agreed," he says. "Look, here's another." A possible entrance edges into the mountain and we squeeze inside, but are promptly thwarted about five feet into it. I kick the rock in frustration and immediately regret it as pain shoots up my leg. I bite my tongue to keep from squealing out loud.

"Breaking your foot is probably not the best idea right now," Ren says with a smirk. I give him a withering look.

"Come on, let's keep looking," I whisper.

We find several more false leads. Frustration pools in my gut until I'm ready to scream aloud. But the reminder of the guards from Bryre hunting us keeps my tongue in check.

When we reach the far side, I notice something odd about a shadowed section of the mountainside. The sun doesn't hit it because of an overhanging ledge, making it appear at first glance to be just another section of rock.

But I think it might be something else.

"Wait, Ren," I say, grabbing his arm. "Look."

I pull him underneath the ledge. His eyes widen. "I almost missed this."

"Me too. It's the perfect place for a discreet entrance."

"After you," he says, as he lights our lone torch.

I step into the darkness, feeling my way forward, but soon our eyes adjust to the torchlight. The opening continues forward and widens, then turns again.

When it begins to slant down, I take Ren's hand, and together we walk into the belly of the volcano.

# CHAPTER 8

**THE HEAT INCREASES WITH EVERY BREATH. CRACKS HIDDEN IN THE** walls serve as natural steam vents, and we have to step around some in the floor of the tunnel, too. I hope we don't encounter any too large to pass. A dragon might have been able to slither over large vents, but the passage was obviously not made for small human feet.

It feels like we walk for miles. The passage gets steeper, and sweat trickles down my spine. It's so warm, my hand slips out of Ren's grasp. I miss the comfort of it, but I don't think I could hold on if I tried.

"Do you think we'll be able to get back up the passage?" Ren asks nervously.

I eye the path in front us—a steep drop. "I hope so," I say, though I'm not as certain as I sound.

To our relief, we soon reach a section that levels out. "I wonder how far down we are," Ren says.

"Perhaps halfway into the mountain?" I guess.

Smoke and steam puff at us from vents in the walls as we reach a large cavern, big enough for a clan of dragons—or one with a particularly large stash of treasure.

Ren holds his torch high, revealing a massive pile of glittering stones that fills the cave. Rubies and emeralds on one side, diamonds and sapphires on another—a whole rainbow of colors winking before us.

I have never seen so many riches in one place in my life—which is saying a lot, since I grew up in a palace.

Ren's eyes are as big as saucers as he takes it all in. "Where do we even start?" he asks, then shivers. "You don't think a dragon could still be alive down here somewhere, do you?"

I notice the warren of tunnels shooting off from this room. I shiver too. "Of course not. Dragons are extinct. The wizards made sure of that. We have nothing to fear."

I hope.

"I'll take the left side." Ren points to the rubies and emeralds. "You start on the right. If it's here, the Wizard's Bane will be in this pile somewhere."

I sigh. "Yes, but we don't even know what it looks like. Not really, just vague descriptions."

The books have described it as a stone of simple beauty. All these stones here are simply beautiful too. How will we know which one to choose? We can't take the entire treasure trove home with us.

Ren dives into the rubies—literally. I stifle a laugh.

Riches are good to have—useful, even—but they've never brought me true happiness. They can't buy me an escape from the wizard.

Ren holds up the rubies, glittering in the glow of the torchlight. "Would it be all right if I take some of these with me?" he says. His face bears an odd expression I can hardly make sense of. Yet I think I know why he asks, and my heart drops into my feet.

"I don't think the dragon will come back to claim them, if that's what you mean," I say.

Ren frowns. "No, if I were—"

"We must hurry," I say, cutting him off. "The guards were right on our tail. They'll find this entrance eventually. We have to locate the Wizard's Bane before they do."

His face falls, but he nods his agreement. Getting the Wizard's Bane is all that matters today. We continue our search in hurried silence, fearful that the guards will discover us any second. Before we find what we need.

I paw over diamond tiaras; rough, uncut gems; and necklaces with stones as big as my fists that would break my back to wear. But nothing that says simple beauty. I toy with the idea that it might be one of the uncut diamonds, but in truth they are not very beautiful at that stage and I toss them aside, disappointed.

Ren makes slower progress through his pile, and I pace the cavern. Could it be hidden in an alcove or somewhere easily overlooked?

Or not here at all?

I push that thought aside and keep walking. It must be here. I can't allow myself to think anything else or I'll curl up on this floor in the awful heat and cry. We've come too far to fail now.

Several small caves branch off from this cavern, and I begin to investigate each one. I don't go too far down any of them, just enough to see where they lead. Most end quickly, while one or two are full-on passages. Some have altars with what appear to be offerings from long ago. Desiccated fruit and spices, more jewels, animal bones, and rock piles dot the caves—more evidence that a real dragon lived here, and that the locals paid it respect.

Something stops me in my tracks.

I return to the last alcove I passed, the one with a small rock formation on the stone altar. They seemed so plain at first glance that I barely gave them a second thought. But on closer examination, they're not all chunks of granite like I assumed. They're set up in a semicircle with four forming a half moon, and one larger rock in the center. It resembles a blinking eye.

At first glance it seemed gray, but up close it has a luminescence to it. In fact, if I stare hard enough, its insides shimmer and swirl. I pick it up carefully, holding my breath and ready for the walls to cave in on us.

The walls remaining standing, but the stone tingles in my palm.

"Ren!" I shout. "Ren!"

He drops the crown he's holding and runs over. He touches the stone tentatively.

"How do you know it's the Wizard's Bane?" he asks.

"Look closer," I say. "Look how the innards move. Like there's something alive inside it. It was in the center of the altar over here." I point to the alcove where I found it. "It was treated like something special."

He eyes the stone warily. "It doesn't look special to me," he says.

I laugh, heady with a certainty I can barely explain. "Here," I say, dropping the stone into his outstretched palm. "See for yourself."

His eyes widen in surprise. He must feel the tingling sensation, a prickling of magic that lies just below the surface.

"I think you're right," he says. I smile.

I take the stone back and slip it into my pocket. "We should go, before the guards drag us from the cave."

Ren gives a longing glance at the piles of jewels before following me up the steep incline of the passage. We have to scramble over sharp rocks in the oppressive heat. It's much harder going up. My foothold slips once, sending me careening down a drop of five feet. I hit the ground hard, but suffer only bruises.

"Rosabel!" Ren cries. "Take this." He pulls a rope from his pack and tosses one end down to me. "Tie it around your waist. We'll keep each other balanced."

"Thank you," I say, grateful he has thought of everything.

Our ascent is slow but steady now. I slip less with the

rope to hold on to and Ren's stable presence ahead. When I begin to believe I'll never be cool again, daylight breaks into the passage. Just a sliver of it is enough to make joy well up in my chest.

"Almost there," Ren whispers.

We reach the bend in the passage and extinguish our torch, but do not dare exit yet. We can't see around the corner without anyone just outside seeing us. We must be mindful of the guards.

"Should we risk it?" Ren whispers.

I shrug. "We can't stay in here forever. We've been inside long enough that they may have moved on by now."

Very slowly, we creep out from behind the corner and into the blinding light of midafternoon.

"Princess," says a low voice that makes my heart sink, "thank goodness we've found you." Hands grab my arm before I can react. Ren is caught too.

"Aron, you can let us go—we're returning to Bryre. You don't have to treat us like captives," I say to the captain of my father's guards. He's one of the few people who know my face, which must be why he was sent to retrieve me. He's always been kind, and is by no means an unreasonable man.

He looks at me sadly. "I'm sorry, Your Highness, but I have my orders to bring you back. I must see that through. Forgive me, but we'll keep you and your friend as comfortable as possible."

We're led back over the lava field toward the forest. More guards hide in the trees than I thought at first. We won't be able to escape this time. But at least we're headed in the right direction. The weight of the Wizard's Bane in my pocket comforts me.

It doesn't matter if my parents lock me away forever. We have what we came for.

# CHAPTER 9

WE REACH THE WOODS BY NIGHTFALL, AND THE GUARDS STOP TO REST.
They keep us in a tent with a heavy watch. I suppose I
should be grateful Mama did not insist on the guards truss-
ing us up. Somewhere in the forest nearby an owl hoots,
bringing to mind the last time I heard one. I shiver, then
pull my blanket tighter around me. I pull out the book containing the spell to invoke the Wizard's Bane and read off
the ingredients.

"One chicken foot. A foxglove blossom. A pinch of
arrowroot. Rowan leaves. Mermaid scale." I sigh. "How on
earth are we going to find all these things?" I moan.

"I think I have a solution."

I raise an eyebrow when Ren pulls a few items from his
pocket. "I remembered the chicken feet and scales in the

spell book, so I grabbed these from the caves before we left."
He opens his fist to reveal a desiccated chicken foot and a
scale of iridescent blue.

I gasp. "How do you know that's a mermaid scale?"

Ren frowns. "Well, I don't, I guess. But it's as close as
we're going to get. They're extinct. It makes sense for the
offering in the dragon's cave to be from something more
powerful than a fish."

"I suppose you're right," I say, grateful he swiped those
things when he had the chance. "But what about the rest?"

Ren's eyes sparkle. "That's the easy part. There are rowan
trees in these woods, and I can grab a few leaves from them as
we pass tomorrow. Foxglove and arrowroot, too."

"I don't recall seeing them when we passed through here
before. I'll keep an eye out." I was so focused on finding the
Wizard's Bane, I neglected the chance to really enjoy my
favorite subject out in the wild.

Tomorrow I'll make a point of giving the forest a much
closer examination, especially for the trumpetlike blossoms
of the foxglove and the arrowroot's leaves.

The guards wake us at dawn and pack up our tent. They
want to move as fast as possible back to Bryre. Is it fear of
the wizard or my parents' wrath that stirs them? I suspect a
combination of both.

Ren and I march in silence while we scan the forest
for the supplies we need to complete the spell. It isn't long
before we pass a rowan tree in bloom, the creamy white
flowers bursting open against the green leaves and white

bark. Ren runs his hand over an overhanging branch and stuffs a handful of leaves in his pocket. The guards think he's a kid, playing with a tree. They have no inkling we have magic in mind.

As midday approaches, mutters roll through the ranks. Nothing specific, just whispers and worried faces.

Something has them on edge. While this concerns me, Ren and I use it to our advantage. They're even less observant of when we stop to pick flowers than before. I pick several wildflowers—including the hanging foxglove—to mask our real task.

When Ren spots a patch of arrowroot, he pretends to tie his shoelace. Then he pulls the plant, roots and all, up from the ground and shoves it in his pack while our guard whispers to another.

I exchange a glance with Ren. Something odd is definitely going on in the forest. I'd bet my life it has something to do with the wizard. I can't help remembering those guards who died without any explanation before we fled to find the Wizard's Bane. The stone is a comforting weight in my pocket.

We can finally do something to help instead of waiting around uselessly.

"What do you think is going on?" I ask Ren when the guards are yet again distracted.

He frowns. "I don't know, but I don't like it. I heard one of them say something about a flock of geese vanishing from a herder's yard. Not the right time of year for them to fly south."

"Strange," I say, more troubled than ever. If the wizard is behind this, and the vanishing goats that farmer mentioned, what could he possibly want with these animals? It makes no sense at all. "We must act quickly," I whisper. "If the wizard is in the woods, he's the only thing with magic around—we should be able to use the spell to siphon off his powers."

"We should see if it says the target needs to be within a certain distance."

"And we'll need to do the spell tonight."

When we stop to make camp for the evening, we're back in familiar territory. The plant life is no longer the strange jungle vines, and our tall trees and leafy branches have returned. The sun sinks below the horizon, and the talk around the campfire takes on the tense tone of the afternoon.

We wait until the chatter trickles off to a smattering of low voices. Then we wait a little longer to be sure all but the two guards on watch have drifted off to sleep.

The items we need for the spell, the book, and the Wizard's Bane are securely packed, and we sneak out of the hole we made in the back of the tent, unnoticed by the guards. The sharp edge of the mermaid's scale sliced through easily. The moon is high above, and it lights our way forward. We want to get closer to Bryre, to where the wizard may be operating.

I haven't had time to finish the book, but according to what I've read so far, the stone will absorb the magic of whoever or whatever is named in the spell. Mama provided that information when she told me about how he wooed her and set us all on this terrible course.

*Barnabas.*

What an evil-sounding name. Fitting for the man who sends my parents into spasms of fear.

Ren and I don't speak as we tread cautiously away from the camp. If something goes wrong, the last thing we want is to harm our own city's guards.

After walking for twenty minutes, we reach a grove far enough away to attempt the spell. As we settle in, sitting across from each other, I realize one odd thing: there are no night sounds at all.

The forest holds its breath.

So do we.

I open the book and read through the spell once more.

"'Combine the ingredients in the exact order listed,'" I read. "'Arrowroot, foxglove, mermaid scale, rowan leaves, and chicken foot.'"

Ren forms a pile, placing each ingredient on top of the last. A chill slinks over my arms, but I keep reading the instructions.

"'Now hold the Wizard's Bane over the ingredients and repeat the spell.'" I set the book down so Ren and I can say it together.

> *"Take these wards, and take this stone*
> *Remove the power that can't be owned*
> *Barnabas is the one we name*
> *So we invoke the Wizard's Bane."*

The stone warms in my hand, quickly growing painful. I'm terrified of dropping it. The book says nothing else after the spell. I don't know what I'm supposed to do with it. The smoky insides shimmer and shake. I look wildly at Ren, but he shrugs helplessly.

A streak of light launches from the stone toward the ingredients below. Flames shoot up from the earth, devouring the offerings. I resist leaping back in fear.

"Is it supposed to do that?" Ren asks. The worry in his voice infects me, too.

"I don't know!"

A high-pitched whine emanates from the stone, and it becomes even more alarmingly hot. Pain sears into my palm, but I refuse to release it. The swirling shimmer inside moves faster and faster.

It bursts out of the stone in a brilliant flash of light, then transforms into dark smoky tendrils that dissipate into the forest. The Wizard's Bane is ash in my hands, coating the blistered burn that remains and slipping between my fingers to the forest floor. I open my mouth in a silent scream.

The *pain*.

It feels as though my hand is on fire, but no flames remain to put out.

Ren grabs his canteen and a rips off a piece of his cloak. His soaks it with water, then carefully wraps it around my hand. The weight of the cloth hurts so much that I want to cry out, but I bite my tongue instead. The cooling effect is welcome, and Ren is only trying to help.

"Do you think it worked?" Ren whispers.

"I hope so," I say. I glance down at the pile of smoking ash. All that is left of the Wizard's Bane. "It was our only chance."

"I didn't expect the Wizard's Bane to do that," Ren says.

"Neither did I."

Ren helps me to my feet, and I wobble unsteadily. That's when we hear it.

At first, it's only a slight creak. Then a louder groaning echoes through the trees. The moon vanishes somewhere behind a cloud, and the darkness is startling.

Then, a ripping sound. Like roots being yanked up from the soil.

Neither of us breathes. Our hearts beat a wild rhythm, and we are all too aware of how alone we are. How exposed.

We run.

We pay no heed to the branches tearing at our clothes or even to the paths themselves. We throw ourselves headlong in the direction of Bryre, thinking only of how to reach the safety of the city's warded walls.

Oh heavens. The guards.

"Wait!" I grab Ren's shoulder. "We have to warn the guards."

"You want to go back?" he pants, catching his breath as he points to the forest behind us. Groans and creaks still echo, sparking prickling shivers over my whole body.

I swallow hard. "Yes. We can't let the wizard hurt them. They need to be warned."

He hesitates for a moment. "All right, come on." We skirt the grove where we performed the spell, but something there catches my eye.

My heart comes to a full stop in my chest.

The ferns in the grove are . . . walking.

They're moving toward us like we have a beacon spell cast on us. I flail for Ren's hand and he squeezes back.

"Do you see what I see?" he asks.

"Oh yes, yes, I do."

I'm rooted to the spot, unable to look away. The realization slowly dawns that the ferns are not the only plants moving of their own accord.

The entire forest is alive. The groaning that frightened us is the sound of the ancient trees pulling up their roots from the ground. The creaking is them stretching their branches like a human stretches her limbs after a long slumber.

Every single one of them slowly advances toward us.

My heart begins to beat again, fast and furious with the pulse of terror.

*We* did this.

Our spell backfired. Somehow it went horribly wrong.

"I don't think we need to worry about the guards after all," I say to Ren as we back away from the grove. "I think they want us."

"This is our fault, isn't it?" Ren says, his face paling several shades in the moonlight.

I don't even nod; I just run.

The groans and creaks increase, and we duck and weave between the trees. Roots rise from the ground near us, flailing over our heads. Limbs reach and swoop, grasping and tearing.

We've never run so fast in our lives.

Finally we near the hidden tunnel we used to leave the city. We glimpse the edges of the city walls through the trees. Bryre hasn't woken up yet.

The large rock hiding the entrance looms, and Ren frantically stomps the dead tree root nearby to unlock it. The boulder opens and we leap inside, sealing the door shut behind us.

"Rocks can't come alive, can they?" Ren asks warily.

"Oh, shut up," I say. But we don't hang around to find out.

# CHAPTER 10

BY THE TIME WE'RE SAFELY UNDER THE CITY WALLS, WE STOP TO REST in the tunnels.

I'm not ready to face my parents, nor to find out whether the horror we brought to life in the forest is still there with the light of day.

Instead we sleep on the old stone foundations, clinging to each other to stay warm. We didn't think to bring our blankets from the encampment, just ourselves, the ingredients, and the old book.

When I wake, I'm not sure what time it is, but I'm certain of what we must do.

In spite of what she did the last time we saw her, I must see Old Mae again. Whether she's willingly in league with the wizard or in his thrall, she knows more than she lets on.

If anyone has a way to undo what we've done in the forest, it will be her. Trees and plants, walking like animals.

I shudder.

We should never have dabbled with magic.

I can think of nothing but why the spell went wrong, and now I believe I understand. How I wish I'd thought this through more before we tried it, instead of rushing off to cast the spell, all to show Mama I could save us from the evil wizard.

What's been troubling me is what happens to the magic the Wizard's Bane siphons off. It can't disappear. The stone contains it. And if the spell is performed with a Wizard's Bane that's already full to the brim with magic, what then?

I don't know for certain, but I fear it's like pouring more water into an already full bucket—magic spills out. And in the worst-case scenario, it could knock the entire bucket over, emptying the contents all over the floor.

We were fools and released the wild magic locked in the stone. All that is left of our hopes to stop the wizard is a pile of ash. We must find a way to undo what we've done.

"Ren," I say softly as I nudge him awake with my elbow. He groans and opens his eyes, then bolts upright. The look on his face makes it clear he remembers everything that happened last night.

"Rosabel . . ."

"Yes, it was real. We woke the forest." Sickening guilt swims in my stomach. Ren puts his head in his hands.

"I was hoping that was only an awful dream."

I grimace, then squeeze his shoulder. "No, but we

must fix it. I have an idea."

It takes a little persuasion, but half an hour later, we leave our tunnels and enter the market, doing our best to keep our faces cloaked. No doubt everyone is looking for us, though most will recognize only Ren.

The flower cart lies ahead, but the old woman is nowhere to be seen. My heart sinks as we approach. Where could she be? Ren and I risked so much. I fear this will be the last time I can sneak out. And now, in this hustling mass of market-goers, she has vanished.

"Perhaps she's getting a bite to eat?" Ren suggests, his face marred by the furrow in his brow.

"Yes, that must be it." I am desperate for some measure of hope.

But when we reach the stall, something's obviously wrong. Her wares aren't fully set out. The curtains surrounding her cart hang haphazardly, as though they have been thoughtlessly displayed. It's nothing like Old Mae's usual meticulous setup.

Fear grips my innards and refuses to let go. One glance at Ren confirms he feels uneasy too. Wordlessly we move to the back of her stall and stop short. A gasp chokes in my throat. I can't look away, until Ren forcibly drags me back to the street.

His hands are on my arms, my face, my back. Despite his kind whispers, I can't stop shaking. The image of the old woman will be forever burned into my eyes.

She's dead. Horrifically, terribly dead. No eyes. And her gut—

I shove Ren away and vomit next to the stall. That distinct metallic smell of blood clogs every pore on my body. I feel as though it's all over me.

But Ren, sweet Ren, he holds my hair and rubs my back as I dissolve on the street. "Come," he says. "There's nothing for us here. Let's go home before we really cause a scene."

Somehow I find my feet again and Ren leads me back to the church and the tunnels.

Old Mae knew who I was. She was the only one who'd risk speaking of magic. Hadn't all the other vendors been terrified to utter even a syllable about the matter? I have no doubt she's dead because of us.

That horror on the street—it's my fault.


We don't bother to sneak back into the palace. Terrified and properly sorry, we limp through the gates and make our way into the front garden. A guard is dispatched ahead of us once Ren is recognized. I hope the ones we left in the forest made it out alive.

Dizziness, gnawing at me for hours, now threatens to completely pull me under. Ren half carries me into the palace.

Magic always has a price. An action and reaction. I suspect this is my price, my reaction, which I experience now. Yet I had to try. How else can we hope to fight magic but with more magic?

My parents run to greet us, a mix of fury and relief on their faces. Mama hugs me too tightly, and I have trouble focusing my eyes on her.

"Where have you been?" she demands.

When she releases me, I sway, and Ren steadies me. "We had to try to break the binding deal with the wizard. We sought out a Wizard's Bane, but it all went wrong when we tried to use it."

Papa takes me by the shoulders. "What happened? What went wrong? Where are the guards we sent to find you?"

I swallow, but my tongue feels sluggish and my mouth horridly dry. "We released magic instead of taking it. The forest . . . it came alive. The trees are walking."

Mama gives Ren a stern look. "What is she raving about? How could you possibly know about Wizard's Banes?"

Poor Ren can only look at the floor. "Your Majesties, we found a secret room in the library and read the books about magic hidden there. We only wanted to learn how to stop the wizard. And now the forest is stirring. We woke it up, but we didn't mean to. It was behind us. If the trees keep moving in our direction, they may reach the walls soon."

Papa does not look as surprised as I expected at the mention of the hidden library, but Mama turns an awful shade of pale.

"The forest is awake? What have you done?" Her eyes burn at me so brightly, I have to look away. "Rosabel, you are never leaving that tower again. No more gardens. No more music lessons with your sister, and definitely no more books."

She grabs my arm as though she means to drag me to my room this instant, and I vaguely hear my father say something I cannot make out. The room spins beneath my feet, and suddenly all I can see is the gilded ceiling above me. Something cold and hard spreads over my back and I realize I am lying on the marble floor in the throne room. Ren's panicked face looms over me, until it's replaced by those of my parents.

My arms and legs feel like lead weights, but I try to reach out anyway. All I can muster is a whisper, "I'm sorry."

# CHAPTER 11

MY HEAD IS STILL FOGGY WHEN I WAKE, AND I'M NOT SURE HOW MUCH time has passed since Ren and I reached the palace—maybe hours, maybe days?—but I do know one thing for certain.

The wizard approaches.

Mama is true to her word, and this time I'm locked away for real. She and Papa took the key and posted a guard in case I try to pick the lock. Fear has swallowed my parents up, leaving only empty husks behind, and now my room with a view is a prison.

Ren told them everything. As his reward, he's forbidden to ever come near me again. Even Delia won't speak to me.

Ren may not be allowed to see me anymore, but the guard has taken pity on him and lets him slip notes under my door, keeping me apprised of the events taking place outside my chambers, and bits of conversations he has over-heard. Mama and Papa have secured the key to the hidden library in the depths of the palace vault. While it was a shock to Mama, it seems Papa already knew. The room is an unpleasant responsibility that has been passed down for generations. My grandfather made Papa swear a blood oath to keep the existence of the books secret and to protect them from falling into the wrong hands, just like every other ruler before him. Moving or destroying them is too dangerous. Though Papa loathes magic, he hates the thought of those books, that knowledge, being in the hands of wizards even more. The key had been lost long before he was born, so he gave it hardly any thought. Until Ren and I discovered it.

The guards we left behind haven't returned. The forest we brought to life spreads slowly like a disease over the mountains and woods. Those who once lived outside Bryre's protective walls have come back to the fold. Strange lights and terrible keening in the woods and hills frighten Bryre's citizens day and night. The living forest hasn't reached Bryre yet, but it will soon.

It is no longer randomly chasing people in all direc-tions—someone directs it toward our city. There is only one who could hope to control the magic we released: the wizard.

All my hopes of finding a way to break the curse, free-ing us from the promise Mama and Papa made long ago, have been in vain. Instead of freeing my family, I caught the wizard's attention. Any chance for another way to save us vanished with Old Mae and the books Mama and Papa will never let me see again. The image of Old Mae in death is burned on my brain, and it flares up again every time I close my eyes. When I sleep, my dreams are haunted by strange creatures, bloodied bodies, and the horrible rustling of walking trees.

Now, all I can do is watch and wait. They say the wizard can't enter the city. That the wards he put into place to protect us from Belladoma's greedy king still hold. No one intending Bryre harm can enter.

But how long can one spell last? The wizard set those wards years ago. What if they start to degrade? He'll squeeze through any chink in our armor he can find.

And with the menacing forest, I fear he intends to do his best to weaken them.

City guards patrol the perimeter at all hours of the day. The ones attacked by the wizard are still frozen solid, and it does not seem likely they will ever recover. Mama and Papa consult with their council debating what to do if the wizard breaches the walls.

And here I sit, waiting for my world to explode while others prepare to lay down their lives to keep me safe. All because of a foolish bargain.

They should have known better than to make a deal with a wizard. Too many people pay the price. I'm not worth such a sacrifice.

The effects of using magic haven't completely worn off, but I pry myself off my bed and make my way to the window on wobbly legs. Even that's locked up tight. Outside my tower, the city is on edge. The streets are empty. Only the guards on the ramparts and gates move and remain busy, no doubt terrified of the monstrous man who approaches.

He's coming for *me*.

As I turn from the window, something else catches my eye. Movement in the forest. From here everything looks miniature. I peer more intensely at the north gate, where it originates. Does the wizard shake the trees with his power? Or does the very earth tremble at the thought of him drawing near?

Watching the foliage makes me long for my garden hidden in the maze. How will those flowers grow without me to tend them? Who else will coddle the empty plot where the Crown-of-Roses seeds are sown, hoping to coax them from the ground at last?

My breath catches. The trees aren't shaking after all.

They're moving. The entire forest shuffles closer and closer to Bryre, one horrifying step at a time. It is almost here.

My breath returns in panting gasps. Is there no end to this terror we've unleashed with our spell? I fear the wizard has seen an opportunity to finish, for his own malicious ends, what we began. I must warn Mama and Papa. They must go to ground, use one of the escape routes and get out of the city. I have nowhere to hide, but they can. I run to the door and pound and scream.

"Mama! Papa! Come quick!"

I scream for five full minutes, but no one comes. I rush back to the window. The forest creeps closer. Thick trees press together in stark lines, forming a circular net around the city walls. This is different, more organized than the wild, haphazard life we gave them, just like Ren told me. It must be the wizard in control now. Even from here there's no mistaking the confused, frightened glances that the guards on the ramparts exchange. The trees are right up to the main gate, blocking the road out of the city. More approach every few minutes, forming row after row of enchanted woods.

The wizard weaves a tight net, and we have no chance of escaping from it. Even if he can't come in, we can't leave. Not without risking the wilds of the woods. I can no longer see between the trunks. All that remains is a looming dark green of waving branches.

The air in the room seems to thin. I slump onto my bed, filled with awful, dizzying certainty.

I will not leave this palace alive.

# CHAPTER 12

BY THE TIME THE SUN SETS, MY MIND IS MADE UP. I MAY NOT LEAVE THE palace alive, but my family will.

Giving myself up to the wizard terrifies me, but I see no other recourse, no other way to keep my city and my family safe.

He's coming for me—if I go willingly, it will buy them time to escape.

Enough people have suffered because of me, first due to the cursed deal and now because of my attempts to play with forces I should never have touched.

It ends now. I will go with the wizard, whatever that may mean. Whether I live or die, I will not let any more people sacrifice themselves in my name.

I rise from my bed, feeling lighter than I expected. A

hollow spot opens in my chest and steadily expands.

I may never see Mama and Papa and Delia again. I may never see Ren again. I cling to their images in my mind, hoping that whatever happens, they're imprinted deeply enough on my heart to endure into the next life or into death.

My nightgown won't do for this endeavor. I select a pale rose-colored gown and dress myself in the mirror. A few cuts mar my face, making me less ladylike than usual.

It doesn't matter tonight.

I take a slip of paper, a pen, and some wax from my desk and sit down to write my final words to my family. My final words to Ren.

*Dear Mama and Papa,*

*Run. Flee Bryre and seek the safety of another country until the wizard is far away from our home. I know you will not approve of what I am doing, but I have made up my mind. Like you told me, Mama, sometimes queens have to make the hard decisions. I may not be a queen yet, but I understand what you meant.*

*Giving myself up to the wizard is the only way to ensure your safety and the safety of our entire city, and that is more important to me than my own. I cannot sit idly by in my tower while you sacrifice yourselves. There is no point. He will win either way. But this way, you at least have a chance.*

*Please, go, and do not let my sacrifice be in vain.*

*Your loving daughter,*

*Rosabel*

*Dear Delia,*

*Forgive me if I have neglected you these past few months. You are one of the dearest people in the world to me. I must leave to keep you, Mama, and Papa safe. If there were any other way, please know I would remain here and be the older sister you deserve.*

*Be brave, sister. You will rule the city one day, and I know you will be a kind queen. Ren will help you. I'm so sorry I won't be here to see it.*

*Love,*

*Rosabel*


*Dear Ren,*

*By the time you read this letter, I will already be gone. Please do not despair for me. I do this willingly and to keep everyone I love safe. I must put duty before everything else, and this instance is no exception.*

*You have always been my best friend and confidant, and as close to me as my own kin. You are as dear to me as I am to you.*

*Please watch over my mother and father, and especially Delia, when I am gone. And my garden.*

*Yours,*

*Rosabel*


I fold each letter carefully, wrapping a tiny piece of my heart in each one. I melt the wax and seal the letters with the personal stamp Father gave me when I was just a child—a perfect rose, imprinted in red wax.

Now I only have to find a way to deliver them.

From the window, I see it happen. First the guards walking along the ramparts crumple to the ground. The forest quakes in its frenzied attempt to reach the castle but meets invisible resistance that prevents it from breaching the walls. Then a man with silver hair down to his jaw walks through the gates.

Horror freezes me to the floor. He found a loophole. But how? The wards should protect against anyone intending Bryre harm. How could he hurt the guards?

Unless he didn't. Some of the men move a little, as though they're only sleeping. . . . Outside the door of my room, I hear a gasp, and then a thud. The guard.

Whatever the wizard did to the guards at the gate must have affected all guards throughout the city. Only one thing can be so specific and travel so quickly to do its work.

Magic.

The enchanted forest. The trees have been trying to get through the walls all day. Could their attack have weakened the wards enough that he was able to slip through? I can only guess at exactly how he's doing it, but if the wizard found a way around his wards, he must be intent on something other than hurting Bryre.

I shiver.

He could only be that focused on one thing: me. Claiming what was promised him. If he gets his promised reward, he won't be able to use that loophole again; the wards will hold against his malice in the future.

It's time for me to go.

I set about picking the lock on my bedroom door. If I had a secret passage in my room, this would be much simpler. I pore over my jewelry case until I find a brooch with a pin thin enough to work. Mama took all the hairpins that I used the last time. It takes a fair amount of jiggering, but after several minutes I'm finally rewarded with a *click*.

I collect my letters and open the door to my fate.

The castle sleeps, which serves my purposes well. I go to Delia first, slipping into her chambers. She's curled on her bed in a pool of moonlight, blond hair spilling over the pillows. She looks serene and utterly unaware of the terror that creeps outside our gates.

A wave of sadness crashes over me. She won't be serene for long after tonight. I'm sorry for it.

I gently press my lips to her forehead and whisper, "Good-bye, sister." I place the letter on the pillow next to her so she'll find it when she wakes. I close her door with a heavy heart, then lock it. The wizard may not know about my sister, and if she wakes up too soon, I can't risk her wandering the halls in search of me.

Ren's note will be trickier. Indeed, I'm not sure where he lives, having never been to his house. But there is one place I know he'll check.

My garden.

With no time to waste, I run soundlessly through the halls in my slippers and take the stairs two at time. In minutes I'm outside, the cool night breeze wrapping around me as if to say farewell. When I reach my hidden garden plot, I'm greeted by the familiar shapes of the rosebushes on either side, the lone surviving sunflower, and the barren patch where the Crown-of-Roses seeds are planted. Sadness plucks at the backs of my eyes. I'd hoped to see what they looked like. Ren will have to care for them for me. I tuck the letter into a rosebush, then hurry back to the palace.

When I enter through the wide double doors of the solarium, a scream reaches my ears and squeezes my heart. Am I too late? Did I spend too much time saying goodbye? I run through the halls, searching for the person who screamed, still clutching the letter to my parents. I stop short in the main hallway. Two guards sprawl unconscious on the floor, and a maid and a butler hover over them.

"What happened?" I demand, unable to hide the tremor in my voice.

"Barnabas—the wizard—he—" The woman shakes so hard, she can't complete the sentence.

"The wizard is here," the butler says. "How did he get through the wards? I don't understand."

I fist my hands in my skirt. "Which way did he go?"

The maid points in the direction of the stairs. This is my one chance to reason with him. To convince him to take me and leave my family alone. I fly up the stairs the same way I took them down—two at a time. Muffled shouts come from the far end of the palace. The wing where my parents' chambers are.

And where mine was when I was a child.

I launch myself in that direction. They insisted Delia and I live in the opposite wing once we were both old enough to walk. I never considered why, but now I understand. The wizard had been invited into their home when he was protecting them from the Belladomans. He knew their habits and the layout of the palace.

He'd know exactly where his promised prize was supposed to sleep.

Another scream.

Mama.

My parents' chambers lie just ahead, the door to their sitting room swung wide open. All the candles are lit, and the glow reaches into the hall, along with their voices.

"Where is my payment?" an unfamiliar man's voice growls. "She is mine—you must give her to me."

The voice slices through me on a cold blade, rending my heart in two and stealing my breath.

"We will give you anything you could possibly want. Money, jewels," Papa says. His voice trembles. "I would even give you the throne and my kingdom instead."

Their moment of hope hangs in the air like a tangible force. The low voice laughs harshly.

"I have named my price, and the deal is binding. You must concede."

I tiptoe closer, heart thundering in my chest. Through the doorway, I see Mama sink to her knees, pleading with the silver-haired man I saw enter the gates less than an hour earlier.

"Please. Please don't take our daughter. Anything but her."

I'm so stunned, I can't move. Never in my life have I seen Mama beg. She's always been the kind, constant backbone of our family. Seeing her grovel like this—for me—shatters my already sundered heart to pieces.

"If you do not hand her over, I will tear this place apart brick by brick until I find her."

"I do not know how you managed to get past the wards," Papa says, "but please take our gold and jewels and leave in peace. Have mercy, and spare our daughter."

The wizard laughs. "The wards did not affect me because I did not enter the city with the intent to harm. I came only to collect. I have spent years learning to focus on that one thing so thoroughly that the wards have a hard time detecting what lies beneath. Besides, the more magic with ill intent the wards have to hold off at once, the weaker they get. I am sure you noticed that even the forest has turned on your kingdom. And now that I am inside the walls, the wards cannot stop me. Anything that gets in my way is collateral damage. I have no need for mercy."

"Have you no heart?" Mama pleads. "I know you were not always so cold. Please, spare her."

The floor quakes under my feet and I brace myself on the doorframe. "You squashed any semblance of warm feelings from my heart, my dear Aria. You made the wrong choice. And now you will pay for it." The chill in the wizard's voice turns my innards to ice.

I step through the doorway into my parents' sitting room. The shock on their faces at my sudden appearance gives them away. A crafty grin spreads over the wizard's face. Now that I'm inside the room and closer to him, I see what I could not before.

Angry, magic heat rolls of the wizard in waves. The floor beneath his feet smokes. A faint crackling sparks from his hands every few seconds, like a barely contained lightning storm.

"Rosabel?" he says.

I nod. "I'll go with you. Just promise you'll leave them alone." I clasp my hands behind my back so that he won't see them quivering.

"No!" Mama cries.

"Please, Rose, don't do this. Run, hide, while you still can," Papa says.

I smile sadly. "There's nowhere to hide. Nowhere is safe from him. Not forever."

"You are a bright one. But what makes you think I will leave your parents alone? Am I not owed interest on my uncollected debt for all these years?"

"Then I won't go willingly."

He steps forward and the air around him sizzles. His silver hair rises from the static charge, lending him a crazed appearance.

"That matters not to me. Besides, you stole something from me too. Who do you think the Bane you found in the volcano belonged to?" He narrows his eyes. "I was furious at first when all that magic was released from my Bane. Though I admit, you did provide an excellent distraction and the perfect way to weaken my wards around the city."

"It was yours?" Shock drains all the color from my face.

"Of course it was. They"—he points to my parents—

"denied me what I needed to take the magic from the realm in one spell, so I've had to improvise. Wizard's Banes drain magic, not just wizards. I turned it on the realm itself, and it's been slowly draining magic for years. It was almost full, too, until you stupidly released it."

Horror makes my knees feel like fragile flower stems in a hurricane.

"Please," Mama begs, "please take our jewels and leave."

Mustering all the bravery I have, I step between them. "No, take me. Let them be."

"I will consider it," the man says. I brace myself when he reaches for me, but Mama throws herself at him.

He shoves her off with a bright light and bang, sending her tumbling to the floor and knocking over a vase of our best blush roses in the process. She lies very still, her back to me amid the falling petals. Her blue silk skirts spread out on the marble floor like flowing water, and sparks of magic flicker over her. Blood pools from where she hit her head on the corner of the table.

The world stands still. Everything is blue and red and her golden hair. I barely register Papa reaching for me or the second blast that sends him flailing.

Mama is dead. An awful certainty takes hold of my insides, making me numb.

Then cold hands grab my arms. Shockingly cold, given the amount of heat those hands burned at my parents. The cooling touch creeps over my skin like thousands of tiny insects, prickling and numbing, and cracking my skin in places. Rivulets of blood trickle down my arms, but I cannot feel a thing. I cannot struggle. I cannot scream. I can only stare at the face of the silver-haired man as his hands wind around my neck and squeeze.

One long, black flash of cold, then oblivion.

# EPILOGUE

THE KING WEEPS OVER THE BODY OF HIS WIFE AND THAT OF THE DAUGH-ter he can no longer find. A sealed letter and a few drops of blood are all that remain where she stood. A bitter end to a vile promise finally fulfilled. Darkness creeps around him, haunting and hollow, filling him up with every sob.

Outside the city walls, the raging forest calms. Saplings and ancient trees alike shamble back to their resting places, where the magic that animated them will return to the one they obey.

In the garden behind the palace stubborn seeds sprout to life. The roots swell below the earth, taking hold of the stones in the foundations, reaching, grasping, ever so slowly. Shoots of black and green pierce the earth, coaxed from their long rest by a sacrifice. Some dark things can only be baptized in blood.

These black, coiling twigs twine around the garden, snaking toward the palace walls, ready to claim what their master truly desires: utter revenge.

# ACKNOWLEDGMENTS

Second books are strange beasts. In some ways they're easier, because you know what to expect, and in other ways they're even trickier. Fortunately, I've had the opportunity to work with an amazing group of people—at HarperCollins, New Leaf Literary, online, and at home—who've supported me and this book the whole way through. My particular, infinite thanks to those noted below:

*Ravenous* would not exist without the brilliant advice of my editors, Rosemary Brosnan and Annie Berger. I can't thank them enough for the tough editing love and for shepherding this book to publication. It's a privilege and a joy to work with them and the entire marvelous, talented staff at HarperCollins Children's Books. Everyone from editorial to design to marketing and publicity put a lot of time, love, and hard work into this book. Truly, I consider myself the luckiest author in publishing!

My agent, Suzie Townsend, for being smart and savvy, and for doing so much more than just selling books. Her insight, advice, and assistance on all aspects of the publication process have proven invaluable. Suzie and the rest of the New Leaf Literary & Media staff are rock stars at everything they do, and I'm so glad to have them in my corner.

Illustrator extraordinaire Skottie Young, for bringing my characters to life on the gorgeous covers for both *Ravenous* and *Monstrous* and in the delightful chapter-heading illustrations inside. His work is incredible, and I can hardly believe how perfectly he captured the mood and feel of both books. My stories could not possibly be better dressed.

My excellent critique partners Mindy McGinnis, R. C. Lewis, Riley Redgate, and Derrick Carmado, who speedily read *Ravenous* and always challenge me to make my books better than I could envision on my own. Also, my critique group and beta readers: Sakura Q. Eries, Amy Trueblood, Michelle Hauck, Christina Busby, Eric J., and Chris Shaw. They may not have all read this particular book, but they have helped make my writing stronger and have been wonderfully supportive along the way.

Speaking of support, there are so many ups and downs and sideways detours on the route to publication, and I'm grateful I had the opportunity to be part of not one but two debut author groups. To all the members of the Class of 2K15 and the Fearless Fifteeners, thank you for the commiseration, for the book love, and for generally being all kinds of awesome. I'm glad we got to share our debut year together!

My local Boston Writers Meetup group, which is also a great source of support and friendship and excellent for ensuring I leave the revision cave at least once a month. Crepes and commiseration go a long way to keeping me grounded.

It would be remiss of me not to include the very kind authors who took the time to read my first book and provide blurbs: Anne Ursu, Natalie Lloyd, Claire Legrand, Rebecca Behrens, and Emma Trevayne. So many thanks for making this newbie author feel like part of the "club" and for taking the time away from their own wonderful books to do so!

My best friends, Trish Ellis and Chandra Reber, for being two of my biggest cheerleaders and always patiently listening as I babble about my adventures in publishing. And, of course, Trish's mom, Diane, for foisting my first book, *Monstrous*, on strangers at every possible occasion. *Ravenous* will no doubt owe more than a few readers to her efforts as well!

My family, for always being excited to hear about this book's progress no matter how many times I talked about it. Also, my extended family—a veritable army of in-laws who came out to many events in support of me and my book.

My husband, Jason, and our pugs, Tootsie and Milo. The pugs for being my foot warmers and plot sounding boards through the months I spent writing this book. And Jason for many, many things, but here notably for naming the Sonzeeki and being the most supportive husband a writer could ask for. You're always my favorites.

And last, but anything but least, all the readers, and the booksellers, librarians, and teachers who've put *Monstrous* and *Ravenous* in their hands. There is nothing better than knowing there are people who love these books and love sharing them. Thank you.

# READ MORE
# SPELLBINDING ORIGINAL
# FAIRY TALES
## from
# MARCYKATE CONNOLLY